OVER THE EDGE

There was no guard rail. On the right, Lang could see occasional tree tops and roofs of the town far below. Twice he saw a large bird below, wings outstretched over the farmland as it coasted along thermals. On this motorcycle, he thought, I'm almost that free.

He was never sure what pulled him from the euphoria of the day. He only knew he was surprised on one of the short straight stretches to see the bike's mirrors filled with a truck. Not the eighteen-wheeled behemoth of American Interstates, but large enough to fill its half of the road.

Lang leaned into a sweeping right-hand turn and set up for a hairpin to the left. No doubt about it, the truck was gaining on them, swerving all over the road as it struggled to stay on the pavement.

Lang searched ahead for a turn-off, even a space between paving and mountainside. There were none. Straight drop right, perpendicular rise left. Nowhere to go.

Taking his left, non-throttle hand from the handlebar, Lang tapped Gurt's leg and pointed behind. He heard a German expletive over the roar of the truck's engine. She squeezed him tighter.

The bike shuddered as its fiberglass rear fender shattered and Lang braced against the impact. The bastard intended to run them over! He opened the throttle to stop.

How had they found him?

THE PEGASUS SECRET

GREGG LOOMIS

LEISURE BOOKS NEW YORK CITY

A LEISURE BOOK®

May 2005

Published by

Dorchester Publishing Co., Inc.
200 Madison Avenue
New York, NY 10016

ISBN 0-8439-5530-9

ACKNOWLEDGMENTS

Thanks to Mary Jack Wald, my agent, whose help and suggestions were priceless, not to mention her efforts to make sure this book saw print. Thanks to Don D'Auria, editor, for his help, too. Henry Lincoln's video on Rennes-le-Chateau was helpful, as were the suggested translation of the Latin puzzle in Poussin's painting by Richard Andrews and Paul Schellenberger's *Tomb of God*.

THE PEGASUS SECRET

PROLOGUE

Rennes-Le-Château
Southwest France
1872

Father Saunière had made a strange discovery.

The roll of vellum parchment was so old that the ribbon tying the sheets together had crumbled into dust when he took the bundle from its hiding place in the altar. He had never seen writing like this, faded lines that looked more like worm tracks than script.

He had been doing some work in the little church, repairs his parish could ill afford to hire out. The roof leaked, a number of the pews were going to collapse without new nails and the altar . . . Well, the altar was older than the church itself.

He frowned as he looked up at the altar. Basically a stone slab, centuries of serving the Holy Eucharist had worn it so unevenly that it was about to fall from the two short plinths supporting it. Even at six feet and over two hundred pounds, he had barely been able to lift the block from its supports. That was when he had discovered that one of the columns was hollow—with the parchments inside.

No one knew the origins of the altar. Saunière supposed it had come from the ruins of one of the many castles nearby. Its intricate carvings were far too elaborate for a church whose poor box rarely yielded more than a few sous at a time.

The area was old. Romans, Templars, perhaps even Moors when it had been part of Catalonia in Spain. The altar could have come from any one of their chapels.

Or Cathars or Gnostics.

The possibility that the altar could have been part of heretic or pagan services made Saunière wince. God alone knew what heathen use the stone might have served. He looked over his shoulder as though someone might be there to reproach him for the thought.

Mere objects could not be evil, he told himself. Still, holding these pages made him uncomfortable. It might be best if they were destroyed. No, that was not his decision to make. He would show them to the bishop on the prelate's next visit, let authority decide.

What harm could mere inanimate documents do, anyway?

The answer came to him as he was conducting evening mass: It had been paper nailed to a cathedral door that had torn the church apart forever.

Part One

CHAPTER ONE

1

Paris
0234 hours

The explosion shook the entire Place des Vosges as well as a good part of the Marais district. Had the thirty-six town houses, nine on each side of the square, been built with less sturdy material than the handmade bricks of four centuries past, the damage might have been greater. Even so, the antique glass had been blown out of every window of the largest of these stately homes, the former Hôtel de Rohan-Guéménée, the second floor of which had been the home of Victor Hugo.

The only real damage, though, was to number 26, the source of the blast. By the time the *pompiers* from the 11th arrondissement, the district fire department, arrived twelve minutes later, the building was four stories of inferno. Saving the house and its occupants was not a possibility.

A line of gendarmes kept spectators a respectful distance from the blaze while others interviewed bathrobe-clad residents. One man, an apparent insomniac, told the officers he had been watching a rerun of the past year's World Cup championship match when he had heard a crash of shattering glass followed by a flash of light brighter than any he had ever seen. Rushing to the window, he had nearly been blinded by the intensity of the blaze.

The glass, the policeman asked, could it have crashed when something was thrown through a window?

The man stuffed a fist into his yawning mouth, his interest diminishing now that the best part of the show was over. How does one distinguish between glass shattering when something is thrown into it rather than something being thrown out? He shrugged as only the French can, conveying uninterested ignorance as well as annoyance at a stupid question. "Je ne sais pas."

He turned to go back home, almost bumping into a middle-aged man in a suit. The spectator wondered what anyone would be doing in business attire at this hour. Not only dressed, but in a shirt freshly starched, jacket and trousers neatly pressed. He shrugged a second time and trudged homeward wondering if TV reception in the neighborhood had been affected by the fire.

The gendarme touched the brim of his cap with a nod, an almost involuntary sign of respect as he wished the new arrival, "Bon soir." A straightening of the back and an air of deference were obvious. It was not every neighborhood fire that drew the attention of the Department of State Security and Investigation, the DGSE.

The DGSE man gave the slightest of nods before staring intently into what was now a smoldering shell. Plumbing, twisted by the heat, poking into emptiness like supplicating arms. The adjacent homes exhibited an ugly black patina of soot as they stared onto the square with windows void of glass. Hot embers hissed with steam as firemen hosed them down. It was as if a shaft straight from hell had broken through the earth's surface where the townhouse had once stood.

"Any idea as to the cause?" the DGSE man asked.

The fireman was fairly certain the nation's security service would not be interested in leaking gas or a match carelessly dropped into the home's supply of kerosene. "No sir, none." He pointed. "The chief fire inspector is over there."

The security department man stood for a moment as though digesting the information before walking over to a short man almost swallowed by his flame-retardant uniform and knee-high boots. The impression was of a child playing in his parents' clothes.

The security man displayed a badge. "Louvere, DGSE. Any idea as to the cause?"

The fireman, too tired to be impressed by what was, after all, just one more bureaucrat, shook his head. "Whatever set it off, it had help from some sort of accelerant. I'd be surprised if it was an accident."

Louvere nodded in apparent agreement. "Ether in an adjoining unit, perhaps?"

The fireman gave a derisive snort. Ether was used in the process of turning cocaine powder into "rocks" of more potent crack. Few narcotic dealers knew (or cared) how to handle the highly volatile anesthetic safely. Misapplication of the heat necessary to the process could and did frequently result in spectacular results.

"In this neighborhood?" He swept a hand, indicating the pricey homes. A three-day tournament had been held here in 1615 to celebrate the marriage of Louis XII. The Place had been home to Cardinal Richelieu and other notables. Duels had been fought in the center of the square while spectators watched from the shelter of the arcades that fronted the buildings. In 1962 President de Gaulle had declared the Place a national historic monument. The prices of homes here, in the rare event one became available, were not set to be attractive to crack labs.

Louvere's eyes followed the fireman's gesture, taking in the perfect symmetry of the pink brick buildings. "I suppose not."

"Besides," the fireman said, "DGSE hardly bothers itself with the dope trade. What's your involvement?"

"Let's say it is personal. I have a friend, an old acquaintance in the States, who asked me to meet his sister, show her around Paris. She was staying with a schoolmate in number 26. Someone I had introduced her to called, said he had heard there was trouble here. So I came."

The fireman rubbed a grubby hand across his forehead. "If she was in there . . . Well, it will take our forensic people a few days to identify whatever's left, probably have to do it by DNA."

The security man sighed as his shoulders slumped. "I don't look forward to making that phone call."

The fireman nodded sympathetically. "Give me your card. I'll personally see to it you get a copy of the report."

"Thank you." Louvere gave one final glance at the gaping cavern that only hours before had been one of the most desirable residences in Paris. Shoulders stooped as though bearing the weight of the world, he walked past the yellow fire trucks that seemed like living animals with each breath-like stroke of their pumps. A short way down the narrow street, a Peugeot was waiting at the curb.

2

Paris
Three days later

The driver reached over the seat to shake his passenger awake. The man in the backseat of the taxi looked even more worn than most Americans the cabby picked up at Charles de Gaulle after a transatlantic flight: clothes rumpled, shirt wrinkled, face unshaven. Once the man was awake, his eyes were the true sign of weariness. Red-rimmed as though from a combination of grief and lack of sleep, they had a stare that seemed to focus on something a thousand miles away until he started counting out euros.

Stuffing the bills in his pocket, the driver watched the man enter a nondescript building across from the Place de l'Opéra.

Inside, the American passed antique elevators to climb worn steps to the second floor where he turned right and stopped. In front of him was what appeared to be an unmarked old-fashioned glass door. He knew the single translucent pane was the hardest bulletproof glass available. Slowly he lifted his head to stare at the ceiling where he was sure shadows concealed a camera. Noiselessly, the door slid open and he entered a small chamber facing yet another door, this one made of steel.

"Oui?" a woman's voice asked through a speaker.

"Langford Reilly to see Patrick Louvere," the man said in English. "He's expecting me."

As noiselessly as the first, the second door opened and Lang Reilly entered one of many offices of France's security force. In front of him stood a man in a dark, Italian-cut suit. The shirt was crisp and the shoes reflected the ceiling lights. In years past, Lang and Dawn had joked that Patrick Louvere must change his clothes several times a day to look so fresh.

Louvere regarded Lang a moment through heavily lidded eyes, eyes that had always reminded Lang of a basset hound. "Langford!" he exclaimed, continuing in nearly accentless English as he embraced his guest. "It has been, what? Ten, fifteen years? Too long for friends to be apart."

He stepped back, a hand still on each of Lang's arms. "You should have called. We could have sent a car."

Lang nodded. "A cab seemed the quickest way, but thanks."

The Frenchman dropped his hands. "I cannot tell you how sorry . . ."

"I appreciate that, Patrick, but can we get started?"

Louvere was not offended by what most of his country-men would have considered brusqueness. Americans were famous for getting to the point. "But of course!" He turned and spoke to someone Lang could not see. "Coffee, please, Paulette. This way, Lang."

Lang followed him down a hall. It had been almost twenty years since he had last been here but other than newer carpet, as cheap and institutional as before, little had changed.

Happily, neither had his relationship with Patrick Louvere. Although their respective governments had frequent differences—the most vocal being the war with Iraq—the American and the Frenchman had remained steadfast friends. Patrick had gladly volunteered to do whatever he could for Lang's sister, Janet, during her visit with a former school chum in Paris. Since Janet was bringing her adopted son, Jeff, the Frenchman had insisted on taking the young boy into his own home daily to play with his own children while Janet and her friend prowled the shops of Rue du Faubourg St. Honore. It had been Patrick's phone call that had shattered Lang's world for a second time.

The DGSE man ushered Lang into the same office he re-membered and slid behind a desk clear of anything other than a slender file folder. Almost immediately, a middle-aged woman appeared with a coffee service and began to set cups on the desk. Although he felt he had consumed a tanker load of the stuff lately, Lang was too tired to protest.

"So, you are a lawyer now?" Patrick asked, obviously making conversation until the men could be alone. "You sue the big American companies for millions of dollars, no?"

Lang shook his head. "Actually, I do white-collar criminal defense."

The Frenchman pursed his lips. "White-collar? Criminal?" He looked as distressed as if he had been forced to mention the words "Australian" and "wine" in the same sentence. "You defend criminals with white collars?"

"You know, crimes that involve business executives. Nonviolent: embezzlement, fraud, that sort of thing."

"The kind of criminal that can pay your fee."

"Exactly."

The woman left the room, closing the door behind her, and Patrick slid the folder across the polished desk top.

Lang looked at it without touching it. "Still no idea who or why?"

Patrick shook his head sadly. "No, none. We found strong traces of aluminum, iron oxide and a nitrogen accelerant."

"Thermite? Jesus, that's not something some nutcase cooks up in his basement like a fertilizer bomb, that's what the military uses to destroy tanks, armor, something requiring intense heat."

"Which accounts for how quickly the building burned."

Patrick was avoiding the subject of Lang's main concern. The news, therefore, was going to be bad. Lang swallowed hard. "The occupants . . . you found . . . ?"

"Three, as I told you on the phone I was certain we would. Your sister, her adopted son and their hostess, Lettie Barkman."

Lang had known it was coming, but the irrational part of his mind had held a flicker of hope that somehow Janet and Jeff had not been there. It was like hearing a death sentence at the end of a trial where the result was a foregone conclusion. It just couldn't be possible, not in a sane world. Instead of Patrick across the desk, he saw Janet, her eyes twinkling in amusement at a world she refused to take seriously. And Jeff, the child his divorced sister had found in one of those fever-ridden countries south of Mexico, Jeff with the brown skin, dark eyes and profile that could have been taken from a Mayan carving. Jeff with his baseball cap turned backwards, over-sized shorts and high-top sneakers. Jeff, Lang's ten-year-old best buddy and as close as Lang would ever come to having a son.

Lang did nothing to wipe away the tears running down his cheek. "Who would want to . . . ?"

From somewhere Patrick produced a handkerchief. "We don't know. The Barkman woman was a rich American divorcée living in Paris, but as far as we can tell, she had no ties to political extremists. In fact, we can find no one among her friends who even knows what her politics were. Your sister was a doctor, a . . ."

"Juvenile orthopedist," Lang supplied. "She spent a month out of every year working in third-world countries where her patients couldn't afford medical care. Jeff was orphaned by an earthquake. She brought him home."

"She also was divorced, was she not?"

Lang leaned forward to stir his coffee. It gave him something to do with hands that seemed useless in his lap. "Yeah, guy named Holt. We haven't heard from him since they split seven, eight years ago. She kept his name 'cause that's the one on her medical degree."

"And obviously robbery was not a motive, not with the total destruction of the house."

"Unless the thieves didn't want anyone to know what was stolen."

"Possible," Patrick agreed, "but Madame Barkman had an extraordinary alarm system with interior burglar bars. Part of having lived in your New York, I suppose. The place was like, like . . . like the place where Americans keep their gold."

"Fort Knox," Lang supplied.

"Fort Knox. I would guess the intent was to destroy rather than steal."

"Destroy what?"

"When we know that, we will be close to knowing who these criminals are."

The two men stared at each other across the desk, each unable to think of something appropriate to say, until Patrick leaned forward. "I know it is small comfort to you, but the fire was intense. They would have died instantly from having the air sucked out of their bodies if the explosion did not kill them first."

Lang appreciated the thought behind the effort and recognized it as a well-intentioned lie.

"The case is actually within the jurisdiction of the police," Patrick went on. "I don't know how long I can continue to convince them we have reason to believe it was the act of terrorists."

Lang wanted the case in the hands of the DGSE for two reasons. First, his friendship with Patrick was likely to evoke more than the routine effort to see the case solved. Besides, the French security force was one of the world's best. Second, the Paris police was a morass of political infighting. Peter Sellers's *Pink Panther* rendition of the inept Inspector Clouseau had some basis in fact.

Mistaking Lang's thoughts for uncertainty, the Frenchman continued, "Of course, every resource . . ."

"I'd like to go to the scene," Lang said.

Patrick held up his hands, palms outward. "Of course. My car and driver are yours for as long as you wish."

"And do you have any idea what they did the day before . . . ?"

Patrick touched the folder. "It is routine to check such things."

Lang pulled the file over and opened it. With eyes stinging from tears as well as lack of sleep, he began to read.

3

Paris
The same day

Lang left his friend's office to go directly to the Place des Vosges. Being here, the last place Janet and Jeff had been alive, somehow brought him closer to them. He paused a long time in front of the blackened cave that was number 26. Head bowed, he stood on grass that had been scorched brown. With each minute, his resolve to see the killers exposed and punished increased. He was deaf to the sound of the grinding of his own teeth and unaware of the scowl on his face. Residents, delivery men and the curious increased their pace around him as though he were potentially dangerous.

"I'll get them myself if that's what it takes," he muttered. "Fucking bastards!"

A uniformed nanny behind him broke into a trot to get the pram and its cargo as far away as possible.

His next stop was to a mortician recommended by Patrick. The service was professional, cool and devoid of the oily faux sympathy dispensed by American funeral directors. He paid for two simple metal caskets, one only half-size, and made arrangements to have the bodies shipped back to the States.

He tried hard but unsuccessfully not to think about how very little of Janet and Jeff those European-shaped boxes would contain.

There was no rational reason to track his sister's last

hours other than a curiosity he saw no reason to deny. Besides, his flight didn't leave till evening and he didn't want to impose on his friend's hospitality. Credit card receipts electronically summoned by Patrick provided a road map of Janet's last day. She had visited Hermès and Chanel, making relatively small purchases: a scarf, a blouse. Probably more interested in souvenirs than haute couture, Lang decided. He did little more than peer through windows at mannequins too thin to be real and draped in outfits that exceeded the average annual American income. The number of Ferraris and Lamborghinis parked curbside dispelled any doubts he might have had as to the extravagance of the goods inside the shops.

The last credit card receipt led him to the Ile St. Louis. Overshadowed literally and economically by the adjacent Ile de la Cité and its towering Notre-Dame cathedral, the St. Louis was a quirky neighborhood in the middle of the Seine. Lang remembered eight blocks of tiny hotels, twenty-seat bistros and small shops filled with oddities.

Leaving Patrick's car and driver in one of the parking spots so rare along the narrow streets, Lang climbed out of the Peugeot in front of a patisserie, inhaling the aroma of freshly baked bread and sweets. He walked southeast along Rue St. Louis en l'Ile until he came to an intersection where the curbs were even closer, Rue des Deux Points. He was trying to match the address on the receipt but street numbers were either hard to see or nonexistent. Luckily, there was only one shop displaying the sign *magasin d'antiquités*, antique shop.

An overhead bell announced his entry into a space crowded with the accoutrements of civilization from at least the past hundred years or so. Oil lamps as well as electric ones were stacked on sewing tables along with piles of dusty magazines and flatware tied in bunches. Bronze and marble statues and busts of goddesses and emperors paraded up and down aisles covered in shag carpet and oriental rugs. Lang resisted the image of cobwebs his imagination created.

The single room smelled of dust and disuse with a hint of mildew. Careful not to dislodge a record player and recordings that Lang guessed dated from the 1950s, he turned around, looking for the proprietor.

"Salut!" A head popped up in front of an amoire. "Can I help you?"

Like most Parisians, the shopkeeper had an unerring ability to recognize Americans on sight.

Lang held up the copy of the receipt. "I'm looking for information."

An androgynous figure in black limped to the front of the shop. A wrinkled hand took the receipt and held it up to a light speckled with dust motes. Spectacles appeared from a pocket. "What do you wish to know?"

Lang thrashed around for a convenient story and decided upon at least part of the truth. "Janet Holt was my sister. She was killed in that explosion over in the Marais a few days ago while she was visiting here. I'm just trying to find out what she bought while she was in the city."

"I'm very sorry." The tradesman pointed to the wall, or rather to a gap between two dark pictures of people in nineteenth-century dress. "She bought a painting."

"A portrait? Of who?" That would have been unusual.

The shopkeeper shook a gray head. "No, a painting of shepherds, of a field, perhaps some religious scene."

That was more in keeping with Janet's taste.

Lang started to ask another question and thought better of it. What did it matter what happened to the painting? Judging from its source, it was doubtful it had either artistic or monetary value.

"That painting," the figure in black continued, "it had not

been here long. In fact, a man came in right after your sister and was very upset it had been sold."

Years of searching out the unusual, of recognizing anomalies, sent up antennae long unused. "This man, do you remember anything about him?"

"Near eastern, perhaps Arab, dressed in nice but inexpensive clothes. He spoke very good French."

Lang ignored the implicit accusation. "Did he say why he wanted the picture?"

"No, but as you can see, I have many beautiful things for sale."

Lang thought a moment. "You said you hadn't had the picture long. Do you remember where you got it?"

Again the shuffling of papers. "From London, Mike Jenson, Dealer in Curios, Antiquities, Etcetera, Ltd. Number 12 Old Bond Street, London W1Y 9AF. We buy inventory from each other."

If it doesn't sell one place, try another, Lang thought. "Could I borrow a pen and some paper?"

He wrote the name and address down, although he could not have explained why he thought it was important. Perhaps because it was the first detail of Janet's last day that had been even slightly out of the ordinary.

"Thanks. You've been a big help."

Outside, Lang began to repeat his path in reverse. So someone had wanted the picture Janet bought. Could it have been the reason for Janet's death? But that made no sense. As Patrick had said, the house on Place des Vosges had been like Fort Knox. It strained the imagination to think someone had been so angry at Janet beating him to the purchase of a painting that he was willing to destroy it and her as revenge.

Still . . .

The buzzing in Lang's mind was becoming louder and

louder. So loud that he was surprised to suddenly realize he really was hearing the sound. He turned in time to see one of the City's ubiquitous motor scooters increase speed and jump the curb. The driver, his features hidden in a full face helmet, must have been drunk or seriously ill, Lang thought.

The machine, still gaining velocity, was headed straight for Lang. As Lang shifted his weight to lunge into a doorway, the rider leaned towards Lang and sunlight flashed from his gloved hand. Lang threw himself away from the rider and felt something scratch his shoulder.

Furious at what he took for criminal negligence, Lang sprang to his feet ready to pursue and knock the driver off the machine's seat. The cause was hopeless. The scooter skidded around a corner and disappeared from sight.

"Monsieur!" The shopkeeper rushed outside. "You are injured!"

"No, I'm fine," Lang replied.

Then he followed the merchant's eyes to where a trickle of blood seeped from a slash in his shirt. The glitter of a blade, the intentional swerve from the street. Someone had come close to cutting his throat.

"We have crime, just like any city," Patrick said later that day.

Lang, his shoulder stiff under what he considered far too much bandaging, snorted. "Yeah, but this wasn't any snatch and run. The fucker wanted to kill me."

Patrick shook his head slowly. "Now why would he want to do that?"

That, thought Lang, was the real question.

CHAPTER TWO

1

Delta Flight 1074: Paris-Atlanta
10:35 P.M. EDT

Lang was exhausted, yet unable to sleep. Without seeing it, he stared at the comedy being shown on the 777's overhead screen. A combination of grief, curiosity and fear of flying had kept him squirming despite the wide seat and ample legroom of first class.

Eyes open or shut, he kept seeing replays of Jeff and Janet. Then a man on a motor scooter with a knife in his hand.

Coincidence? His earlier training had taught him to distrust seemingly unrelated events. But who would want to kill a woman who devoted her life to her adopted son and other small children across a troubled globe? For that matter, who would want Lang himself dead?

An old grudge? He couldn't think of any that would have survived fifteen years.

"Get you something?" The flight attendant had put on a smile along with fresh lipstick.

Lang shook his head. "I'm fine, thanks."

But, of course, he wasn't.

He forced the thoughts of Janet and Jeff from his mind as a parent might send unruly children outside to play. Thinking of the two metal boxes in the plane's cargo hold wasn't going to get him any sleep. Think of something pleasant, something soothing. . . .

Had it been only two nights ago, just hours before that phone call from Patrick?

He had spent the evening with Father Francis Narumba. They had dined at Manuel's Tavern, a funky bar that was a hangout for students, politicians and the self-proclaimed local intelligentsia. It boasted a warm if seedy collection of wooden booths and worn bar stools. The food had never been great and the atmosphere less, but it was a place where a black priest and a white lawyer could argue in Latin without anyone noticing.

Lang and Francis had their own campaign to keep alive the language of Virgil and Livy. Both were victims of a degree in the classics, Lang because he was too stubborn to be pushed into business school, the priest because the language had been required in seminary.

Their friendship was based on mutual need: there were too few people around who viewed history as something older than last week's *People* magazine. Although Lang tended to consider anything that happened after the first sack of Rome as current events, Francis had an astonishing recall of the medieval world. The Catholic Church's role in that world provided a fertile field for friendly argument.

The priest had listened politely as Lang blew off more than a little steam about the inefficiency of the Fulton County prosecutor's office, a matter motivated by more than the purely altruistic concern of a good citizen.

Having a client under indictment for over a year wasn't good for business, particularly the client's. An indictment works as a hardship, since in the public eye the accused is presumed guilty until proven otherwise.

"If the DA is as incompetent as you say, how'd he get the office?" Francis asked, regarding a badly overcooked filet of salmon. He shrugged at the hopelessness of Manuel's cuisine. *"Fabas indulcet fames."*

Latin aphorisms were a fiercely competitive game of one-upmanship.

Lang had ordered a hamburger, something requiring effort to screw up. "Hunger does indeed sweeten beans but you'd have to be pretty hungry to enjoy that," he said. "In answer to your question, the DA owes his job to who he knows, not any ability, *Ne Aesopum quidem trivit.*"

"He has not even thumbed through Aesop?"

Lang was pouring from a pitcher of room temperature beer. "Believing in all those saints makes you literal. More liberally, he doesn't know zip."

The priest sipped from a glass that had to be as tepid as Lang's. *"Damnant quod non intelligunt."*

They condemn what they do not understand.

After dinner, Lang lost the coin toss for the check for the third straight time. Sometimes he thought Francis had special help in such matters.

"Janet and Jeff okay?" Francis asked as they walked to the car.

His interest was more than polite. Since her divorce, Janet had, paradoxically, become a staunch Catholic, active in Francis's parish. Lang suspected she believed that the church's position on remarriage might impede another poor choice. Jeff's very foreignness made him special to Francis, a native of one of Africa's less desirable homelands.

Lang reached in his pocket for the key to the Porsche. "Both fine. Took Jeff to the Braves' opener last week."

"Looks like you could afford a real car instead of this toy," Francis grumbled as he contorted himself into the passenger seat.

"Enjoy the ride or take MARTA," Lang said cheerfully. "By the way, Janet got Jeff a dog last week, the ugliest mutt you'll see at the annual blessing of the animals."

"Beauty is, as the saying goes, only skin-deep."

Lang turned the key in the ignition. "Yeah, but ugly goes all the way to the bone. I think Janet picked the dog out as being the least likely to be adopted from the pound."

Before reaching the part where Lang got home, he dropped into a dreamless abyss. He didn't regain consciousness until the same flight attendant, with the same smile, shook him awake and reminded him to raise his seat back for landing.

2

Atlanta
Two days later

Lang thought he had grieved as much as a man could when Dawn died. The lingering illness, the agony of watching the woman he loved slip away had, he thought, seared his soul against further loss.

He was wrong.

As he watched the two caskets, one only half the size of the other, being lowered into the red Georgia clay, he lost the stoic exterior southern custom required of men. Instead, he wept. First wet eyes, then tears he made no effort to staunch. If anyone thought less of him for his anguish, screw 'em. He was not weeping only for Jeff and Janet, of course. He was crying for himself just as much. The last of his family gone. The thought filled him with loneliness he had never known existed.

He had lost friends and acquaintances before; any adult had. He had also known a few guys, fellow employees, who had perished in the occupational hazards of his former work, too. And he had lost Dawn, but he had had months to anticipate the inevitable. But his younger sister and nephew had been snatched away with a suddenness and in a manner that was incomprehensible.

The funeral had an air of unreality, something staged for his consumption alone. He watched the service as though witnessing someone else's bereavement, perhaps in a film. But he was no mere spectator to the anguish that chewed at him like an animal gnawing its way free from a cage.

The holes that would receive Jeff and Janet were next to the marble with Dawn's name on it, not yet weathered, the inscription as sharp as the loss he felt every Sunday when he placed flowers on the impersonal hump of earth. He would have two more graves to visit as Jeff and Janet shared eternity with Dawn on this same hillside.

Instead of hearing the words Francis read from the prayer book, he replayed every video game he had shared with Jeff, saw again every gold-starred homework assignment. He missed them both, but the death of a child was the bit of evidence that condemned the universe, that denied a sparrow-watching god.

By the time the mourners, mostly neighbors or Janet's medical peers with a scattering of parents of Jeff's friends, had finished their sincere if meaningless condolences, his grief had metabolized into fury. Whoever had done this would pay in spades. No matter how long it took, how much time was required, how far he had to travel, he would find him. Or them.

They had screwed around with the wrong family. He had no experience in law enforcement but he did have a unique repertoire of acquaintances, people who had access to information unavailable to police. If he had to call every one of them to find the guilty party, he'd do it.

The anger was strangely comforting. It brought order to an otherwise senseless world. He imagined the taste of revenge against persons unknown, ignoring the growing impatience of the cemetery's crew. His lingering at graveside was postponing the removal of the Astroturf that had concealed the mound of raw dirt from sensitive eyes, the return of the backhoe that would push the mound of soil onto coffins that had remained closed during the service.

A gentle hand touched his shoulder. His thoughts scattered as Francis patted him on the back. Lang had asked him to officiate not only as Janet's priest and friend but also as his own friend.

"Lang, you need to be thinking of Janet and Jeff, not revenge."

Lang sighed. "That obvious, huh?"

"To anyone who looks at your face."

"I can't just walk away, Francis, forget what happened. Someone did this, killed two innocent people. And don't tell me it was God's will."

The priest shook his head, staring at the two graves. "I assume you asked me to perform the service because you wanted to involve a higher force than yourself. I . . ."

"Oh, bullshit!" Lang growled. "Your higher force was notably absent when needed."

He instantly regretted the remark, the result of grief and anger as well as a sleepless night or two. Although Lang professed no particular faith, there had been no need to belittle someone else's.

"Forgive me, Francis," he said. "I'm a little raw right now."

If the priest had been offended, he didn't show it. "Understandable, Lang. I also think I understand what you're thinking. Wouldn't it make more sense to let the French police handle it?"

Lang snorted derisively. "Easy enough for you to say. To them it's just two more homicides. I want justice and I want it now."

Francis studied him for a moment, large brown eyes seeming to read his thoughts. "Just because you survived one risky occupation doesn't mean you're qualified to track down whoever did this thing."

Lang had never told Francis about his former employment. The priest was smart enough to guess that a lawyer who had attended law school in his thirties and had a blank spot almost a decade long in his resume likely had a past he didn't want to discuss. Francis had surmised the truth or something very close to it.

"Qualified or not, I have to try," Lang said.

Francis nodded silently and turned his head to stare down the gentle slope before giving his usual parting shot. "I'll be praying for you."

Lang managed to tweak his mouth into a grimace that didn't quite reach a smile as he gave his usual reply. "Can't hurt, I guess."

It was only as he watched Francis walk down the slope that Lang realized he had made a commitment to himself. Not a promise born in fury, not some feel-good resolution to be forgotten, but a commitment.

How he was going to fulfill it, he had no idea.

3

Atlanta
An hour later

Lang went from the funeral to Janet's house.

He would have to put it on the market, of course, although he was avoiding doing so. Janet had worked hard as a single-income parent for this place where she could give her son a home of his own. It was a part of both of them with which Lang was reluctant to part.

The grass needed cutting, he noted sadly, a condition Janet would never have tolerated. In back, he almost wept again when he saw the swing set he and Janet had erected two years ago. The effort had consumed most of a hot summer afternoon and a cooler of icy beer. Only last month, Jeff has confided to his uncle that he was too big now to play on swing sets like little kids.

Lang unlocked the door, noting that the place had that stuffiness that unused places seem to acquire. Telling himself that he needed to make a thorough inspection, he wandered upstairs and down, winding up in Janet's living room. He smiled wanly. It was far neater than he had ever seen it. The walls were covered with her paintings: mournful saints, dour-faced martyrs or bloody crucifixions. Janet collected religious art and Lang was the one who had started it.

Years before, a defector from one of the Balkan countries had brought with him part of his art collection, painings he had no doubt stolen from some Communist-banned church and was selling with an enthusiasm only a recent convert to capitalism could muster. The pictures, as Lang recalled, were of a bloody and recently severed head of John the Baptist and an equally gory body bristling with arrows. Saint Sebastian, he supposed. The colors were remarkable, the style early Byzantine and the cost at the London auction quite reasonable. In light of Janet's recent conversion to Catholicism, the gifts had seemed appropriate. Or at least the source of a good laugh.

They were a bigger hit than Lang had contemplated, igniting an interest that would last the rest of her life. Janet was not a particularly religious person, her Catholicism notwithstanding. She did, however, enjoy the portrayals of the sundry saints in all their miseries of martyrdom. It was the only sort of art, she explained, she could really afford. Impressionists and their contemporary progeny far exceeded her finances. There was enough church art on the market to keep the price of even some of the earlier pieces within her range.

She also got a certain amount of pleasure out of Lang's not always successful efforts to translate the Latin that frequently appeared in the paintings.

He understood the interest in collecting. In his various travels, Lang had managed to gather together a small group of objects connected to the classical world he found so fascinating: a Roman coin with Augustus Caesar's image on it, an Etruscan votive cup, the hilt of a Macedonian dagger that might have belonged to one of Alexander's soldiers.

He was locking the front door when the mail truck pulled up to the curb. Lang watched as the postman stuffed the mailbox and drove off.

Sara, Lang's secretary, had come by the past few days to collect the mail, mostly a stream of advertising flyers that seemed to proclaim that life, for the buying public, continued as though nothing had happened. The irony of Janet's existence being reduced to bits on some huckster's mailing list was a bitter one. As her executor, there were a few bills which Lang intended to pay before saying farewell on her behalf to AmEx and Visa.

The mailbox contained a postcard announcing a sale at Neiman's, the midtown neighborhood paper and an envelope with the name "Ansley Galleries" printed on it. Curious, Lang opened it, extracting a computer-printed letter informing "Dear Customer" that the gallery had been unable to reach anyone by phone but the job was complete.

Ansley Galleries was a small storefront down around Sixth or Seventh Street, a few minutes from where he was standing. There seemed no point in having Sara make an extra trip.

The teenaged girl behind the counter had spiked purple hair, lipstick to match, a butterfly tattooed on her neck and a ring through her left eyebrow. Looking at her made not having children of his own easier to bear. She glanced at the letter, then at him. Her jaws stopped masticating a wad of gum long enough to ask, "You're . . . ?"

"Langford Reilly, Dr. Holt's brother."

She looked back down at the letter in her hand and then back at him. "Jesus! I read in the paper . . . I'm sorry. Dr. Holt was a sweet lady. Bummer."

He had had enough condolences for a lifetime, let alone today. Still, it was nice of the kid. "Thanks. I appreciate that. I'm taking care of her estate. That's why I'm picking up . . ."

He pointed to the paper in her hand.

"Oh! Sorry! I'll get it for you."

He tracked her progress between the shelves behind the counter by the sound of popping gum.

When she returned, she had a package wrapped in brown paper. "Dr. Holt sent this from Paris, had us frame and appraise it for insurance." She tore off a small envelope that had been taped to the paper. "This is a Polaroid of the painting and the appraisal. You'll want to keep them somewhere safe and we'll keep a copy." She put both envelope and package on the counter and consulted a sales slip. "That'll be two sixty-seven fifty-five, including tax."

Lang handed her his plastic and watched her swipe it through a terminal as he stuffed the envelope into his inside coat pocket. What was he going to do with some piece of religious art? Selling it was out of the question;

Janet had bought it in the last hours of her life. He would find a place for it somewhere.

He signed the credit card receipt, wadded it into a pocket and took the package under one arm. Stopping at the doorway, he let his eyes acclimate from the dark of the shop to the bright spring light outside.

Something out there was not quite right, out of place.

The old sensitivity which made him habitually aware of his surroundings had become so much a part of him that he no longer noticed it, like a deer's instinctive listening for the sound of a predator. His mind noted the doorman of his condo standing on the left instead of the right side of the door, a jalopy in an upscale neighborhood where Mercedes and BMWs belonged.

It took a second for him to realize he had stopped and was staring at the street and another to realize why. The man on the other side, the derelict who appeared to be sleeping off the demons of cheap wine in the paper- and glass-littered doorway of one of the neighborhood's empty buildings. He sat, facing Lang, eyes seemingly closed. The worn camo jacket, tattered jeans and filthy, laceless sneakers were in character. The man could have been one of the city's thousands of wandering homeless. But how many were clean-shaven with hair cut short enough not to hang below the knit cap? Even assuming this one had recently been released from a hygiene-conscious jail, it was unlikely he would be here so close to noon when the church down the street was giving away soup and sandwiches. Also, he had gone to sleep in a hurry. Lang was certain the bum had not been there when he arrived at the gallery, yet he had found a suitable spot and dozed off in two or three minutes. Even the gut-corroding poison purchased with dollars panhandled from guilty yuppies wouldn't knock him out that quickly.

Of course, Lang told himself, he could be mistaken. There were plenty of beggars in Midtown and he could have failed to notice this one. But it was not likely.

Raising a hand as though to shade his eyes, Lang left a space between his fingers, keeping the sleeper in view as he walked to where the Porsche was parked. The knit cap slowly turned. Lang, too, was being watched.

In the car, he circled the block. The man was gone.

Lang reminded himself that paranoia doesn't necessarily mean someone really isn't after you.

CHAPTER THREE

1

Atlanta
That afternoon

Lang knew Sara, his secretary, would have alerted him to any emergency in his practice. It was as much as to occupy his mind as to see things for himself that he went to his office, a suite high in one of downtown Atlanta's taller buildings.

She had been full of teary condolences at that morning's funeral, and Lang expected Sara to begin weeping again. She had, after all, known Janet and Jeff well. To his surprise, she greeted him with, "Kennel called. Janet left this number as an emergency contact. The dog, Grumps, been there over two weeks. Want me to pick it up? What kind of a name is 'Grumps,' anyway? What ever happened to Spot or Fido?"

"Name Jeff picked out, I guess." Lang had no idea what he was going to do with one large, ugly dog. But Grumps

had been Jeff's friend and he sure as hell wasn't going to
see the animal sent to the pound. Actually, when he
thought about it, having the mutt around might be like
having a little part of his family back. "No thanks. I'll pick
him up on the way home."

He sat down behind a desk covered with files bearing
Post-Its.

Once he had retired from his previous occupation, he
and Dawn had agreed the law was an appealing second
career. His small pension plus her salary saw him through
school. The idea of working for someone else was unap-
pealing. Upon graduation, he set out his own shingle and
began working the phones with old acquaintances for
clients.

Word spread. His practice became profitable, enabling
Dawn to quit her job and open the boutique of which she
had always dreamed. No longer subject to the unpre-
dictability of his former work, he was home almost every
night. And when he wasn't, his wife knew where he was
and when to anticipate his return.

They pretty much had it all, as the Jimmy Buffet song
says: big house, money to do what they wanted and a love
for each other that time seemed to fuel like pouring gaso-
line on a fire. Even after five years, it hadn't been unusual
for Dawn to meet him at the door in something skimpy—
or nothing at all—and they would make love in the living
room, too impatient to wait to get to the bed.

It had been embarrassing the evening Lang brought a
client home unannounced.

The only real cloud on their horizon was Dawn's inabil-
ity to get pregnant. After endless fertility tests, they
arranged for an adoption that had been only months away
when Dawn began to lose both appetite and weight. The
female parts that had refused to reproduce had become
malignant.

In less than a year, her full breasts had become empty sacks and her ribs looked as though they would break through the pale skin with the next labored breath. This was the first time Lang realized the same universe that could give him a loving, helpful wife could dispassionately watch her degenerate from a healthy woman into a hairless skeleton in a hospital bed where her breath stank of death and her only pleasure was the drugs that temporarily took away the pain.

As the cancer progressed, he and Dawn spoke of her recovery, the things they would do and places they would go together. Each of them hoped the other believed it. He, and he suspected she too, prayed for speed to reach the end that was inevitable.

Lang suffered in the certain knowledge of her mortality and in the irrational guilt that he was unable to give her comfort. He had more time than anyone would have wanted to prepare for her death.

As he remembered, he wondered which was worse: the torture of certain death or the sudden snatching away of his sister and nephew.

At least for the latter, he could dream of revenge, of getting even with the powers that had caused their deaths. That was a satisfaction he would never have for Dawn.

Over the years since his retirement, he had diminishing need to use his former contacts. How many of his old cohorts remained, he wondered as he groped in a desk drawer. His fingers found the false back and he slid a wooden panel out of place. Behind it was a small booklet which he pulled out and opened on the desk. Who was left? More importantly, who was left that owed him a favor?

He dialed a number with a 202 area code, let it ring twice and hung up. Somewhere, Lang's own phone number would appear on a computer screen. In less than a second, that number would be verified with Lang's name and location. That is, if the number he had called still belonged to the person he hoped he was calling.

Within a minute, Sara buzzed him. "There's a Mr. Berkley on the phone, says he's returning your call."

Lang picked up. "Miles? How they hangin', ole buddy?"

The reply took a split second longer than an ordinary call. The call had been routed through one of a number of random relays scattered around the globe and was completely untraceable.

"Jus' fine, Lang. How th' hell you doin'?" Through the years, Miles Berkley had clung to his southern drawl as though it were a prized possession.

"Not so good, Miles. I need some help."

Lang knew his words were being compared to old voiceprints. Or verified by some technology that had come along since his departure.

Pause.

"Ennythin' I can do, Lang . . ."

"There was a fire in Paris three days ago, looked like thermite was used."

"So I heard."

Miles still read local papers. Anything abnormal, anything that might be the precursor to possible activity of interest, was noted, examined and catalogued. Miles apparently had the same job.

Grateful for that bit of luck, Lang asked, "Any military stores missing? Any ideas where that shit came from, who might have weapons like that on hand?"

"What's your interest?" Miles wanted to know. "Think it might be a client of yours?"

"It was my sister, her friend's house. She and my nephew were in it."

There was a pause that was too long to attribute solely to a relay. "Shit, I'm sorry, Lang, Had no idea. I can see why you'd wanna know but we don't have zip so far. No break-ins at military installations, no inventory missing, far as we know. 'Course about ennybody could walk off with half the Russian arsenal without the Ruskies knowin'. Your sister into something she shouldna been?"

"Nothing more than her kid, her medical practice and her church. Hardly criminal."

"That makes it tough to guess at a motive. Say, you're not thinking of coming out of retirement, are you? Hope not. Whoever these bastards are, they're likely to be pros. No way you can take 'em on by yourself, even if you knew who they were."

"Wouldn't think of it," Lang lied. "You can understand my interest. Any chance you can keep me posted, you find out anything?"

"You know I can't do that, not officially, anyway. Asshole buddy to asshole buddy, I'll see what I can do."

For several minutes after he hung up, Lang stared out of the window. He had just begun and already he was at a dead end.

2

Atlanta
Later the same day

Park Place was not a very original name: the developer of Lang's condo building had taken it right off the *Monopoly* board. There was no Boardwalk nearby. Putting up a high-rise that looked like a stack of square checkers probably was not a new idea, either. Having a doorman in a comic opera uniform was, however, a first for Atlanta and a bit rich for any place south of New York's Upper East Side.

When Lang got home, Richard the doorman wasn't as much an amenity as an obstacle. He was inspecting Grumps with the same expression he might have used for garbage dumped in the building's marble foyer. The dog's wagging tail and imploring brown eyes did little to diminish the disdain.

Grumps didn't much look like a pet of the affluent, Lang grudgingly admitted. The dog could have been claimed by almost any breed, with his shaggy black coat and white face. One ear was pointed, the other folded over like a wilted flower. Straining at the end of his new leash, Grumps was sniffing a bow-fronted boulle chest that Lang had long suspected might have been the genuine article. Had the dog not already anointed the boxwoods outside, Lang would have been nervous about the Abkhazian area rugs.

He figured a fifty would turn contempt to gratitude and he was right.

"He was my nephew's," Lang explained apologetically as he handed over the folded bill. "I didn't know what else to do with him."

Richard pocketed the money with a smoothness of one accustomed to residents' largess beyond the Christmas fund. No doubt he was aware of Janet and Jeff's deaths. Like all the building's employees, he seemed to know what was going on in the lives of those he served.

He winked conspiratorially. "Looks like he weighs under ten pounds to me."

The condominium association's rules forbade pets in excess of ten pounds, a weight Grumps clearly exceeded five or six times.

"The gift is to make sure your powers of estimation don't deteriorate," Lang said with a wink.

"Count on it. Can I help you with the package?"

Richard was referring to the wrapped painting Lang had under the arm that wasn't holding the leash.

Lang thanked him but declined, in a hurry to reach the

elevators before any of his more realistically sighted neighbors appeared.

Once the dog had inspected every inch of the condo, verifying that he and Lang were the only living creatures present, he slumped into a corner, staring into space with one of those canine expressions that is subject to multiple interpretations. Lang would have guessed he missed Jeff.

A good feed would cheer him up. But what to feed him? Lang had neglected to stop by the store for dog food, even had he known what brand Grumps preferred. Guiltily, Lang transferred a pound of hamburger from the freezer to the microwave. His offering received no more than a polite sniff. The mutt really did miss his young master.

"You don't want to eat, it's okay with me," Lang said, instantly feeling foolish for trying to strike up a conversation with a dog.

Grumps's only acknowledgement was shifting his mournful brown eyes in Lang's direction. Lang sat on the sofa and wondered what he was going to do with a dog that wouldn't eat and a painting he didn't want.

Grumps began to snore. Swell. Nothing like a dog for companionship.

Lang gazed around the familiar space. The door from the outside hall entered directly into the living room. Across from it, floor-to-ceiling glass framed downtown Atlanta. To his right were the kitchen and dining area. On his left was the door to the single bedroom. Most of the available wall space was occupied by built-in shelves loaded with an eclectic selection of books that demanded more space than the small suite had to give. He had been reduced to buying only paperbacks because he could not bear to discard hardbacks but had no place to put new ones.

What little wall space remained was given to oversized landscapes by relatively unknown impressionists, paintings he and Dawn had purchased together. His favorite, a reputed Herzog, hung in the bedroom where its rich greens and yellows could brighten the mornings.

The art was among the very few things he had kept after the sale of the house he and Dawn had hoped to fill with children. Most of her antiques were too large for the condo, their fussiness too feminine for his taste and the association too painful. He had kidded himself into believing the hurt would be diminished by getting rid of things familiar.

Shedding the furniture had been an epiphany in a sense, though. It had led him to recognize furniture, clothes, appliances as mere stuff, objects rented for a lifetime at most. Dawn's death had made him acutely aware of the futility of material possessions: they were only things you had to give up in the end. Not that he had become an ascetic, shunning worldly delights. But if he could enjoy the better restaurants, live in the place of his choice, drive the car he wanted, the rest was excess baggage.

Lang had replaced antiques with contemporary pieces of chrome, leather and glass, retaining only two items, both predating his wife: a golden oak linen press, which housed the television and sound system, and a small secretary, the pediment of which bore the carved lazy eights that were the signature of Thomas Elfe, Charleston's premier cabinetmaker of the eighteenth century. Behind the wavy, hand-blown glass was his small collection of antiquities and a few rare books.

He forgot Grumps's snores for the moment while he considered the brown paper package leaning against the wall by the door. Might as well have a look.

He found pretty much what he had expected: a canvas of about three by four feet depicted three bearded men in robes and sandals. They appeared to be examining an oblong stone structure. The two on either side held sticks or staffs while the one in the middle knelt, pointing to an inscription carved into the rock, *"ETINARCADIAEGOSUM."* Latin. "I am in Arcadia" was Lang's tentative interpretation, but that left over the "sum." Why would there be a superfluous word? An incorrect translation was the answer that first came to mind. But he couldn't make sense of the words any other way.

The fourth figure, a woman richly dressed, stood to the right of the men, her hand on the shoulder of the one kneeling. Behind the figures, mountains dominated the landscape, chalky hills instead of the verdant foliage of most religious pictures. The geography seemed to converge on a single gap, a rugged valley in the hazy distance.

There was something about that gap. . . . He turned the picture upside down. The space between the mountains now resembled a familiar shape, roughly similar to the profile of Washington on a quarter. A small peak made the long nose, a rounded hill the chin. It was a stretch, but that was what it looked like.

The painting had no meaning he could see, Biblical or otherwise. He crossed the room to where he had tossed his suit jacket across a chair and took the appraisal out of the pocket, putting the Polaroid on the secretary. *"Les Bergers d'Arcadie*, copy of the original by Nicholas Poussin (1593–1665)," read the note from Ansley Galleries.

Did that mean the work was a copy of Poussin's work or that Poussin had made the copy? Had the copy been made between 1593 and 1665 or had the artist lived seventy-two years? Whichever the case, the appraiser at Ansley Galleries had put a value of ten to twelve thousand dollars on the painting which Lang assumed included the two-hundred-buck-plus frame he had paid for. Whether the value was real or merely a feel-good for a customer, he could only guess.

No matter. It wasn't going to fit easily here. He stepped

back to take another look before moving the painting from beside the door. Where could he put it where it wouldn't be in the way in the small apartment? Nowhere, really.

He set it on the fold-out desk of the secretary, stood back and stared at it again. *Bergers*—French for shepherds, perhaps? That would explain the staffs or crooks but not the woman who was far too well-clad to herd sheep. *Arcadie*? Acadia? A name given to part of Canada by eighteenth-century French settlers, wasn't it? He was almost certain. When the English expelled them, they had immigrated to the nearest French territory, Louisiana, where they became known as Acadians or 'Cajuns. Longfellow's epic *Evangeline* and all that. But the British hadn't conquered Canada by 1665, had they? And what the hell did Canadian shepherds have to do with anything?

Curious, he searched the bookshelves until he found a historical encyclopedia. The province in Canada had been named for a part of Greece. Great. Now he had shepherds that were Greek instead of Canadian. Lots of help that was.

Leaving the puzzle of the painting on the secretary, he took the appraisal and Polaroid into the bedroom and put them in the drawer of his bedside table, making a mental note to take them to his lock box next trip to the bank. Exchanging his suit for a pair of jeans, he headed back into the living room as he buttoned up a denim shirt.

3

Atlanta
The next day

When Lang got home from work the next day, he noticed scratches on the brass plate of the lock on his front door, small marks that an untrained eye would never have noticed. Squatting so his eyes were level with the doorknob, Lang could tell that these were no random marks left by a careless cleaning crew. Each tiny scrape led to the opening of the lock. Someone had tried to pick the mechanism.

Lang stood. He had almost succeeded in dismissing the incident on the Ile St. Louis as a botched robbery attempt. But not quite. Someone from his former life? It was still unlikely they would have waited this long to conclude whatever business they might have had. Besides, he was in America, not Europe. As if that still made a difference.

The more important question was, had they succeeded and how many were "they"?

Lang made himself swallow hard, giving himself time to dissipate the outrage of having his personal space violated. Bursting in on one or more possibly armed burglars might make for a great scene from a Bruce Willis movie but it wasn't a move towards a longer, healthier life.

Call the cops? He was reaching for the cell phone on his belt and paused. The Atlanta police? It would take them forever to arrive and if there was no one in his unit, he'd look like a fool.

He turned and went back to the elevators.

At the concierge desk in the lobby, he waited until the pimply-faced kid in the ill-fitting uniform finished making a phone call and turned to him.

Lang shrugged with an embarrassed smile. "I locked myself out."

"Your number?" The kid was already looking under the desk for one of the skeletons. With the number of geriatric residents, Lang's problem was not unusual.

On the ride back up, Lang felt a twinge of guilt. If burglars were in the apartment, there was some possibility they were armed. Maybe he should have summoned the law after all. Involving this young man in a possible robbery, exposing the lad to potential physical harm, wasn't a nice thing to do. Conversely, facing one or more red-handed felons alone was stupid. Heroes died young.

Accustomed to the idiosyncracies of the wealthy, the concierge never asked how Lang had managed to engage the dead bolt from outside in the hall. Instead, he pushed the door open and gestured Lang inside. "There we are, Mr. Reilly."

Lang's eyes were searching the small space as he handed a folded bill over. "Thanks."

"Thank *you,* sir." From the tone, Lang must have given him a larger tip than he had anticipated.

Lang noticed nothing unusual until he turned to face the interior wall. The painting was gone. He hurriedly glanced around in the unlikelihood he had misplaced it. How do you lose a canvas that big in an apartment this small? You don't.

He took two steps, stopping at the counter that separated kitchen from living room. Enjoying the coolness of Mexican tiles on his stomach, Grumps looked up and yawned.

"Great guard dog you are," Lang muttered as he started to turn towards the bedroom.

He stopped again. Beside Grumps was a large grease spot. The intruders had occupied the dog with something to eat. As verifying the fact, Grumps burped loudly.

"Excuse you, bribe-taker. You better hope they didn't lace that hunk of meat with rat poison."

Unabashed, Grumps stretched and belched again.

At first, the bedroom seemed untouched.

Then Lang noticed that one of his silver hairbrushes was on the side of the dresser opposite where he normally left it. A photograph of Dawn faced the room at a slightly different angle. Someone had been careful but not careful enough.

Stepping around the bed, Lang opened the single drawer of the bedside table. The Browning nine-millimeter he had carried for years was where he kept it. Besides the gun and a box of ammunition, the drawer was empty.

Lang was certain he had put the Polaroid and appraisal of the picture there for temporary safekeeping. Who would steal a Polaroid?

The memory of the smoldering ruin in the Place des Vosges was his answer: someone who wanted to leave no trace of that picture.

He shook his head. Stealing the painting and the photo . . .

Lang took a quick inventory of his home. A few items were an inch or so out of place but nothing else was missing. Perhaps the disappearance of the three items made a sort of illogical sense. The thief had been unhurried but left the sterling silverware, a pair of gold cuff links and studs, and the pistol. The purpose of the break-in had clearly been the Poussin and all evidence of it.

Why?

Lang had no idea but every intention of finding out.

CHAPTER FOUR

1

Atlanta
The next day

Lang was waiting at Ansley Galleries when it opened the next morning. The same purple-haired girl was behind the counter with the same bored expression.

"Our copy?" she asked. "Good thing we keep copies of all our appraisals, like I told you. You'd be surprised how many people keep 'em in the house. There's a fire or something and both the art and the appraisal's gone."

"And the Polaroid," Lang asked, "you said you keep an extra of it, too?"

She nodded, chewing a wad of gum. "Yeah, the Polaroid, too."

He smiled weakly and shrugged, a man embarrassed by his own ineffectiveness. "Dumb me. Can't remember where I put the envelope with them in it. Be happy to pay for copies."

The gum snapped. "No problem."

A minute later she was back. The copy of the photograph, though not in color, was remarkably clear. He handed her a twenty.

She shook her head. "Happy to help. You lose that, we'll charge for the next set of copies."

Outside, he pretended to search his pockets for car keys while he checked up and down the street. If there were watchers, they were out of sight.

2

Atlanta
An hour later

"High Museum as in art museum?" Sara asked incredulously. "You want me to get the number of the art museum?"

Lang settled behind his desk, speaking through the open door. "What's the big surprise? I go to the museum, theater, ballet, et al, regular culture vulture. You don't remember my getting tickets for you for the opening of the Matisse exhibit?"

Sara shook her head without a gray hair moving out of place. "Lang, that was years ago. And it was one of your clients who got the tickets."

"Just find out who the director is, okay?"

Two hours later, Lang parked in the MARTA lot behind what appeared to be white building blocks dumped into a random pile by a giant child. The contemporary edifice had to be one of the ugliest in a town not known for its architectural treasures. Lang's theory was that Sherman's destruction of the city a century and a half before had given Atlanta an atavistic insensitivity to structural aesthetics. The High Museum was named for the donors of the site, the High family, not for any preeminence in the art world. In fact, the concrete and glass housed a collection surprising only in its modesty when compared to similar institutions in comparable cities.

Lang passed by the circular ramp inside the main hall and took an elevator to the top floor. Exiting, he passed a modern mural on canvas that an alert janitorial crew anywhere else would have recognized as a painter's drop cloth and hauled outside to the Dumpsters. At the end, he found a door marked "Administrative Offices."

Lang had the impression he had stepped through Alice's looking glass. Hair of every color, rings in every visible orifice, clothes from *Star Wars*. The clerk at Ansley Galleries had been conservative in comparison.

A young woman with half her head shaved and polished, the other covered by Astroturf-green hair, glanced up from the computer terminal on her desk. "May I help you?"

"I'm Langford Reilly. I have an appointment with Mr. Seitz."

The woman jabbed a dagger-length fingernail painted an ominous black. "In there." She picked up a phone. "Mr. Reilly's here to see you."

A man stepped from a doorway. Lang wasn't sure what he had expected but Mr. Seitz wasn't it. Instead, he was normal looking. Well-tailored dark suit, red power tie, shiny black wingtips. He was slender, just under six feet tall. Early forties, judging by the dove-wings of gray over his ears. His chiseled face had recently seen the beach. Or the inside of a tanning booth.

A gold Rolex competed in dazzle with jeweled cuff links as he extended a manicured hand. "Jason Seitz, Mr. Reilly."

"Thanks for seeing me on such short notice," Lang said. "Quite a colorful crew you have here."

His eyes followed Lang's stare. "Art students. We try to

hire from the art school," he said as if that explained the costumes. "Won't you step this way?"

They entered an office that was as traditional as the employees outside were weird. Seitz indicated a leather wing chair where Lang could admire the wall of photographs: Seitz shaking hands with or hugging local business leaders, politicians and celebrities. He slipped behind a dining room table–sized desk littered with snapshots of paintings, sculptures and some other objects Lang didn't immediately recognize.

Seitz leaned back, made a steeple of his fingers and said, "I usually don't have the pleasure of meeting with people I don't know, but Ms. . . . ."

"Mitford—Sara Mitford, my secretary."

Seitz nodded. "Ms. Mitford was quite insistent, said it was urgent. Fortunately, I had a cancellation. . . ."

His gaze had the practiced sincerity of someone used to soliciting money. It fitted nicely with the favor he wanted Lang to know he was doing him.

"I really appreciate your taking the time. I'm sure running this place keeps you busy."

The museum director smiled. Lang would have been astonished had he shown anything but perfect teeth. "Actually, the board of directors runs the museum. I am their humble servant."

"Yeah. Well . . ." Uncertain how to respond to the ill-fitting humility, Lang opened his briefcase and leaned forward to hand the copy of the Polaroid across the expanse of mahogany. "I was wondering if you could tell me about that."

Seitz frowned, squinting at the picture. "I'm afraid I don't understand."

"*Les Bergers d'Arcadie,* Nicholas Poussin. Or at least a copy of it."

Seitz nodded. "Mid–seventeenth-Century French, if I recall. The original of that picture hangs in the Louvre. What specifically is it you want to know?"

Lang had what he thought was a plausible explanation. "I'm not sure. That is, I'm a lawyer and I have a case involving . . ."

The director held up his hands, palms outward. "Whoa, Mr. Reilly! The museum is not in a position to authenticate art for individuals. As an attorney, I'm sure you can understand the liability issues."

Lang shook his head, eager to calm what he recognized as a bad case of legal anxiety syndrome. "I apologize. I didn't make myself clear. All I want is to learn the history of the painting, what it's supposed to depict."

Seitz was only marginally calmed. "I'm afraid I can't be of much help." He whirled his chair around, removing a book from the antique table behind him that served as a credenza. Thumbing through it, he continued. "I can say, I think, that what you have there is a picture of a copy, and not a particularly authentic copy, either. Ah, there . . . Not quite the same, is it?"

He was pointing to a photo of a similar picture. At first Lang saw no difference. He looked more closely. The background was smoother; there was no upside down profile of Washington.

"Religious art, late Renaissance, not my specialty," Seitz continued, shutting the book with a thump. He brought Lang's copy closer to his face. "Those letters on the structure, they look like Latin."

Lang moved to look over his shoulder. "I think so, yes."

"Obviously, they mean something. For that matter, the whole painting may well be symbolistic. Artists of that era often had messages in their paintings."

"You mean, like a code?"

"Sort of, but less sophisticated. For instance, you've seen

a still life, flowers or vegetables with a bug or two, perhaps a wilted blossom?"

Lang shrugged noncommittally. It wasn't the sort of art he would remember.

"It was popular about the time Poussin painted. A certain flower or plant—rosemary for memory, for example. A beetle might be reminiscent of an Egyptian scarab, symbolic of death or the afterlife or whatever."

Lang went back and sat down. "So you're saying this painting has a message of some sort."

This time it was the director who shrugged. "I'm saying it's possible."

"Who might know?"

Seitz slowly spun his chair to face the window behind him and gazed out in silence for a moment. "I don't really have an idea." He flashed the Rolex. "And I fear we're running out of time."

Lang didn't budge from his seat. "Give me a name, if you would. Somebody likely to be familiar with Poussin, preferably somebody who might be able to decipher whatever symbolism there might be. Believe me, it's important. This is no academic exercise."

Seitz turned back to stare at him, a frown tugging at his mouth, no doubt because he wasn't used to being delayed. Then he returned to the row of books from which he had taken the first one before snatching another one up and paging through it, too.

"It would appear," the art director said, "that the leading authority on Poussin and on late Renaissance religious art, too, is a Guiedo Marcenni. He's written quite a lot about your man Poussin."

Lang pulled a legal pad out of his briefcase. "And where do I find Mr. Marcenni?"

The frown had become a sardonic smile. "Not 'mister,'

but 'Fra.' Brother Marcenni is a monk, an art historian with the Vatican Museum. Vatican, as in Rome." He stood. "Now I really must ask you to excuse me, Mr. Reilly. One of the young ladies will show you out."

He was gone before Lang could thank him. Thank him for nothing. Lang was more puzzled than ever.

3

Atlanta
That evening

Lang was so absorbed in his thoughts that he almost missed the elevator's stop at his floor. Still thinking, he took the few steps to his door and stooped to pick up the *Atlanta Journal-Constitution*. He froze, key in hand.

"FIRE GUTS MIDTOWN DISTRICT," the above-the-fold headline screamed. An aerial view showed a pillar of smoke towering from a block of one-story, flat-roofed buildings. The one in the middle was—had been—Ansley Galleries.

Lang let himself in and dropped into the nearest chair, oblivious to Grumps, who was more than ready to go outside.

A fire leveled an entire block of Seventh Street early this afternoon as the result of a faulty gas stove, according to Capt. Jewal Abbar, Chief Investigator for the Atlanta Fire Department.

Three shops, Ansley Galleries, Dwight's Interiors and Afternoon Delites, were totally destroyed. Other establishments in the popular in-town shopping area were severely damaged.

Abbar said there were no serious injuries, although several people were treated at Grady Memorial Hospital for smoke inhalation.

Maurice Wiser, manager of Afternoon Delites, a vegetarian restaurant, was quoted as saying the stove exploded when turned on.

Lang didn't finish the article, but dropped the paper and stared at the wall. It was possible, he conceded, that the stove exploded in an amazing concurrence of accident and coincidence. Just as it was possible someone had fire-bombed the house in Paris, he had nearly had his throat slit, and his highrise had been burglarized just to steal a painting—and a copy at that. Now the gallery that had kept a copy was also a fire casualty.

If all of that were coincidence, the Poussin made the curse of the Hope Diamond look like a lucky shamrock.

Instead of coincidence, he saw an emerging pattern, frightening in its simplicity: Whoever possessed that picture, or knew something about it, was in jeopardy. Including Lang.

But why? The original Poussin, the one in the Louvre, must have been seen by millions. The slightly different background in Janet's copy, then, was the reason someone wanted that particular painting. And if they wanted it badly enough to commit indiscriminate murder and arson for it . . .

Lang knew four things: They were intent on erasing every trace of that painting, they didn't care who got hurt, they had an international intelligence system as good or better than most poilce forces, and they were well prepared for the task.

The last two observations were the most frightening. Intelligence and preparation indicated a professional and a professional indicated an organization. What sort of an organization would burn and kill just to destroy a copy of the Poussin? An organization that had a very strong interest in whatever secret the canvas held.

His train of thought was derailed by Grumps's insistent pacing. "Okay, okay," he said. "Gimme a minute."

He went into the bedroom and opened the drawer in the bedside table. He took out the Browning. Easing back the slide, he confirmed there was a round in the chamber. He checked the safety and stuffed the weapon into his belt. From now on, it was going to be like the credit card: Don't leave home without it.

Tomorrow he would have to go apply for a permit. But for the moment, being caught without the gun had more dire consequences than being caught with it.

As Lang left the apartment with Grumps on a leash, he stopped in the hall to leave two telltales. The first was a tiny strip of plastic tape stretched between the door and jamb, a device any professional would anticipate and find fairly easily. Then he licked his hand and wiped it on the knob, sticking a hair to the brass. Virtually impossible to see and it would fall loose at the slightest touch.

If his reasoning was anywhere near correct, he could expect company soon.

4

Atlanta
A few minutes later

When Lang and Grumps came back in, he nuked a frozen enchilada in the microwave and fed Grumps the dog food he had finally remembered to buy. From the sounds of voracious eating, Lang judged he had made a good choice.

Lang's meal was laced with so many chilies it could have constituted an act of war by the Federal Republic of Mexico. He scraped his leftovers into Grumps's bowl. The dog gave him a reproachful glare and retreated to a corner, Lang's offering untouched. Apparently Lang was more a connoisseur of canned dog food than international cuisine

Lang selected a tubular steel chair with minimal padding, one in which it was unlikely he would be very comfortable, putting it just to the side of the door to the outside hall. As the door opened, the chair would be behind it. Then he moved a three-way lamp to the other side of the entrance, its lowest setting enough to silhouette anyone coming through the doorway but dim enough not to spill into the hall outside. He put the Browning in his lap, although he didn't intend to use the automatic unless he had to. He wanted answers, not bodies.

Then he began to wait.

There wasn't enough light to read. So he just sat, observing Atlanta's skyline. Far to the south, he could see jets, pinpricks of light, as they approached or departed Hartsfield-Jackson International. Somewhere between Lang and the distant airport, beams of searchlights aimlessly crisscrossed the night sky. He resisted the impulse to check the luminous dial of his watch. Time passes more slowly when you keep track of it.

Maybe he was mistaken; maybe he was in no danger. Maybe, but unlikely. Whoever had obliterated the place in Paris and started a fire in Midtown wasn't likely to spare him. The only question was when it would happen.

Well after what Lang estimated was midnight, past the time he usually turned out the lights and retired, he detected, or imagined, something from the floor beside him, not so much a sound as an undefined interruption of clinging silence. A growl from Grumps, increasing until Lang put a comforting hand on the furry head. The dog had taken Lang's rebuke after the burglary to heart.

Lang stood, silently moving the chair aside and putting the Browning in his belt again. Caterpillars with icy feet were marching up and down the back of his neck where muscles were tightening in anticipation. Years had gone by since he'd last had that feeling. He had missed it.

A series of soft clicks came from the door. Lang was glad he hadn't had time to install a new lock. The replacement would have alerted whoever was on the other side of that door that the occupant knew the intruder could gain entry, make him even more cautious than committing a burglary would.

Lang tensed and tried to breathe deeply to relax mind and muscles. Tension begot mistakes, his long-ago training had taught. And mistakes begot death. Tension and training were both forgotten as the door slowly opened inward, a square of darkness against the pale, buttery light of the lamp.

Lang resisted the impulse to lunge and throw his weight against the door, pinning the intruder against the jamb. Too easy for him to escape into the hall. Or shoot through the door. Instead, Lang waited until he could see the entire form of a man, a dark mass, arm extended as it entered and quietly shut the door. Something glittered in the man's hand.

A weapon, Lang was certain. He felt the fury for Janet and Jeff boil up in his stomach like bile. But he made himself wait.

Wait until the intruder turned from closing the door. Then Lang moved, pivoting to face him. Before Lang's brain even registered the shock on the invader's face, Lang's left hand came down like an ax against the other man's right wrist in a move designed to shatter the small, fragile carpal bones. Or at least knock a weapon loose. Simultaneously, Lang smashed the heel of his open right hand into the throat. Done correctly, the blow would leave an opponent helpless, too busy trying to force air into a ruined larynx to resist.

Lang was only partially successful. Something clattered

to the floor and there was a gasp of breath as the man, still a solid dark form, staggered backwards. Lang's weight had shifted with his attack and he followed through, pirouetting to put his full bulk behind a fist aimed at where he gauged the bottom of the intruder's rib cage would be, the place where a blow to the solar plexus would double him over like a jackknife.

Lang hit ribs instead.

Lang's opponent lurched sideways, stumbled over the mate to the chair in which Lang had been sitting, and sprawled onto the floor. Lang flipped the light switch.

The man on the floor, scrabbling to his feet, was dressed in black jeans and a black shirt, with leather gloves. He was about Lang's size, his age difficult to guess. He backed away, reaching into a pocket as he measured the distance to the door.

Lang thumbed the safety off the Browning as it came out of his belt and he assumed a two-handed shooting stance. "Don't even think about moving, asshole."

There was a click as a switchblade flashed in the light. The stranger lunged forward clumsily, his legs still shaky from Lang's punches.

Like a matador evading the charge of a bull, Lang sidestepped, spun and brought the heavy automatic down across the back of the man's skull with all the fury accumulated since the night Janet and Jeff had died. On one level, Lang wanted to split his head open even more than he wanted answers.

The impact reverberated through the Browning and set Lang's hands trembling. The stranger went down like a marionette when the strings are cut.

Lang stamped a heel into the hand holding the knife, forcing the fingers open. A kick sent the weapon skidding across the room. Lang straddled his unwanted visitor's back, his right hand pressing the muzzle of the Browning against the man's cranium while his left explored pockets.

Nothing. No wallet, no money, no keys, no form of identification, the absence of which was a form of ID itself. Professional assassins carry nothing that yields information as to their own persona or those who hire them.

There wasn't even a label on the inside neck of the T-shirt. But there was a silver chain around the man's throat, the sort of plain strand that might carry a woman's locket or lavaliere. Lang bunched it in his hand to snatch it free.

The guy bucked and rolled violently, tossing Lang aside like an unwary bronco rider.

Lang rolled up on his knees, the Browning in both hands again. "Give me an excuse, asshole."

The intruder shakily got to his feet, his eyes darting to the door at Lang's back. Lang thought he was going to rush him, make a try for the hall outside. Instead, he spun, staggering for the glass door that separated the living room from a narrow balcony outside.

Lang got to his own feet in a hurry. "Hey, wait, hold it! You can't . . ."

But he could. With a crash, he went through the glass and over the edge. The room's light played off knifelike shards to make patterns on the ceiling as Lang struggled with the latch to the sliding glass door. There was no need, he realized. Lang simply stepped through the jagged hole the man had made. He heard traffic twenty-four floors below and the tinkle of the remaining broken glass falling from the door frame.

People were already gathering in a tight bunch below, six or seven of them obscuring all but a leg twisted at an impossible angle. Lang recognized the uniform of the night doorman as he looked up, pointing an accusing finger. In the landscape lights, his mouth was an open, black "O."

Lang went back inside to dial 911, only to learn a police

car had been dispatched along with an ambulance. He returned the Browning to its drawer before conducting a hurried inspection of the living room. Two chairs were overturned, the rug in front of the entrance bunched as though from a scuffle. The switchblade glistened evilly from under an end table. In front of the couch, the light caught another knife, this one a broad dagger with a curved blade and a narrow, decorative hilt. A *jimbia,* the knife carried bare-bladed in the belts of nomadic Arabs, a weapon worn as commonly as a westerner wore neckties.

It wasn't until he was on the way to answer the insistent buzzing of the doorbell that he noticed something shining from the folds of the wrinkled rug.

"Coming!" Lang shouted as he stooped to pick it up.

The silver chain. It must have spun free when the intruder threw Lang off his back. He held it up. A pendant swung from the thin strand. An open circle about the size of a twenty-five-cent piece was quartered by four triangles meeting in the center. Lang had never seen anything exactly like it, yet it seemed vaguely familiar, perhaps very similar to something else.

But what?

He shoved it into his shirt pocket to consider later and opened the door.

Three men were in the hall, two of them were in uniform. The third was a wiry black man in a sport coat who was holding out an ID wallet.

"Franklin Morse, Atlanta police. You Langford Reilly?"

Lang opened the door wide. "Yep. Come in."

Morse took in the disheveled room at a glance. "Wanna tell what happened?"

Lang noticed the two uniforms had spaced themselves so that, should he try, he could not attack both at the same time. Standard procedure when you don't know if the person being interviewed is the perp or not.

Lang shut the door. "Sure. Have a seat?"

Morse shook his head. "No thanks. Crime scene crew'll be here any minute. So, Mr. Reilly, let's hear it."

Lang related what had happened, omitting any reference to the pendant he had found. He didn't want to have to surrender the only clue to what he suspected was an organization far beyond the understanding or reach of the local cops. He saw no reason to mention the early warning of the invasion, either. The last thing he wanted was to provoke further interrogation based on what would be perceived as some nut's conspiracy fantasy.

As he finished, there was a knock at the door. Morse opened it, admitting a balding white man with futuristic-looking photographic equipment and a young black woman with a suitcase. Lang felt marveled at how quickly they made themselves at home.

As though agreeing with someone Lang hadn't heard, Morse nodded to him. "Broke in here with two knives and winds up taking the quick way down rather'n stay in the same room with you, Mr. Reilly? That your story?"

"And I'm sticking to it."

"Hard to believe perp'd kill hiss'sef like that rather'n take th' collar. Way the courts work, wasn't even facing major time. Sure you didn't use some kinda persuasion to throw him out, jujitsu him through the glass there? You sure as hell be justified, him breakin' in here like he did."

Lang shook his head. "Nope, like I said, I knocked the knife outta his hand, hit him a lick on the back of the head and he dropped the other one. He jumped through the glass door."

Morse ran a hand across the bottom half of his face. "You about the baddest ass I've seen. Where you do your workouts, Parris Island? Where you learn to handle a man with a knife?"

"Navy SEAL," Lang said. The story was as verifiable as it was false.

Morse eyed him with renewed interest. "SEAL, huh? Thought them guys were career. You don' look old enough to take retirement."

"Was in Desert Storm in '90, took a raghead bullet clearing Kuwait City harbor."

Morse's crime scene crew was poking around the room, moving objects on the secretary with pencils, inspecting the bottoms of furniture. Lang couldn't even guess what they hoped to find. Grumps watched with declining interest.

"Lemme get this straight." Morse was consulting his note pad. "That dog growls, you hear somebody foolin' with th' lock. 'Stead o' callin' 911 then, you jus' wait for him to come in. Like, meybbe you want to bust him yo'seff?"

Lang straightened the rug with his foot. "I told you: there wasn't time. If I'd been on the phone instead of ready for him, there's a good chance the homicide would be here instead of down there."

Morse's eyes were searching the room again. "You got a phone in the bedroom. All you had t' do was lock yo'seff in an' call the police."

Lang chuckled, although he couldn't put much humor in it. "That's what you'd do, put your life in the hands of the local 911 operators, same ones let a man croak of a heart attack last month while they argued about whose jurisdiction he was dying in? I'd be better off calling the San Francisco police."

"Okay," Morse admitted with a raised hand. "Meybbe all the bugs ain't worked out yet."

"Yet?" Lang asked, incredulous. "System was installed in '96. The 'bugs' are the mayor's friends, sold it to the city."

"You own a firearm?" the detective wanted to know.

The change of subject almost caught Lang off balance just as he surmised it was supposed to. It was standard practice for the Atlanta cops to confiscate, or at least hold as long as possible, every handgun they could find on whatever excuse they could manufacture. This wasn't a time to be unarmed.

"You got a warrant?" Lang parried.

Morse sighed. "Not only you dangerous to be around, you a smartass, too. You want a warrant, I can get one."

He apparently intended to bluff it out.

"From whom, the Wizard of Oz? You got zip for probable cause."

Morse gave Lang a glare. "Okay, keep your artillery. We ain't gettin' ennywhere thisaway. You ever see this dude before?"

Lang set the overturned chair upright and sat in it, motioning Morse to the other. "Never."

The policeman sat as he shook his head. "You sure? Ain't easy believein' perp goes to all the trouble to sneak into the buildin', come up here jus' to kill a stranger. You tellin' me ever'thin'?"

"Sure," Lang said. "Least I can do to assist our law enforcement personnel."

Morse grunted. " 'Nough wise-assin'." He grew serious. "You mus' think I'm some kinda stupid, I'd believe a guy come up here t'kill a perfect stranger an' wind up taking a long walk off a short balcony. You know somethin' you not tellin'. You know itsa crime, lie to the police?"

Lang's hand touched the pocket with the pendant in it. "You think I'm being less than candid?"

Morse leaned forward. "You know somethin' you not tellin'."

The bald photographer and the woman with the suitcase were standing by the door, their investigation complete.

Lang went to the door and opened it. "Detective, I give the police every bit of credit they're due." He extended a hand. "Nice to have met you, although I can't say much for the circumstances."

Morse's grip was strong, consistent with what Lang would have expected of the lean body, like a runner's. It was easy to imagine the detective winning a foot race with a fugitive.

"We may well be back."

"Any time."

5

Atlanta
Later that night

Lang was too tense to sleep. Instead his mind spun in what seemed like endless circles.

Was the pendant a clue or simply a bit of personal jewelry? Lang was unaware he was shaking his head no. A man who didn't even carry a wallet would hardly wear an individualized item.

Unlikely Lang was dealing with a sole person. A lone individual would have a hard time conducting twenty-four-hour surveillance, a harder time planning the theft of military thermite.

And why would a reproduction of a painting by a minor artist be worth the lives of whoever possessed it? Whoever they were, they had the fanaticism of zealots, a willingness to die for something Lang did not understand.

Yet.

It was all too bizarre. Perhaps it involved wackos, nutballs who had a serious if irrational grudge against that picture and anyone who had anything to do with it.

Lang had already made up his mind to find out.

If there was an organization, people other than the body on the pavement below his condominium, responsible for Janet and Jeff, he had to know or be looking over his shoulder the rest of his life. And given the murderous nature of these people, that might not be very long. Besides, if others were involved, Janet and Jeff demanded he get even.

Lang knew precious little to begin with, but he was fairly certain the answers were not in Atlanta. He was due a little vacation anyway.

Once at the office, he had Sara begin preparing requests for a leave of absence in each of his cases. He had to specify the time, so he gave himself a month. He didn't have to state where he was going, though. Just as well. He wasn't certain.

He wasn't certain what he would be searching for, nor for whom. What did the painting have to do with it? Was the pendant significant?

He was certain of only one thing: The vendetta had begun.

THE TEMPLARS: THE END OF AN ORDER

An Account by Pietro of Sicily
Translation from the medieval Latin by Nigel Wolffe, Ph.D.

1

THE CROSS AND THE SWORD

The crimson cross on his surcoat was elongated, emulating the huge sword that required both hands to wield, yet the cross he cherished was the small one of equal arms, the one in the silver circle he wore about his neck, the one described by the four equal triangles.

But I confuse my sequence in hastily composing these, my last notes. I shall commence again, this time at the beginning.

I, Pietro of Sicily, write of these things in the Year of Our Lord 1310,[1] three years after my arrest and false accusation and the false accusation of my brethren of the Order of the Poor Knights of the Temple of Solomon and the issuance of the Papal Bull, *Pastoralis praeminentia*, which commanded any Christian monarch to seize our lands, our chattels and all other goods in the name of His Holiness Clement V.

In past years, to write of myself would have constituted pride, a sin in the eyes of God. Now I am unsure there is sin and, heaven help me for my blasphemy, if there is God at all.

The events of which I write or those that have led me to apostasy are those I set out herein, not because I, God's humble servant, deserve note but because I have observed that the powerful write the histories and those who have caused the downfall of my brothers are powerful indeed.

Although it is not important, just as I am not important, I was born to a serf of a minor lord in Sicily in the fourth year of the reign of James II of Aragon, King of Sicily.[2] I was the youngest of six children, the one whom my mother died birthing. Unable to support his family, my father took me to a nearby house of Benedictine friars that they might succor me, raise me in the faith and benefit from such labours as they, and God, might choose for me.

Would that I had cleaved to our founder's admonition that, to attain purity, one must "seek solitude, submit to fasting, vigils, toils, nakedness, reading and other virtues."[3]

The monastery was given largely to farming, close enough to the town to see the three towers of a new castle built on heathen ruins. Like all such institutions, it was dedicated to intercession for its patrons and the souls of its benefactors and caring for the poor.

I was taught skills beyond those known to villeins of my birth: the making and reading of letters, the understanding and speaking of Latin and Frankish and the knowledge of mathematics. It was at this last skill that I, with God's help, became most proficient. By my twelfth summer, I kept the accounts for the cellarer:[4] the volume of grapes and olives harvested, the number of loaves made, the poor donations from those who sought our prayers, even the quantity of plates fired in the kiln.

It was also that summer I was to end my novitiate,[5] becoming a full member that fall. If only I had not succumbed to the sin of ambition, I would be there yet and would not be facing the cruel fate that awaits me.

It was in August when I saw him, Guillaume de Poitiers, a knight on a magnificent white horse and the most beautiful man I had ever seen. I had been outside the monastery walls, measuring the quantity of sheep dung to be put on the vegetable garden, when I looked up and there he was.

Despite the heat of the day, he wore full armour, including a hauberk,[6] underneath his flowing white surcoat which was emblazoned front and back with the blood-red cross-pattee, announcing to all that he had been to and returned from the Holy Land. His garments thereby proclaimed him to be a knight of the Order of the Poor Knights of the Temple of Solomon, the most fearsome and holy soldiers of the Church.

On his left hip was strapped a long dagger of a design foreign to me, with a curved blade wider than the hilt, which I later learned was a weapon of the heathen Saracens. On his right was a very short knife.

His esquire, mounted on an ass, led two other horses, mighty creatures far larger than the beasts I had seen. Across their backs were strapped a lance, a long, two-edged sword, and a Turkish mace, as well as a triangular body-shield which was adorned by a crimson cross also, this one squarish with perfect triangles for arms.

I followed as he rode through the open gate into the cloister, dismounted and knelt before our poor abbot as though he were paying obeisance to the pope himself. He asked for a night's shelter and food for his man and animals. He requested these for himself last, after his horses and esquire, as was proper for men of God as were we and was he.

As he knelt in supplication, I noted his hair was long and unkempt, his armour beginning to rust and his robe and cape covered with the dust of travel. Travel he had, as I was to learn later. He had survived the fall of Acre, the last Christian city in the Holy Land, the year after my birth. With the former residents of Jaffa, Tyre, Sidon and Ascalon, he and his remaining brethren had fled in Venetian ships along with Grand Master Theobald Gaudin who brought with them such treasure and relics as the Order had.

Guillaume had waited in Cyprus for the papal pleasure of Boniface VIII, thinking that once again it would please God to send the Knights to cleanse the infidel from Jerusalem.[7]

When it became apparent this would not take place soon, he was ordered to return to his original monastery in Burgundy. He was on his way there when I saw him.

Risking the sin of jealousy, I managed to kneel next to him at Vespers that evening, the better to admire the accoutrements I have described. I could not but notice the sun's dark mark on his face and a star-shaped scar at his neck, a wound his esquire told me he received from a heathen arrow and survived only by God's grace.

It was then I observed the circlet of silver encompassing what I had first perceived as four triangles. It was only later he explained to me the triangles described the equal arms of the Templar cross, symbolizing the Holy Rood with the equality of all the Poor Brothers of the Temple of Solomon. It was the only adornment the Order allowed its members.

He also noticed my interest in his scar, for after the last prayer, he touched the discolored skin and said, "Only the low-born kill at a distance, young brother. Knights look into the souls of their enemies."

"Souls?" I said, curious. "The heathen, the accursed of the true God, have souls?"

At this he laughed, drawing the attention of Brother Larenzo, a devout man and prior of the abbey. "He is human, young brother. And do not forget, those figures you use in your calculations instead of Roman letters come from the infidel as do your calculations of the seasons. He is a worthy foe. And, at least for now, he holds all the Outremer,[8] having ousted the best Christendom could muster."

Brother Larenzo was making no effort to conceal that he

was listening to the conversation. I was already the subject of his ire since silence and meditation after Vespers is the rule. I had had more than one beating at his hands for sacrilege, so I replied, "But surely Christ's Church will ultimately prevail."

Guillaume laughed again, to the prior's great annoyance. Laughter was as rare inside these walls as the wealth we had all foresworn. "The trouble is not with Christ's Church, it is with Christ's kings and princes. They fight among themselves instead of uniting against the nonbelievers. They are wont to worry more about the power of rival sovereigns than domination of the very home of Jesus by heathens." Here he moved his hand in a rough estimation of crossing himself. "Many such kings even fear us, the Poor Knights of the Temple."

Would that I had listened with a sharper ear to this last! Had I heeded it and all it implied, I would not now be facing the fate that awaits me, a stake surrounded by brush to be lit.

I confess again to the sin of pride when this brave knight who had so valiantly served the cause of Christ chose to accompany me, rather than the abbot, to the refectory for the evening meal. I could feel all eyes upon me as I genuflected before the crucifix behind the abbot's table to give thanks.

Once seated, our guest gave his bowl of porridge a look of disgust. "No meat?" he asked, interrupting the reading from the lectern.[9]

The entire room went silent, so shocked were we that anyone less than a nobleman would expect to find meat, even more so in a weekday supper.

The abbot was an elderly brother, his voice little more than a wheeze across toothless gums. He coughed, making an effort to be heard from the dais where he shared a table with the elder and governing brothers.

"Good brother," he said, "Christ's last meal was only bread and wine. How much more nourishing is this? Be thankful, for there are many who have not even this simple repast."

Once again Guillaume gave that laugh as he raised his clay

cup of watered wine. "You are right, good abbot. I am thankful for this meal and for the hospitality you afford a poor knight returning from the service of Christ."

Satisfied, the old abbot continued to gum the mush of cereals that was our lot more often than not.

Without lifting his eyes from his bowl and spoon, Guillaume muttered to me, "I did not expect the killing of the fatted calf but even the laziest of men can snare a hare and I have seen countless roe in the forest hereabouts."

Fascinated by words that would have earned me a beating for impertinence if not sacrilege, I asked, "And you Templars have hare or roe with weekday suppers?"

"And with the noon meal also. Or beef or pork. Mush like this does not sustain a man's body."

"It does keep his soul, however," a brother on the other side whispered.

Guillaume shoved his bowl away hardly touched. It is a rich man who passes up food. Or a foolish one. "Souls do not fight the Saracen, bodies do."

After the meal, the order's rules required a retreat to the chapel for confession and then to individual cells for private prayer before Compline.[10] I had been given a dispensation to work in the order's small counting room. The olives were near harvest and it was necessary I calculate how many *boissel*[11] the order would have to press into oil for sale. I was completing my initial figures on a slate and preparing to transfer them to the permanence of sheep parchment when I became aware of Guillaume.

He gave me a smile filled with perfect teeth and entered to look over my shoulder. "These figures of the infidel, you understand them?"

I nodded. "You do not?"

He looked at them from one angle, then another, frowning. "A knight does not trouble with figures or letters. They are for priests and monks."

"But you are a member of a monastic order."

Again the laugh. "This is true, but a special order. You note I do not wear sackcloth that stinks and crawls with vermin, and that, dusty from travel, I bathe. The Knights of the Temple do not live like other monks."

"You certainly are not reputed to accept Our Lord's command to turn the other cheek, either," I said with unaccustomed boldness.

"Nor do I believe the meek shall inherit the earth. I do not believe our Lord ever said such a thing. It is cant, false dogma to keep serfs and vassals subservient."

Such talk made me uneasy, for it bordered on heresy. Yet he was a knight whose neck bore physical witness of his willingness to die for Church and pope.

"Obedience," I said, "is one of the basic vows of our order."

"And without it, chaos would result," he said. "An army marching to more than one set of orders cannot survive the enemy. It is meekness I deplore, not obedience."

This made me feel more comfortable.

"Besides figures, you also can understand written language?"

"If it is in Latin or Frankish and written boldly," I said modestly.

He seemed to withdraw within himself for a moment before he spoke again. "You have not taken your final vows here?"

I had no idea why he asked but I answered truthfully, "I have not."

"My order needs men such as yourself."

I was astonished. "But, I am not noble-born, know nothing of arms such as you bear."

"You do not understand. For every knight, there must be provisioners. For every temple, there must be those who can count money and goods, scribes who can read and write languages. It is this post you can most surely fill. Come with me to Burgundy."

He might as well have suggested I visit the moon. I had never been more than a day's travel by foot from where I now sat.

"I cannot," I said. "These are my brothers who need me to do God's work."

A smile, not entirely devout, tugged at his lips. "I have learned that God usually gets what He wants, no matter the efforts of man. I am offering you three meals a day, two of which have meat. You will never go hungry. You will sleep on a clean bed, wear washed clothes that are not a nation of lice, fleas and ticks. You will do calculations of figures the likes of which you have never dreamed. Or you may remain here, as mean, dirty and hungry as any beast. Either way you will serve God, of that I am certain."

God nearly struck me dumb. I could not answer. Had I prayed, sought His guidance as I should have, I would have realized He was trying to tell me to remain. But, like many young men, the idea of such luxury turned my head.

"I leave right after Prime,"[12] Guillaume de Poitiers said, "before washing myself and before light, please God. You may share my esquire's ass. Or you may remain here, serving God in a lesser manner and a great deal more squalor."

The next morning, I left the only home I could remember, a cell only large enough for a straw mattress, with a ceiling so low I could not stand in it.[13] Since poverty is one of the vows of the Benedictines, I took with me no possessions other than the rude sackcloth gown I wore. And the things that infested it. Would I had chosen to endure the vile life to which I had become accustomed.

Translator's notes:

1. All dates have been converted to the Gregorian calendar for the convenience of the reader.

2. 1290.

3. Actually, this directive came from St. Cassian. St. Bene-

dict (ca. 526) founded the first order of monks who lived in a community rather than alone.

4. The monk in charge of provisions for the monastery.

5. The word used by Pietro is Middle Latin, *noviciatus*, which means the place where novices are trained. It is doubtful a rural monastery would have such a luxury.

6. A tunic of chain mail. The full battle dress of a Templar knight is described by surviving copies of the French *Rule*. In addition to what Pietro describes, it would have included: helmet (*heaume*), armour protecting shoulders and feet (*jupeau d'armes, espalliers, souliers d'armes*).

7. The City of Jerusalem fell to the Sultan of the Baybars in 1243. It is doubtful Guillaume or any of his contemporaries had ever even seen the Holy City, although it was the avowed goal of the Templars until their dissolution in 1307.

8. The name both crusaders and Templars gave to the Holy Land, which they viewed as simply another country under the reign of the Pope.

9. The Bible was read at all meals.

10. The last mass of the day, usually said right before bed.

11. It is assumed this Frankish word is the origin of the English bushel. The exact quantity denoted is lost to antiquity.

12. An early morning mass, usually around five A.M. The first masses of the day, Matins and Lauds, were said shortly after midnight. After Prime came Terce, then Nones, Sext, Vespers, etc., for a total of six a day.

13. Many monastic cells were intentionally constructed so the occupant was always bowed when in it, thereby enforcing the virtue of humility.

Part Two

Part Two

CHAPTER ONE

Dallas, Texas
The next day

Lang hated flying. He felt helpless and out of control belted into an airline seat.

Gloomily, he sat in the waiting area for gate twenty-two of the American Airlines terminal at the Dallas–Fort Worth Airport and watched the man with the little boy.

The guy, midforties, mousey gray hair retreating from front and top, slightly paunchy, was the sort who would be the last to be noticed in a room full of people, just the sort of person Lang had been trained to watch first. The child was blond, four or five, and didn't look enough like the man to be related. Having the kid along, though, was good cover. Somebody had been clever.

Lang had paid them minimal attention when the man had puffed his way to the Delta counter in Atlanta and bought the tickets, explaining he *had* to make the flight, a family emergency.

An emergency where?

Lang had booked the ticket to Dallas, paid by credit card, gone to the American counter and used cash and a false, if expired, passport from his past as ID to buy a seat from Dallas to Fort Lauderdale. He planned to cab from Lauderdale to Miami International, then catch a plane to Rome via JFK. The circuitous routing had paid off in shaking the tail out of the crowd of travelers.

In Atlanta, there had been no reason to consider the pair to be anything other than what they seemed. When they had gotten on the same tram in Dallas to go from the Delta terminal to the American terminal, Lang became suspicious. They had not had time to collect the single bag they had checked in Atlanta, although the boy had the same bright yellow backpack he had carried on board. Seeing them at the gate for the flight to Lauderdale got Lang's attention.

Even with the airlines' price wars, Atlanta–Lauderdale via Dallas was a bit unusual.

Lang watched the guy go to the bank of pay phones, no doubt to alert someone to be on standby in Florida. The fact that he chose a land line rather than a cellular denoted that he was either one of the few people in America without a mobile unit or wanted security for his call. Lang pretended interest in the view of the tarmac from a window next to the pay phones, a position from which he could hear every word. The man glared and hung up without saying good-bye.

When the man took the little boy to the men's room, Lang went to a newsstand and bought a *USA Today*. He browsed the candy, selecting three foil-wrapped Peppermint Patties. Then he followed the guy into the toilet and shut himself into a stall. From the outside, it would look as though Lang was reading the paper as he did his business.

Lang only needed a little luck for the guy not to have time to make another call before he got back.

Returning to the waiting area, Lang glanced around as though trying to find a seat. He selected one next to the kid, who was engrossed in a Game Boy. Moving the child's backpack slightly with his foot, Lang sat so that the little boy was between Lang and the boy's companion. Lang swiveled in the seat so that the yellow pack was partially obscured by his legs.

"Whatcha playin'?" Lang asked the child.

He wasn't shy of strangers. "In-ig-ma," he said without looking up.

Lang watched the blips scramble across the tiny screen. He could feel the adult's question: Did Lang know? But there wasn't a whole lot Lang's shadow could do without attracting attention.

"How d'you play?" Lang asked innocently.

He listened to an explanation surprising in its detail for a child that age.

"Sounds like it would be more fun for two," Lang suggested.

"That's mighty nice of you, mister," the man said, "but you don't have to . . ."

Lang couldn't place the accent but it certainly didn't come from Atlanta.

"But I want to," Lang said. "Reminds me of my own son." He managed a pained expression. "He was about this age when he died of leukemia."

The eyes of the white-haired woman in the seat across from Lang instantly glistened. There was no way the man could gracefully get Lang to leave the little boy alone. From the expression on his face, that had occurred to the minder, too.

"May I?" Lang held out a hand.

The child looked at the man for approval and handed the game over.

"Oops!" Lang dropped it.

As he reached under the seat to retrieve the little electronic box, Lang slid something out of his pants leg and into his hand.

Lang suddenly jerked erect and pointed down the concourse. "Isn't that Mel Gibson?"

Heads snapped around in unison. Lang slipped the object into the backpack and retrieved the Game Boy.

"Guess I was mistaken," Lang admitted sheepishly. "Show me one more time how this works."

Lang was getting soundly thrashed when the flight was called a few minutes later.

As a first-class passenger, Lang went to the head of the boarding line, noting the table that, since 9/11, always stood ready for random searches. When he handed his ticket to the gate attendant, he also leaned forward and spoke in low tones. From her reaction, he might have made a lewd proposition.

She hurriedly turned her duties over to one of the ticket agents and scurried away.

Lang waved to the little boy and boarded.

He was sipping Scotch and trying to find his place in a paperback novel when a woman slipped a thin bag into the overhead bin and slid into the seat beside him. She wore a business suit, a matching gray jacket and skirt. Lipstick and a slight blush were her only makeup. Her ash-blond hair was gathered into a chignon by a tortoiseshell comb. The important finger sported a diamond that anywhere other than Texas would have been vulgar. She was young, twenty-something, but puffing like an octogenarian climbing his third flight of stairs.

Lang smiled at her as he put down the drink glass. "Sounds like you ran the whole way."

She gulped a lungful of air. "I thought they were gonna cancel the flight and I have to, absolutely have to, get to Fort Lauderdale."

If the ring hadn't been a tip that she was a native of the Lone Star State, the flat drawl was.

Lang mustered his very best surprised expression. "Cancel the flight?"

The few stray hairs outside the comb waved like an insect's legs as she bobbed her head. "Guy tried to smuggle a gun on board."

"No!"

"Yeah, in his son's backpack. Somebody tipped Security to bring one of those portable X-ray machines an' there it was, big as life, right in the child's pack."

Lang gasped in amazement. "You see it, the gun?"

"No, but they, the security people, were hauling the guy away, said they were gonna search the kid's backpack in a secure area. Wanted to make sure he didn't have a chance to use a weapon with all the people around, I guess. Feel real sorry for the little fella."

Lang lifted sympathetic hands. "Pretty low, involving a child in something like that."

It was at that moment he noticed he still had smudges of chocolate under his fingernails. It had gotten there while he sat on the john, waiting for his palms' heat to soften the outside of the Peppermint Patties so he could fashion them into the *L* shape of a pistol before using the tinfoil wrappers, highly X-ray–reflective, to encase his creation.

International intelligence or not, they could be outwitted.

Lang stood, stooping to avoid bumping his head. "Reckon I've got time to wash my hands before they make us strap this airplane on?"

CHAPTER TWO

1

Leonardo da Vinci International, Rome
The next morning

Rumpled and gritty-eyed, Lang disembarked, relishing the cool spring morning after the fetid, recirculated air of the L-1011. It was a relief to be outside even if the smell of diesel fuel filled his nose. At the base of the stairs pushed against the plane, he watched vehicles scurry across Leonardo da Vinci International like bugs across a pond's surface. Along the airport's perimeter, perpetual smog turned distant trees into gray lace.

A herd of busses chugged to a stop and his fellow travelers clamored aboard. For reasons as mysterious as the Poussin, the Italians rarely used jetways that allowed passengers to enter the terminal directly from the aircraft. He suspected the owner of the bus company was well connected.

Speaking of connected, the Rome airport had been a

joke in years past, construction ongoing in what Lang and his peers had assumed was a permanent political boondoggle. Now it was finished. White concrete slabs, bowlike angles and portholes of tinted glass gave the international terminal a slightly nautical appearance. Inside, another surprise awaited. Elevators, escalators and stairs were also new, although their multidirectional confusion was much the same as before.

Under the bored gaze of customs officials at the nothing-to-declare exit, Lang submitted his passport to cursory inspection before ducking into the first available men's, both from necessity and to see who from his flight might follow.

No one.

Opening his single bag, he swapped his Levi's and button-down shirt for French jeans and a shirt with the distinctive Italian taper. Oxblood Cole Haan loafers were exchanged for the Birkenstock sandals European men insist on wearing over dark socks. A mirror splattered with hairspray and streaked with substances best not inquired into gave him back the reflection of a man dressed in Eurofashion, the combination of the worst a common market had to offer.

The unfavorable exchange of dollars for euros at the airport posed a financial hit. Still, he was willing to pay for the opportunity to see if anyone he recognized lingered while a machine completed what amounted to small-scale extortion.

Another series of people-moving devices deposited him into the train station, the one place unchanged since his last visit. A pavilionlike roof sheltered four tracks and a small arcade. He bought espresso from an old woman and a ticket from another machine. Then he sat, waiting for both the caffeine high and the train into Rome. Predictably, the coffee did its work before the Italian Railway.

The train was as refreshingly new as the airport. Comfortable seats upholstered in tasteful blue fabric had replaced dirty and cracked vinyl. Instead of small, dusty windows and cramped aisles, the cars boasted panoramic views on either side of a generous aisle.

The ride was unchanged. Lang inevitably expected a countryside dotted with ruins of temples and crumbling arches, alabaster badges of glories past. After all, this was Rome, the Eternal City. All he ever saw from train windows were weed-infested switching yards, rusting rolling stock and the backs of drab housing projects. The same disappointing intrusion of the twenty-first century every time.

When he had brought Dawn here, she had found even the blight exciting. She had almost exploded with anticipation at each dreary stop, thrilled by the very names along the route.

Dawn.

She had enjoyed every second of life, delighted in the smallest detail. He saw her not in the modern coach but the old one, relishing the filthy vinyl of the seat, alternately staring at the Italians on board and craning her neck to make sure she missed nothing of the industrialized suburbs of Rome. For the forty-five minutes the trip took, her fascination with a foreign country's banalities never subsided.

Later, she admitted she found even the smells of the crowded coach exotic. Anyone thrilled by the aroma of fifty or so unwashed bodies reeking of garlic and hair tonic truly loved life.

Dawn.

He and Dawn stayed at a tiny hotel that had shared a piazza with the Pantheon for half a millennium. Then, the city had been romantic, fascinating, full of treasures at every turn. Now all he saw were the crowds and grime of one more big town, a place full of painful memories.

The train was creaking to a stop for Tiburtina, the end of the line, as he managed to set memories of Dawn aside as gently as he might handle fine porcelain. Where to stay? He rationalized that the place Dawn and he had enjoyed so much was too touristy, too likely to be found were someone searching for him. The big hotels, the Hassler and Eden, were even more obvious, places that catered to Americans. A number of smaller establishments were clustered along the remnants of the northern wall, hotels that offered modest prices and a view of the Borghese Gardens over the crumbling bricks of Rome's ancient perimeter. No good: haunts for Americans on package tours and budgets, students, academics and retirees. Worse, these hostels were within blocks of the embassy, their prices and location ideal for use by old acquaintances. He preferred not to encounter former comrades by accident. Too many questions to answer.

Assuming the people he sought weren't Italian, he needed a place where a foreigner would be rare, easy for him to spot as he tried to blend into the fabric of the city. There were a number of small, pricey inns along the Via del Corso, places where Armani salesmen from Milan and glass manufacturers' reps from Venice would stay to service the stores along one of Europe's most chic shopping districts. A possibility.

As the train shuddered to a final stop, he decided upon none of the above. Instead, he chose the Trastavere district. Lang remembered it from pre-Dawn days. Like some other urban areas separated from the main city by a river, the Trastavere considered itself different, more Roman than Rome, just as Brooklynites prided themselves on being the real New Yorkers or the residents of the Rive Gauche the true Parisians.

He had originally found the area's charm in its history. In the sixteenth century, it had been Rome's blue-collar neighborhood, home to the artisans who built the cathedrals, painted its frescoes and carved its monuments. Michelangelo and Leonardo had both stayed in the Trastavere. In modern times it had become a haven for the bohemian lifestyle, the residence of unemployed musicians and artists looking for patrons.

There was a trattoria on the Piazza Masti where he had shared pasta with a Czech defector. The food had been abysmal, the decor worse, featuring photographs of those two Italian-American icons, Sinatra and Stallone. The piano player had mangled American tunes of the fifties. He never considered taking Dawn there.

Next door had been a *pensione,* a few rooms in a district that made little accommodation for visitors, certainly none for the luxury demanded by Americans.

Perfect.

He spoke only a little Italian, mostly the tourist vocabulary of directions to the men's room and complaints about prices. And the universal "Prego," a chameleonlike word that could mean anything from "in a hurry" to "you're welcome." Unfortunately, his Latin was of about as much use as Chaucer's English would have been in today's America. Not that it mattered at the moment. The driver of the Opel taxi he took at the station was even more unfamiliar with the native language. Whatever the cabbie's linguistic shortcomings, it quickly became obvious he had acclimated to driving in Rome, using horn and gestures rather than brakes. Intersections without stoplights were tests of testosterone levels.

Since only about a fifth of the streets were wide enough for vehicles larger than the ubiquitous Vespas and bicycles, the ride was circuitous. From experience, Lang found it easier on the nerves to close his eyes, hold on and pray to Mercury, the Roman god of travelers in peril.

The cab lurched suddenly and Lang winced in anticipation of metal grinding against metal. Instead, he heard a stream of Italian invective fading behind them. He opened his eyes. The cab was on a bridge, the Ponte Palatina. The dull green Tiber, lined with trees, sloshed listlessly along in its concrete prison below.

Lang remembered an observation Dawn had made: Unlike Paris, London or even Budapest, Rome did not show its best face along its river. The Tiber was more like the city's backyard, she maintained, a nuisance towards which no major buildings faced, distant from the center of ancient, medieval and modern Rome. As happened so often, she had verbalized a thought he had never quite completed. One more reason she left a gap in his life that he doubted would ever be filled.

Ahead and to the right, the dome of Saint Peter's floated on a brown sea of smog, coolly serene above the mass confusion of early morning traffic. A right turn and the river was replaced by three- and four-story buildings, their worn stucco roseate in the early sunlight. He recognized the Piazza di Santa Maria di Trastavere by its Romanesque church. The small square was full of grandmothers pushing baby carriages and men unloading trucks. The neighborhood was groggy, stretching and yawning as it recovered from the previous evening. Tonight, dark would again send the older folks and children inside while jazz musicians, mimes, and the young swingers took their places. By night, this piazza was Bourbon Street, the Left Bank, anyplace funky.

The Opel dashed down an alley into which it barely fit and then came to an uncertain stop. Shabby buildings huddled around a small square paved with stones that could have been placed there centuries ago or yesterday. Shadows gave the area an ominous feeling as they stubbornly retreated from the morning.

Lang got out, paid the cabby too much and crossed the

square, wondering if he could have chosen a better loca-tion. The trattoria he remembered had not yet opened but next to it the *pensione* was advertising a vacancy. He slammed the huge brass knocker twice against the mas-sive panels of the door. From inside, bolts began to slide, one, two, three before the door groaned open on iron hinges.

Lang had forgotten the locks.

Either the city experienced a perpetual wave of burgla-ries or its citizens were fascinated with locks. It had not been unusual to have to open two or three to get into his hotel at night, another pair to access the proper floor and two or three more on each room. A guest in one of the smaller hotels, one which did not have a night clerk on duty, was weighted down by more keys than the average jailer.

"Si?"

Lang was looking at an old man, his frame so small Lang was surprised he could open the mammoth door.

"Una camera?" Lang asked. *A room?*

The old man inspected Lang carefully. Lang knew the look. The innkeeper was trying to guess how much he could charge for the room. Stepping aside, the old man motioned his potential guest inside. "Una camera. Si."

Lang was trying to disguise his American accent. "Con bagno?" *With bath?*

The old geezer had apparently decided Lang had po-tential above his average guests: students, the traveling poor. He shook his head, no, the room didn't come with a bath. "But come with me," he gestured.

Lang followed him up a dark staircase and down a hall to an open door. Inside, the furnishings were about what Lang would have expected of a *pensione*: double bed, its sheets and pillows rolled at the foot; a dresser against the wall, its imitation wood veneer scarred by cigarette burns. Above it hung a mirror in a plastic frame. An armoire, also with a mirror, matched the dresser only in age.

Lang crossed over to the single window and was delighted to find himself looking down into a courtyard, one of those Roman surprises hidden from the noise and grime of the street. Like many such places, this one had been turned into a compact and fertile vegetable patch, an Italian specialty. Even though it was only April, round red tomatoes peeped out from lush vines. Some eggplants already bore purple fruit. There were greens Lang didn't recognize along with the basil and oregano without which no Italian garden is complete.

The old man spewed out words so fast Lang would have had a hard time understanding him even if he had been fluent in the language. Lang surmised he was describing the amenities of the room.

"Non parlo Italiano," Lang said sadly as though admitting one of his life's greater failures. "Sprechen Sie Deutsch?"

Being German would explain the edge Lang had put on what little Italian he had spoken. After years in Bonn, Frankfurt and Munich, Lang's German was pretty good.

There were a number of other reasons to assume a German identity.

The old man shook his head, reappraising his guest. Lang guessed he might well be old enough to remember the German-Italian Axis, Hitler and Mussolini. The Italians did not find it inconsistent to recall *Il Duce* as a builder of roads, the only man ever to make the trains run on time, while blaming the devastation of their country on Hitler. In fact, the anniversary of the collapse of the Fascista was a holiday every April, called Liberation Day. The national pretense was that the people themselves had had nothing to do with World War II. True or not, the old hotelkeeper was not likely to admit he knew the language of the country's former oppressors.

Neither historic revision of Orwellian proportions nor the more recent Common Market had reduced the awe with which the Italians regarded the German people. Teutonic trains ran to the precise second; their automobiles were reliable and their economy and government stable. Germans were not like Italians.

Even more distinct was the German's lack of interest in the haggling that was part of every Italian purchase. Lang could see the disappointment in the old man's eyes as he stepped into the hall to display what he considered the room's most salable feature: it was adjacent to the guest bath.

With a gesture, Lang declined his host's offer to inspect the facility. Lang had seen enough *bagno* to anticipate he would stand and use the shower hose rather than sit in a tub that might receive a weekly cleaning.

Lang nodded. He would take the room.

"Quotidano?" Would Lang pay by the day?

"Si."

The innkeeper named a number, disappointed when Lang's lack of reaction indicated he had started too low. He held out his hand for Lang's passport. Like most European countries, Italy required establishments renting rooms by the night to make records of their guests' nationality papers, information entered into a computer by the local police and checked against lists of wanted criminals and other undesirables such as suspected terrorists or couples staying together without benefit of clergy.

"Ho una ragazza," Lang said with a salacious wink. *I have a girlfriend.* Lang tendered several large bills in excess of the night's rent.

Lang didn't have to be fluent in the language to read the old man's mind as he inspected the cash and leered, communicating his understanding of illicit romance with a wink. This guest, he was thinking, is a German and therefore wealthy. He wants only to spend a night or two with a woman not his wife without the potential inconvenience of that fact being stored in endless government records. The question was not one of morality but of economics. How large would be the bribe to the local police to forget this minor infraction of an onerous law that did nothing but invade personal freedom anyway?

Such questions were frequent in Italian business.

Lang headed for the stairs, pretending to be leaving, before the old man grudgingly agreed to accept what had been offered. He handed Lang a ring of keys along with another incomprehensible string of Italian and left the floor, his muttering trailing up the stairs behind him like malodorous smoke from a cheap cigar.

Lang locked the door and stretched out on the bed. Through the open window, the sharp noises of traffic were smoothed into a sleepy drone. He inhaled the fragrance of freshly turned earth mixed with a bouquet of herbs.

He thought of Janet and Jeff.

In less than a minute, he was asleep.

2

Portugal
0827 hours the same day

Hundreds of miles away, at about the same time Langford's plane touched down, fog swirled against rippled and nearly opaque windowpanes, condensing into tiny rivers of silver that ran along the leaded edge of each piece of ancient glass. The mist, not yet dissipated by a monochromatic sun, made gray stone resemble a grainy black-and-white photograph.

From a window, a light, muted into quicksilver by the moist haze, danced across the otherwise still fog. The light took on a bluish tint as a computer screen flickered alive, an event so starkly anachronistic with the hand-carved stone, battlements and turrets as to be disturbing had anyone been watching.

The man in front of the screen might also have been from another time. He wore a coarse robe with a hood, something from a medieval monastery, perhaps. Despite the chill, his feet were clad only in thong sandals. He waited impatiently for the Macintosh to boot up before typing an eight-letter password. A series of letters, five to a group, appeared. These groups were completely arbitrary to anyone without decryption software. When he was certain the message was complete, the operator touched a series of keys. The indecipherable letter blocks were replaced by a single sentence.

The man wagged his chin up and down as though agreeing with what he was reading. An unauthorized and virtually undetectable entry into worldwide airline reservation systems had revealed that Langford Reilly had flown into Rome from Miami. Similar hacking into credit card records failed to disclose hotel reservations. Presumably his whereabouts would soon be available from police computers into which his passport would have been entered. The information could be picked as easily as grapes from the vine.

The operator scowled. He didn't like to wait; that wasn't what computers were all about.

A breeze parted the fog outside like a curtain and rattled the windows in their hand-forged lead casements like a spirit seeking entry.

The man didn't notice. He reread the message as he un-consciously twisted the silver chain around his neck. From the chain hung a pendant with four triangles. He input in-structions to his electronic correspondent: *Find Reilly. See who his past contacts in Rome might be. The authorities will shortly be looking for him also. Before you kill him, see what he knows, who he has told.*

CHAPTER THREE

1

Rome
1300 hours

Lang woke up refreshed, having made up for the sleep he had missed on the plane and the change in time zones. Outside, the hum of traffic was missing. A check of his watch told him why. Thirteen hundred hours, one o'clock, the time in the afternoon when businesses, museums and even churches close for three hours.

Lang swung his feet off the bed and unlocked the door. He stepped into the empty hall and gently rapped on the door of the communal bath. With no response, he ventured in. It was every bit as bad as he had anticipated. After washing his face in the cracked porcelain sink, he did his business before venturing out of the *pensione*.

Standing in the shadow of the doorway, Lang checked the piazza for anyone who didn't seem to belong. Little boys shouted as they kicked a scruffy soccer ball. Crones

in black ꓘ
etable stall.
across the w
with watery e
very young and
lunch inside befo

As he crossed t
trattoria next to the
and worse art, had fe

As he walked, he wa
most symbolic of Rome
end but an ordinary hous   leg-
long to anyone if, indeed,   . But they all
looked well fed and healthy.   .iat's why he didn't
see any rats. Small fountains, n more than cement bowls
with flowing pipes, were placed on almost every block so
that the cats, and the occasional dog, wouldn't go thirsty.

The only thing more numerous than cats were Gypsies,
dark-haired women extending roses for sale, reaching for
palms to read, or suckling infants. Or muttering curses at
passersby uninterested in whatever was being offered.
Gypsies, Romans believed, made their real living as pick-
pockets and thieves. True or not, Lang shifted his wallet to
his front pocket.

It was a rare piazza that did not have its own unique
church, stature or fountain. Likewise, each of those minia-
ture neighborhoods had its own odor. Brewing cappucino
might dominate one, while a block away, an open-air market would scent the air with ripe vegetables.

The smell of fresh bread stopped him cold. He was hungry, hadn't eaten since the soggy, unidentifiable mess the
airline had proclaimed a meal. He made a right turn down
another alley-width street, dodged a Japanese motorcycle
under less than complete control by its driver, and arrived
at the Osteria den Berlli, a restaurant on the Piazza San

a still had the quality

...pped back into the sunshine, the
...us clinging to his palate. He strolled
...more Roman letting lunch settle in his
...until he reached the traffic-choked Via Della
...azone, the wide boulevard that leads to the Vatican.
...en in April, before the tourist season started, the sidewalks were jammed. Shops displayed religious trinkets, small busts of the Pope, cheap crucifixes. Lang would not have been surprised to see St. Peter's Basilica in a snowglobe.

Before leaving Atlanta, he had made one more call to Miles, this time asking about common acquaintances in Rome.

Miles had been guarded. "You're going to Rome for a vacation and just want to renew auld lang syne, right? This doesn't have anything to do with the thermite or your sister's death, right?"

"You're overly suspicious, Miles."

"Comes with the job, remember? Besides, I'd get shit-canned, I told who the Agency people in Rome were. Maybe shot."

"They don't do that any more," Lang had said. "Just cancel your government pension and benefits."

"Years I put in, that's worse."

"Besides," Lang said reasonably, "I didn't ask who was Agency in Rome, I asked whom we knew in Rome."

"Typical lawyer hairsplitting. Why you wanna know, anyway?"

"I need an introduction at the Vatican, figured the Agency'd know whom to contact."

Miles made no effort to even sound as if he believed him. "Vatican, like where the Pope hangs? You want to fill out the forms for future canonization, right?"

"Miles, Miles, you are letting cynicism poison your otherwise bright and cheerful disposition. I simply want a brief conference with one of the Holy Father's art historians."

The phone connection did nothing to diminish the snort of derision. "Right. Like I would engage only in intellectual conversation were I alone on a desert island with Sharon Stone."

Lang sighed theatrically. "Miles, I'm serious. I have a client who is about to spend a fortune on a work of religious art. The world's most renowned expert on the artist is in the Vatican. Would I lie to you?"

"Like I would if my wife found lipstick on my fly. Okay, okay, I can't give you a roster of Rome assets, don't have the clearance to call it up, anyway. Just so happens, though, that I heard Gurt Fuchs is presently assigned to the trade attaché at the Rome embassy."

Lang couldn't remember if he had taken the time to thank Miles before hanging up the phone. There had been a time when Gurtude Fuchs had made him forget everything else.

Lang's first career had been with the Agency, the job he referred to in his mind as being an office-bound James Bond. Like most embryonic spies, he had trained at Camp Perry near Williamsburg, Virginia. Known as the Farm by its graduates, there he had learned the arcane arts of code, surveillance and the use of weapons ranging from firearms and knives to garrote and poison. His performance had been either too good or too poor (depending on the point of view) for a posting to the Fourth Directorate, Ops. Instead, he had been sent to a dreary office across the street from the Frankfurt railway station where he spent his days with the Third Directorate, Intelligence. Rather than cloak and dagger, his tools had consisted of computers, satellite photos, Central European newspapers and equally humdrum equipage.

In 1989, Lang had seen his future in the Agency shrunk by the much-heralded Peace Dividend and changed by shifting priorities. Even the grime-encrusted office with a view of the *Bahnhof* in Frankfurt would be a source of nostalgia when he was forced to learn Arabic or Farsi and stationed in some place where a hundred-degree day seemed balmy. Dawn, his new bride, had drawn the line at including a floor-length burka in her trousseau.

He had taken his retirement benefits and retreated to law school.

Gurt, an East German refugee, had been a valued linguist, analyst and expert on the German Democratic Republic, who was also stuck in the Agency's Third Directorate.

Gurt and Lang had joined several couples for a ski weekend in Garmish-Partenkirchen. In his mind, Gurt would always be associated with the Post Hotel, Bavarian food, and the slopes of the Zugspitze. The resulting affair had been hot enough to burn out a few months later when he met Dawn on a brief trip back to the States.

To Lang's surprise and chagrin, Gurt had seemed more relieved than jilted. They had shared a friendship ever since, though, a relationship renewed as scheduling and posting allowed: an occasional drink in Frankfurt, a dinner in Lisbon until his resignation. By that time she was due a promotion to management, a result of the Agency's begrudging and Congressionally mandated sexual egalitarianism more than her acknowledged abilities. Her talents were not limited to language but ranged from cryptography on the computer to marksmanship on the firing range.

On mature reflection, perhaps it was just as well Gurt did not take the end of their romance too seriously.

When Saint Peter's was only a couple of blocks away, Michelangelo's dome filling the northern horizon, Lang looked for a pay phone. He was thankful he wasn't in one of those European countries where public phones are hoarded like treasures, available only in branches of the national postal system. In Rome, pay phones were plentiful if functioning ones were not. He had chosen this part of the city from which to phone. A trace of any call made from here would lead to one of the most heavily visited places in the world. Though not impossible, it would be difficult to pinpoint the specific location of any one phone quickly enough to catch someone involved in a conversation of only a couple of minutes.

If anyone were tracing the call.

He dialed the embassy number and listened to the creaks, groans and buzzing of the system.

When a voice answered in Italian, Lang asked for Ms. Fuchs in the trade section.

The voice smoothly transitioned to English. "May I tell her who is calling?"

"Tell her Lang Reilly's in town and would like to buy her dinner."

"Lang!" Gurt shouted moments later. If she wasn't happy to hear from him, she had added acting to her list of achievements. "What carries you to Rome?"

Gurt still had not totally mastered the English idiom.

"What brought me here was seeing you again."

She gave a giggle almost girlish in tone. "Still the *Shiest* . . . , er, thrower of bullshit, Lang." He could imagine her cocking an eyebrow. "And have you brought your wife with you to see me?"

No way to explain without staying on the line a lot longer than he intended. "Not married anymore. You free for dinner?"

"For you, if not free, at least inexpensive."

She had mastered lines that died with vaudeville.

They had no common history in Rome, no place he

could designate by reference in case someone was monitoring the perpetual tap on all Agency lines. Lang's choices were a secluded place where he could be sure neither had been followed or a very crowded spot where they would be more difficult to spot. The more potential witnesses would also mean more safety.

Crowds won.

"The Piazza Navona, you know it?"

"Of course. It is one of the most famous . . ."

"Fountain of the Three Rivers. Say about eighteen hundred hours?"

"Isn't that a bit early for dinner?"

Most Italians don't even think about the evening meal until nine o'clock, 2100 on the twenty-four-hour clock common in Europe. They do, however, begin to consume appertifs long before.

"Want to see you in the sunlight, Gurt. You always looked best in the light."

He hung up before she could reply.

Like most lawyers, Lang was connected to the womb of his office by the umbilical cord of the telephone. He could have no more failed to call in than a fetus could fail to take sustenance. He had not had the time to purchase an international calling card, so the call was going to require considerable patience in dealing with an overseas operator whose English might be marginal.

Sara answered on the second ring. "Mr. Reilly's office."

Lang glanced at his watch and subtracted five hours. It was shortly after nine A.M. in Atlanta.

"Me, Sara. Anything I need to know, any problems?"

"Lang?" Her voice was brittle with tension. "Mr. Chen called."

Chen? Lang didn't have any client . . . Wait. He had had a client, Lo Chen, several years ago. The man had been accused of involvement with the growing number of Asian mobs in the Atlanta area. Not believing any authority would be stupid enough not to tap the line of the lawyer representing a man accused of a crime, Chen had insisted Lang use pay phones to call him at a rotating list of phone booths. Complying with his client's wishes, Lang used one of the phones in the lobby of the building.

What did Sara mean?

"Do you remember Mr. Chen's number?" Sara sounded as though she was about to cry.

"I'm not sure. . . ."

Sara said something, words directed away from the phone.

A man's voice asked, "Mr. Reilly?"

"Who the hell are you?" Lang demanded, angry that someone would interrupt a call to his own office.

There was a mirthless chuckle. "Surprised you didn't recognize me, Mr. Reilly."

Lang felt his lunch sink. There had to be something wrong, terribly wrong. "Morse?"

"The same, Mr. Reilly. Now, where be you?"

"What the hell are you doing in my office?"

"Trying to find you, Mr. Reilly."

"You got more questions, I'll answer 'em when I get home. Or on your dime."

"And just when might you be coming home?"

There was something in the tone, a come-here-little-fish-all-I-want-to-do-is-gut-you quality to the question that activated Lang's paranoia like a tripped burglar alarm.

"You're asking so you can meet my plane with a brass band, right?"

There was a pause, one of those moments the writers of bodice-rippers described as pregnant. Lang would have called this one plain ominous.

Then Sara apparently took the phone back. "They're here to arrest you, Lang!"

"Arrest? Lemme talk to Morse."

When the detective was back on the line, Lang's concern was beginning to outweigh anger. "What is this B.S.? You sure as hell can't begin to prove I've obstructed your investigation."

In fact, with the Fulton County prosecutor's conviction rate, it was doubtful he could convince a jury of Hannibal Lecter's violation of the Pure Food and Drug Act.

There was another dry chuckle, the sound of wind through dead leaves. "Proovin' not be my job, Mr. Reilly. Arrestin' is. Shouldn't come as any big surprise I got a murder warrant here with your name on it. Where were you 'round noon yesterday?"

On my way to Dallas with a false passport as ID, Lang thought sourly. There would be no record that Lang Reilly had been on that plane.

"Murder?" Lang asked. "Of who, er, whom?"

Even stress doesn't excuse poor grammar.

"Richard Halvorson."

"Who is he?"

"Was. He was the doorman at that fancy highrise of yours."

Lang had never asked Richard's last name. "That's absurd! Why would I kill the doorman?"

"Not for me to say. Mebbe he didn't get your car fast enough."

Just what the world needed: another Lennie Briscoe.

"And I didn't hear you say where you were yesterday," Morse added.

"I barely knew him," Lang protested.

"Musta known him fairly well: left your dog with him. And he was shot with a large-caliber automatic just like the Browning be in your bedside table."

Lang fought the urge to simply drop the phone and run. The more he knew, the better he could refute what appeared to be absurd charges. "If you've been into my bed-side table, I assume you had a warrant."

"Uh-huh. Nice and legal. Got it when your fingerprints showed up on the shell casings. Gun's been fired recently but ballistics report won't be back till tomorrow. I'm bettin' be your gun killed him." Morse was enjoying this. "You got somethin' to say, you come back here an' say it. FBI gets involved, you become a fugitive. You don't want them on your trail."

Me and Richard Kimble, Lang thought.

Lang knew he should sever the connection as quickly as possible but he couldn't, not just yet. "The dog I left with Richard . . . ?"

Apparently Sara could hear at least part of the conversation. Her voice was clear in the background. "I've got him, Lang, don't you . . ."

Lang hung up with at least one problem solved and walked away in a daze. They had done it, of course, killed Richard with his Browning—the one Lang had loaded, leaving his prints on the shells—and replacing it where it was sure to be found. Clever. Now every cop connected to the Internet anywhere in the world would be looking for him. Interpol, the Italian Policia, everyone would be doing their work for them.

How long had Lang been on the phone? Long enough for a trace? Unlike the old movies, computers could race through area switchboards with the speed of light. But an international call involved satellites, no wires connected to specific telephones. The best the computer could do was give general coordinates as to location. The bad news was that a trace would reveal Lang wasn't in the U.S. of A., something Morse would have had to wait to find out after getting the record of the Miami-Rome flight in the check of credit cards that was standard procedure in any fugitive hunt. Without a current bogus passport, Lang had had to use his real name and plastic for that leg. In today's terror-conscious environment, paying cash for an international flight would have subjected him to scrutiny he had not wanted.

2

Atlanta
Twenty minutes later

Detective Franklin Morse stared at the fax again, although he had already studied every detail of both pages. The quality was poor, but good enough to recognize a copy of an airline ticket from Miami to Rome. The name of the passenger was clear enough: Langford Reilly. So was the transmitted photograph, grainy and streaked.

Reilly looked like he was walking past some sort of official on the other side of a booth, maybe customs or immigration in an airport. That would make sense if Reilly had fled to Rome, if that was where Reilly was when the detective had spoken to him not half an hour before.

What didn't make sense were the two pieces of paper themselves. They had arrived on the machine used exclusively by the detectives in the squad room in Atlanta's City Hall on East Ponce de Leon. Not a state secret but not exactly a published number, either. Verification of the numbers at the top of the pages led to a public facsimile machine in Rome.

Okay, so Lang Reilly was in Rome and someone wanted Morse to know that. But who and why?

A criminal warrant was a matter of public record, but not a lot of citizens scoured the court dockets. Morse had hoped to keep it quiet, not spook the lawyer. Until Reilly had fled, that is. Still, whoever had sent this fax didn't get the information from the media that there was a want out on Reilly, not yet, anyway.

That led to the conclusion that the sender had a source inside the department. Morse shot an involuntary glance around the room, gray furniture on gray carpet in gray cubicles in what had been the appliance floor of a Sears & Roebuck. People came and went, phones rang, and computers clicked in a familiar cacophony.

Not exactly high security. Anyone could have mentioned that Langford Reilly was a man the Atlanta police would like very much to speak with up close and personal.

Granting that the word had gotten out, Morse had been on the job too long to accept anonymous tips at face value. People who ratted from some sense of civic duty rarely did so without a desire for recognition. Sometimes the bad guy was given up because someone wanted to get even for some wrong, real or imagined. Most often, information came for a price, either cash or expectation of future favors.

Morse was willing to bet none of those reasons applied here. Your usual snitch didn't travel to Rome. Nor did he send anonymous tips by paying the cost of transatlantic faxes. No siree Bob, there be something else at work here.

But what?

Morse pushed back from the metal government-issue desk. No point in wasting time inspecting the dentures of free horses. For whatever reason, he had information that a suspect in a murder case was in Rome, had fled the country. Standard procedure was to notify the FBI who would then send a want to the country involved. Assuming the foreign country wasn't involved in a major war, the crime in question had no political ramifications, and the local dicks had nothing more pressing on their collective plates, the police would add the name of the wanted person to a list of criminals, known illegal aliens and other miscreants.

Once and a while, a perp actually blundered into the arms of the Poletzei, gendarmes, constabulary or whatever and got taken back to the United States. Usually the perp got busted for another crime or was spotted in an airport or train station.

Morse was less than optimistic as he went across the room to wire the Fibbies. Reilly didn't look like a one-man crime wave. But he could have killed Halvorson because the doorman knew he had had a reason to throw that guy off his balcony. Whatever. Except for the real fruitcakes, the odds of a perp killing more than once were nil.

The detective was still thinking when he returned to his cluttered desk. Back to the question of why the anonymous informant had gone to the trouble of letting the cops in Atlanta know that Reilly was in Rome. Only reason Morse could see was that somebody wanted Reilly caught.

The interesting question was why. Answer that and you might get all sorts of helpful information.

Morse leaned back in his chair and regarded the patterns years of water stains had made on the ceiling. But where to start? Man was a lawyer, probably had more than a few people like to see him in jail. Could check the court records, see if Reilly'd lost a case or two he shouldn't have.

Nah, didn't seem right. Something told him to try Reilly's service records, one of those unexplainable, irrational hunches he had learned to trust.

Navy SEAL, the man had said. Small, elite corps. Couldn't be too many of those around. Let's see who Mr. Langford Reilly, Attorney at Law, might have pissed off in the service of his country. Morse looked around the room again, this time trying to remember who had the phone number for the military service records place in St. Louis.

3

Rome
1750 hours

Lang got to the Piazza Navona early, giving himself plenty of time to spot a trap if one was being set. To Lang, the Navona was the most beautiful and historic piazza in a city crammed full of beauty and history. The long elliptical shape recalled the stadium of Diocletian, which the present piazza had replaced. Ancient architecture existed harmoniously with Romanesque, Gothic and Baroque. Of Bernini's three marble fountains on the piazza, the largest was the Three Rivers in the center. It was also the easiest to locate among the mobs of tourists, artists entertainers, and natives who watched the whole scene with detached amusement.

Lang chose a table outside a taverna and picked up an abandoned newspaper, over the top of which he could watch the shifting crowd of tourists taking pictures, artists selling paintings and entertainers seeking tips from an appreciative audience. He hoped he looked like one more Italian, whiling away an afternoon over a cup of espresso.

Gurt was hard to miss. She turned more heads than the American Chiropractic Association. She stood nearly six feet, pale honey hair caressing shoulders bared by a well-filled tube top. She approached with long, regal steps, designer sunglasses reflecting the sinking sun as her head turned back and forth, searching the piazza.

As she came closer, Lang was glad to see that ten-plus years had not changed the long face, angular chin and high cheekbones. She carried an aura of untouchability that made men keep their distance. Perhaps it was a dose of the arrogance for which her countrymen are noted.

Or a desire to invade France.

Either way, Lang could see her on German travel posters.

There had been a time when his fantasies had placed her in less public places.

She lowered her glasses long enough for her blue eyes to lock onto his before she resumed what appeared to be an idle glance around the piazza. She was waiting for him to make the first move, to let her know if it was safe to acknowledge each other.

Lang vaulted out of his seat and walked over to her, unable to keep a stupid grin off his face. Without having to lean over, he kissed her cheek.

"You look great, Gurt."

She returned his kiss with somewhat less enthusiasm. "So I am told."

He took her left hand, surprised at how gratified he was not to find a ring on it, and led her back to where his coffee cup and purloined newspaper waited. He reclaimed the table with a sudden sideways move that would have done credit to an NFL running back, earning glares from an American couple who had not yet learned that in securing taxis and taverna seats, quickness and daring are everything. Gurt sat with the ease of royalty assuming a throne, dug into an oversized handbag, and placed a pack of Marlboros on the table.

"I'm surprised you still smoke," Lang said.

She tapped a cigarette from the pack and lit it with a match. "How could I not? I am brain-laundered from all the ads your tobacco companies run here because they cannot show them in the States."

Not exactly true. A number of European countries had banned tobacco ads.

"Not good for your health, Gurt."

She let a stream of smoke drift from her nostrils and

once again he was reminded of the golden years of cinema. And lung cancer.

"Smoking is not as unhealthy as the business you were in when I last saw you."

"Third Directorate, Intelligence?" Lang asked. "Biggest risk was getting poisoned by the food in the cafeteria."

"Or dropping a girl like a hot . . . cabbage?"

"Potato."

"Potato." Those blue eyes were boring into his so hard that Lang looked away.

"I wish I could say I regretted it. I fell in serious love with Dawn."

"And with me?"

"Just-as-serious lust."

She took another puff and waited for the server to take their order before taking a new line. "If the people back at the embassy knew I was meeting with a former, er, employee who, I am sure, wants something, I'd go Tolstoy."

Go Tolstoy, being required to fill reams of paper with details of anything that didn't fit routine, usually filled with self-serving fiction.

The waiter reappeared with two glasses of Brunello. The dying sun reflected from the red wine to paint spots of blood on the tabletop while they watched people watching people. Rome's favorite pastime. A battalion of Japanese followed their tour leader, a woman holding up a furled red umbrella like a battle flag. They broke ranks to photograph the magnificent Bernini marbles.

When her glass was half empty, Gurt spoke with a nonchalance so intensely casual Lang knew she had been straining not to ask before now. "You are divorced?"

"Not exactly."

He explained about Dawn, only partially successful in trying to relate her death in an emotionless narrative.

Sometimes being a man isn't easy. Gurt picked up on the still-sharp grief, her eyes shimmering. The Germans are a sentimental lot. SS guards who had joked while exterminating women and children in the morning wept at Wagner's operas the same evening.

"I'm sorry, Lang," she said, her voice husky with sympathy. "I truly am."

She put a hand over his.

He made no effort to move it. "You never married?"

She gave a disdainful snort. "Marry who? You don't meet the best people in this job. Only lunatics."

"Could be worse," Lang quipped. "What if you were working for the penal system?"

She brightened. "There is such a thing?"

"Corrections, Gurt, the U.S. prison system."

"Oh." She sighed her disappointment. "Well, my not getting married is not why you are here. I think you want something."

He told her about Janet and Jeff and the man who had broken into his condo.

"Who are these people that would kill your sister and your nephew?"

"That's what I'm trying to find out."

They were quiet while the waiter refilled glasses.

When he departed, Lang took the copy of the Polaroid from a pocket and pushed it across the table. "If someone could tell me what the significance of this picture is, I might be on the way to finding the people responsible."

She stared at the picture as though she were deciphering a code. "The police in the States, they cannot help?"

He retrieved the picture. "I don't think so. Besides, this is personal."

"You were with the Agency long enough to learn revenge is likely to get you killed."

"Never said anything about revenge, just want to identify these people. The cops can take it from there."

"Uh-huh," she said, not believing a word of it. "And how do you think I can help?"

"I need an introduction to a Guiedo Marcenni—a monk, I think. Anyway, he's in the Vatican Museum. Who does the Agency know in the Vatican these days?"

Lang remembered the well-kept secret that the Vatican had its own intelligence service. The Curia, the body charged with following the Pope's directives in the actual governance of the Church, maintained a cadre of information gatherers whose main functionaries were missionaries, parish priests or any other face the Church showed the public. Even though the service had not carried out a known assassination or violent (as opposed to political) sabotage since the Middle Ages, the very number of the world's Roman Catholics, their loyalty and, most importantly, the sacrament of confession, garnered information unavailable to the spies of many nations. Like similar organizations, the Agency frequently swapped tidbits with the Holy See.

Gurt fished another cigarette from the pack. "And what am I to tell my superiors? Why do I want to introduce a former agent to this monk?"

Lang watched her light up and inhale. "Simply a favor for an old friend, a friend who has specific questions about a piece of art he wishes to ask on behalf of a client."

"I will think about it."

They ordered bean soup and eggplant sauteed in olive oil along with a full bottle of wine.

As they finished, Lang said, "Gurt, there's something else you ought to know."

She glanced up from the small mirror she was using to repair her lipstick. "That you are wanted by the American police? Close your mouth, it is most unattractive hanging open. I saw the bulletin this afternoon."

One of the duties the Agency had assumed rather than face extinction upon the demise of its original enemy was cooperation with local authorities and Interpol in locating American fugitives abroad. The FBI, sensing a turf invasion, had protested loudly but futilely.

Lang felt his dinner lurch in his stomach. "You mean the Agency knows?"

She checked the result of her effort, turning her head to maximize the light supplied by tabletop candles. "I doubt it. The message was misfiled. The screw up won't be discovered for a day or two."

"But why . . . ?"

She dropped the mirror back into her bag. "I have known you a long time, Lang Reilly. A call from you after all those years made me alert. I did not think you would have called me unless you wanted something. Then I read the incoming and made a connection. I hunched right."

Her mangling of the idiom did nothing to diminish his surprise. "But you could get fired. . . ."

She stood and stretched, a motion he guessed she knew emphasized shapely breasts. "You are an old friend, one of the *Komraden*. I have few of those."

He looked up at her, feeling a smile beginning. "Even when I'm an international fugitive?"

"Why not? I was willing to help when you called and I knew you were a lawyer."

Everybody was into lawyer-bashing.

Lang left several bills on the table as he stood up. "A walk before I put you into a cab?"

She stepped closer. He could smell the sourness of tobacco smoke as she spoke. "Have I gotten so old I no longer interest you?"

Coquettishness had never been among Gurt's charms.

"If looks are what you mean, you've aged better than good whisky. I'd hardly call what I feel 'interest.' "

"Good," she said. "Then we can take the same cab to wherever you're staying."

Being a Southerner, Lang was a little uncomfortable when he realized he was the one being seduced. Scarlett O'Hara was a steel magnolia, not a New Woman.

He took her hand. "This way, *Fraulein*. And by the way, the charge is murder. I'm innocent."

She slipped her bag over her shoulder. "I knew that before I came here."

Later that night, Lang lay on top of skimpy covers, sweat drying on his chest. Beside him, Gurt's breathing was deep and regular, the sound of peaceful sleep. They had made love without inhibition, a noisy performance he was fairly certain dismissed any doubts his host might have had about the reason he had not wanted his passport entered into the system.

The murder charge, he thought, could be disproved easily enough. Show Morse the bogus passport and let him check the airline's passenger manifest. The Agency would be less than happy to find a former employee was using false papers it had created, but the Agency wasn't his problem. Lang's problem was that he would have to return to Atlanta to demonstrate his alibi. That, he wasn't ready to do. Not yet, anyway.

4

Rome
1230 hours the next day

"Your Brother Marcenni isn't at the Vatican."

Lang put down his square of pizza, swallowed and asked, "Then, where is he?"

Gurt had gone to work that morning and then met him at an outdoor table on the Via del Babulno in view of the

Spanish Steps, a hundred yards by a hundred yards of white travertine angles, straights and terraces in their spring garb of pink azaleas. As always, the steps were the roost of hordes of young people: students and artists, who seemed to spend their days sitting, smoking, photographing each other and lazing in the sun.

Gurt, obviously enjoying Lang's concern, was prolonging it. She poked a fork tentatively at her salad. "Orvieto, he's in Orvieto, supervising the restoration of some frescoes."

Lang took a sip of beer. Orvieto was an hour, hour and a half north of Rome just off the *Auto Strada* to Florence.

He put down his glass. "Want to spend a day in Umbria, just being a tourist?"

Finished with her salad, Gurt was firing up another Marlboro, the second Lang had seen since she had joined him that morning. "Why not? But do not think I believe this tourist shit. You cannot communicate with this priest unless he speaks English or I translate for you."

Once again, Gurt had read him with disquieting accuracy. Among several other languages, she was fluent in Italian. At the Vatican, finding a translator would have been no problem. In a small hill town, it might be impossible.

"Is that a 'yes'?"

She nodded, looked vainly for an ash tray and flicked ashes onto her empty plate where they sizzled in the salad's oil. "It is."

"We'd best go by car. The international fugitive bulletin you saw probably's been disseminated to the local cops and I'd just as soon stay away from choke points."

Choke points, places where he could be squeezed into narrow quarters. Like train or bus stations. Or airports.

She tilted her chin and jetted smoke skyward. "I would think a motorcycle would be more desirable. The helmet is a perfect mask and nobody would expect you to be on a bike."

Lang grinned. "I wouldn't expect me to be, either. Have you looked at those things lately? Cafe racer bars, competition-faring, rear-mounted pegs. You have to ride the damn things like you're making love to them. Besides, riding anything on the *Auto Strada* without being encased in iron is suicidal."

"There was a time when you had motorcycles happy, liked them. You even owned one, a Triumph Bonneville. Called it the crotch rocket."

"That was over ten years ago," Lang said. "I've gotten smarter in my old age."

She ground out her cigarette in the plate. "Or duller."

"You didn't think I was dull last night."

"I was being polite."

A shadow on the table made them look up. The waiter was following the conversation with obvious interest.

"Lovers' quarrel," Lang explained.

"We are not in love," Gurt said.

"You adore me."

"In your dreams."

The waiter fled. Gurt and Lang burst into laughter at the same time.

When he could be serious again, Lang said, "Too bad radio comedy is dead. Did you mean what you said?"

"About not being in love?"

"About the motorcycle."

"It would be a good disguise. Nobody would suspect a man your age would be on a bike."

Lang suspected he had just been insulted. "That mean you're willing to ride on the back all the way to Orvieto?"

"The fresh air will do us both healthy."

"You're on. But can we find a machine we can sit on instead of hunch over?"

CHAPTER FOUR

1

Rome
The next morning

Lang didn't expect a fine Italian bike, a Ducatti or Moto Guzi. They were far too expensive for the average Italian and most were exported to the States. He anticipated one of the small Japanese machines common to Rome's narrow streets.

He was mistaken.

She arrived the next morning on a BMW 1000, old but well kept. The machine wasn't known for its acceleration, but it excelled in reliability, smoothness of ride and lack of noise. BMW had been the first to employ the shaft drive now used by most touring bikes in place of the vibration-causing, maintenance-high chain.

Had it not been for the braid of blond hair hanging down the back of the green-and-white leathers, Gurt's full face helmet would have made recognizing her impossible.

Lang watched with equal parts amusement and surprise as Gurt dismounted. She was the only woman he had ever known strong enough to hoist a bike that big onto its floor stand. Matter of fact, he don't think he'd ever known another woman who drove a motorcycle.

He was appraising the BMW as she pulled off her Bell Magnum.

"Nice, yes?" she said.

"Makes the trip worth taking. Don't suppose you have an extra set of leathers?"

Europeans biking the highways wore colorful two-piece leather outfits rather than the jeans preferred by Americans. Without the proper costume, Lang would be conspicuous.

She pointed. "In the Krausers."

Krausers were the saddlebags attached to the frame. With the turn of a key, they could be detached to serve as luggage.

"And an extra helmet." One identical to hers was hanging on its loop beneath the seat.

"I don't know what you had to do to get someone to loan you their bike plus all this," Lang said, taking the leathers out of the saddlebag, "and I'm sure not going to ask."

Gurt laughed. "Why would I borrow it? It's mine."

Lang felt a twinge of jealousy that he was pulling on pants an unknown number of other guys had worn. "I suppose you'll insist on driving, then."

"And make you sit behind a woman?" She found this immensely funny. "You would be, what's the word, castigated?"

"Castrated."

"That, too."

Lang was surprised at how well the trousers fit. The jacket was snug but it would zip shut. His reflection in a shop window showed a typical European, ready for a cross-country ride. Except for the Birkenstocks.

"Damn! Forgot my shoes."

Gurt smiled. "I have no extra boots."

"I've got a pair of shoes back at the *pensione*. They aren't motorcycle boots but they're better'n sandals."

The slow run through the narrow streets and alleys served as a refresher course in motorcycle driving. By the time they reached the *pensione*, Lang was eager to get on the road where speed would make the BMW far more stable than the wobbling pace the crowded city streets required.

He was in and out of the room in seconds while Gurt straddled the bike, studying a road map. Lang's Cole Haans hadn't been intended for shifting a motorcycle's gears but they would do. He turned to the east towards the Tiber and let out the hand clutch as he turned the throttle.

2

The old *pensione*-keeper had been watching from behind a curtained window. How strange these Germans were! The man would only pay for a room at this modest establishment to fuck his whore, yet he was riding a BMW worth two or three months' salary for the average Italian. Where had he been keeping that expensive machine? He certainly had not arrived on it. Clearly the man and woman were used to riding together. They had matching leathers, something the German's wife might like to know and be willing to pay to learn.

He would have to discover the man's identity. Perhaps there were papers in the room. . . . But he would have to be careful. There was something about the occupant of the room next to the bath upstairs, a mannerism, the hardness of his eyes, that said he was a man not to be angered.

A knock at the door, the flurry of banging of someone in a hurry. Let them wait. With all three rooms full, there was no reason to risk falling in a rush to turn someone away. The noise became more persistent as the old man shuffled to the door.

The man standing outside wore coveralls, the uniform of the European working class. He could have been a plumber or truck driver. It was unlikely he wanted a room.

"Si?"

The workman shoved his way inside and shut the door before he held up a photograph. The old man recognized the German.

"You have seen this man, an American?" the stranger asked. The accent was not Roman, perhaps not even Italian.

"I am the information bureau?" the old man sneered. Like any other commodity, information had a value, was not something to be given away. Perhaps this man was working for the German's wife. "Out, go ask your questions elsewhere or show me your police credentials."

The stranger reached into the top of his coveralls. When his hand came out, it held a pistol. The gun was pointed at the old man's head.

"Here are all the credentials I need, you old fart. Now, once again before your meager brains are splattered all over this entryway, have you seen this American?"

The old man was frightened. He had seen such things happen on the American programs on television. And this man might be American. Worse, by the way he butchered the language, he could be Sicilian. Either way, dying on behalf of a guest's privacy was not included in the rent. If only this man would go away and leave him unharmed, he would say a hundred Hail Mary's at Saint Peter's.

He nodded and pointed to the picture of his guest. "I thought he was German."

The truck driver, or plumber, or whoever he was, with

the gun said angrily, "I don't give a shit what you thought. Is he here?"

The old man felt his bladder release. Warm urine was running down his leg, becoming cold as it soaked his pants. He hoped the man with the gun didn't notice. He would go to Saint Peter's on his arthritic knees if this evil man would just go away.

"He left seconds ago, right before you came. He and a woman."

The old man felt weak with relief as he saw the gun returned to inside the coveralls.

"The couple on the motorcycle?"

The *pensione* owner nodded vigorously. "Yes, yes. That was them. They were headed towards Florence."

The stranger was suspicious. "And how do you know that?"

Had he not been frozen with fear, the old man would have kicked himself for saying anything that kept this intruder here one second longer. If he would go away, he would crawl on his belly like a snake to Saint Peter's.

"I saw the color of the border of the road map the woman was looking at. It only shows Rome north to Florence."

The gunman/workman's eyes narrowed. "You have good eyesight for an old man."

He had said too much, the old man was sure of it. He was going to be found dead in the *pensione* that represented his entire life's savings. He would not only crawl to Saint Peter's, he would take every bit of money paid by the accursed German/American and put it in the poor box as thanks for his deliverance.

The man with the gun spun on the heels of his work boots and left the old man gaping after him. He had been spared. A good thing, too. Had the bastard with the gun remained one second longer, the old innkeeper would have had to attack, snatch away the gun and shoot him with it like the American policeman he had seen in the film on television. What was it the American policeman had said? Oh yes: "Go ahead, make my day."

3

Umbria
Two hours later

Off the *Auto Strada*, they passed a cluster of motels that would have been at home anywhere along an American interstate. They followed a procession of trucks through modern Orvieto before turning off the main road and beginning the climb uphill.

Orvieto was the only hill town Lang had ever visited that was not hilly. Instead, the old walled city perched on top of a rock formation that was flat on top, a geological phenomenon any resident of the American Southwest would recognize as a mesa. There was little traffic. Tourists had not yet discovered the place, although the huge empty parking lot below the main piazza gave an indication of the citizens' aspirations.

Winding through the narrow streets, Lang guided the BMW into the Via Maurizo and the Piazza Dumo, a square dominated by the cathedral. The late morning sun danced along the gilt mosaics covering the facade of the exuberantly Italian Gothic building. Unlike the more famous towns of Tuscany to the north, there were few cars on the square. Lang parked and held the bike steady as Gurt swung a long leg over the seat to dismount.

They entered the narthex of the church, standing still while their eyes acclimated to the dim light. Inside the nave, candles flickered in side chapels, shadows giving movement to frescoes. A brightness came from somewhere beyond the choir, the raised platform where the transept crossed the main body of the church.

An elaborate altar held more candles, their wavering light making Christ seem to writhe on His cross. To the right of the sanctuary, another side chapel blazed with electric floodlights anachronistic in a setting centuries old. The floor was covered with dropcloths. Brushes, putty knives and bottles of pigment were scattered everywhere. Even the clutter did little to detract from richly colored figures tumbling into the abyss, that favorite of Italian frescoes, the Final Judgement.

No matter whether painted by Michelangelo, Bernini or some other artist, the subject always reminded Lang of late Friday night at a singles bar.

On scaffolding halfway up the wall of anguished souls consigned to damnation (or those who would sleep alone), three men were examining one of the figures. Two wore overalls. The third was in a paint-splattered cassock.

"Fra Marcenni?" Gurt called.

The man in the cassock turned. He could have been one of the saints pictured throughout the church. His white hair stood around a pink circle of scalp, catching the powerful light in an electronic halo. He was small, about the size of the *pensione*'s owner and about the same age.

"Si?"

"Do you speak English?" she asked, shading her eyes as she looked up at the top of the scaffolding.

The halo shook: no.

Gurt fired off a burst of Italian.

The monk smiled and replied, pointing behind Lang and Gurt.

"He says he'll come down in a minute or two, that he'll be happy to speak to us. We are to enjoy the art of this magnificent church while we wait."

Lang's lack of interest in religious art applied equally to the magnificent or otherwise. So, instead of feeding coins into boxes to illuminate the paintings in the various chapels, he amused himself by deciphering the Latin epitaphs marking the tombs of prelates and nobility who had contributed generously to this church. The burial places of the poor, no doubt, had long since been forgotten.

The meek might someday inherit the earth but it will be one that doesn't remember them.

Lang studied a small glass vial embedded in the altar, trying to ascertain what holy relic might be enshrined there. A nail from the True Cross, a finger bone of St. Paul?

He never found out.

Gurt took him by the arm. "Fra Marcenni is taking a break. We'll have coffee on the square."

The good brother preferred wine.

They sat alfresco at a table only a few yards from the massive doors of the cathedral. Gurt and the monk exchanged what Lang supposed were the banalities of commencing a conversation with a stranger.

Signalling for a second glass, the old monk said something to Gurt and looked at Lang.

"He would like to see the picture we have come to ask about,"she translated.

Lang handed it across the table. "Tell him I need to know what it shows."

The monk stared at the Polaroid while Gurt spoke. He replied and Lang waited impatiently for the English.

"Three shepherds are looking at a tomb."

Lang had never considered this possibility for the enigmatic structure. "The woman, who is she?"

The old man listened to Gurt and crossed himself as he replied.

"A saint, perhaps the Blessed Virgin herself," Gurt said. "She is watching the shepherds at the tomb, perhaps the tomb of Christ before He arises."

Swell. Lang had come all this way to understand another religious painting. Although the tomb of Christ had always been pictured as a cave, one from which a stone could be rolled. The difference was hardly worth the trip.

He was reminded of the two shipwreck survivors floating in a lifeboat in a fog. Suddenly, they see shore and the figure of a man.

"Where are we?" shouts one of the men in the boat.

"At sea, right off the coast," comes the answer.

"Imagine that," the other man in the boat says. "Running into a lawyer out here."

"Lawyer?" his companion asks. "How the hell do you know he's a lawyer?"

"Because the answer to my question was absolutely accurate and totally worthless."

Like the old priest's answer.

Brother Marcenni must have sensed Lang's disappointment. He took a magnifying glass from somewhere in his cassock and squinted at the picture before speaking again to Gurt.

"He says the letters on the tomb are in Latin, written without spaces in the manner of the ancient Romans."

This was again telling Lang he was at sea. "That much I knew."

As though understanding the English, Brother Marcenni read in a slow, quivering voice, *"Et in Arcadia ego sum."*

"Makes no sense," Lang said to Gurt. "Both *sum* and *ego* are first person. *Sum* means 'I am' and *ego* is the first person pronoun."

Gurt looked at him as though he had grown another head.

Lang shrugged apologetically. "Latin is sort of a hobby."

"I never knew that."

"It didn't seem relative to the relationship. We usually communicated in grunts and groans. Ask the good brother if *sum* and *ego* aren't redundant."

After treating Lang to a glare that would have singed paint, Gurt and the monk exchanged sentences. He gesticulated as though his hands could solve the mystery.

Finally, Gurt nodded and said, "He says the second denotation of the first person is perhaps for emphasis. The phrase would translate as 'I am also' or 'I am even' in Arcadia but is peculiar usage. Perhaps the artist was speaking alle . . . alle . . ."

"Allegorically," Lang supplied.

"Allegorically. As if he were saying, 'I am here also,' meaning that death is present even in Arcadia."

"The tomb of Christ is in Canada or Greece? Ask him how that might be."

In reply to Gurt's question, the monk motioned the waiter for yet another glass of wine and laughed, hands moving expansively.

"He says the artist, Poussin, was French. The French are too busy with women and wine to be exact about geography. Besides, Arcadia was frequently symbolic for a place of pastoral peace."

Or anything else, by Lang's observation.

Since he had to drive back down that curving road, Lang was drinking coffee. His cup had gone cold and he motioned to the waiter as Brother Marcenni produced a metrically numbered straightedge and began to measure the Polaroid. He turned the picture sideways and upside down, nodded and spoke to Gurt.

"He says this is not only a picture but a map."

Lang forgot about warming up his coffee. "A map? Of what?"

After another exchange and much waving of hands by the monk, Gurt answered, "Many of these old paintings were maps. The shepherds' staffs are held at an angle that forms two legs of an equilateral triangle, see?" She pointed. "If we draw the third leg, the tomb is in the center.

That means the painting, the map, directs the observer to the tomb itself, wherever located."

"He's sure?"

Another question in Italian.

The old man nodded vigorously, laying the straightedge along one axis of the picture, then another.

"He's sure. Shepherds' staffs, soldiers' swords, other objects that are straight were often used as clues. It would not be a coincidence that two legs of the triangle would be at geometrically correct angles."

"A tomb's located between the staffs of two shepherds?" Lang was skeptical.

Gurt shook her head. "No, no. Notice the trees lead from the mountains in the background? If you continue the line of those trees, they reach the tomb, too. Trees also frame that jagged gap in the mountains, see? Brother Marcenni says that if you were in this place and lined the mountains up to match the painting, you would be standing where the tomb was."

The monk interrupted.

"He says it is also significant that the background is not as he remembers it, that the Poussin painting with which he is familiar was different. It would not have been unusual in the artist's day to do several similar works."

None of this had convinced Lang. "He's telling us that this painting was done as a map to Christ's burial place in Greece?"

Gurt again spoke in Italian. The old man shook his head, crossed himself again and pointed to the picture, the sky and himself.

"He says of course not. The Holy Sepulchre is in Jerusalem and has been empty since the third day after the crucifixion when Christ rose before ascending into heaven. The tomb in the picture could mean anything, a treasure, perhaps where a vision appeared to someone.

When the painting, or the original from which it was copied, was done, symbolism was fashionable, as were hidden meanings, puzzles and secret maps. If you knew where those mountains were, perhaps in Greece, you might find whatever the tomb symbolizes."

This was a little better than telling Lang he was at sea.

"So," he said, "that's why my sister and nephew died. Someone wanted to make sure they didn't figure out they had seen a map leading to treasure, or something worth killing for."

"Or dying for," Gurt said. "Like the guy who jumped."

They sat in silence for a moment. Lang was trying to guess what was worth that long step from his balcony. The monk regarded his empty glass wistfully, stood and bowed as he spoke.

"It's time for him to get back to work. Those lazy plasterers will do nothing unless he is there," Gurt translated.

Lang stood. "Tell him he has sincere thanks from this heretic."

Gurt's translation made the old man smile before he turned and crossed the piazza.

Lang sat back down and drained the dregs of his cold coffee. "I'd say somebody has gone to a lot of trouble to make sure nobody lives long enough to figure out that picture."

Gurt gave the square a worried glance. "I'd say you better do as you Americans say, watch your ass." Her face wrinkled. "How do you do that, watch your own ass, without straining your back?"

4

Orvieto

They drove downhill, the narrow mountain road unwinding in front of the BMW like a black ribbon. Even with

Gurt's weight on the back, the machine bragged of its stability as Lang braked, downshifted and accelerated through each curve. The combination of precise engineering and a place to test its limits occupied his attention. He had even forgotten Gurt's arms around him, breasts pressed against his back, sensuous even through leather.

There was no guardrail. On the right, Lang could see occasional treetops and roofs of the town far below. His view across the Umbrian valley was virtually unobstructed, a patchwork of shades of green until it reached smoky hills on the horizon. Twice he saw a large bird below, wings outstretched over the farmland as it coasted along thermals. On a motorcycle, he thought, I'm almost that free.

To his left, Orvieto was disappearing behind its walls until there was nothing to see but a bank of dirt or retaining stones.

He was never sure what pulled him from the euphoria of the day, the scenery, the company. He only knew he was surprised on one of the short straight stretches to see the BMW's mirrors filled with a truck. Not the eighteen-wheeled behemoth of American interstates, but large enough to fill its half of the road. Behind the cab, a load on a bed was covered by canvas, its corners flapping in the wind as though the truck, bed and cargo might suddenly take flight.

Where had it come from? Either Lang had been totally distracted from driving or the truck was moving far too fast for the twists of the tortured road.

Lang leaned into a sweeping right-hand turn and set up for a hairpin to the left. No doubt about it, the truck was gaining on them, swerving all over the road as it struggled to stay on the pavement. Lang could see the bed swaying wildly, almost enough to turn the rig over. He listened for the hiss of air brakes, a sound that didn't come. Maybe the driver was drunk or the brakes had failed. No sober, sane person would risk running off the road where the shoulders between asphalt and empty space were so thin.

Lang searched ahead for a turnoff, even a space between paving and mountainside. There were none. Straight drop right, perpendicular rise left. Nowhere to go.

Tiny, cold feet of apprehension began to walk up Lang's back. The truck got bigger in the mirrors.

The bike made a right-hand turn and entered a straightaway of perhaps two hundred yards. Its mirrors no longer reflected the entire truck. Lang could clearly see the prancing lion of Peugot on the grill. Over the hiss of the airstream, he could hear the truck driver shifting through higher gears.

The idiot had no intent of slowing down.

Taking his left hand from the handlebar, Lang tapped Gurt's leg and pointed behind. He heard a German expletive over the roar of the truck's engine. She squeezed him tighter.

The bike shuddered as its fiberglass rear fender shattered and Lang braced against the impact. The bastard intended to run them over! He opened the throttle to the stop.

How had they found him? How could they have possibly known he was driving a motorcycle to Orvieto? Lang shoved the questions from his mind. Right now, he needed to concentrate on keeping the Beamer on the pavement.

If he could beat the truck into the next curve, it would either have to slow down or be flung off the side of the mountain by centrifugal force. Too bad he wasn't on a machine known for speed rather than comfort.

He sensed the massive bumper inches from the rear wheel again as he swung wide, the better to straighten the line through the curve. The bike's speed pushed it to the outside, well across the center line. If something were on the other side of the blind turn, headed uphill, they would meet it head-on. A risk he had to take or be crushed.

They flashed through the shadow of the hill, relieved to finally hear the snort of air brakes as they reentered sunshine. They had gained a hundred feet or so.

Lang tested the throttle again, making sure it was still as open as it would go. The grip was wet with sweat and his hand slipped. He wished he had found a pair of gloves.

The mirrors were empty only for a second until the ugly snout of the truck poked around the turn like a beast seeking prey. Lang was trying to remember the trip up, how far he and Gurt were from the bottom. If they could make it to a flat road where the Peugeot would not have a downslope to add to its speed, even the BMW's indifferent acceleration would leave the truck behind.

If.

The truck closed the gap again, its engine bellowing in triumph. The motorcycle simply could go no faster.

Gurt shifted. She had to know movement could destroy the balance of the bike, send them flying into space. Lang wanted to turn around and scream at her to be still but he couldn't take even that brief second away from watching the road. Not at this pace.

He felt one arm clasp around his chest while Gurt seemed to be bending over. The Krausers. Christ, this was no time to be searching through the saddlebags for something she might have forgotten to bring!

Lang could see in the periphery of one mirror as she stood on the rear pegs and turned to face the truck, using the arm around Lang to sustain her balance. The interruption of the BMW's airstream, the added resistance of her erect body, made the front end shimmy. Had Lang not needed to fight to maintain steering, he would have risked taking a hand off the bars to snatch her back onto her seat.

Not that it mattered. The grille of the truck looked like a chrome mouth about to open and devour them both. And there wasn't a damn thing Lang could do.

One, then two pops were snatched away by the wind, muted both by helmet and rushing air. A blowout! Lang instantly anticipated the loss of control that came with losing a tire at high speed. Instead, there were three more sounds, a shallow noise like slow clapping. The BMW's only wobble was from Gurt standing in the airstream.

A flick of his eyes from the road to the mirrors saw the truck rapidly receding, the sun a million diamonds on its crazed windshield. In near disbelief, he watched its swerving increase in ever larger curves until, amid a wail of protesting rubber, it launched itself over the side of the road like a huge rocket. It seemed to hang in emptiness before its nose pointed down and it was swallowed by space like the souls in the fresco. Lang thought he felt the road quiver with a series of impacts downhill.

Gurt sat back down and returned her arm to his waist. He detected a whiff of cordite before the wind devoured it, and he realized what had happened.

As the slope gentled, the road widened until it reached a verge wide enough for Lang to pull off and stop. He pulled out the BMW's ignition key. Neither he nor Gurt moved or spoke, letting the heat from the cylinder heads seep through their leathers as the cooling machinery ticked.

Lang finally took off his helmet and turned to watch Gurt unbuckle hers. "I had forgotten you won the Agency's shooting competition in eighty-seven. Pistol *and* rifle, if I recall."

She smiled demurely as though he had complimented a new dress. "Eighty-eight and eighty-nine also. After that, I quit competing."

"What happened to the gun?"

"Over the hillside along with the *Schweinhund* in the truck. When the police find the wreck, they are likely to start interrogating anyone in the area. There are bullet holes in the windscreen. I didn't want to have a weapon on me."

"The gun is clean?"

She was leaning forward, inspecting her makeup in the bike's mirrors, more like a debutante than someone who had just made a shot James Bond wouldn't have dared. "It is Agency-issue. My gloves prevented my fingers from printing on it or powder marks on my hands for paraffin to detect. I need only to also dispose of the extra clip in the Krausers."

"Should we go back, see what happened to the driver?"

She turned from the mirror to ruefully regard the cracked fiberglass of the BMW's rear fender. "And have the authorities show up while we're poking around? I do not think they would listen to the explanations of an international fugitive."

Lang thought about that. "There may be a clue as to who he is, was."

"Perhaps if you take off your leathers, put them back in the bags, I will go back alone. If the police come, they will never connect a woman to such a shooting. They are, after all, Italian. They will think it was an attempted high-john."

"Hijack."

"Him, too. I will see if the driver has any identification. I will also make sure he is unable to tell anyone what happened."

He watched her ride off. Kipling, he thought, must have known someone like Gurt when he wrote that "the female of the species is more deadly than the male."

5

The Umbrian Auto Strada
Thirty minutes later

Lang waited in one of the road stops that litter the *Auto Strada*. With its islands of gas pumps, cafeterias and bathrooms reeking of disinfectant, it could just as well have been on the interstates of New York or on Florida's Sunshine State Parkway. Why does America export only the tacky? Lang had a theory that someday all of Europe would look like Kansas or, worse, California. With that to look forward to, how could anybody be in favor of globalization?

He was thinking of something else that day, however. The cappuccino in front of him was simply his ticket of admission, the price to be paid for a seat at the bar. The caffeine provided a small high, lost in the tide of adrenaline that was just now beginning to ebb. How had he lived this long without the rush only danger gives? Even if his job at the Agency had never involved a life-or-death situation, a shoot-out, or a high-speed chase, it had been exciting to plan the smuggling of a defector across an armed border. Even guessing an opponent's next move on the chessboard of Europe had its thrills before the red king and its pawns were swept from the table.

Now all he had to look forward to was verbal fencing in a courtroom, a competition as highly stylized as any Kabuki performance. At this moment, he missed the game more than he had ever anticipated. The fast-paced developments and the challenge had faded into a memory he suspected was tinted by nostalgia as he had pursued the crushing sameness of law school and practice. At the time, it had been more than an even swap: the certainty he would becoming home every evening in exchange for broken promises and a wife sick with worry when he could only tell her he would be gone for an undetermined period.

Dawn wasn't here anymore and Lang was involved in a game with stakes higher than he would have chosen. Even the Reds, those world-threatening hoards of Godless communists, the Agency's raison d'être, had not been fanatics.

At least, not the ones he had known. He had never heard of an opposing agent willing, let alone eager, to die for Marxism like a mujahideen ready to sacrifice all for Allah. They, the name Lang had unconsciously pasted on the unknown group, They were as zealous as any bomb-toting Arab terrorist. His would-be assassin had dashed across the room to jump, to meet whatever maker he contemplated, rather than risk capture. The driver of that truck could not have expected to survive the crash his speed made inevitable on that winding road. He had only hoped to take the two motorcyclists with him to whatever place he thought worth his life on earth.

For what?

To Lang, such fervor implied religion, a religious group, more likely a cult. History was replete with dismal examples: the Moslem cult of Assassins, from whom we take the word, who had greeted the Crusaders with nocturnal knives, the Hindu Thuggee, stealthy stranglers of the imperial English, Japanese kamikaze dying for their emperor-god.

Brother Marcenni's explanation had given Lang an idea why They might want the picture, might kill to get it. All sorts of wealth could be hidden somewhere, Poussin's painting the key to its location. But he'd never heard of martyrs for material riches. Men died for causes, for ideas, for vengeance. But for earthly wealth they would never possess?

But then, the old monk hadn't said the picture was a map to pirates' gold, buried treasure or the like, had he? But why else would a painting, one that did not even exactly copy the original, be worth killing for? Something of ideological value?

Like what, the holy grail?

There were some facts of which Lang was fairly certain. They wanted the painting and intended to eradicate anyone who might have learned its secret. That secret had to do with the physical location of something of great value to Them. Lang was interested in what that something might be. It could lead him to whoever had killed Janet and Jeff. And tried to kill him. Now that he knew the painting might have a secret, he needed to find out who was guarding the truth the enigma concealed. And why.

He had a plan.

There was a hush in the crowded room as Gurt entered and took the vacant seat at the bar beside Lang. A six-foot Valkyrie in motorcycle leathers was apparently not a common sight. Oblivious to the eyes following her every breath, she lit a Marlboro and motioned to the man behind the bar, pointing to Lang's cup. She also wanted cappuccino.

Lang would have bet that was the fastest service the barman had provided in weeks.

He grinned as the hum of conversation resumed. "You make quite an entrance."

She took a deep drag from the cigarette, speaking through the haze of her own tobacco smoke. "They'll get over it."

He waited impatiently for her to tell what she had found. She waited until she tasted her coffee.

"Well?"

With her free hand, she reached into a pocket and held up a silver chain. From it dangled the same design Lang had seen in Atlanta, four triangles meeting in the center of a circle.

She let the pendant twirl on the chain. "No papers, no wallet, no identification other than this."

"I take it he was . . . ?"

"As a herring."

"Mackerel."

"Why should one fish be more dead than another? The jewelry mean anything to you?"

"Same as the man who broke into my apartment in Atlanta had."

She stubbed out her cigarette and put the circle on its chain back into a pocket of the leathers. "Would have been easier to have used a rifle than a truck. Any guess why he tried to run us under instead of taking an easy shot from behind a tree?"

Lang wasn't eager to question the wisdom of the decision that had left Gurt and him alive, but he said, "Maybe there was some reason for us to die in a traffic accident."

Gurt shrugged as though it was a matter of no consequence. "Dead is dead. And we aren't. What's next?"

"I need to get out of Italy, go to London."

Lang saw an instant of uncertainty. There is no word for "go" in Gurt's native tongue. Germans fly, walk, drive, etcetera. The means of transportation denotes going. One would not, for example, *gehen,* walk, to the United States but would *flugen,* fly.

"Not easy," she said. "By now your picture will be in the hands of every police force in Europe."

She was right. But Lang said, "Since the Common Market, no one guards borders anymore." He signaled the barman for two more coffees. "If I could get on a plane at an airport that doesn't have flights to or from places outside Europe, there would be no customs and immigration. I'd only have to worry about being recognized by an airport cop and a half-decent disguise would solve that problem."

"You'd still have to show your passport to get on the flight."

"Seems I remember someone who . . ."

She looked around, apprehensive that the conversation might be overheard. "Yes, yes, the engraver behind the jewelry shop on the Via Garibaldi. If there were two of us, your disguise would be even better. The police aren't looking for a couple."

"Thanks, but I don't want you at risk."

"Risk, he says!" Those eyebrows arched again. "And what do you think we were in back there on the road, an English tea party?"

"You want to help, see if you know someone in S&T who can fix up a disguise."

Science and Technology, the Agency's Second Directorate, the L. L. Bean of espionage, equipping agents with everything from radio transmitters that fit into the heel of a shoe to umbrellas that shot poison darts.

She stared hard at her cup. "Either I go with you or you'll get no help from me. I'm not going to assist in your getting killed."

Lang pondered this development. Gurt was no damsel in distress whom he would have to worry about every minute. She had just proved that. Still, exposing her to Them . . .

"Your engraver," she added as though aware he was weighing his options. "He is in prison for counterfeiting."

"You're very persuasive," he said. "You can get S&T's help, assuming they still do that sort of thing?"

She drained her cup, making a face at the bitterness of the dregs. "Science and Technology are still with us, yes. They could certainly come up with a disguise your mother wouldn't recognize. But for who? I mean, they are not going to help an ex-employee evade the police. And there are requisition forms, authorizations . . ."

The Agency, like any branch of government, ran on a high-octane mixture of paperwork and red tape. As part of the Peace Dividend, employees like Lang had been allowed to retire without replacement. Except in the First Directorate, Administration, the home of the paper shufflers, where bureaucrats were still plentiful as cockroaches.

And, like the insect, could survive anything, budget cut or nuclear attack. These were the people who required the endless forms that justified their existence.

"Not worth the trouble," Lang conceded. "I still remember how to make myself over so you wouldn't recognize me."

"With your clothes on or off?"

He ignored her. "I'll need some cash. Quite a bit, actually, since I can't use an ATM. Withdrawals from my account can be too easily traced. I'll need clothes and stuff, too, since mine are at the *pensione*. It wouldn't be smart to go back there. That leaves the passport and the usual: driver's license, credit cards, etcetera. You can get all that?"

"As long as you understand I'm coming with you."

"You drive a real bargain."

"It is for your own safety. You cannot, as you say, watch your own ass."

"You can just take off?"

"I have vacation time coming."

Lang knew when he was whipped, the value of a strategic retreat. "Okay, let's go back to your place in Rome and get what we need. Just remember, I warned you, this isn't some sort of war game."

She smiled sweetly, speaking with that mellifluous Southern accent much imitated by those who have never been south of Washington. "Why, mah deah, that is the most gracious invitation Ah have evah received."

Lang didn't even try to guess what Rhett might have replied.

THE TEMPLARS:
THE END OF AN ORDER

An Account by Pietro of Sicily
Translation from the medieval Latin by Nigel Wolffe, Ph.D.

2

Even before the sun had reached its zenith, the heat per-
suaded Guillaume de Poitiers to shed greave and sabaton,[1] remaining armoured only in breastplate, pallette and brassard[2]
over his hauberk. Over all his military garments was the
white robe that floated about him like a cloud.

He professed no discomfort, relating to us some of the
hardships encountered in combating the abominable Turks:
the land deserted, waterless and uninhabitable. Therein he
and his comrades found not the manna God provided the Is-
raelites in the wilderness but prickly plants with scant moisture or nutriment. More than once, he and his fellows had
eaten their warhorses and left mangonel,[3] ram, scaling lad-
ders and other implements of battle in the sand for want of a
means to transport them.

His esquire, a young man a few years older than I, had been
christened Phillipe. He had, just as I did, no memory of tem-
poral family, having been raised as a child by the Knights of
the Temple.

In the dust raised by Guillaume's steed, we toiled along on the heavily laden ass. Phillipe entertained me with tales of exotic lands far beyond my mean knowledge. He had been with his master since Cyprus and had shared the privations of the voyage from there. Twice they had been beset upon by pirates from Africa; twice their faith and a wind sent by God had delivered them.

At the risk of the sins of gluttony and greed, I asked Phillipe again and again about the food and quarters I could expect. He verified what his master had said: Meat was served twice a day, and brothers, whether knights, esquires or others slept on pallets stuffed with straw which was changed weekly. There was a stream nearby so that one might bathe should the weather not be intemperate. Indeed, it may have been at this time I became so engrossed in the luxuries awaiting me that I almost forgot that my purpose was to serve God, not my own desires. It may well be for this that I am to be punished.

We made our way up Monte San Giuliano, a name that seemed to bode well, being nearly the same as our knight's in the local dialect.[4] At the top was the city of Erice, encased in the walls built by the Norman kings.[5] Here we spent the night in an abbey not unlike the one I had departed. So enraptured was I by the promises of things to come that I was disappointed by fare identical to that I had consumed all my life.

So mean had places dedicated to worship and meditation become to me in my anticipation that I was impatient for Prime to end so we might come one day closer to Burgundy. Once again, our departure was made in the dark.

The morning was not yet bright enough to illuminate the road down the mountain, a path so tightly convoluted as to make it impossible to see around the next turn. I was glad to be riding the ass whose agility far exceeded that of the lumbering horses which we had to guide carefully lest they misstep and fall into the valley below.

We had gone a scant dozen furlongs[6] beyond the city's gate when we came around a bend and encountered men in the road. The morning had by then acquired just enough light to show the cudgels[7] they carried. Even in the sheltered life I had led, I knew that men upon a public road without beasts or women were more likely to be miscreants than travelers.

I clasped the rosary around my neck and began to pray for St. Christopher's intercession, for, although I had nothing worthy of stealing, I had heard men such as these usually left their victims dead or nearly so. Indeed, was that not the lesson of Our Lord's parable of the Good Samaritan?

If the poor light and devious road had prevented us from seeing these vile knaves, it had likely prevented them from seeing that one of our number was a knight with all the armour and weapons of that state.

As they advanced, Guillaume de Poitiers turned his white charger and trotted back to us so serenely as to deny he was about to enter the arena of battle.[8] From the impedimenta upon the back on one of the tethered horses trailing behind Philippe and myself, he drew his great sword and lifted his shield. Holding the blade in one hand and the shield in the other, he turned his horse and spurred it towards those who meant us harm.

"God's will be done!" he shouted as he thundered down the narrow path.

A knight on horseback is more than a match for men on foot armed only with clubs and short knives, as I was about to witness.

The men in the road apprehended their fate and began to scatter, condemned by their choice of location. There was no means for them to escape other than down the road or over the precipitous edge to near-certain destruction.

Our knight stood in the stirrups and swung that mighty blade, cleaving one man's head and shoulders from a body that ran one or two more steps before falling in a sea of his own blood. The next man shared his companion's fate. Two more jumped into the abyss rather than being skewered like swine above a fire.

Although I had seen men die of the fever or simply because God had willed it, I had never witnessed souls depart this life with so much blood. Even though these men had meant us evil, I was distressed there was no priest available to administer a final unction. I said a speedy prayer for these robbers in hopes of preventing eternal torture of their souls, a revenge no Christian could desire even for those as foul as these. We are, after all, brothers in that we are children of the Lord of Heaven.

If Guillaume de Poitiers harbored such thoughts, he did not reveal them. Instead, he stood in the stirrups again, signalling us to move forward with his sword.

"Are you well, m'lord?" Phillipe asked his master as soon as we had drawn near enough to be heard.

The knight gave us that laugh as he handed his bloody sword, hilt first, to Phillipe. "Praise God, as well as a man can be who has just sent scoundrels to their proper place in hell. We must hasten to find the rest, for surely their encampment is nearby."

I am ignorant as to how he knew this to be so but it was not my station to question the judgement of a knight of God. And as the land became flat, we smelled smoke. A trace of it could be seen against the sky, now brilliant with morning's full light. At the edge of the road, he bade us be quiet, took a fresh mount and led us into a forest so thick it was as if twilight had come.

Shortly we came a clearing. A few mean twig huts were gathered around a central fire over which a hind was roasting, poached from the local lord. These varlets ate far better that those in the service of God.

About the fire were a number of women, some suckling infants. The only men to be seen were old or visibly disabled, no doubt from a life of knavery. Upon seeing our knight, those that could scattered like a covey of partridge. The balance retreated into the crude shelters.

Guillaume de Poitiers disdained following those who had fled. Instead, he leaned from his great warhorse, taking a burning faggot from the fire with which he lit the hovels. As we left, I could hear the screams of those trapped with the conflagration.

"Sir," I asked, "I can understand your putting to flight those who would have robbed us, but is it not unchristian to put to the torch those who have done us no evil?"

He inclined his head as he stroked his beard before replying. "Those who would have robbed us are succored by those we have destroyed. They are but vile creatures, serfs illegally escaped their master who intend to live a life causing mischief to travelers such as we. Their destruction is no more than the killing of vermin in the grain house."

This did not comport with my understanding of the teachings of Our Lord that even the lowest among us are as brothers. But I was young, ignorant and in the company of a man who had fought and bled for Christ, so I changed the direction of my query.

"But sir, you did not look into the eyes of those you killed here," I said, remembering the remark he had made about his wound. "They died in their huts, baking like so much bread."

He nodded, that smile on his lips. "You remember well, little brother. But there are exceptions to every rule. Those men in their shelters died of fire, one of God's four elements."

I knew the four elements consisted of fire, water, wind and earth, but I knew not what pertinence this had to killing. I indulged myself in the sin of pride. I was ashamed to admit I knew not.

Within a few hours we entered the city of Trapani, the name meaning "sickle" in Greek because of the crescent shape of the harbor there. As I have said, until this time I had never been more than a day's journey by foot from my home. I had, of course, heard of the sea, but that is different from seeing it. Thinking of those waters like those on which Our Lord walked and in which His apostles fished, I had not imagined anything like what greeted us. I am ashamed to admit my faith was so little that I could not have imagined the fashioning of anything so deeply blue, so restless or so vast. I had been used to seeing hills and mountains, trees and streams. But here I could see to the very edge of the earth.

Nor had I seen ships before, huge carts that floated upon the water with great white sails, each vessel with enough cloth to blanket the abbey I had left. There seemed to be thousands of these craft, crowding each other as they rose and fell with each breath of the mighty ocean.[9] This huge fleet, I was told, belonged entirely to the Templars who, after paying what amounted to extortion to the Venetians to leave the Holy Land, had decided to purchase their own ships.[10] Those members who had not already done so had gathered here to journey to their home temples.

For days we waited for a wind that would take us northward along the coast of Italy to Genoa and then to the coast of Burgundy. But even the size of these craft to the vastness of the sea, even my faith did not prevent me from becoming trepidant. This I recognized as my weakness, my failing, that I was unable to be comforted that God's will would be done.

During the time in Trapani, I came to realize Guillaume de Poitiers was not alone different from the poor monks with whom I had lived. All his Templar brethren lived well. Although it is hardly man's place in God's scheme to judge, I noted humility and poverty did not number among their attributes. They enjoyed great quantities of unwatered wine (which they were quick to condemn as inferior to the wines of other regions) and were profligate in their habits. Gaming was as common among them as prayer as was recounting stories in which the narrator was the hero, usually a little bit more so than his predecessor.

I was to learn a number of the Holy See's rules did not apply to this Order. This may well have carried the seeds of its fall from grace, a fall as disastrous if less spectacular than Satan's from Heaven.

Translator's Notes

1. Armour shielding leg and foot
2. Armour covering the arms, shoulders and upper body
3. A device for throwing large rocks, like a catapult
4. The Italian equivalent of William is Guglielmo
5. 1091–1250
6. Approximately 650 meters
7. The word Pietro uses is *cycgel*, Frankish for either a short heavy club or a weapon used to beat upon an opponent. In this context, it is doubtful these people would have weapons more sophisticated than could be fashioned from readily available material.
8. The author uses *liste*, a Frankish word which later came to include the areas used for knightly competition. Since the sport of jousting between knights was unknown at the time of Pietro's narrative, the earlier meaning of the word is used.
9. The hyperbole here is Pietro's, not the translator's.
10. There are no consistent records as to the number of ships owned by the Templars, but it is unlikely that the entire fleet would have been at an obscure Sicilian port at once or that all the ships in port would have been theirs.

CHAPTER FIVE

1

Atlanta
The same day

Morse was slouched in his chair, studying another fax, this one from the Department of Defense, Bureau of Records, St. Louis.

Reilly's dates of service matched what Morse remembered him saying, even confirmed a bullet lodged between the seventh and eighth cervical vertebrae. If Morse understood the medical jargon correctly, the examining doctor had adopted an attitude of "if it ain't broke, don't fix it." Attempting surgery to cut the damn bullet out could sever some nerve with a long name. Made sense.

Morse sat up so suddenly the casters on his chair slammed against the gray carpet with a thud, causing the detective in the cubicle next to his to look up from her computer with a glare.

"C-seven and C-eight?" he said to no one in particular

before he picked up the phone and dialed the medical examiner's number from memory.

The first person he spoke to confirmed his suspicion: There was no eighth cervical vertebra. The thoracic spine began after the seventh cervical disk.

Mistake?

Could be.

He reached into the inside pocket of the suit coat draped over the back of his chair and produced his notebook. It didn't take long to find the number for Reilly's office. Now, if he could just get the minimal cooperation if the lawyer's secretary . . .

2

Atlanta: Offices of Arnold Krause, M.D.

Morse hated doctors' offices even when he was not a patient. The worn and outdated magazines and the cheap furniture were almost as bad as the receptionist's, "The doctor'll be right with you," a promise uniformly and cheerfully given but rarely kept. He had a theory that there was a school somewhere that recycled lobotomy patients to work the front desks of physicians' offices.

His badge made a difference. He hardly had time to settle in with a month-old copy of *People* before he was ushered into an office where diplomas and certificates covered more of the walls than the dark paneling.

"Arnold Krause." A short man in a white coat entered the room right after Morse and circled him to stand behind a desk and extend his hand. "Understand you're interested in Mr. Reilly's records."

Morse savored the nervousness most people exhibited around policemen. "That's right, Doctor. There be no doctor-patient privilege in Georgia. . . ."

Krause plopped into a leather chair behind the desk and slid a manila folder and a large envelope across the polished mahogany. "As I'm well aware. Still, we don't usually turn over medical records without a subpoena. But where a patient is subject to an investigation . . ."

Morse sat in a wing chair across the desk and began to thumb through the file. "I appreciate your not insisting on the formalities."

"We try to cooperate with law enforcement," the doctor said, closely watching where Morse directed his attention.

Morse read the typed notes of last fall's physical. Reilly seemed to be in good health. Impatiently, he opened the envelope, dumping X rays onto the desk. He held them up one by one to the light from the office's only window until he found the one he was looking for.

He handed it to the doctor. "This be the neck, right?"

Krause whirled in his chair to place the X ray on a viewer built into the wall. Fluorescent light flickered and came on. "The bottom of the cervical spine, yes. Actually, the picture is a chest X ray."

It was obvious the doctor wanted to ask why Morse wanted to know.

Morse ignored the implicit question. "And there be no foreign objects imbedded in Mr. Reilly's cervical spine, right?"

The doctor's face wrinkled into a puzzled frown. "Foreign object? Like . . . ?"

"Like a bullet."

The doctor paled visibly. "A bullet?"

Morse leaned across the desk. "What I said, a bullet. If one were there, we'd see it, right?"

Krause nodded. "I'd certainly think so. But why . . . ?"

"In your examination of Mr. Reilly, you never saw a scar, anything that would indicate he'd either been shot there or had a bullet removed?"

The doctor shook his head. "No, nothing. But why . . . ?"

Morse stood, hand extended. "You've been very helpful, Doc."

Krause took the extended hand gingerly, as though he thought it might break. "You think Mr. Reilly has been shot in the neck?"

Morse turned to go. "Somebody sure does."

3

Atlanta: Parking deck of Piedmont Medical Center

Morse handed over a wad of bills and the gate out of the parking lot lifted. It was one of the rare times he didn't count his change. He was too preoccupied with a wound shown by records but not by physical exam.

He had no trouble with a man making up a military career. Lots of men did that, pretended they had been in combat when they hadn't gotten any closer to the enemy than the officers' club. Or claimed military service when they hadn't worn a uniform since the Boy Scouts. But he'd never seen the service itself fabricate a Purple Heart.

Why would they do that?

He fiddled with the air-conditioning in the unmarked department-issue Ford, grimacing when warm air came out of the vents. He sighed and rolled down the window.

They would do that because Mr. Reilly had never been a SEAL, probably never been in the navy, because someone preferred Mr. Reilly's past not be subject to scrutiny.

That was the only answer Morse could come up with.

He grimaced again, this time from the thought of the can of worms that thought opened up. If some nameless, faceless bureaucrat had given Reilly a bogus past, his real past would, most likely, come under the huge and ill-defined umbrella known as national security. In a word, Mr. Reilly had been some sort of a spook. Or still was.

And if Mr. Reilly was still in the spook business, he didn't have to have a reason to kill Halvorson. Or throw the other guy from his balcony, either, for that matter. Somebody in Washington could have decided the doorman was actually an agent for some terrorist cell and ordered him terminated. Or that the alleged burglar was bin Laden's brother-in-law, for that matter.

Morse slammed on the brakes, almost running a red light.

National security or not, people didn't get away with murder, not on Morse's watch. He'd report his suspicion to the federal boys to add to their international alert. Maybe they could pry something out of the cloak-and-dagger crowd, find out who Reilly knew in Rome, where he might be hiding.

Part Three

CHAPTER ONE

1

London
The next day

The *ping* of the seat belt and "no smoking" lights woke Lang from a deep sleep. He rubbed stinging eyes and leaned across Gurt to peer out the window. A sea of dirty clouds was rising to meet the MD 880. Across the narrow aisle, a young couple of Eastern European origin were unsuccessful in comforting a howling infant. The British Airways flight attendants were scurrying to collect the last plastic drinking cups before trays were ordered back into their upright positions.

He let the seat up and ran a finger across his upper lip, making sure the moustache was still glued into place. Graying hair and thick glasses aged him a bit, Lang hoped. Bits of foam rubber stuffed into cheeks made his face match the jowly photograph of Heinrich Schneller on the German passport in his pocket.

Gurt and Lang had the picture taken at a photographer's shop a block from the embassy. The glue on it had hardly been dry when she applied a copy of the official stamp to the blank passport.

Facial hair was a new sensation for him. He had always believed it silly to cultivate on an upper lip what grew wild elsewhere.

The ticket clerk at Milan's Malpensa Airport had given their documents a cursory glance before wishing them a cheerful *arrivederci*. The only attention from the gray-uniformed *Policia* with their gloss polished gun belts and boots had been appreciative stares at Gurt.

A blunt-cut dark wig and a slight stoop to minimize her height were the only disguise to which she would agree. There was, after all, no reason to think They had ever seen her face. Still, she was worth the unabashed gaping for which Italian men are notorious.

Herr Schneller and his wife, the much younger-looking Freda, had departed Milan on a flight to the relatively new City Airport in Docklands just outside London. Had any-one checked with the company whose name was on the credit card paying for the tickets, Frau Schneller was ac-companying her husband on a trip to price carpet-grade wool in Milan and then London, from where they would proceed to Manchester.

Lang had no idea if the address for Herr Schneller's em-ployer even existed, but he knew from experience the Hamburg telephone number would be answered by some-one speaking credible *Hochdeutsch* and probably sitting in a room in Virginia. He also knew the passports and drivers' licenses would pass scrutiny. Anyone attempting to verify the Visa or American Express cards would find valid ac-counts, although he had had to promise not to use them for anything other than identification. Gurt had called in a number of favors to get the paperwork and plastic. Making charges to the account would overstep whatever agreements she had made.

It was comforting to have the chicanery of professionals on his side.

As the aircraft trembled, Lang cinched himself tighter into the seat, a Pavlovian response to the airlines' implicit assurances that no problem could not be solved by a fastened seat belt. On a rational level, he knew the plane's bucking and groaning was due to the deployment of flaps and landing gear, and that the aircraft was the consummate product of American engineering. Still, he could take little comfort from the quality of American-made parts that would litter the countryside should something go wrong.

Lang had become no fonder of flying.

The landing and subsequent taxi to the terminal were uneventful and blood began its normal circulation through Lang's hands once he relinquished his death grip on the arm rests.

As anticipated, there were neither customs nor immigration facilities. Within minutes, Lang and Gurt were handing their bags to a smiling cabby for storage in the boot of his shiny black Austin Motors taxi. Lang gave him the destination, thankful London cab drivers were not only required to speak English but also to possess an encyclopedic knowledge of the city.

It might have been April in Italy, but winter was reluctant to release its hold on England. The sky was the color of the bottom of a cookie sheet, with burned spots for clouds. The cab's wiper moaned across wet glass as they headed for the West End.

London had not been a favorite of Dawn's. That had been largely Lang's fault. He had brought her there for Christmas with visions of a Dickensesque holiday, complete with fresh snow, plum pudding and yule logs. Instead they got fog, darkness at three-thirty in the afternoon, and runny noses from a cold induced by their hotel's archaic heating system.

Even the Victorian opulence of one of the Savoy's River Suites, exquisitely furnished and oval shaped, could not compensate for the gloom that met every morning's glance from the window. Lang and his wife spent an afternoon at the Tower, watched the changing of the guard, and endured overcooked beef at Simpson's, all the tourist activities he thought she would enjoy.

The weather was a blanket that smothered any enthusiasm she could muster.

The couple had dinner with Lang's friends from MI6 at their clubs, evenings of drinks and war stories; they spent an afternoon of extravagance at Harrods. Neither lifted Dawn's mood, as dark as the view from the window.

Lang had been frustrated. London had been one of his favorite cities in the world. He and Dawn had their first and only fight. They went home early, on Boxing Day, notwithstanding Ben Jonson's observation that he who tires of London has tired of life. According to Dawn, Dr. Jonson obviously enjoyed beastly weather and worse food.

The day they left, the weather was as bad as the day they arrived.

Lang remembered that trip with particular pain, for it had been only a week later that Dawn experienced menstrual cramps that curled her into a fetal position. Another week and she was under the doctors' death sentence.

Lang had never returned to London until now.

Changes in the city were obvious. Every vista included building cranes. New office space, new dwellings for the City's new e-millionaires. Lang had recently read that London was outstripping the rest of Great Britain combined in construction, prosperity and expansion.

He watched the West End from the moisture-streaked

windows of the cab until Buckingham Palace flashed by. On the other side of the car, the Victoria Monument was alive with rain slickers and umbrellas, tourists seeking a vantage point for the changing of the guard. A quick left onto St. James Street and the area of the same name. They were only blocks from Piccadilly Circus, the entrance to Soho, the shopping, restaurant and theater district. Just past the crenellated twin Tudor towers of St. James's Palace, the cab turned into a small mew, made a right and stopped in front of an unimpressive brick building, identified only by a brass plaque announcing it to be the Stafford Hotel.

Small, cheap accommodations hadn't helped Lang evade Them in Rome. He was certain he had been followed from the *pensione* to Orvieto. This time he was choosing an upbeat hotel, a place Herr Schneller might stay with his wife, what the guidebooks called "moderate to expensive," well located. The deciding factor had been its location in a cul-de-sac, a short street that hosted one private club, two small hotels and a few businesses. No shops, no restaurants. Anyone loitering there would be obvious.

A doorman who could have stolen his uniform from the set of *A Christmas Carol* took their baggage from the cabby. While Gurt dispensed tips and checked in, Lang inspected the lobby. It was as he remembered. Past the reception area, the parlor of a Victorian manor house was set for tea. Behind it was someone's idea of an American sports bar–*cum*–men's club. Helmets from each NFL team were placed around the top of the bar, which faced stuffed chairs far more comfortable than anything to be found in a North American counterpart. Neckties, each displaying school or regimental colors, hung from the ceiling like striped stalactites. Photos of European athletes adorned the walls along with a single print of a B-17 landing on a snow-lined runway, presumably a British aerodrome of

World War II. French doors opened onto a small courtyard. Since Lang's last visit, apartments above a garage had been built on the other side.

He wasn't happy that the only exits from the hotel were through the front door or those units. There's safety in numbers and nowhere is that more true than when it comes to ways to get out.

By the time he had completed his tour, Gurt was waiting at the elevator. Their room was small, neat, clean and well furnished. Once Gurt had hung a couple of dresses in the closet, she lit a Marlboro and headed for the bathroom.

"I'm going to change before I go to Grosvenor Square," she announced over her shoulder.

The U.S. Embassy and, therefore, the Agency Chief of Station were in Grosvenor Square. Even on their own time, Agency employees had to check in upon arrival in a country other than that in which stationed. Conventional wisdom was that the requirement discouraged operatives from launching projects of their own just as Gurt was doing by accompanying Lang.

"Take a cab or you'll get drenched," he advised the closed bathroom door. "The nearest tube station is almost as far away as the embassy."

The door cracked open and Gurt's disembodied head appeared along with a cloud of tobacco smoke. "You know this or are you reading from a guidebook?"

"Where the nearest subway station is? I know. I used to spend a fair amount of time here."

She nodded, seeming to evaluate the information. "Thanks for the point."

"Tip."

"Whatever. It does me happy you care."

The door closed, leaving him to reflect that in English, people were happy. Or were made happy. Only in German were they done happy. The difference said something about the nationality. Someday he might take the time to figure out what.

2

London, St. James

Half an hour later, Lang stepped out of Fortnum and Mason, opened his new umbrella and thanked the top-hatted doorman who was holding the door open for him. His acquisition would not only shelter him from the persistent drizzle but it would also blend into the umbrella-toting crowd lining the curb, waiting for a break in the traffic.

To Lang's right, the neon of Piccadilly Circus bled into the wet pavement, making the black asphalt dance with color. A doubledecker bus blocked then revealed the stature of Eros, the Greek god of love, who had presided over the circle for over a century.

Horns hooted as busses, trucks and cars came to a stop. Not quite used to having to check his right, rather than his left, Lang stepped in front of a bright red Mini Cooper. The driver's hair was cut Beatles fashion, a cigarette bobbing in his mouth as he shouted into a cell phone. Lang picked his way around the rear of a Rover and two Japanese motorcycles before he got to the opposite sidewalk.

Half a block to his left was Old Bond Street. He saw the sign before number 12: Mike Jenson, Dealer in Curios, Antiquities, Etcetera. He pushed open the door and went in.

3

London, the West End

Miles away in the West End, a man scanned black-and-white television screens on which pictures of city streets flickered, stopped and rolled on to various urban scenes. Occasionally a picture was commanded to freeze, a white halo surrounding a face until the controller told the machine to proceed.

Most Londoners did not know that, on average, their likenesses were transmitted forty times a day as they commuted to and from work, ran errands between buildings or simply window-shopped. The cameras were a legacy of IRA terrorism. Thousands had been posted around the city in discreet locations, cameras little different from those used as security devices in department stores. The sheer number of images had been overwhelming, far too many to be scanned by London police.

The age of technology had come to the rescue with face-recognition software. A picture of a face could be programmed into a computer and assigned numerical values: a number for the space between the eyes, another for the length of the nose and so on. Once a face was "recognized" in the cameras' pictures, an alarm went off and the countenance in question was highlighted, its location appearing on the screen.

Since major components of facial construction—occipital arches, mandible, rhinal bones—can be altered only by surgery or trauma, the computer could, in most instances, see through changes such as hair loss, weight loss or gain, or the most relentless force of all, age.

With the reluctance of governments everywhere to relinquish power once acquired, the London police had elected to let those few who knew of the devices forget them once the Irish Question had been temporarily resolved by tenuous agreement. On the few occasions when the subject arose, officials quickly pointed out that cameras in less-than-prosperous neighborhoods were responsible for an impressive number of arrests. Removal of surveillance equipment from "safe" areas but not from oth-

ers was likely to offend the historic British sense of fair
play, and, more likely, cause a political firestorm in the city
council. The occasional citizen who publicly bemoaned
the loss of privacy was condemned by authorities as an an-
archist opposed to municipal security.

Identical technology was used by the Tampa, Florida,
police as an "experiment" to identify no less than nineteen
Super Bowl fans with criminal records at the 2001 game.

The London police would have been the last to admit
that anything transmitted was subject to interception or, in
this case, hacking.

It was just such an interception that the man in front of
the screens was watching.

Lang Reilly turned just as he entered the shop, present-
ing both full-face and profile shots to a lens mounted un-
obtrusively on a rooftop. The man monitoring the screens
stopped the motion in the picture and squinted at the
highlighted or "haloed" area before punching numbers
into a cell phone.

"You were right," he said. "He's tracked it back to Jenson.
What do you want done?"

He listened for a moment and disconnected without another word. He hurriedly entered another number.

"Jenson's," he said without identifying himself. "Make
sure everything is sanitized, Jenson included. No, we've
changed that. We want Reilly alive, see what else he
knows."

4

London, Old Bond Street

A bell tinkled as Lang entered the shop, a room about
twenty feet by twenty. Oils and watercolors shouldered
each other for space on the simple plaster walls. Regi-

ments of dark-wooded furniture paraded in orderly ranks and files, dividing the room into squares as neat as any formed by the British infantry. There was a smell of lemon oil.

He heard footsteps on the wooden plank floor and a curtain at the back was brushed aside. A short man in a dark suit came out, his hands clasping each other as though he were washing them. A long, pale face was topped by lifeless dark hair shot with silver. His smile revealed teeth crooked enough to make an orthodontist salivate.

"Mornin', sir," he said in an accent Lang would have attributed to Jeeves the butler. "I help you or you jus' browsin'?"

"Mr. Jenson?" Lang asked.

There was a furtive flicker of the eyes, the look of someone in need of an escape route. Lang would have bet Mr. Jenson had unhappy creditors.

"An' who might you be?" he wanted to know, his tone more defensive than curious.

Lang smiled, trying to seem as nonthreatening as possible. "A man looking for information."

The caution in Jensen's voice was not dispelled. "An' what sort of information would that be?"

Lang admired a highboy, running a hand across mahogany drawers inlaid with satinwood. He pulled out the Polaroid, using the marble top of a commode to smooth out the creases. "I was wondering if you could tell me where you got this?"

Jenson made no effort to conceal his relief Lang wasn't there as a bill collector. "Some bloody estate or winding-up sale, I'd imagine. Not some place where you can't likely get another if it's genre religious work you fancy."

"I'm a lawyer," Lang explained, his hand still on the cool marble on which the small photo lay. "I have a client to whom the origins of the painting shown there could be very important."

As Jenson inspected the snapshot, his eyes narrowed, giving his long face the appearance of a fox scenting a hen house. "Don't usually keep records of art sold lyin' about. Space considerations, and all that, y'know. Have to look it up, check my books. That'll take a spot of time, if you take my meaning."

Lang did. "I, my client, that is, would expect to pay you for your time, of course."

Jenson treated Lang to that picket-fence-in-bad-repair grin again. "I'll have it for you"—he produced a pocket watch—"after lunch. You come 'round a coupla hours from now."

5

London, St. James
An hour and a half later

Lang had lunch wrapped in newspaper at a fish and chips take-away. It wasn't the best meal available, but it was the quickest. Which meant he had time to kill. Wiping the grease from his chin with a thin paper napkin, he entered the nearby Burlington House, home of the Royal Academy of Arts, where he spent half an hour staring with total lack of comprehension at the current visiting exhibition of abstract art.

Best Lang could tell, there were two schools displayed here. First were the splattists, distinguishable by paint applied by flinging it in the general direction of the canvas or whatever surface was involved. The paint splattered as it hit, forming shapes and patterns dictated by centrifugal force and gravity rather than design. The other was the smearists, artists who preferred to glob paint at random and then smear it into whorls, lines or anything else as long as it was not in a recognizable form. Then there were the truly avant-garde, who defied definition by simply coloring the canvas a single, uniform color.

All works that very much resembled the result of Jeff's efforts with finger paints at age three.

Jeff and Janet. For the last few days, Lang had concentrated on finding their killer rather than dwelling on the emptiness their deaths had left in his life. His fists clenched. By God, he would find the unknown They. He would have vengeance.

A schoolmarmish woman, her white hair gathered in a bun, gave him a frightened look and scurried away, turning her head to make sure he wasn't following. Lang realized he had spoken out loud.

Conceding he was no culture vulture and that contemporary art was beyond his ken, Lang retreated to the sculpture promenade to admire a Michelangelo relief.

After the abstractionists, it was just that: a relief.

As he started back towards Old Bond Street, it stopped misting. The sky was a little lighter with a hint if not a promise of sunshine to come. Umbrellas were now furled, used as walking sticks or carried underarm.

Once again, the bell tinkled his entrance. Lang busied himself inspecting the furniture as he waited for Jenson to come out from behind his curtain. Machined rather than planed surfaces and cast rather than forged nails betrayed most pieces as reproductions, reflections of revivals of the past century: a Savonarola chair, its fish-rib back more likely made for the fashions of the 1920s rather than fifteenth-century Florence; an Irish Chippendale table from the craze of the fifties, its claw feet matching more perfectly than could have been done by any eighteenth-century craftsman.

Lang soon grew tired of the game and checked his

watch. He had been waiting ten minutes. Jenson had to have heard the bell. Perhaps he was in the midst of a lengthy phone conversation.

"Mr. Jenson?" Lang called.

No response.

The man had to be there. He wouldn't have left his shop unlocked.

Lang called again with the same result. He was getting a little angry at the man's rudeness.

Lang crossed the room and pulled back the curtain.

Two naked bulbs, the low-wattage sort the English prefer, hung from the ceiling. Dust-speckled light created an archipelago of shadows around tables, chairs and chests, all in various states of repair. Ornate but empty picture frames, some large enough for life-size portraits, leaned against furniture with a haphazardness at odds with the order of the showroom. The dimness and the dark spots gave Lang the creeps.

To his right, light seeped around a door. An office, no doubt. No wonder Jenson hadn't heard him enter with the door shut. Lang made his way over, using touch as much as sight to avoid his shins colliding with some very unforgiving wood.

Lang reached the door and knocked. "Mr. Jenson?"

Receiving no response, he knocked again, this time harder. The door swung open.

Lang had often heard the smell of blood described as coppery. To him it was reminiscent of the taste of steel, a smell like the taste of your tongue running across the blade of a knife. However it smelled, there was blood everywhere.

Jenson sat at an old rolltop desk that was swamped in papers. Were it not for the blood, he could have been napping, head tipped against the back of a chair. Blood covered his shirt, his jacket and his trousers. Blood formed puddles on the desk and covered the bare planks of the floor. Blood was splattered across the wall in a display not unlike the art exhibition. An oozing gash separated Jenson's chin from his throat. Eyes not yet dull gazed in surprise into the darkness of the ceiling.

Next to the desk, a safe yawned open, a trickle of papers spilling onto the floor. More papers were scattered across the desk and floor, some already reddish as the fibers sponged up the fluid of Jenson's life. It looked as if, in a final fit, Jenson had taken every scrap of paper he could find and tossed them into the air.

Lang leaned the umbrella against a wall and touched the back of his hand to Jenson's slack jaw. The skin was still warm. Jenson hadn't been dead very long. Lang glanced nervously around the room. The killer could well have been hiding in those shadows on the other side of the door. Moving to face that way, he hurriedly sifted through the papers on the desk.

A quick peek showed mostly bills. Lang almost gagged from the overpowering stench of blood and tried to breathe through his mouth. He was probably wasting his time. Why would They kill Jenson and leave the very information they were trying to cover up?

Answer: They wouldn't, and Lang sure didn't want to be here when the next customer walked in.

He took a last sweeping look and noticed something on the floor under Jenson's chair, a sheet of paper soggy and red. It would not have been visible to someone standing over the unfortunate antique dealer. Lang picked it up gingerly, trying to get as little of Mr. Jenson's blood on his fingers as possible. These days, blood can kill, depending on what unpleasant virus it might be carrying. The paper was soaked, virtually unreadable. A DHL shipping bill. Lang was about to drop it and wipe off his fingers when the word "Poussin" made him forget his squeamishness. There

were a list of items, some too blurred to read, but Lang
guessed the painting had been one of a number of items
of furniture and furnishings sold in bulk. The only other
words were "Pegasus, Ltd"—the shipper—and an illegible
address.

Either Lang was looking at a list totally unrelated to the
people he was searching for—or he had gotten lucky.
Which was the more likely, that Jenson had handled more
than one Poussin or that his killer hadn't seen the paper
Lang was now holding? Although hardly active in the art
world, Lang had never heard of Poussin a month before
and the shipping bill had been where someone standing
over Jensen might not have seen it, particularly if Jenson
had put it on the desk and pushed it over the edge onto
the floor when his muscles gave their final spasms.

Lang didn't have a lot of time to decide. The bell over
the door announced another arrival. Or departure. The
killer could be escaping and there wasn't a lot Lang could
do about it.

Or maybe there was. Stuffing the bloody paper into a
pocket, he cautiously went back into the storage and repair room. Whoever had sliced Jenson's throat would be
covered in blood, judging by how much had splattered the
office.

Unless he had managed to steal a car, or have one waiting at the curb, Jenson's killer was going to be easy to identify if Lang could catch up to him before he could change
clothes.

Of course, he could have still been in Jenson's shop, too.
The possibility slowed Lang as he edged towards the showroom, his back to the wall in case the bell had meant an
entry rather than the killer's departure.

As he reached the curtains separating the show area,
Lang saw something on the floor. For an instant, the dim
light gave the illusion of another body. He felt himself

tense until he realized he was looking at nothing more than a bundle of clothes, coveralls stained red with blood.

Lang was certain he would have seen them had they been there when he came in. He picked them up, quickly searching. He would have been surprised to find anything useful, but he had to look. The idea the murderer had been there when he arrived, watched him go into the office, was enough to make the fish and chips lurch in his stomach.

Why not try to finish what They had failed to do in Atlanta?

Lang's question was answered soon enough. A police constable in the traditional four-button jacket and high, rounded hat was looking around the showroom. He held an automatic pistol pointed in Lang's direction.

Lang's first thought on seeing the weapon was that the killer had remained, disguised as a police officer. Then he remembered that the London police had abandoned tradition and begun to carry arms a few years ago.

"Someone called, said there'd been . . ." The cop's eyes widened and Lang realized he was still holding the bloody clothes.

"Look, I didn't . . ." Lang began, all too aware of how lame he sounded.

Judging by the tremor in his voice as he spoke into the radio transmitter fixed to the lapel of his jacket, the constable was more frightened than Lang was.

"Backup, more chaps 'ere in a 'urry," he shouted in an East End accent that would have done Eliza Doolittle credit. "'Urry th' bleedin' backup! I got the bugger whot done it right 'ere. Number Twelve Auld Bond Street."

Lang dropped the incriminating coveralls and backed through the curtains into the storage area, his hands extended so the policeman could see he was no threat. "I just walked in here, found him."

The officer was young and clearly nervous. The muzzle of his weapon—a Glock nine-millimeter, Lang guessed—wavered. "An' I'm th' bleedin' Queen's Consort. Right where you are, Yank, 'old it right where you are."

Lang took another step backwards and came up against a large piece of furniture. The cop followed slowly. Maybe he was afraid if he let Lang get too many steps away he would miss if he had to shoot. Lang put a hand behind his back to feel his way around the obstacle. His fingers touched one of the picture frames he had seen earlier.

"'Ands up where I can see 'em," the constable demanded.

Lang was betting the cop wouldn't pull the trigger unless forced to, a risk Lang wouldn't have taken in Atlanta. Lang wasn't going to submit to arrest if he could avoid it without doing the young policeman any great harm. When and if Lang could be proved innocent, the tracks he was following would be cold. Besides, he had had more than enough experience with the criminal justice system to know it for the crapshoot it was. Lang's fingers ran along the ornately carved frame as the officer came closer. The hand that wasn't holding the gun was fumbling behind him—for handcuffs, Lang guessed.

"Both 'ands, I said. . . ."

Lang took a deep breath and shifted his weight to his front foot. He gave a high kick that the Rockettes would have envied and the Glock spun from the officer's hand and clattered to the floor. As the officer spun to retrieve it, Lang swung the picture frame over his own head and the policeman's. It could not have fit better. The officer's arms were pinned to his sides by the gilded wood. The constable could do little more than glare.

"Trust me," Lang said, headed for the door, "I had nothing to do with this and I'd like nothing better than being able to stick around and prove it."

The constable didn't look much like he believed him.

Lang could already hear the pulsing sirens used by police all over Europe, the ones that reminded him of the movie *The Diary of Anne Frank*. It might as well have been the Gestapo coming for him: if he was caught, he wouldn't be sent to Auschwitz but he sure as hell would be going somewhere behind barbed wire where They could reach him at their leisure.

Lang stepped outside and walked away, resisting the impulse to run like hell. He was two blocks down the street before he realized he had left his umbrella.

6

London, St. James
Ten minutes later

There was a note waiting at the Stafford:

> Gone shopping. Dinner at Pointe de Tour. Tea here at 1600 hrs.
> Gurt

Attached was part of an article clipped from a magazine, informing Lang that the Pointe de Tour was one of the new London restaurants, located on the south side of Tower Bridge. French cuisine, multiple stars. Expensive.

Waiting around for Gurt didn't seem wise. He went to the room and packed his bag. He felt guilty as hell but she had no place in his plans. They had set him up, killing Jenson and calling the police to nab him virtually in flagrante delicto, as lawyers say.

Well, as some lawyers say, those who remember the phrase from law school.

Every law enforcement agency in Europe as well as the

United States would have a reason to be looking for Lang once the fingerprints were lifted from the umbrella and it was traced back to Fortnum and Mason. Being part of a couple wasn't going to be sufficient cover, anyway, once the constable got to a police artist who could draw Heinrich Schneller's face.

Once run through Interpol, the fingerprints would put the Herr Schneller persona to rest for good.

Lang pocketed the cash Gurt had left in the room's safe, wrote her a note he knew was inadequate, and left.

Crossing the Mall to St. James's Park, he spent a few minutes pretending to watch the birds on Duck Island. No one else showed an interest in him or the waterfowl. He walked along Whitehall and the edge of the brown pea gravel of the Horse Guards' parade ground and the Paladin facade of Banqueting House, the site of royal revels. That princely party boy, that swinging sovereign, Charles I, had been beheaded there. Today, Lang wasn't nearly as interested in history as he was in anyone who might be following.

Of course, the fact he couldn't see Them didn't mean They weren't there. Lang appreciated Their cleverness. Jenson's killer could have killed Lang in the shadows of the shop. In a country with fewer annual homicides than, say, Montgomery, Alabama, such a murder would have raised more questions than merely the death of the antique dealer would have. They had arranged to have Lang sought as the culprit.

Once Lang was in custody, he suspected They would know where to find him. A criminal organization with members in America and Europe would have access to police records and, quite likely, any jail in which he might be incarcerated. And what could he do? Who was going to believe a suspect in two murders who raved about international conspiracies and secrets hidden in pictures?

Clever.

Lang used a doorstep to pretend to tie his shoe, taking the opportunity to look behind without being obvious about it. A group of Japanese, cameras clicking amid bird-chirp voices, stopped to photograph everything in sight. Lang left them behind as he turned right, hoping to disappear among the traffic, pigeons and milling crowd that was Trafalgar Square.

Lang had at least one advantage, small though it might have been. They didn't know about the bloody paper with the company name on it, presumably the source of the painting. They had killed Jenson to stifle the vary information They had overlooked.

At Charing Cross, a huge shopping plaza and office building rose over the Underground station. Lang stopped at a public phone, an uninteresting steel box similar to the ones in the States. Most of the old red phone boxes had long since become decorations in bars in the U.S., he supposed. At least that was the only place he still saw them. Unlike American phones, the directory was still attached. Lang found the number and dialed, keeping an eye on the small bag of possessions he had brought from the hotel.

By the time the brief conversation was complete, an anemic sun had broken through the clouds, its appearance more aesthetic than warming.

Once he hung up, he continued down The Strand until he reached the Temple Bar Memorial, an iron griffin that marked the place the actual City of London met Westminster, two of the municipalities generally lumped together as "London." Here The Strand became Fleet Street, the former center of London's newspaper publishers.

Lang wasn't here for newspapers. For that matter, the press had long since departed for the suburbs: shorter commutes, lower rents and more modest salary demands from unions.

One last check behind him and he turned into a narrow street, more of an alley, Middle Temple Lane. From here an even more confined byway led to a small park surrounded by the buildings of the Temple Bar, the site of the offices of almost every barrister in London.

Lang let his memory lead him up a marble staircase worn uneven by centuries of clients seeking potential rectification of injustice and certain diminution of their money. At the top, a half-glass door bore flaking gilt letters, "Jacob Annulewicz, Barrister."

Barrister Annulewicz's business spilled into the shabby waiting area. Two chairs covered in a chintz popular in the 1940s, worn almost beyond recognition, overflowed with stacks of paper. Files were piled on a much-abused table. The secretary's desk was surprisingly neat, its peeling veneer visible under an over-sized computer monitor, the only indication Lang was still in the twenty-first century.

If there was one, the secretary was gone, dismissed for the duration of Lang's visit.

"Reilly!"

An older man stood in the doorway to the inner office, dressed in a black gown, a starched white split dickey at his throat and a short white periwig perched on an otherwise bald scalp like a bird's nest on a rock.

"Jacob!" Lang set his bag down to return a bear hug. "When did you join a Gilbert and Sullivan revival?"

Jacob stepped back, releasing enough pressure to allow at least shallow breathing. "Still the smartass, I see."

"And you're still defending the indefensible," Lang said, indicating the robe. "What's with the costume? I thought you only wore it to court or with a mask on Guy Fawkes's Day."

"And where do you think I was just before you called, the Mayfair Club?"

"Not unless they've substantially relaxed their membership requirements."

Jacob beckoned Lang into his office, a small room that reeked from the briar pipes dead in an ashtray. "Not likely," he said without rancor. "Still no women, Jews or Labour MPs. And you have to have a letter from at least five members, two of whom must be deceased."

Jacob's office was as cluttered as the outer room. He moved a stack of files to look under it, set it down and lifted another. This time he uncovered a small wooden box into which he put the wig.

"Clubs. It is still difficult, being one of Jehovah's chosen among the Gentiles."

Lang moved papers from a chair and sat on genuine Naugahyde. "From the looks of your waistline, you haven't encountered any good pogroms lately. I take it you're still away from the Promised Land by choice."

The son of Polish Holocaust survivors, Jacob had been taken to Israel as a child. He subsequently immigrated to England, becoming a British citizen, an act that did not deprive him of his Israeli citizenship but made him a prime candidate to become one of the Mossad's undercover agents stationed in friendly and unfriendly countries alike. If history had taught the Jews anything, it was the uncertainty of alliances with goyim. Consequently, they spied on friend and foe alike with admirable evenhandedness.

Jacob's brief had been to keep an eye on Arab diplomats in London, to pass along to his handlers the snippets of information from which the tapestries of international affairs are woven. The information might or might not be passed along to the intelligence community of the United States, which hosted no Iraqi, Iranian or Liberian embassy of its own upon which to spy.

Somewhat less well known was Jacob's ability with explosives, learned during his time in the Israeli Army before his migration to England. Unconfirmed rumor had it that he was the one who had gotten into the hiding place of one of Hamas's more notorious terrorists and wired T4 to the telephone's dial. The next call blew the man's head off without so much as cracking the mirror on the wall. True or not, Jacob had the reputation of being the duke of detonation, a prestidigitator of plastique.

The Americans as well as the British had suspected his duties included spying on them as well. All potentially aggrieved parties—CIA, FBI, MI5, MI6—agreed he was now retired, no matter how odd his choice to spend his final years in the practice of law that had been his first love, or, odder still, his preference for London drizzle over Mediterranean sun.

Jacob opened doors behind his desk, revealing a small cupboard, counter and gas ring upon which sat a teapot. "Still lemon, no sugar?"

Lang had to smile. "Age hasn't taken your memory."

Jacob poured into porcelain mugs. "Not entirely a blessing. I can still remember whom I dislike but my eyesight's gotten so bloody bad, I can't see the blokes coming." He opened a tin and shook his head sorrowfully. "Out of biscuits, I'm afraid." He extended a steaming mug and lit one of the malodorous pipes. "So brief me on the last ten years, Langford. You might include the reasons for that ridiculous moustache, what I hope are false jowls and that dreadful German-made suit."

Lang glanced around the room and touched his ear.

Jacob nodded. "Ah, yes, 'tis a lovely spring day outside. Why don't we take our tea out to the courtyard. Who knows, we might even hear a lark sing, although the last of the poor creatures I saw in London was years ago, dying of the smog, he was."

The sun had grown no warmer and Lang shivered as they entered the courtyard. "If you think your office is bugged . . . ?"

Jacob's head bobbed solemnly. "Was it not your poet

Robert Frost who observed some people believe good fences make good neighbors? In our business . . . our *former* business, good listening devices make good neighbors. Your Agency, MI5, the others, do not fear what they think they know. So I let them listen in to what happens in my office. It must put them to sleep. I have nothing to hide anymore. Besides, had it not been for your countrymen . . ."

"You'd be dead," Lang finished.

Years ago, Lang's employers had known from bugging Jacob's phone that he was going to be nearby at the same time a Hamas group planned to explode a car bomb at the Israeli Embassy. Unknown to the would-be terrorists, the building had long previously been rendered impervious to anything smaller than a nuclear blast and the most serious damage would be to the surrounding neighborhood. Arresting those planning to join Allah in paradise would have tipped the fact the Arab group was seriously infiltrated. Lang had insisted no point was to be served by letting Jacob be reduced to his composite atoms and had warned him clear.

"I would indeed be dead," Jacob agreed, "a fate only marginally worse than old age. Now, the last ten years, what have you been doing that you worry about being overheard?"

Lang told him.

Jacob shook his head. "My sorrow for the loss of your family. Your sister, nephew, I didn't know. But Dawn . . . A name from the poetry books. You will remember I had the wisdom to ask her what she saw in you when you two visited London some years ago. Lovely person.

"Now you are a lawyer in America, wanted for murders you did not commit both here and there. How may I be of help?"

They had walked the short distance between the law offices and an old round structure, the Temple. Lang pulled open the heavy door and motioned Jacob inside.

"I'm cold," Lang said. "There's no one here and I doubt anyone has bugged this place."

The Temple was just that. Built in the twelfth century by the Order of Knights Templar, it was round with an inner circle supported by columns. In the middle of the circle, several stone effigies reposed on the worn limestone floor, swords clasped to their armored chests. No inscription gave a clue as to their identity. Lang had always assumed they were Templars.

Jacob and Lang circled the room as Lang finished his story.

"Pegasus, Limited," Lang finally said. "The only clue I have, or at least the only one I understand. If it does business in Europe, Echelon would know."

Jacob stopped. "Echelon? Your National Security Agency doesn't share that information with any agency where I might find out."

The National Security Agency was the most secretive of the secretive. Its operatives were computer jocks, its weapons high technology. It participated in no active espionage in the conventional sense but maintained a heavily guarded satellite monitoring station just outside London which had the capability to intercept every fax, e-mail and phone call made in Europe. The information was shared only among England, Canada, Australia and New Zealand.

Lang smiled. "Of course, your retirement. Plus Mossad naturally has no means of intercepting Echelon and would be reluctant to do so if it could. I wouldn't want to impose on our friendship by asking . . ."

"You cannot get this information from your former employers or their friends at MI6?"

Lang shook his head. "My former employers don't owe me a favor, particularly not the London Station. It's the plumb of the service, draws all the Harvard-Yale types, guys that wouldn't dream of being seen with someone who graduated from a state college." He wrinkled his nose, giving his very best imitation of an upper-class British accent. "As for MI6, old thing, why they're just too, too. Hardly can understand the blighters, talking through their Cambridge-Oxford noses, y'know. Just too tiresome, dealing with a bloody Yank. No sense of . . . Well, old stick, you know what I mean."

Jacob chuckled as he held up a hand in surrender. "Okay, enough. What makes you think this Pegasus can be found by Echelon?"

"Because there are no electronic transmissions it doesn't pick up. That's how Boeing beat Airbus in the bidding for new aircraft for several Mideast countries."

"You know American intelligence agencies are forbidden to do such things, Langford. They assure us all they only use such technology to keep track of terrorists, bin Laden, North Korea, sale of missiles to certain Arab nations."

Lang rolled his eyes. "And of course diverting billions of dollars to U.S. companies would not be sufficient incentive to deviate from that policy."

Jacob glanced around, making sure no one had entered the building since the conversation began. "Even if what you say is correct, how could a single name be sorted out? There must be millions of transmissions daily."

"Done easily enough by programming keywords into the computer."

"Like 'bomb'?"

"Like. Story a few years ago was that an Irish comedian was playing on stage in Soho. Opening night, called his girlfriend in Belfast, was nervous about his act. Said he was afraid he was going to bomb out. Two blocks were cordoned off before he even got to the theater. Bomb squad, dogs, the works. MI5 blamed it on that all-time favorite, the anonymous tip."

Lang could hear fingernails rasping against a heavy five-o'clock shadow as Jacob scratched his chin. "So, if some-one were to have the ability to intercept Echelon's product, 'Pegasus' could be a keyword, any communica-tions concerning it gathered in. A tall order, as you say, for a small, poor operation like Mossad."

Lang chuckled. "Small, yes. Poor, perhaps. Most efficient in the world, undoubtedly."

Jacob was staring somewhere past Lang. "This is all you know about these people who have killed so many, that they are somehow connected to this Pegasus?"

"And that's only a hunch." Lang reached into a pocket and showed Jacob the medallion from the truck driver. "This is the only thing I'm certain of, that the two men who tried to kill me were wearing one of these, four triangles meeting at the center of a circle. Hardly a coincidence."

Jacob squinted at the medallion. "No, no coincidence. Not four triangles, either."

He had Lang's undivided attention. "Oh?"

"Try a Maltese cross in a circle."

"How d'you get that?"

He pointed. "There, all around you."

Lang turned, half expecting another assassin. Behind him, carved into the walls, the device was evenly spaced. The centuries had almost obliterated them and he hadn't noticed until now.

Lang felt as though his jaw was hanging open. "I don't get it."

Jacob stepped over to the wall and rubbed his fingers across one of the circled crosses. "This was a Templar church, one of only two or three in the world that haven't been destroyed, let fall into ruin or radically altered. It would seem reasonable that the design has something to do with them."

"Impossible!" Lang blurted. "The Templars were fighting monks sworn to protect pilgrims in the Holy Land from Moslems. The order was disbanded by papal decree in the fourteenth century."

Jacob pursed his lips. "Impossible or not, you see the symbol, same as you have in your hand."

This was beginning to sound like time travel out of bad sci-fi. Next, Lang would discover Richard the Lion-Hearted was the one who wanted him dead. "Why would a monastic order from seven, eight hundred years ago be interested in a painting? And if they exist, they're a holy order, not murderers. How does any of that make sense?"

Jacob shook his head. "My friend, as a Jew, I have little interest in Christian holy orders. Too many of them served their religion by killing practitioners of mine. But I do have a friend who might have an answer, a fellow at Oxford, Christ Church. He teaches medieval history. Oxford is, what, an hour's train ride?"

"Great. Except I'd just as soon stay away from train stations. I'm sure the police are watching them."

Jacob scratched his chin again. "I'll call him tonight, tell him you're coming. Stay with me and tomorrow you can have my Morris. Hopefully there won't be another truck trying to run over you. Maybe I'll have some information from Echelon by the time you return."

As they walked back to Jacob's office, Lang noticed a man on a bench reading one of London's tabloids. "Murder in the West End," the headline screamed. He couldn't be sure at that distance, but Lang thought he recognized his own picture, the one from his Agency service file.

7

Westminster
1650 hours

The afternoon sun was streaking the pewter gray of the Thames with orange, or at least that part of the Thames Inspector Dylan Fitzwilliam could see from his office at Scotland Yard six floors above Broadway. He stood at the window a moment longer before returning to the papers on his desk.

After four years with the fugitive squad of the Metropolitan Police, he was fully aware how unlikely it had been that he would be able to accommodate that American chap. What was his name? Morse, yes that was it, Morse with the Atlanta police. The Met had more than enough criminals to keep it busy without larking about looking for those the Yanks had let slip through what he perceived to be rather loose fingers.

That dreadful murder of the antique dealer in the West End, Jenson. Constable had just about caught the killer in the act, red-handed, one might say if one found puns amusing. Wonder the lad hadn't slit the constable's throat as well. The description the frightened young policeman had given the artist had fit rather well with a picture in the international fugitive file in the computer if one ignored the moustache and chubby cheeks.

Overrated things, computers. Admittedly, Fitzwilliam would never have recognized the chap, not with what was a disguise making him look older, heavier. Professional job, that disguise. As it should be, turned out. The information that came from the States said that the bloke was former CIA, Yank equivalent of MI6. Didn't know what was the most surprising, that the fugitive was one of that cloak-and-dagger lot or that the CIA had admitted it. Dreadfully embarrassing that, to have one of your old mates go 'round the bend, kill two people for no apparent reason. No reason if, in fact, this Reilly chap really was no longer one of them.

Computers. Fact was, Reilly would have eventually been identified by old-fashioned, thorough police work. Even without all the modern glitz, the fingerprints on that umbrella had been confirmed by Washington. They were Reilly's. And the brelly, well, now, that had been lucky. Just bought that day, it turned out, at Fortnum and Mason, paid for with a credit card belonging to a Heinrich Schneller, nobody the chappies at Visa had ever heard of. That was a bit of information Fitzwilliam was going to keep close to his chest, as the Yanks said, quietly put out a trace to be notified if that card were used again. And make sure every copper at every major international airport had a picture of Herr Schneller, with and without his bloody moustache.

Fitzwilliam sat down with a sigh, his eyes on the face staring up at him from his desk. Amazing resolution these days—photo could have been a shot from someone's holiday last week. Pushing the picture aside, the inspector reread the material that had accompanied it.

This Reilly chap had spent some time in London before, had a list of acquaintances. And an odd lot they were. A Mossad operative, probably retired by now; a German national he had been boffing, a rather striking woman from the picture he guessed came from her service jacket; and any number of publicans where he had his pint as regular as any working-class sod. Fitzwilliam's forehead creased in a frown. It was going to be a spot of bother, pulling men off investigations to go 'round and chat up all these people.

He reached for the phone. Best get to it. The cousins were waiting and they were an impatient lot. Worse, they believed their own cinema, that Scotland Yard had the ability to do anything asked of it. He snorted as he punched in numbers. The Yard should have the resources of the sodding Yank FBI.

THE TEMPLARS:
THE END OF AN ORDER

An Account by Pietro of Sicily

Translation from the medieval Latin by Nigel Wolffe, Ph.D.

3

Nothing I learned from the cellarer had prepared me for the manner of provisioning a ship. Each vessel was but ten rod[1] in length and half that high at bow and stern. A single mast carried a single sail,[2] all other space being crowded with as many as one hundred people. Each person required two barrels of water as well as a mat of straw, a quilt, meat, cooking utensils, and spices as would make the meat fresh to the taste such as ginger, cloves and mace. The cost of this provisioning paid to the merchants of Trapani was, according to Guillaume de Poitiers, forty ducats for a knight.

He also said the unwary paid as much for the worst as for the best, this in reference to the mat and quilt. A man paid five ducats for those items but they were sold back to the merchants by arrivals for half that, so that many were worn and rife with vermin.

The upper stage of the vessel was desirable over the lower, the latter being smoldering hot and sultry. But it was in these lower quarters the low-born such as Phillipe and I were quartered. I was to suffer greatly, for this lower deck was also the repository for horses, oxen, swine[3] and other animals, the stench of whose excrement never left this area.

The days at sea were such as to try my faith. The ship rolled and pitched in such a devilish manner as to nearly toss me into the waters when I ventured from my pallet beneath the deck. Most of my time I spent suffering from a malaise I learned to be common to many who venture upon the waters for the first time. The vapors of the sea cause the stomach to tighten, refusing to retain whatever victuals are put in it while trying to reject that it has already sent forth.

Such was my misery that the captain of our vessel, a heartless, vile man who delighted in the misery of others, took great glee in calling down to those of us ill in the lower deck, "Shall I make you meat anon?"

Then he would laugh as he told all that would hear, "They have no use for the meat they have purchased. Better we should consume it than it go bad."

It is God's mercy that after some period of time, the body develops an imperviousness to these atmospheres of the sea that cause such illness. Thanks be to heaven and its merciful Lord, such proved to be the case and I was delivered from such suffering as I had never before experienced and know now that I never shall again. The agony that I face is of a different sort.

By God's will we reached Genoa where we replenished our supplies and set out for France.

With God's kindness in abating my illness, I took note of my surroundings. I had never had the opportunity to observe the workings of a ship. Most interesting were the maps used by the navigator on which lines were drawn, dividing the portions of the earth into squares,[4] in which the ship was placed by careful nocturnal observation, thereby demonstrating our position on the sea in relation to points of land. These charts gave me pause as being not those sanctioned by God.[5]

I was to learn this was not the only rule of God that found its exception among these Knights of the Temple.

We disembarked at Narbonne in that region of Burgundy known as the Languedoc. As we journeyed away from the sea, we traveled along a valley where the soil was as white as the Knights' surcoats. To our left the River Sals ran south to the ocean we had left.

As we progressed, I became increasingly aware of a huge castle[6] crouched atop a mountain on the far side of the river. I was told this was Blanchefort, an edifice that had been in the hands of the Knights since it was given by a family of that name to Hughes de Payens, Grand Master of the Poor Knights of the Temple of Solomon in the year of his return from The Holy Land.[7]

"The Blancheforts were truly devout servants of God," I remarked to Guillaume de Poitiers when he trotted his charger to the rear of the train to verify that Philippe and I were keeping up. "The gift of such an estate to the Order would surely find favor in heaven."

He leaned from his saddle to check the bindings of the load carried by one of the horses. "The abbey at Alet as well as barracks at Peyrolles. Master de Payens was a rich man indeed."

"You mean the Order was enriched," I said.

He looked at me in silence before he replied, "No, little brother, those are not the words I spoke. Master de Payens was given those lands himself so that the Order might profit as he saw fit."

"But the vow of poverty . . . ?"

He shook his head. "Think you instead of the vow of obedience which forbids asking your betters impertinent questions."

He left me to ponder how a member of a holy order could own such riches as the properties as the aforementioned. Once again, the monastic vows I understood did not seem paramount to this Order.

We rested and encamped for the night outside the village of Serres. At daylight, we forded the river and made a rearwards turn. I could not help but note that the morning sun was on my left just as it had been on my right the day before.

"Are we not but returning from whence we came by another path?" I asked one of the older esquires.

"Indeed we are progressing to the south," he said, "just as we marched to the north yesterday. Serres was the nearest place to cross the water and now we are proceeding to the castle at Blanchefort."

Shortly thereafter, we began an ascent up a mountain. Where vegetation failed to cover it, the soil was as chalky in colour as it had been in this region since we left sight of the sea. It was claylike to the touch and I pondered what victuals might grow in dirt so different from the loamy black humus of Sicily.

At the top, we halted in front of towering walls of white stone while the knights with us exchanged words I did not understand with those on the ramparts. During this conversation I noticed the walls were not stones crudely piled like the boundary of the abbey I had departed but carefully fitted so that each rested upon the other. I was later given to understand that the knowledge of how to make this so came from the Saracens.[8]

Above the grand entrance was a portal of pure travertine of almost a rod[9] square upon which was graven the likeness of a winged horse rampant, so cunningly done in detail that I would have not been astonished to see it leap from the stone in which it was encased. I had seen graven images occasionally on buildings of antiquity, those edifices erected in pagan times, which Christ's Church had not yet replaced with Christian monuments, but I would have never expected such a likeness to dominate the entry to a place consecrated to a holy order.

"It is Pegasus, the mythical horse of the Greek," Guillaume de Poitiers explained. "It is the symbol of our order."

Once again, my surprise overcame my humility. "Is it not blasphemous to have a pagan symbol in such a place?"

Rather than taking offense at my boldness, he smiled. "It is the worshipping of such images our Maker proscribes, not the observation. Besides, Pegasus reminds us of our humble origins."

It was difficult for me to comprehend how an order which owned castles such as this could possess any origin not majestic. "How so, m'lord?"

He sat back in his saddle, his eyes not leaving the fixture of the horse. "When our order was young, we could afford but few horses. When two brothers traveled the same way, they shared a single animal. At a distance across the sands of the Holy Land, the two white surcoats flowing in the breeze resembled nothing so much as a winged horse. The emblem so reminds us of that humility and poverty which our order embraces as virtues."

I had observed neither among the order but for once held my tongue.

Just then the portcullis rattled open and we entered an area reminiscent less of a humble cloister such that I had departed than of the inner baileys of the few nobles I had visited while soliciting alms for the abbey or assisting one of the brothers in some task for which we had been summoned. There were no asses, horses, or other animals at liberty therein nor the smell of the ordure of farm animals. Instead, the fragrance of orange trees greeted our entry, mixed with rosemary, thyme and lavender which grew in sculpted beds planted on the south side of the cloister to receive the sun's full warmth.

An elaborately carved fountain gave forth the musical sound of water from its place in the center of the cross formed by paths that divided the garth into quadrants. The yard was encircled by an arcade, shady and cool behind its columns and open spaces.

Windows were not shuttered against the elements but were filled with glass, an extravagance I had never witnessed outside of the cathedral at Salamis, the city on an island near the place of my birth.

The interior was richly furnished with Venetian silk and Flemish tapestries, and blessed with the most holy of relics: the roasted flesh of Saint Lawrence, albeit turned to powder by the years since his martyrdom, an arm of Saint George, an ear of Saint Paul and one of the jars holding the water which our Lord turned into wine.

As was the wont of my former order after a journey, I went to the chapel to offer thanksgiving for my safe arrival. I was surprised to discover that it was round, a complete circle rather than the shape to which I had become accustomed. I subsequently learned that all Templar churches are of this design, as was the Temple of Solomon in Jerusalem. The room was surrounded by columns of serpentine and red marble. The altar was in the middle, a wondrously carved solid block of the purest white marble, unveined, on which devices were carved depicting scenes from the Holy City. The cross thereon reflected the lights of a hundred tapers, for it was of solid gold. The cost of this place alone would far exceed the worth of the entire abbey from which I had come.

Nor was this end of excess. The occupants of this most marvelous place greeted the return of their brethren with a feast shared even by humble esquires such as Philippe and myself. For the first time in my life, I tasted the meat of lampreys, partridge and mutton, accompanied by a wine so strong it made me giddy.

All was as or more than Guillaume de Poitiers had promised. The meat I have described. I was given a cell larger than the sum of any two at my previous abbey and a bed soft with wool stuffed with straw.

Would I had given my soul the same consideration as my flesh. Perhaps I would not be at the dismal place at which I find myself.

Translator's Notes

1. 5.029 meters.
2. He describes a typical two-decked thirteenth–fourteenth-century galleon-type vessel used in the Mediterranean.
3. Medieval ships carried their own sources of food for all but the shortest voyages, as the means of preservation of meats and vegetables were uncertain at best. Servants such as Pietro would have shared quarters with both the horses and other animals as may have been aboard for purposes of food.
4. Roman cartographers devised a method roughly similar to the present system of latitude and longitude by the use of *kardo maximus*, which ran north–south and *decumanus maximus*, running east–west. Although latitude as we know it today was known by the ancients, it was not until the late eighteenth century that Thomas Fuller, an English watchmaker, devised an accurate measure of longitude.
5. Medieval maps were absurd in their simplicity. In the seventh century, Isadore, Bishop of Seville, designed a world that was like a disk, with Asia, Europe and Africa sharing unequal quadrants with Jerusalem always at the center, based upon Ezekiel 5:5: "This is Jerusalem, which I have set in the midst of the nations and countries that are around about her." This practice or similar ideas persisted until the Renaissance. Fortunately for Western civilization, the Arabic world both admired and continued to use the Ptolemaic method of cartography, partially described in 4 above. The Templars, no doubt, learned this method while in Palestine as they did the mathematics, engineering and navigation known in the an-

cient world but lost or suppressed by a Church that did not trust knowledge of a pagan society.

6. The actual word used is *castellum*, which could include a palace as well as a castle. The translator has chosen the word with the connotation of fortifications.

7. 1127

8. See 5 above.

9. 5.029 meters. The medieval measurement was likely somewhat smaller.

CHAPTER TWO

1

London, St. James
1600 hours the same day

Gurt reread the note before she wadded it up and sent it flying into the trash can.

That bastard! She slung her purse across the room where it smashed against the far wall with gratifying violence. She had saved his ass in Italy and used her connections, not to mention her money, to get him to London.

He thanked her by dumping her like a one-night stand.

She almost wished she could cry, so great was her hurt and humiliation. She sat on the edge of the bed and lit a Marlboro, staring at the rope of smoke spiraling towards the ceiling.

As the minutes passed, her rational nature began to take control. Lang had made her no promises, had in fact tried to talk her out of coming here. How typically male: gallantly concerned about exposing her to danger while ignoring the fact someone needed to watch his back. Old-fashioned chauvinism, though charming, could get him killed.

Would serve him right, too.

She could shoot better on her worst day than Lang ever could, was current on modern trade craft and, most importantly, was someone the opposition, whoever they were, probably did not know was a player. With his picture on the front of a dozen newspapers, he needed the cover of being part of a couple more than ever.

Men in general and Lang in particular were capable of phenomenal stupidity. The thought made her feel somewhat better.

You need me, Langford Reilly. You need me, Schatz. And the Dumkopf factor does not diminish this fact in the least.

She reached for the phone on the other side of the bed, stopped and stood. Stubbing out her cigarette, she left the room, trying to remember where she had seen the nearest pay phone.

2

Oxford
1000 hours the next day

Late the next morning, Lang turned the ancient Morris Minor off the M40. The sixty miles from London had been as uneventful as possible in a car the size of a shoe box. A small shoe box. His only problem, other than cramps in muscles he didn't even know existed, had been a major case of flatulence, the result of an Indian meal Rachel, Jacob's wife, had insisted on preparing for dinner. In the intelligence community of the past, Rachel had been known as one of the world's worst and most enthusiastic cooks. Her dinner invitations had inspired legendary excuses.

Last night, she had prepared a version of Bombay aloo, a fiery potato dish, the heat of which had mercifully seared Lang's taste buds, rendering him impervious to her latest culinary disaster. All in all, he had probably gotten off lightly with only gas.

The Magdalen Bridge was, with typical British disregard for the number of letters in a name, pronounced "maudin." However articulated, it gave Lang a picture-postcard view of the honey-colored spires and gothic towers that were Oxford. He could have been looking at a skyline unchanged in five hundred years. The town, of course, had changed. The Rover automobile factory, among others, was located here. Still, the town had a medieval quality that its residents, both town and gown, intended to preserve.

Unlike American universities, Oxford was a composite of any number of undergraduate and graduate colleges, all more or less independent. Christ Church was one of the oldest and largest.

Just off the Abington Road, Lang found a rare parking spot among the bicycles that are Oxford's most popular form of transportation. He entered the Tom Quad, the university's largest quadrangle, named for the huge, multiton bell that chimes the hours there. Not only do the British ignore letters, but they also like to name towers and bells.

He had written Jacob's directions down and read them over before proceeding along one of the paths that formed a giant X across the neatly trimmed grass. On the other side, two young men tossed a Frisbee.

He entered an arch and climbed stone stairs as worn by centuries of student feet as those to Jacob's office had been by lawyers and clients. Down a poorly lit corridor, he found a tarnished plaque that informed him he was standing at the entrance to the office of Hubert Stockwell, Fellow in History. He was reaching to knock when the door swung open and a young woman emerged, her arms full of books and papers. She gave Lang a startled look before dashing for the stairwell.

Lang was fairly certain the expression on her face had nothing to do with his digestive tract problems.

"Come in, come in," a voice boomed from inside. "Don't stand about in the hall."

Lang did as ordered.

His first impression was that he had walked into the wake of a tornado. Papers, books and magazines were scattered across every surface, including the floor. This place was the brother to Jacob's office. There was an odor, too: the smell of old, stale documents Lang recognized from his occasional foray into the court clerk's archives at home. Bound and unbound papers were stacked on a mound he subsequently identified as a desk behind which sat a round-faced, bearded man peering at him through thick horn rims. He could have passed for a young Kris Kringle.

"You must be Jacob's friend," he said. "Look too old to be one of my students."

Lang extended a hand which the man ignored. "Lang Reilly."

"Hubert Stockwell," the man behind the desk replied without getting up or reaching out his own hand. "A pleasure and all that rubbish."

He started to say something else, but stopped and his face wrinkled as he sneezed. "Bloody old buildings! Drafts, damp, cold stone floors. Bleeding wonder we don't all die of pneumonia!"

He produced a soiled handkerchief, wiped his button of a nose and returned the cloth to wherever it had come from, all in a single motion so quick Lang was unsure he had seen a handkerchief at all. Lang would not bet on any shell game the good professor ran.

"You'd be the chap interested in the Templars."

"I understand you're an authority."

"Rubbish," Stockwell said, enjoying the compliment anyway. "But they did traipse through a period of history about which I know a little. Yank, aren't you?"

The change of subject made Lang shift mental gears before responding. "Actually, I'm from Atlanta, where a lot of people might resent being called that. Has to do with a Yankee general who was careless with fire."

Stockwell's head bobbed, reminding Lang of one of those dolls given to the first five thousand to enter a baseball game. "Sherman, yes, yes. *Gone With the Wind* and all that. Didn't mean to offend."

"You didn't. About the Templars . . ."

He held up a hand. "Not me, old boy, not me at all. Had an associate, chap named Wolffe, Nigel Wolffe, was fascinated by the blokes, translated some sort of manuscript, scribblings supposedly written by a Templar before he was put to death. Beseeching God for mercy, confession of sins, contrition, all of the claptrap of the medieval church, I'd imagine."

"And of today's Catholics," Lang said.

Stockwell's jaw slackened and the glasses slid to the tip of his nose. "Oh dear, I didn't mean . . ."

Lang smiled, an assurance they were perfectly comfortable together, just two antipapists. "You said you *had* an associate."

Stockwell sighed heavily. "That's right, past tense. Poor Wolffe is no longer with us. Splendid chap, played a killer hand of whist. Tragic, simply tragic."

Lang felt a chill not entirely caused by the drafts Stockwell had complained of. "I don't suppose Mr. Wolffe . . ."

Stockwell sneezed, doing the trick with the hankie again. "Dr. Wolffe."

". . . Dr. Wolffe died of natural causes?"

Stockwell stared at Lang, his eyebrows coming together like two mating caterpillars. "How's that?"

"I was asking how Dr. Wolffe died. An accident, perhaps?"

"Yes, yes. You must have read about it, seen it on the telly."

"I'm sure I did."

The professor turned to gaze out of the only window the cramped space had. There was a look of longing on his face, as though he were wishing he could go outside and play. "They said he probably left the bloody ring on after making tea. Explosion knocked out windows all the way across the quad."

"There was a resulting fire?"

Stockwell managed to pull away from the view outside. "Extraordinary memory you have. Mr. . . ."

"Reilly."

"Reilly, yes, yes. Surprising you would remember that from a newspaper or television account months ago."

Lang leaned foreword, hands on the paper-swamped desk. "His work on the Templars, it burned, too?"

Stockwell's Santa Claus face was masked with melancholy, the loss of scholarly work more lamentable than that of a colleague. "I'm afraid so. The original of the manuscript, notes, everything except his first draft."

Maybe Lang hadn't made the trip for nothing after all. "Where might that draft be?"

"The University library."

"You mean I can just go to the library and read it?"

Stockwell stood and looked around as though he might have forgotten where he had parked his sleigh. "Not exactly, no. I mean, I'll have to get it. Poor Wolffe ran me a copy on the machine, asked for help. Chap could never edit his own work. I was working on it when he . . . Well, he won't be publishing anyway, not now, will he? I left it at my carrel, planned to finish it up, submit it in his memory. Let's be off, shall we?"

Lang would have been surprised had the good professor been wearing something other than a tweed jacket with leather elbow patches. He reached behind the door and took a tweed cap from a coat rack. His universal uniform of academia was now complete.

They dodged bicycles until they turned into Catte Street. Before them was the massive fourteenth-century Bodleian Library, the repository of an original draft of the Magna Carta, innumerable illuminated manuscripts and at least one copy of every book published in Great Britain.

Stockwell pointed to the adjacent round building of enthusiastic Italian Baroque architecture, featuring peaked pilasters, scrolled windows and a domed roof. "Radcliffe Camera," he said. "Reading room. Meet you there soon's I collect Wolffe's papers."

Lang entered through a heavy oak door, ducking to get under a lintel no more than five and a half feet high. Anyone who doesn't believe in evolution should try smacking their heads on a few medieval doors, he thought grimly.

The Camera served as a general reading room. Oak tables, built to modern proportions, lined two walls. In the center, some of the library's more famous contents were on display in cloth-covered glass cases. Light struggled through opaque glass windows and filtered from miserly overhead lamps. The quiet was tangible, a dusty deafness interrupted by the occasional sound of a page being turned or the beep of a laptop. A lurch in the gastrointestine made Lang wonder where the men's might be, the loo, in Britspeak. This was not the place he could pass gas and escape undetected. He had been in noisier graveyards.

Lang waited for Stockwell, lifting the light-shielding cover from one case and another. A few Latin phrases greeted him like old friends, but most of the writing was

Saxon, Norman French or some other language he had never seen.

He was concentrating on an elaborately illustrated, hand-lettered Bible in what, he was guessing, was Gaelic when the professor appeared at his elbow so suddenly he might have dropped down a chimney.

He took a sheaf of papers from under one arm and tendered them to Lang. "Here you go. Drop the lot off at my office when you're done."

Lang took them, scanning the first page. "Thanks."

Stockwell was headed for the exit. "Pleased to do it. Friend of Jacob's and all that."

Lang sat at the nearest table, concentrating on what he was reading. For the second time in a very short period, he experienced a jolt in his stomach. But this one had nothing to do with Rachel's cooking.

THE TEMPLARS: THE END OF AN ORDER

Account by Pietro of Sicily
Translation from the medieval Latin by Nigel Wolffe, Ph.D.

4

I shed my novice status shortly after our arrival at Blanchefort, taking my vows as a Brother of the Order of the Poor Knights of the Temple of Solomon before the autumn harvest. I shed also my innocence and my faith, now I realize.

True to the inducements I had been offered, I supped on meat twice daily and bathed myself twice weekly until All Hallows' Eve, when the air's chill made it impractical to do and I was subjected to the body's natural vermin once again. Even these deprivations seemed trivial, for I was allowed to change my vestments[1] for clean ones weekly, thereby ridding myself of my small tormentors.

Not only did my belly grow with victuals far richer than those consumed by others in God's service, but my knowledge increased its girth as well. I know now that I should have remembered Eve's original sin in thirsting for forbidden knowledge, but like hers my mind possessed an unquenchable thirst. Uncontrolled lust for knowledge, forbidden or not, can be as deadly as carnal lust, as I was to discover all too late.

The castle had a library the likes of which I did not know existed except, perhaps, under the direct keep of the Holy Father in Rome. I had become used to one or two manuscripts illustrating both in word and picture the Holy Writ. The Brethren's collection included volumes with scribbling resembling worms with brightly coloured ornamentation, which, I was told, was the wisdom of the Ancients preserved by the heathen Saracen.

When I asked why works of pagans and heretics were allowed in consecrated quarters, I was told that writings forbidden most Christians were permitted here. It was a refrain I was to hear repeated often, that the Knights were not bound by the same dictates as the rest of Christendom.

In acting as scribe and counting house clerk, I made another discovery. The Brothers had a system by which a Christian on a pilgrimage might both protect his money while being able to use it when he wished. A traveler could deposit a certain number pieces of gold or silver with any Temple and receive therefore a piece of parchment bearing his name, the amount deposited and a secret sign known only to the Brethren. When this parchment was presented at any other Temple, be it in Britain, Iberia or the German duchies, a like amount as the pilgrim had deposited would be paid over to him, thereby preventing the common scourge of robbery upon the highways or piracy upon the seas.[2]

For this service, the Temple issuing the parchment and the one rendering value for it received a fee. This seemed to me like the sin of usury, a practice forbidden Christians but allowed the Knights. Worse, the Temples were in the business of letting money out for profit, the same as any heathen Israelite.[3]

More curious were the sums of money that came from Rome in regular increments. Unthinkable riches arrived to be placed in the Temple's treasure room. This wealth was not distributed as alms to the poor as Christ admonished but went to purchase lands, arms and such excess as the Brethren might desire. Even so, a substantial fraction of the Holy See's bounty was not spent but rather accumulated for purposes I only now understand.

At first I feared to corrupt my soul, for gluttony takes many forms, including the wanton dissipation of wealth. I sought out Guillaume de Poitiers and interrupted his gaming with other Knights. Indeed, gaming, eating and the consumption of wine occupied more of the day than did practice with the sword, pike or lance.

He invoked the name of several saints along with consigning to hell the wooden cubes which he and his fellows constantly rolled, wagering on the outcome. "Ah, Pietro, little brother," he said, his voice full of the aroma of the grape. "I see by your face you are disturbed. Do the figures in your counting house become amok?"

At this, there was much gaiety among his companions.

"No," I said solemnly. "I am overcome by such curiosity as I cannot bear in silence. The Holy Father sends us great sums as he does to all Temples. Yet it is the duty of the body of the Holy Church to remit to Rome what they can for the sustenance of that same Holy Father. I understand not."

"In the beginning of our Order," he said, "we had no choice but receive support from Rome were we to equip and maintain ourselves against the infidel."

"But now the Holy Land is lost, by God's unknowable will," I said. "The Order can no longer protect pilgrims to Jerusalem any more than it can attack Saracens from here."

He nodded and pointed to a nearby window. "See you Serres there? And on the other side is Rennes. It is the Holy Father's pleasure that we guard those towns. For that he sees fit to reward us."

"Guard from what?" I asked. "There are no hostile armies nearby and the time of the barbarians is long hence."[4]

"So you might think," he said. "But it is not our place to question Rome. Only one prideful would do so."

I took his meaning and felt my face flush with shame.

He put his hand on my shoulder. "Besides, it is not always armies or barbarians we have to apprehend. This is the area of two pernicious former heresies that could have destroyed the Holy See as surely as any band of armed men: the Gnostics and the Cathars."[5]

"And we must guard Cardou from their successors," spoke Tartus, a German.

"But that is but a mountain, bare and empty," I said.

Guillaume de Poitiers gave his brother Knight an abashing glare. "So it is. Brother Tartus has enjoyed God's gift of wine to excess, I fear. We guard towns, not empty hills."

Tartus appeared ready to speak again but did not. I was aware there was a secret that was being kept from me. There I should have allowed the matter to stand. Would that I had not continued so or that I had sought God's help before relying upon my own.

At the first opportunity, I repaired again to the library to ascertain who these Gnostics and Cathars might be.

I found both had their origins in the Holy Council of Nicea,[6] at which the early Church adopted the four books as gospel, rejecting others. One of those rejected was that of Thomas, who wrote that Jesus instructed his followers to adhere to the leadership of James upon His death.[7]

This Thomas might have been he who was the doubter, insisting to touch Our Lord's wounds, for it is from him these Gnostics and Cathars drew their loathsome heresy which, though such was not their purpose, denied the Holy Scriptures, many of which were writ in the blood of martyrs.[8]

I was at first unable to discover the reason these apostasies found such sustenance here in the Languedoc as would require the maintenance of the Knights at such great expense.

Days later, I came upon the answer, a manuscript apparently taken from a Gnostic heretic shortly before his soul was sent to hell and his body to the stake. Rolled rather than bound, it consisted of a single scroll of vellum,[9] badly spelled, poorly written and greatly faded. Had I not let my curiosity overcome my devotions, I would have realized this diabolic writing had been placed in my hands by the devil himself, just as he tempts many of the unwary with the promise of knowledge, for this document was obscene to all Christendom.

The Gnostic author of this abhorrent writing gave not his name but spoke of earlier writings which he purported merely to translate from the ancient Hebrew and Aramaic. They bespoke as follows:

After the Crucifixion of Our Lord, Joseph of Arimathea,[10] who was Jesus's brother, and Mary Magdalene, who was Jesus's wife,[11] fearing persecution also, fled to the far end of the Roman Empire which was then called Gaul. The area was peopled by a number of Jews including the exiled Herod.[12] They brought with them only that which could be carried. Included among this impedimenta was a large vessel, the nature of which they kept secret and which they hid in the hills of this region near the River Sens and the mountain called Cardou, the same as the mountain Tartus had said the Brethren guarded.

It is here that this narrative denoted its heretical source which I dared not repeat lest my soul be forever damned for such blasphemous utterances. I did, however, seek out Guillaume de Poitiers and tell him some of the things of which I had read, though not the part that would damn me forever should I speak it. He was undistressed by it, saying the ravings of madmen had naught to do with us and our duty of loving and protecting The One True God.

But they did, as I was to learn to my sorrow.

Translator's Notes

1. The Latin *vestimentum* meaning clothing, is the word used. Since Pietro would have worn robes, the translator has chosen a literal translation.

2. This was, no doubt, not only the first system of cheques or drafts, but the first travelers' cheques.

3. By Papal decree, only Jews were permitted to charge interest on loans. This explains the rise of the Jewish European banking houses.

4. Although he uses the Latin word for barbarian, it is likely he refers to the Vikings whose raids extended even to the Mediterranean from the eighth until the tenth century.

5. From the Greek word for knowledge, *gnosis*. The Christian Gnostics believed that Christ was mortal, born of Mary and was touched by God. His spirit, not his corporeal body, ascended into heaven. The Cathars believed Christ was an angel who never really existed in true human form. The potential damage either belief might have done the early or medieval Christian church, which had committed itself to the Pauline doctrine of the physical resurrection and ascension of Christ into heaven, is obvious.

6. 325 A.D. The major question addressed by this early conference of Christians was whether Jesus was created by God or was part of God. A seemingly academic distinction, the question had endless theological implications as will become apparent. The latter belief, i.e., that Jesus was "begotten, not made," being of one substance with the Father prevailed.

7. The so-called Nag Hammadi gospels were unearthed in Upper Egypt in 1945, encased in terracotta jars like the Dead Sea Scrolls at Qumran. Translation of these remarkable documents, fifty-two in all, was not completed until 1977. They also refer to a Gospel of Thomas which contains such an admonition.

8. See 5 above.

9. *Veelin*, Frankish for lamb or lamb skin specially prepared for writing. It was not uncommon to also use calfskin or kidskin.

10. Aram, was the ancient Hebrew name for Syria but it is unlikely that a sibling of Christ could have come from there.

We must assume Arimathea was a city in Palestine, the ancient name of which is lost.

11. This is not the first time the question of Christ's marital status has arisen. Jesus, as a Jew, would have followed the Jewish law's commandment to marry. In fact, the controversial Lobineau documents registered in the Bibliothèque Nationale in Paris make the argument that Jesus arrived in the Languedoc alive and *en famille* and was founder of the Merovingian dynasty of Frankish kings.

12. The Roman province of Aquitainia, subsequently Aquitaine in southern Gaul, including today's Languedoc, was a convenient place for Roman emperors to exile those fallen from grace. Ironically, Pontius Pilate was also banished there.

CHAPTER THREE

1

Oxford

Lang knew he was holding Wolffe's death warrant, the reason They had killed him. The thought made him glance apprehensively around the room before he began to read. First, he forgot his digestive problems, then where he was. The only interruption was that spoor of academia, annoying footnotes.

By the time Lang finished reading, he had some theories as to the painting's riddle. The question was whether he was going to live long enough to try them out.

2

London, South Bank
1630 hours

A dirty carpet of clouds was threatening rain by the time Lang wedged the Morris into the Strand's afternoon traffic and crossed Waterloo Bridge to South Bank.

Located along the inside of the bend of the Thames, South Bank was actually east rather than south of London. Until extensive urban renewal by the Luftwaffe in World War II, the area had been warehouses and factories. For the next fifty years, little was built there. Now it displayed high-rise offices, music halls, galleries and housing for those who enjoyed contemporary surroundings. The skyline could have been that of any number of American cities.

Lang went straight down Waterloo Road to St. George's Circus, one of those traffic circles the British seem to prefer to traffic lights. After two circuits, he worked his way to the outside and exited onto Lambeth Road, where the Imperial War Museum's two massive naval guns filled his windshield.

Off Lambeth, he crowded the Morris into a rare parking spot, killed the engine and watched the rearview mirror. Like most London streets, this one was one way, giving him a clear view of approaching vehicles. After five minutes, it was clear he hadn't been followed. He was fairly certain nobody but Jacob, Rachel and the professor knew he had gone to Oxford, but in light of what he had learned there, it would be an obvious place for Them to watch.

He cranked up the Morris and drove into a parking garage beneath an apartment building that would have been at home on Riverside Drive or East Seventy-first Street. He left the car in Jacob's space and followed the signs to the lift, as the English call elevators.

Jacob opened the door. Even in the hall, Lang could smell something besides his pipe. Rachel in the kitchen.

Jacob gestured Lang inside, his glance up and down the hall more of a nervous tic than a conscious movement. "Glad you're back safely. Stockwell any help?"

"He was, yes," Lang said, handing over the keys to the Morris as he crossed the threshold.

The apartment was the antithesis of Jacob's office. The furniture was contemporary, glass and chrome that made Lang nostalgic for home. Lucite shelves along one wall held a few books and several pieces of modern sculpture that possibly had begun life as engine parts. Two walls held art that bore a resemblance to the splattist works Lang had seen the day before. The remaining wall was glass, through which Lang could see a small deck and a panorama of the Thames that, in the darkening afternoon, reminded him of Monet's *Houses of Parliament*.

Jacob was waiting for further explanation but Lang asked first, "What did you learn about Pegasus?"

Jacob settled onto a sofa, leather slung like a hammock on a chrome stand, and fumbled a pipe from the pocket of a shabby sweater. "Quite a bit, actually."

Lang sat and waited impatiently as Jacob went through the ritual of lighting up.

"Pegasus," Jacob said among puffs of smoke, "Pegasus, of course, was the winged horse of Greek mythology that caused the stream Hippocrene to spring from Mount Helicon with a blow from his hoof."

Lang shifted in his seat, hoping Jacob would get to the point sooner rather than later.

"I have no idea as to the relationship between a mythical animal and a commercial enterprise," Jacob admitted, "but the company is interesting in several respects. First . . ."

Sucking loudly, he stopped to dig in the briar with what

looked like a nail. Lang suppressed an urge to throw the
damn pipe out the window. "I know the relationship with
the mythical animal. But the company . . . ?"

". . . A Channel Island corporation, based in Jersey." Jacob arched those buglike eyebrows in an implied question.

"You mean it has bank and corporate secrecy," Lang
said. "By law, the identity of the shareholders and officers
are confidential and any transactions on the Channel Islands aren't taxed."

Jacob had his pipe smoldering again. "Just so. Legally,
we would have no way of knowing that the company has
annual receipts of several billion dollars. Quite extraordinary considering it produces nothing, performs no ascertainable services."

Lang let out a low whistle. "Jesus, that's an income larger
than the gross national product of a lot of countries.
Where does it come from?"

"Even more interesting: a number of sources, all either
overtly Roman Catholic, like the Pope's investments and
discretionary funds, or strongly influenced by the Church,
like a number of Catholic relief agencies."

Lang realized he was gaping, then asked, "For what? I
mean, that pays off a lot of winning bingo cards."

Jacob shrugged. "Unfortunately Mossad is an intelligence source staffed, by definition, by those unlikely to be
privy to the workings of the Catholic Church, the Vatican or
the Papal State. Whatever Pegasus does, it doesn't do it by
phone, e-mail or fax, anything Echelon monitors. Mossad's
known about it for years, never found it interesting."

Never found it threatening to the Jewish State, Lang
thought. "Any idea where the money goes?"

Jacob was probing the pipe again, this time with a
wooden match. "Geographically? Europe mostly. A chain
of sausage restaurants in Germany, petrol dealers in the

U.K., ski and sea resorts in France. Too many businesses to track just out of curiosity, and communications between them are encrypted. They don't seem to be breaking any laws, pay taxes when they can't be avoided, that sort of thing."

Lang thought for a moment. These were all businesses with high cash potentials. "Sounds like money laundering to me. Any contacts in Asia, South America, places where narcotraffic is heavy?"

Jacob was sucking on his pipe again. He shook his head.

"Any individual names?"

"As I said, Mossad isn't particularly interested. I had to call a lot of favors due to get what I did."

"What about Jersey? Is the island just a mail drop or does Pegasus have some sort of operation there?"

"Can't say. I can tell you that a disproportionate number of communications go through a Lisbon exchange. Could be just a switching point, could mean they do business there."

Impatiently, Lang watched his friend apply yet another match to the bowl of his pipe and suck until blue smoke poured out of it.

"One really strange thing," he said at last. "Little hamlet in the southwest of France, Burgundy. Rennes-le-something . . . Rennes-le-Château. Wire transfers there to what I'd guess is a dummy corporation. Small amounts but on a regular basis. They've got no operations there we—Echelon—could find."

Lang leaned back in his chair, more leather slung on a chrome frame. "Rennes-le-Château? Never heard of it."

"I found it in the atlas. Somewhere near the Pyrenees."

"The Languedoc region?"

Jacob was knocking the pipe's contents out into a glass ashtray that seemed fragile enough to shatter from the effort. The intensity in Lang's tone made him look up. "I think so, yes."

The American stood. "The atlas, you have it here?"

Jacob was clearly puzzled at Lang's sudden interest in geography. "Well, yes . . ."

The doorbell rang.

Jacob carefully laid his pipe in the ashtray and went to the door, squinting through the peephole. "Sure you weren't followed?"

"Followed? By whom?"

Jacob's eye was still against the hole. "Coppers, by the look of 'em."

3

London, Mayfair
At the same time

The computer screen washed Gurt's face in blue light. Overhead, the glare of the unremitting fluorescent bulbs made the basement of 24 Grosvenor Square resemble an operating theater. In its own way, the room was as antiseptic as any surgery, as clear of electronic bacteria as a hospital of the conventional kind. Electronically swept daily, every inch was videotaped on a continuing twenty-four-hour reel. Even so, the room was partitioned off by seamless glass, a feature that prompted its regular occupants to refer to it as "the fish bowl." It was the most secure part of the American embassy's secured sections, the part where the Agency did its work.

Gurt's security clearance was high enough to access the information she was seeking, a closed personnel file, but clearances did not impress the cybergods who dictated the time required to comply with a request of the system. She hit the "enter" key for the second time in a fruitless effort to speed a response, impatiently muttering a curse to which her native tongue gave special emphasis. As though she had spoken a magical password, the file she sought appeared. Scanning it, she committed parts to memory. Note-taking of any sort was forbidden.

She was about to close out when a blinking red light at the bottom of the screen caught her attention. She frowned, entering another access code.

Someone had managed to hack into the system, into this specific file. Unbelievable! The network's complexity made the Pentagon's look like a child's puzzle in comparison. Ten minutes' further investigation was useless. This was a case for the Agency's supernerds, cybergurus who, unknown to the public, had successfully traced the worldwide Love Bug and Melissa viruses of a few years back to their authors.

As with those viruses, the intruder had routed his inquiries through a number of computers belonging to individuals and companies across the globe, innocent hosts for electronic burglary. But whoever he was, the Agency's reverse cookie had made certain he had left cyberevidence of his entry and departure, the time and date. The date, she saw, was yesterday.

Presumably the hacker wanted the same information she had just garnered. Gurt exited the system hurriedly. She didn't have a lot of time. Lang's ass was slung worse than he knew.

4

London, South Dock
1645 hours

"Cops?" Lang asked, pointing to the kitchen. "Where does that lead?"

There was a loud knock, the sound of the door being struck with something harder than a human hand. A gun butt came to mind.

"Leads to a back staircase," Jacob said. "Want to wager they don't have it covered?"

Rachel had come out of the kitchen, started to ask what was going on and decided against it. Her years of marriage to Jacob had taught her to question little. She was, however, following the conversation with astonishment that Lang would be wanted by the police.

Lang stepped to the glass wall, sliding it open.

"There's no way down from . . ." Jacob cautioned.

On the narrow balcony, Lang climbed onto the metal railing about four feet above the cement, using a hand against the building's wall to steady himself. The balcony below was identical, too narrow. Even though it was only twelve feet or so below, it would be too easy to miss if he jumped.

From inside Jacob's apartment, Lang heard renewed and determined banging on the door, accompanied by loud and demanding voices.

Jacob shot him a glance before shouting, "I'm coming, I'm coming!"

The adjacent balcony was too far to simply step over onto it. But a good jump . . . Lang didn't have a lot of choice. He resisted the urge to close his eyes as he stooped, coiling his leg muscles, and sprang into empty space.

The sole of his shoe slipped on the edge of the concrete and Lang grabbed for the iron railing as he fell. His weight yanked his arms straight with a jerk that felt as though they were tearing from the sockets. For what seemed an eternity, Lang's fingers grasped for purchase on the cement and he tried not to notice how far away the street looked twelve stories below.

Through the open glass, he could hear voices above. Jacob's sounded angry. He sensed, rather than heard, footsteps. It hadn't taken the police long to conclude Lang was no longer in Jacob's place and search elsewhere.

Like outside.

Finally Lang was able to grasp one of the railing's uprights. He tugged gently, making sure the slender metal would hold his hundred and ninety pounds. His other hand found a second upright and he slowly began to chin himself up as though on a crossbar.

As his head was coming level with the cement floor of the balcony, he heard something that made him turn his head. On Jacob's balcony, a pair of shoes were at eye level, the soles and rubber heels unevenly worn. Lang extended his arms, lowering his head below balcony-level and hoping his hands weren't visible in the growing dusk. He was hanging in a twelve-story void but they would hardly look for him beneath the adjacent balcony. Jacob's balcony would block out the rest of him unless someone came to the very edge and looked over.

Scuffed toe caps the color of butterscotch turned away and a voice announced, "Bloke's not 'ere. Sure we 'ave the right flat?"

Lang couldn't make out the words of the reply but the tone was affirmative.

He heard the glass door to Jacob's apartment slide shut, and he glanced upward, risking the paleness of his face showing against the dark background if anyone were still outside. He was alone. Once again he chinned up until one hand, then the other, could reach the top of the railing and he could pull himself up, over and onto firm footing.

The drapes on the glass were pulled, so Lang couldn't tell if there were lights burning inside. He put an ear to the cold surface. No voices, human or electronic. Either the occupants were the rare ones who didn't watch the BBC news at this time of day or the place was empty. He tugged at the grip. Locked. Who would lock a door on the twelfth floor, he asked himself as he took a credit card from his wallet. Someone seriously paranoid, came the answer as he inserted the card and pressed back the latch.

Thankful that few homeowners in England had firearms, Lang stepped into total darkness.

Guided by a sliver of light under the door to what he surmised was the common hallway, he moved forward, arms outstretched. His hands missed the low coffee table that smacked his shins so painfully he had to bite his lip to suppress a curse.

He was reaching for the door to the hall when shadows moved across the ribbon of light underneath it. The click in the lock nearly immobilized him like headlights are supposed to transfix a deer. As he frantically tried to think of a hiding place in the dark, he remembered his sole experience in the matter, an encounter on a dark road in the Black Forest, had resulted not in an indecisive buck but a badly damaged Volkswagen.

Lang did the only thing he could think of: take a position next to the hinges, a place where the opening door itself would momentarily hide him. Then the lights flashed on, blinding him for an instant. When he could see again, he was looking at a woman carrying a basket, the plastic kind Europeans use for grocery shopping. She saw him as she turned to close the door.

Her eyes opened to a size Lang had thought impossible anywhere except in the comic strips. She made a sound more like a squeak than a scream. It wasn't loud enough to mask the smashing of glass when the basket slipped from her grip and hit the floor.

Lang smiled the most nonthreatening smile possible as he stepped out from behind the still-open door and into the hallway. "Sorry, wrong flat." He almost slipped on something that crunched under his foot. "Sounds real fresh. You'll have to give me the name of your greengrocer."

She found her voice, as indicated by the scream that followed him as he fled down the hall.

He decided not to use the elevator. No idea how long it would take to get down and the police might very well be responding to the poor frightened woman right now. He made a dash down the stairs. At the lobby, he summoned the stuffy dignity so dear to the English to stroll for the door outside and enter the fresh darkness of early evening.

How the hell had the cops known he was at Jacob's place, Lang wondered as he walked towards the nearest tube station. He was certain no one had followed him to Jacob's. And if they had, where did they pick him up? If he had been recognized at Oxford, why hadn't he been arrested there? Because they had somehow known he was coming here, to Jacob's.

The thought made Lang shiver more than the chill of the evening. To know he would seek out Jacob, someone would have had to look over his long-closed service record, something the Agency's pathological penchant for secrecy made unlikely. The London police, Scotland Yard, would have known that, probably wouldn't have even bothered to ask, assuming they had been aware of his former employment. But he was almost certain he had seen his photo from his service jacket in the tabloid the man on the bench had been reading at the Temple. How did the paper get it? That raised an even more disturbing possibility: Someone had exhumed his record, buried under years of bureaucratic sod, and was supplying the police with the information. They. They who wanted him arrested, imprisoned where They could tend to him in their own sweet time.

Lang's thoughts were interrupted by the protest of tires under brakes. A sedan, something the British would call a saloon car, ran onto the sidewalk, blocking his path. Two men got out, pistols pointed.

"Mr. Reilly, I believe," the taller of the two said, holding up a leather folder with a badge on one side, a photograph on the other. "Scotland Yard. You're under arrest."

"Wow!" Lang said, raising his arms. "All my life I've dreamed of this, actually meeting someone from the Yard. A real Kodak moment."

The streetlights' halogenic jaundice showed that the larger man had suffered a bad case of acne at some point in his life. His suit was ill fitting. The look of something bought off the rack and poorly tailored? No, the jacket had been hurriedly altered to fit around the clearly visible shoulder holster. Not the tailored British look Lang associated with English inspectors. The gun was wrong, too, a Beretta. Scotland Yard, like most American police forces, favored the Glock nine-millimeter, a weapon lighter, faster and holding more rounds than the Italian-made automatic.

The other man was behind the first, shorter and heavy, Costello to his companion's Abbott. He wore the recognizable butterscotch shoes. Holstering his gun, he stepped to Lang's rear, pulling his arms behind him. Lang expected to hear the snap of handcuffs. Instead, Costello tightened his grip as Abbott put his weapon away also.

"You'll be coming with us, Mr. Reilly," Abbott said politely. "The lads at the Yard have a query or two for you."

"Don't suppose it'd do any good to tell you I didn't do it," Lang said, testing the man's grip by pretending to struggle.

"An' which would be that you didn't do, now? The one in America or the poor sod in Bond Street?" Abbott was reaching inside his suit jacket.

The light was far from good but sufficed for Lang to see Abbott produce a syringe.

"Since when did Scotland Yard start sedating its prisoners?" Lang asked.

"Easier and more humane than clubbing or pistol-whipping like your coppers do the poor black blokes," Abbott, said, concentrating on testing the needle. The lights turned the tiny stream of liquid into gold. "Now this won't hurt a bit."

Lang felt tingling along his neck just as he had when the would-be killer entered his place in Atlanta. As then, the Agency's basic training returned like a poem memorized and long forgotten.

Lang suddenly threw his weight forward. Costello's reaction was the natural impulse to resist by planting a foot forward, the better to pull Lang back. At that instant, Lang shifted his bulk to his back leg, lifted his front foot and brought the heel of his shoe and every bit of one hundred ninety pounds he could manage down on Costello's instep.

Only an instant separated the sound of crunching bone and Costello's scream. His grip relaxed and Lang hurled himself forward. Costello took a single hop and fell to the sidewalk where he lay moaning.

Abbott had dropped the needle and was reaching for his Beretta. Lang feinted with a left jab, delaying his draw by the instant it took to lean away. Crouching to make sure the blow would land where he aimed it, Lang placed a right hook right below the rib cage.

Abbott folded as neatly as a jackknife, his knees hitting the pavement in a posture that would have resembled prayer had his hands not been trying to embrace the liver Lang hoped was ruptured by the blow. He gave Lang a baleful look before doing a face-plant on the sidewalk.

As he writhed on the ground, moaning, something fell from his shirt. Lang wasn't surprised to recognize the Maltese cross in a circle.

Lang used a foot to roll him over, stooped and picked up the Beretta before walking over to the lamppost Costello was using to try to pull himself upright. Lang disarmed him, too, tossing his weapon into some bushes, before jamming the muzzle of Abbott's weapon into his mouth.

"Who the fuck are you?"

The only fear was Lang's when he saw none on the man's face. Just like the man who tried to kill Lang at home, death wasn't a very scary possibility to these people.

"Who sent you?" Lang could feel his frustration becoming anger. "Answer me, or by God your brains'll be splattered all over that lamppost."

His assailant's answer was a smile, or as much of one as he could manage around the gun's muzzle.

Lang's fury at Them was boiling. These pukes were from the organization that had burned Jeff and Janet to death as they slept, had tried both to kill him and frame him for two other murders. If this bastard was so willing to die, Lang was more than willing to accommodate him. His finger tightened on the trigger and his passion to bring pain, destruction and death grew. Revenge was less than a hundredth of a millimeter away.

The man's eyes moved from Lang's face, focusing for only a split second on something over Lang's shoulder. It was enough. Lang dropped to one knee and spun around. Abbott, *jimbia* in hand, collided with Lang, falling over the top like the victim of a shoestring tackle. Still off balance, he imbedded the blade meant for Lang up to its hilt into his comrade's chest.

A geyser of arterial blood, black in the streetlight, spurted from the shorter man as he slumped to the ground. He made a sound that could have been a sigh had it not come from around the knife that was splitting his sternum. Eyes open but becoming lifeless stared above.

The accident didn't seem to shake Abbott at all. He scrambled to his feet in the same motion with which he snatched the knife from the still body. It came free with a sucking sound that made Lang's stomach heave. Painted with his companion's blood, Abbott whirled towards Lang, the blade raised for another try.

Still on one knee, Lang raised the Beretta in both hands. "Hold it right there."

At that moment Lang became aware of three things. First, his attacker wasn't going to be intimidated by the gun. Second, he had no idea if the weapon had a bullet in the chamber. Third, there was no time to pull the Beretta's slide back or check its safety to make sure it was ready to fire.

Lang squeezed the trigger.

5

Jacob stared at the statuesque woman in his doorway. "Lang who?"

Gurt shoved past him into the apartment. "I don't have time for sport, Mr. Annulewicz. Lang is in imminent danger. I need to know where he is."

Jacob shrugged. Besides his natural suspicion, it was his instinct to evade questions asked in German accents, slight as the inflection might be. "A most popular man. Second time this evening somebody's popped 'round looking for him. Beginning to think I'd like to meet the bloke m'-self."

Gurt stepped closer, maximizing her six-inch height advantage "You were Mossad; Lang, Agency. Thirteen years ago, Hamas planning to bomb the Israeli embassy. You were scheduled to be in the neighborhood. Lang convinced the Agency to let him warn you. You always joked that you wondered what he would have done if they had refused to let him."

Jacob's eyes widened. "You do know him! I'm sorry . . ."

Gurt gave him the briefest of smiles. "Apologize later. Right now I need to find him. He's in more trouble than he realizes."

Jacob had recovered sufficient composure to begin working on his pipe. "Not likely he doesn't know he's in a spot of bother. He left right ahead of the coppers."

"Unless he was uncharacteristically careless, I doubt that's who they were. The Agency gave his edited service records to the police but someone else accessed his service file, someone besides the police. That's how they found out about you, your friendship. Someone needs to tell him that his past, his contacts are known to these people."

Jacob sat down hard on the leather-and-chrome hammock, his pipe temporarily ignored. "Bloody hell! If they have his service records . . ."

"He has no place to go in London they don't know about," Gurt finished. "I need to warn him."

Jacob looked up at her. "I have no idea where he might have gone. He left here in a hurry." He pointed the pipe's stem at the balcony. "Took the quick way down."

Gurt walked over, sliding the glass open as though she expected Lang to still be there. "What did you two talk about before the 'cops' arrived?" She made quotation marks in the air.

Now Jacob remembered his pipe and was stoking it with a match. "He'd just come back from Oxford, went to meet a chap I know, history fellow. Wanted to learn something about the Templars."

Gurt turned from the opening onto the balcony, her forehead wrinkled. "Templars? As in Knights Templar?"

Apparently despairing of getting the briar going again, Jacob set it down. "The same. He found . . ."

There were two pops from the street below, sounds distinct from the murmur of the city. Jacob and Gurt rushed onto the balcony. If the noise had come from just below, its source was masked by shrubbery and shadows. Both turned and made a dash for the door and the elevator down.

6

London, South Dock

Lang had never killed anyone before. He would never forget each tiny detail, as if everything had slowed to a dreamlike pace. The Beretta bucked as though it were trying to escape his grasp, fell back to center the sight on the dark splotch on the white shirt and jumped again, all before the first shot had echoed off the nearby buildings. Brass shell casings, catching the light, sparkled like twin shooting stars as they arched into darkness.

His attacker grunted in surprise and pain. Unlike the movies, the bullets' impact didn't even slow him down. If it hadn't been for the two red flowers blooming on his shirt, Lang would have thought he had missed. The pistol's front sight centered again and he was about to squeeze off another round when the man's knees buckled. As in a slow-motion film, his legs gave way and he hit the ground like a felled tree. His body was sprawled in a position that made Lang wonder if his bones had turned to liquid.

In any major American city, the sound of gunfire would make the neighbors burrow deeper into the safety of their homes. But not in London, where street shootings were still a novelty.

Above Lang's head, lights were coming on, windows were opening and the curious were calling out, asking each other what had happened.

Lang hurriedly checked both men's pockets, finding

only the bogus police ID. Tucking the Beretta into his belt, he took one last look at the two bodies. He expected exultation or at least some degree of satisfaction for the small measure of revenge. Instead he felt a faint nausea. He made himself think of those two open graves on the hillside in Atlanta, but it didn't help much.

Three of them for the persons he had loved. Scorekeeping was useless. He turned and walked quickly in a direction away from the approach of pulsating sirens.

7

London, South Dock

Inspector Fitzwilliam arrived in a less than jovial mood. These things always seemed to happen during the BBC newscast, calls that took him away from the telly and returned him to a dinner long since gone cold.

A crowd silhouetted by flashing lights was his first view of the crime scene. His next, after shouldering his way through the throng of spectators, made him forget both news and supper. Bodies were scattered about like some red Indian massacre in one of those American Westerns he had enjoyed so much as a lad. Two victims, one bloody as a freshly butchered beef, the other with neat, round holes in the breast of his shirt.

This was London, not New York or Los Angeles where street gangs conducted wars the police were impotent to prevent. What the hell . . . ? But the two victims didn't look like street criminals. They wore suits with ties.

The detective in charge spotted Fitzwilliam and came over, notebook in hand, wrapped in an odor of curry. The sweat glistening on his dark face made Fitzwilliam suspect this was the first truly grisly murder the young man had seen.

" 'Lo, Patel," Fitzwilliam said, "Any idea what happened?"

"Like the shootout at the bloody OK Corral," Patel said, the whites of his eyes large in contrast to his brown skin. "Both poor sods had shoulder holsters, police identification. I checked, the identities are false. We found one gun, a Beretta, in the shrubs over there," he pointed. "Other pistol, if there was one, has gone missing."

Fitzwilliam nodded, digesting this information. The U.K. did not permit the carrying of handguns, let alone concealed handguns, by anyone other than police, military and a very few security types. The presence of weapons and bogus ID indicated organized crime, quite possibly the so-called Russian Mafia that threatened to overrun Europe, or, worse, a part of a Colombian drug cartel.

The inspector walked over and took a closer look at the bodies. Even in this poor light, neither had Slavic features nor the coloring or strong facial characteristics of many Latinos. "Don't suppose they had any other means of identification on them?" he asked.

At his elbow, Patel shook his head. "Not so much as a National Health card."

Fitzwilliam squatted beside the body that had been shot. Suit was off the rack as were the shoes. The Russians favored tailor-made Italian toggery; the Colombians, fancy boots. He'd bet these men were neither. The fact that both holsters were empty would indicate they hadn't been ambushed, were at least trying to defend themselves. But how do you get stabbed while you're carrying a pistol?

He stood, taking in the entire scene with weary eyes. There was something about this South Bank neighborhood off Lambeth Road. He was certain he had never been here before, yet . . .

Annulewicz, the former Mossad agent who had been a friend of Reilly's. Didn't he have a South Bank address? The inspector began to pat his pockets in the vain hope he might have Annulewicz's address.

"Can I help you, Inspector?" Patel offered solicitously.

Fitzwilliam gave up the search but he was sure Reilly's former friend lived around here somewhere. If the American were involved, that might explain something, although Fitzwilliam was unsure what.

"No, thank you," he said crisply, beginning to scan the growing crowd of spectators.

His search was almost immediately rewarded. A woman, blonde and tall enough to stand out. Pretty, like the photograph of Reilly's woman friend, the German. He made his way to her side just as she was moving to the outer ring of spectators, about to leave.

"Miss? Pardon me, miss." He had his identification hanging from his jacket pocket but he removed the leather wallet with the badge to hold out where she couldn't miss it. "Miss Fuchs?"

She had to hear but she gave no indication. Remarkable control, he thought. "I know who you are, miss. I'd prefer to have a word with you here than at the station."

That stopped her. It was only when she turned that he realized she was a full head taller than he.

"Yes?"

"I'm Inspector Fitzwilliam, Metro Police," he began as though the badge weren't inches from her face. "We're looking for an old friend of yours, an American, Langford Reilly."

The coldness of the stare she fixed on him was undiminished by the poor light. "And what makes you think I know where he might be? If you know who I am, you also know I have not seen him in nearly ten years, maybe more."

"May I remind you, Miss Fuchs, that harboring a felon is a crime?"

She nodded slowly. "I'll bear that in mind in case he comes looking for a harbor."

Even the woman's back managed to convey indignation as she took long strides into the darkness.

Fitzwilliam motioned to one of the uniformed officers, gave him instructions and returned his attention to the two bodies.

Moments later, the constable returned, pointing towards one of the high-rise buildings. "Residents' names'r listed inside, just beside the lift. He's on the twelfth floor."

Fitzwilliam thanked the man and went inside.

In response to his ring, the door cracked open. The inspector could see a bald scalp and spectacles precariously perched on a nose. "Mr. Annulewicz?" Fitzwilliam held his badge up to the door. "Metro Police. Might I come in?"

The door shut and a chain lock rattled. The door opened again and Fitzwilliam entered a small living room in which two women sat on a couch. He guessed one was Mrs. Annulewicz. The other was Miss Fuchs. He dipped his head in recognition and introduced himself to the others.

Annulewicz shrugged in response to Fitzwilliam's question. "Haven't seen him, Inspector. What's he done that would have Scotland Yard at my door?"

"Police matter," Fitzwilliam said, willing for the moment to perpetuate the charade that they didn't know. "We'd like to talk to him."

Annulewicz turned to the German woman. "Gurt, d'know our old mate Langford Reilly was in town?"

She shook her head. "Not until this gentleman asked me if I had seen him."

"I see," Fitzwilliam said, as indeed he did. "And when was the last time you were in the U.K., Miss Fuchs?"

She shook her head again. "I am unable to remember exactly."

"Ten years or so ago, Miss Fuchs, according to immigration records. I suppose you were suddenly overcome with nostalgia."

"It had been too long," she said.

"I don't suppose either of you have any idea what happened right outside your window, down there on the street?"

"We heard a noise and went downstairs," Annulewicz said. "I came right back up as soon as I saw someone had been hurt. But the police came before I could place a call."

Fitzwilliam reached into a coat pocket and produced a pair of business cards. "I won't bother you further, particularly since it's been so long since the two of you have seen each other. But if you hear from Mr. Reilly, ring me up."

They were both nodding as he left.

Amazing how chummy the two of them were, Fuchs and Annulewicz, Fitzwilliam thought bitterly. Truly amazing since, according to the information he had from the CIA, the two had never met.

8

London, South Dock

Lang went down the steps of the Lambeth North Underground Station at a pace unlikely to invite attention. He took the first train. There were few passengers, probably because it was after working hours in what was largely a residential neighborhood. He rode for a few minutes before checking the multicolored diagram of the Underground posted in each car. Brown, Bakerloo Line. Three or four stops and he'd be at Piccadilly Circus, only a few blocks from where Mike Jenson, Dealer in Curios, Antiquities, Etcetera had been murdered only . . . when? Had it been only yesterday?

Lang figured Piccadilly was as good a location as any, better than some. Dinner and theater crowds would provide protective anonymity. And maybe, just maybe, he would get lucky. Maybe an old acquaintance would still be there, one that he doubted was in his service file.

The train shuddered to a stop. A teenaged couple boarded, he with purple hair and an intricate tattoo of a dragon writhing beneath his tank top, she with green spikes of hair along her scalp like the dorsal ridge of a dinosaur. Her gender was ascertainable only by breasts pressing brown nipples against a T-shirt that had been laundered into gossamer. Both kids dripped rings and pendants from various pierced body parts.

And Lang thought the girl at Ansley Galleries had been weird.

He might as well have been invisible. The two sat at the far end of the coach, oblivious to anything but themselves. How they managed what the tabloids call intimate embraces without entangling body jewelry was a mystery.

The faces of the only other passengers, two middle-aged women without wedding rings, managed to express disapproval, curiosity and envy all at once.

Lang was watching what was about to become what he termed *coitus terminus subterra interruptus*—having sex interrupted by a subway stop—as he reviewed the information he had gained. The translation of the Templar papers indicated that area of France, the Languedoc, might be the place he needed to search. Pegasus's business in a largely rural part of Burgundy was hardly coincidental.

Pegasus.

Did a modern, multibillion dollar corporation take its name from the symbol of a monastic order that had been officially disbanded seven hundred years ago, or was it an incarnation of the Templars themselves? Pietro had described the Templar organization in terms that also fit Pegasus: receiving a shitload of money from the pope. Could a secret two millennia old account for everything, both in

Pietro's time and Lang's, a secret whose key lay in a copy of a religious painting by a minor artist?

The questions were enough to make his head hurt.

Hand in hand, the adoring punkers got off at Westminster. The two spinsters looked as though they were thankful to have survived a particularly nasty epidemic.

Even with the Templar papers, as Lang mentally referred to them, he knew way too little. He had learned during his stay with the Agency, old aphorisms notwithstanding, what you didn't know was anything but benign. Classic example was Kennedy's decision to withhold air support, uncommunicated until troops were already on the beaches of the Bay of Pigs. Bet you couldn't find a veteran of that fiasco who believed what you didn't know couldn't hurt you.

EDFA, the Agency's acronym for "Educate yourself as to the problem, Decide upon the desired result, Formulate the plan most likely to achieve that result, Act."

Sure. Nothing is impossible for he who doesn't have to do it.

Lang had only part of the information he needed. He knew that an organization, possibly of historic origin, certainly of vast economic power, wanted him dead, dead like Jeff and Janet. The desired result was to make the bastards wish they had never heard of Lang Reilly: a payback of cosmic proportions.

And Lang still hadn't done the hard part, formulating a plan. Time to go back to the "educate" stage and start over. Without understanding Pegasus, he would never be able to put a hurt on it. To learn if Pegasus really was somehow connected to the Templars.

Pretty heavy stuff.

Lang had never been particularly religious, probably because as a child he had been dragged out of bed every Sunday morning and forced to spend an hour on the most

uncomfortable pew that ever existed in the entire Episco-
pal Church. Admittedly, he was a little old still to be re-
belling. Even in the hours spent in involuntary worship, he
didn't remember ever hearing about Jesus being married,
let alone surviving the crucifixion like that Lobineau guy
Dr. Wolffe mentioned in one of his footnotes.

Medieval religious orders in the twenty-first century?
Pretty bogus.

Education.

So far, more questions than answers.

Like, how had They known to come to Jacob's flat? Lang
was all but positive he hadn't been followed to the Temple
Bar or from Oxford. But if not followed, how? What was it
Sherlock Holmes said? Something like, "If you eliminate all
possible solutions, only the impossible remains." Impossible someone had discovered his relationship with Jacob
through his service records. Impossible.

Therefore the answer?

Lang had been thinking along those lines already when
he decided to renew another old acquaintance, one who
wouldn't be in any service file.

Lang checked his watch as he climbed up the steps to
street level. Quarter after nine, just after four in Atlanta.
When he had called the office from Rome, Sara had referred to Chen, the client Lang had called from the pay
phone downstairs in his building. With the cops in the office, she hadn't been able to expressly mention the pay
phone but that would have been the only reason to name
a client from four or five years ago.

From a public phone in the station, he made a collect
call, a somewhat easier job than it would have been
through an Italian-speaking operator. He assumed there
was a tap on the office phone, so he made the call brief.

"Sara, remember Mr. Chen?" he asked. And hung up.

If they could trace that, technology had really improved

more than he thought. Star-69, of course, didn't work with international calls. By the time computer records of calls to his office could be searched, he could go around the world on a very slow boat.

He switched phones and used Herr Schneller's Visa card to charge the call. Happily, Gurt hadn't terminated his credit quite yet. Lang was hoping he remembered the right phone number in the office building, that he wasn't calling the deli across the lobby.

"Lang?"

Sara's voice could have been an angel's, he was so happy to hear it.

"It's me. You okay?"

"Fine now. I thought that detective was going to bring his toothbrush and move into the office, much time as he spent there. What about you? I understand you've been accused of a murder in London as well as the one here."

"To paraphrase Mark Twain, the reports are much exaggerated. Listen, I can't talk long. Call the priest, ask him to stand by tonight. I need to speak with him."

"You mean Father . . ."

"No names!" Lang almost shouted with a harshness he regretted. He could imagine Echelon's programming listening for names of his current friends. Unlikely but possible. "This call is being transmitted by satellite. It isn't secure."

Sara was willing to take his word for it. "I'll alert him. And Lang . . . I know you didn't kill anybody."

Lang had a vision of two bodies lying in the street, one with two bullets he had fired. "Thanks, Sara. It'll all work out."

Lang hoped he sounded more confident than he felt.

CHAPTER FOUR

1

London, Piccadilly
1740 hours

Cloaked in Piccadilly's evening crowd, Lang stopped to look at window displays every few feet. He didn't see any faces reflected more than once. He circled the block delineated by Regent Street and Jermyn Street twice, pausing to examine an equestrian stature of William of Orange apparently in the dress of a Roman emperor. Despite his problems, Lang smiled. The king in drag. Before the royal scandals of the late nineties—Di, Fergie, the lot—the English took their monarchs way too seriously.

Lang still recognized no faces from a few minutes earlier.

He checked his watch and hurried along like a man suddenly realizing his wife is waiting at dinner or the theater. At 47 Jermyn, he stopped at an unmarked door. A column of names and bell buttons were to the left next to the rusted grille of a speaker. Lang had to squint to see the names. He was in luck; she was still here.

When he pressed a button, a woman's voice, tinny over the wire but Cockney accent nevertheless clear, replied, " 'Oo's there?"

Lang leaned close to the speaker, both not wanting to be overheard by people on the street but to be sure to be understood by the voice at the other end. "Tell Nellie an old friend, the one who looked but didn't touch."

The speaker clicked off.

Nellie O'Dwyer, formerly Neleska Dwvorsik, had been the madam of one of London's more exclusive call-girl rings since before Lang had known her. Although prostitution was technically illegal, the Brits were smart enough not to waste time and money battling a business no government had ever completely suppressed. As long as Nellie's girls caused no complaints, she was left alone to operate her "escort" service.

Once safely out of some East European workers' paradise, a significant number of defectors' first wish was a woman. Whisky came in a distant second. A relaxed and happy man was a lot easier to debrief than one tense and resentful. When Lang had first been stationed in London, it had fallen his lot as low man on the pole to find a regular source to satisfy the need. The item was creatively entered under "counseling" in the expense accounts that were subject to Congressional oversight.

It was unlikely this service to his country appeared in Lang's service jacket. If somebody had his file, he doubted they would see Nellie's name in it.

As one formerly accustomed to the machinations of Marxist-Leninist states, Nellie had expected Lang to demand a percentage, or at least a sample of the goods. It didn't take a genius to see the downside of being a partner—or a customer—of a brothel keeper. Not smart when employed by a nation with Ozzie and Harriet morality.

Instead, Lang had thanked Nellie for what she had perceived as generosity, even if it would have been at her girls' expense. "I'll just look and not touch," he had said.

The phrase had become a joke in more languages than Lang cared to count, as scantily-clad women repeated it in accented English every time he came to pick up a "date" for the Agency's most recent acquisition.

Nellie still thought it was funny. Her voice squealed with an enthusiasm little diminished by the age of the electronics. "Lang! You have come back to your Nellie!" There was a buzz and the bolt clicked back. Lang swung the door open as Nellie's voice commanded, "You come up here right this minute!"

He could only hope Nellie and her girls were too busy to pay attention to the news on the telly, or at least not enough to have seen him on it. As he climbed the wooden stairs, his fingers closed around the Beretta still in his belt.

What if Pegasus had learned about Jacob through some means other than his records? Would they also know about Nellie? Lang glanced back down the stairs at the only escape route. Once he stepped into Nellie's parlor, even that would be closed.

If They were waiting for him . . .

2

London, South Dock

By the time Jacob and Gurt exited the elevator of his apartment building, blue lights were swirling through the night. Without exchanging a word, they shoved through the growing circle of people. Four uniformed constables, their faces towards the crowd, kept the inquisitive at a distance from where two men in suits were kneeling beside two bodies on the sidewalk. A third was writing in a notebook as an elderly woman spoke.

Gurt strained to hear. ". . . One man ran away . . . too dark . . . looked out the window soon's I rang up the police."

Gurt turned her attention to the two forms sprawled on the pavement. The closest to her was far too bulky to be Lang. The other was facedown. Damning the morbidly curious who were blocking her view, she pushed to one side.

"Look 'ere . . ." a man growled over his shoulder. He turned, took in her size and expression, and got out of her way without regard to how many of his fellow spectators had to be jostled.

The taste of blood surprised Gurt. She had no idea how hard she had been biting her lip. She had had no chance to see the bodies before that policeman had accosted her, sending her back to Jacob's apartment before he could see how upset she was. She had been in torment until she could get back outside, see for herself. Damn Lang Reilly! Leaving her without so much as a good-bye when he obviously needed help. Serve him right if that were him there. She lifted her eyes for an instant. No, she didn't really mean that. *Please don't let that body be his.*

"Not him," Jacob whispered at her elbow, startling her. She hadn't realized he had followed in the wake she had left in the crowd like a passing ship. "Neither one of 'em."

"How can you be sure?" she asked quietly.

"Those are the pair that came to my flat looking for him, the ones you doubt were the police. Looks like they caught up with him, after all."

Gurt had not been aware she had been holding her breath. "Gott sei danke!" she muttered in an uncharacteristic lapse into German.

She was equally thankful she was not viewing the mortal remains of Langford Reilly and shocked at the thought he could have killed anybody. Lang had taken the Agency's training in self-defense, even learned to kill, but he definitely was not the lethal type. He was a wiseass, not an assassin.

"We need to find him," she said, turning away from the corpses. "Any ideas?"

Jacob was patting his pockets, no doubt searching for the pipe he had left in his apartment. "No more than I had a few minutes ago. I'm afraid."

Gurt closed her eyes, a gesture several bystanders mistook for a horrified reaction to Americanlike violence on the streets. Shit. She had left her cigarettes in her purse in Jacob's flat. If ever she could have used a Marlboro . . .

3

London, Piccadilly

The door at the top of Nellie's stairs opened into what could have been the lobby of a tourist-class hotel: unmatched chairs scattered in view of a cheap television set, a certain worn quality to the few end tables, magazines carelessly tossed about. The girls were the ones who relaxed here. Customers rarely saw the room.

Had the place been done in antiques, the furniture still wouldn't have gotten Lang's first attention. Young women, most in their teens or early twenties, lounged. Every skin color the world had to offer was on display with a minimum of cover. Most wore short pajamas or bra and panties. A few were done up in more exotic garb such as embroidered kimonos or shifts in vibrant African colors. Nellie's inventory reflected the ethnic diversity London embraced.

None of them gave Lang more than a bored glance. Nothing like being ignored by a roomful of partially dressed women to shrink the old ego.

Nellie emerged from a hallway opposite from him, squinting at Herr Schneller's moustache and jowls. They inspected each other as warily as a couple of dogs meeting on the street. Lang was surprised she looked pretty much the same as he remembered. Not a thread of silver streaked the blue-black hair that seemed to sparkle with green and amber like a crow's wing in the sun. Her face was smooth, devoid of the little wrinkles years try to sneak by. Her chin was sharp, unblunted by the wattles of age. Her only concession to the passage of time was a dress that reached her knees, instead of the microskirts Lang remembered. Even so, her calves were slender, well-turned and without the mapping of varicose veins.

Her important parts had defied gravity as well as old age.

Lang took her gently in his arms and planted a wet one on her cheek. "You're still a young girl, Nellie."

She displayed teeth that must have put at least one orthodontist's kids through university. "You compliment both me and my unbelievably expensive plastic surgeon."

There was still a trace of the Balkans in her voice. She cocked her head, leaned back and regarded him like a specimen in a jar. "But you . . . you don't look the same."

"Not all of us age as well as you."

Her rich, thick hair had always been her best feature— or at least of those Lang could see. She shook her head, the silky strands caressing her shoulders. "That's not what I mean, luv."

Lang touched the moustache and padded cheeks. "Let's just say you're the only person in London I want to recognize me."

A smile twitched the corners of a sensuous mouth. "I thought you had left your position with . . ."

He let her go and managed to drag his eyes off her long enough to make sure there wasn't anybody there who didn't belong. A little late. If Pegasus had been waiting for him, he'd be dead. He'd been far too interested in the scenery to notice potential danger. Death by carnal desire.

Lang stepped back and shut the door. "I did. It's the cops I'm dodging."

She treated him to those teeth again. "The police, is it, luv? You've come to the right place."

"That's what I hoped you'd say."

A second look around the room and he didn't see any familiar faces, faces from the past. Attrition was fierce in Nellie's line of work.

"I'd like to spend the night," Lang said. "Make a telephone call if I could."

She raised manicured eyebrows. "Make a call and spend the night, would you?" She swept a hand in an arc. "Are my girls so ugly you need to call in talent?"

Lang grinned sheepishly. "No, no. I need to speak with a friend in the States, a priest, actually."

Nellie laughed, a blunt coughing sound. "A priest? We know about priests, what they do. No wonder you never wanted any of my girls."

She said it loud enough to get the attention of several of the young women nearby. If he hadn't been so occupied with Pegasus, Lang might have blushed.

She took him by the hand to lead him into the hall she had come out of. It was lined with doors like a corridor in a hotel, except there were no numbers. They stopped in front of one while Nellie fished around in her blouse. Lang was about to make the obvious crude comment when she produced a key and unlocked the door.

"Sue Lee's room," she explained. "She's on the coast of Spain with a client."

She wrinkled her nose at a faint odor Lang couldn't identify. "Been cooking in here on her wok. Vietnamese, Japanese, something like that. You'll get used to the smell."

She ushered him inside. "Sure you don't want company, luv?"

The room looked like one in a girls' dorm. A vanity with light-studded mirror was built into one wall. A plain wooden chair, a metal chest of drawers and a single bed completed the furnishings. It wasn't exactly the place Lang would have imagined a high-price hooker spending her off time.

Nellie had been following his appraising look around. "The girls don't entertain in their rooms. The traffic would make it hard for the coppers to look the other way. They use hotel rooms or have their own flats. She pointed to a door on the other side of the vanity. "The loo. Connects with the next room. Mind that unless you want a surprise. Help yourself to the telephone."

"Thanks."

She started to close the door and stopped. "Sure there's nothing I can get you?"

Lang smiled. "Thanks, but no."

She looked at him as though seeing him for the first time. "On the run from the law, bet you haven't eaten. Some of the girls always get fish and chips, Chinese, some sort of take-away. No trouble to get something for you."

The mention of food reminded him he hadn't eaten since . . . since Rachel's gut-cramping Indian fare the night before. He must have fully recovered because he was suddenly hungry enough to risk another had it been available. Fortunately, it wasn't.

"You talked me into it," he said, pulling some bills out of his pocket. "Surprise me."

Finally alone, Lang reached for the telephone, one of those cutesy ivory-and-gold ones that is supposed to look like an antique. He picked it up, happy to hear a very contemporary dial tone. He dialled 00, international, 1 for North America, and 404, one of Atlanta's area codes, and then information. Never before had he paid particular notice to the toneless voice of the computerized information service. It had an American accent.

After a series of astral clicks and whirs, a familiar voice was on the line, words so clear they might have been spoken from across the room rather than across the Atlantic. "Lang?"

"It's me, Francis, your favorite heretic."

Francis's chuckle was audible an ocean away. "Glad to hear from you, although I've been reading some pretty disturbing things in the local fish-wrapper."

Lang was thankful the phone's cord extended to the bed. He stretched out. This was going to take awhile. *"Fama volat,* Frances, rumor travels fast. Besides, you know the media: accused on page one-A, acquitted somewhere in the obituaries."

"I suppose," the priest said, a rueful note clearly detectable. "They publish accusations but not the rebuttal."

"If it bleeds, it leads," Lang said. "Gotta pump the ratings for the six o'clock news and sell advertising for the paper."

"Somehow, I don't think you had your secretary have me wait for your call just so you could tell me you didn't do it."

Lang took a deep breath and exhaled. "No, you're right as usual."

"You've recognized your feet are set upon the road to hell and you want me to hear your confession."

Even the fatigue that was beginning to fog Lang's mind couldn't suppress a chuckle. "You don't have enough time left on this earth to hear my full confession."

"Then it's my pastoral skill and brilliant intellect you seek."

"Don't you guys take some sort of vow of humility? But, yeah, sort of. First, listen to what I have to tell you. Pay attention. There'll be a test later."

It took Lang the better part of twenty minutes to explain. He only paused to answer an occasional question and thank the young woman who brought him chopsticks, a box of steaming rice and another box of food, the contents of which he tried not to speculate about.

Lang finished his meal and story about the same time.

"Templars?" Francis asked skeptically. "Over a billion dollars a year from the Vatican?"

Lang was licking his fingers, more an effort to remove the inevitable grease than because he had enjoyed the meal. "I don't suppose you know anything about that?"

"The money from the Vatican? Not likely that sort of thing would be shared with a lowly parish priest. I know a little about the Templars and this area of France, the . . ."

"Languedoc."

"The Languedoc and the castle this monk Pietro mentions, Blanchefort. Some people think the holy grail is hidden somewhere in that area."

Lang forgot greasy fingers. "Holy grail? Like, the cup Jesus used at the Last Supper?"

"That's what it was to Richard Wagner and Steven Spielberg. Remember the opera and the Indiana Jones movie? It was a cup in Arthurian legend, too. But it could be anything. The earliest legends describe it as a stone with mystical properties and some scholars think it relates to the ark of the Covenant which disappeared from Jerusalem a thousand years before Christ. Hitler thought it was the lance of Longinus, the spear that pierced Christ's side. No reason it couldn't be the 'vessel' your friend Pietro found in the Gnostic document."

"But you don't think such a thing exists?" Lang asked.

Francis was just warming up. He always saved the best part of his arguments for last. "I don't know the Church's position on the subject, guess they haven't had to address the matter in a few hundred years. Me, I say, why not? What

I do know, there was a parish priest in the area we're talking about, a little town called, called Rennes-le-Château, I
think. I'm fairly sure the man's name was Saunière and he
lived around the middle, last part of the nineteenth century."

"You remember all this like you do your catechism? I
mean, that's remarkable you could recall all that along
with all the mumbo-jumbo you have to memorize."

"I'll ignore that, although it might calm your heathen
breast to know I actually went to the place a couple of
year ago, was in France as part of an international Church
council and I traveled around for a couple of days until I
could get the cheap airfare home. Saunière was pretty
much a tourist industry. If you can keep still, I'll tell you
why."

"I'm quieted, I'm quieted."

"He, Saunière, was a poor priest in a poor parish. He
was doing some minor restoration work in the church
building himself because they couldn't afford professional
help. Anyway, part of the altar came loose. Inside was a
sheaf of old parchments. He seemed excited, showed
them around but wouldn't let anyone read them. Not that
the locals could have; they were supposedly in Latin or
Hebrew or something. Maybe the Gnostic document that
Templar was talking about.

"Almost immediately his little parish had funds to repair
the church, build a hotel-size guest house, more money
than anyone ever thought was in the whole Languedoc. A
steady procession of cardinals began visiting. We're talking
about the ecclesiastical equivalent of Podunk, a place
those cardinals would never have heard of a year earlier.
Saunière's personal lifestyle crossed the poverty line like a
rocket on the way up, too. New vestments, housekeeper,
wine cellar. All of those things a true prince of the church
might have."

"Like a choice of little boys or concubines?" Lang couldn't help it. Francis was too easy a target for the church's peccadillos.

"Any more vulgarities from infidels and I'm gonna hang up and say my rosary. Anyway, Saunière never revealed the source of his sudden wealth. He died under mysterious circumstances as did his housekeeper."

"Don't tell me," Lang said, "let me guess: He died in some sort of accident involving fire."

He could tell Francis was puzzled. "Actually, he drowned when a small boat turned over. Nobody ever knew what he was doing in the middle of a river. Why?"

"Pietro mentioned the four ancient elements of fire, wind, water and earth. Go on."

"The locals speculate the parchments were some sort of treasure map, but they were never found. Once he died, both money and church dignitaries were never seen again in the area."

Lang stretched, fighting the urge to simply go to sleep. "So the man got lucky, found a buried treasure or the altar was full of winning lottery tickets. What does that tell me about the Templars?"

Lang could barely hear Francis's throaty chuckle. "Oh ye of little faith! The story goes on. In the sixties, the nineteen sixties, that is, somebody published a book speculating that Saunière had found treasure belonging to the Templars. They were active in that part of the Languedoc and this castle Pietro describes is one of theirs. Saunière could well have found some of the immense wealth those dead white boys left when they had to make a fast getaway."

"Wealth? Treasure?" Lang asked. "Until I read that Oxford fellow's translation, I had always thought the Templars were a monastic order, sworn to poverty, chastity and other unpleasantness."

"They were, at least initially. They went to the Holy Land

to protect pilgrims from the Moslems, joined in the Crusades and all that. Order was founded in the early eleven-hundreds, I think. Like other monks, they took a vow of poverty. Things changed in the next two hundred years. The Order acquired wealth, I mean a lot of it. Nobody really knows how or from where.

"A number of Europe's kings noticed these fighting monks had castles, lands, even their own ships. By the time the last Christian outpost in Palestine fell and the Templars all returned to Europe, they were pretty much a nation unto themselves. A lot of rulers, Philip of France, the pope, were both covetous and a little fearful.

"In 1307, Philip had his sheriffs seize Templar castles in France and imprison the knights. The pope, Clement V, knew which side of his bread had the butter on it. Philip was the most powerful monarch in Europe and Clement wanted to make sure he stayed on the right side of him. So he issued a bull condemning the Templars on a number of trumped-up charges.

"As you can imagine, most of the other kings and emperors were eager to follow suit, since the Order's holdings would become theirs. A number of the brothers were rounded up and tortured until they confessed to all sorts of things, homosexuality to blasphemy. Eventually, those who had been caught were burned at the stake, at least in France. Edward of England and Henry of Germany weren't into confessions produced by torture and the Templars' holdings there weren't as rich as in France.

"A number of brothers escaped by disappearing before Philip's order, no doubt had advance warning. Anyway, their private fleet and whatever treasure they had were never found."

Lang was quiet a moment, thinking. "And people think they left that treasure around the Languedoc?"

"People who really are into the subject are all over the

board. Some think the escaped Templars made it to Scotland where the king, Robert the Bruce, was already excommunicated and therefore not on particularly good terms with Clement. Others think they took their treasure with them and sailed to an island off what's now Nova Scotia. Even others don't believe there ever was a treasure as such, that the Templars' riches were their real estate holdings."

"And what do you think?"

There was a sigh on Francis's end of the line. "I've never really had an opinion. The Templars are an interesting bit of history as far as I'm concerned, but no more than that. As for their treasure, I think you could make a better investment in time and money by buying one of those reproductions of a map to the place Captain Kidd supposedly hid his treasure on Long Island Sound."

"At least Captain Kidd isn't killing people."

"And the Templars are just as dead, although the Masons and Rosicrucians claim some relationship with the Order. They both have secrets supposedly guarded by members' lives."

Lang snorted in derision. "I don't think I'm up against guys in funny hats or nutcases upset about Prozac and I haven't read about throats slit at your neighborhood Masonic Temple. No, these Pegasus guys are serious. They very much have something they're willing to kill to keep to themselves. I'd bet it has something to do with the money from the Vatican. And that just might be related somehow to this place in France where this guy . . ."

"Saunière."

"Saunière. Where Saunière hit the local lotto."

"Maybe," Francis agreed, "but what about the picture, the shepherds? That's supposed to be in Arcadia, Greece, not France." He paused for a moment. "But then, Arcadia's also used in poetry as a synonym for any place of pastoral beauty and peace. Could be metaphoric rather than geographic."

Lang knew from the intelligence business that only in fiction do all the pieces of a puzzle fit. There was almost always some bit of information that turned out to be unrelated to the problem at hand, perhaps to another, perhaps useless. But here? The Poussin had tripped whatever wire was set to guard a secret Pegasus wanted to protect.

"Could be anywhere," Lang agreed, "but that Templar, Pietro, and what you're telling me now both point to the Languedoc. I'm not sure how the painting fits in, although it must have some connection. Otherwise, Pegasus wouldn't kill to prevent anyone from understanding whatever the hell it means."

Francis grunted affirmatively. "Yeah, but what?"

"Think maybe it has something to do with the Gnostic heresy, Joseph of Arimathea being Jesus's brother and Mary Magdalene His wife?"

"That's two questions," Francis said. "First, the Scriptures, at least the ones the Church recognizes as gospels, are silent about Jesus's brothers and sisters. Since Jews of biblical times tended to have large families, it's more likely than not that He had siblings. There's always been speculation about a wife. Hebrew law required young men, particularly a rabbi as Jesus must have been, to marry. Some scholars speculate the wedding in Cana, the one where He turned water into wine, to be his own. Problem with siblings and a spouse is that they raise troubling questions about lateral and direct descendants, questions the Church had rather not deal with. That professor Wolffe who did the translation is correct about the Merovingian dynasty who ruled that area of France for a century or two after the collapse of Rome. They claimed to be descendants of Christ, no small problem for the papacy back then.

"The Gnostics were a group of heretics who believed

God created Christ mortal, that after His death, His spirit, not his body, ascended into heaven, contrary to Jewish Messianic prophecy. No physical resurrection, no Messiah. The Gnostic view had been specifically rejected by the Council of Nicea along with proposed gospels supporting it, hence the heresy in proclaiming the doctrine."

Lang nodded to the priest on the other side of the ocean as he struggled against weariness to understand what he was hearing. His jaws stretched in a monumental yawn. "Interesting church history, but I don't see how it fits whatever the painting portrays. If it means anything at all. Pegasus seems to think it does. Whatever. I intend to solve the puzzle of the picture, or at least find out what Pegasus is trying to protect. Only way to get even for what they did."

There was an audible sigh, the sound of disapproval. "Lang, revenge can backfire. I wish you'd let the police handle it."

"Francis, you dream," Lang snapped back. "The Paris police are clueless. I want results, not a murder case gone cold. You seem to forget those people, Pegasus, tried to kill me in Atlanta and I'm fairly certain it wasn't friendly conversation they wanted this evening. And let's not forget they managed to get me accused of a couple or murders. I'd say I owe 'em big time."

"You know you should give yourself up to the authorities before you have to kill someone else, before anyone else dies. God will see you through."

"Rumor has it He helps those who help themselves, Padre."

"How about advice from a friend, forget the Padre business?"

"I am, as they say, all ears."

"Illigitimi non carborundum."

"Francis, you can do better than some sort of liberated Latin for 'don't let the bastards wear you down.' "

"Then watch your ass."

Despite his problems, Lang was grinning when he hung up the phone. He was waging a losing battle with sleep but found enough reserves to take the Polaroid of the painting from his wallet. Crumpled from wear, the figures were still as enigmatic as the Latin inscription.

He yawned again, wondering when he might be sleeping in his own bed again. The thought of home triggered a seemingly unrelated thought. He wanted to sit out on his balcony with his morning coffee, looking out over the city and reading the paper.

The paper.

Lang routinely worked a syndicated puzzle where letters were scrambled. If solved, a familiar phrase appeared. What if the Latin inscription were like the puzzle in the paper, an anagram in which a seemingly superfluous word supplied letters necessary for the message?

ETINARCADIAEGOSUM.

ET IN ARCADIA EGO (SUM).

His exhausted body and mind protested as he got up from the bed to rummage through the chest of drawers until he found a sales receipt from Harrods. Further search located the stub of an eyebrow pencil on the vanity. Using the blank back of the sales slip, he began rearranging letters. He started with the one the shepherd's finger was touching, so that each version began with the letter A.

Twenty minutes later, Lang was staring at what he had written, sleep forgotten. Could he be reading this correctly? His Latin was good enough for competitive aphorisms but he had to be sure he had this right.

He snatched the door open so fast he startled a young woman walking the hall in a fire-engine-red teddy.

"Where can I find Nellie?" he asked as if the world depended on the answer.

Recovering with the aplomb demanded by her profession, she pointed, speaking with an accent Lang didn't recognize. "The office, end of the hall."

Nellie's face had an unhealthy pallor, a reflection of the blue of the computer screen inches from her eyes. The world's latest technology was now in the service of its oldest profession.

She swiveled around, the casters on her chair squeaking. "Change your mind about . . . Bloody hell! Look like you seen a ghost, you do."

Lang guessed the office had previously been a closet. There wasn't room for both of them, so he stood in the doorway. "In a way, I suppose I have. I've got a really strange request."

She gave him a lopsided smile, a conspiratorial nod and said, "Strange requests are part of the business, luv. Leather, chains?"

"Even stranger. Any place you could put your hands on a Latin-English dictionary this time of night?"

She was shocked, quite possibly for the first time in her professional career. "Latin? I'm running a university now, am I?" She thought for a moment. "There's a bookstore down by the university, though it's not likely open this hour."

Lang was too excited to wait. If he was right . . . The prospect overcame his better judgment. "I'll go see. Keep the room open for me."

She put a restraining hand on his arm. "Don't bother, luv. I've got a girl visiting a customer in Bloomsbury. She'll ring in shortly 'n' I'll have her pop over to Museum Street. No need you riskin' bumpin' into the law, now is there?"

Museum Street was a collection of cafes and small shops selling old books and prints. Many of them kept hours as eclectic as their inventory.

"Thanks."

An hour later, Lang put down a tattered paperback

Latin-English dictionary, shocked to discover he had been right. The painting was an enigma no more, although it was going to take an Olympic-quality broad jump of faith to believe its message. But Pegasus sure as hell did. That was why they were willing to kill.

Pietro's narrative and the enigmatic inscription said the same thing, as unbelievable as it might be. Now all Lang had to do was evade the cops and some very nasty people long enough to locate a specific spot among thousands of square miles and verify the tale of a monk dead seven hundred years.

He was on his way to France.

THE TEMPLARS:
THE END OF AN ORDER

An Account by Pietro of Sicily
Translation from the medieval Latin by Nigel Wolffe, Ph.D.

5

And so did the days fly by on the wings of falcons. Such time as I could spare from assisting the cellarer as his seneschal, doing sums on the abacus and making inventory of such produce as the Temple's serfs produced.[1] Such time as I could, I stole from my labours to spend in the library, learning more about the Gnostics and their pernicious apostasy, documents so vile that at least one was secreted not in the library but in a hollow column. Its existence was revealed to only a few brothers. How I wish I had not been one of them! I was not amused by the irreverence shown the Holy Gospels as much as I was curious as to the contents of the vessel mentioned in those ancient volumes. I also was curious as to the reason the Holy See would send what amounted to tribute to a single Temple whose only duty was to guard Serres and Rennes, two simple villages which appeared to apprehend no danger.

Thus did the Gnostic documents tempt me as the serpent did Eve, induce me to seek knowledge of that better left in obscurity.

One sin begot another and I began to journey far from the Temple, my peregrinations taking me even beyond the boundaries of the Temple's fiefdom and along the River Sals and among the hills and mountains, particularly the white mountain called Cardou. I chose this path because it was the one most similar to the one described in the writings of the heretics as being the ancient Roman road and the one taken by Joseph of Arimathea and Mary Magdalene when they came into these parts.[2] I compounded these derelictions of my duties to my brethren and to God by wantonly lying to my superiors, falsely testifying that I was but walking the metes and bounds of the Temple's estates. Much more the sin because I was seeking forbidden knowledge.

Directions could not be had from the villeins thereabout, for they spoke in a dialect I could not comprehend. Had they been conversant in Frankish or Latin, it is improbable they could have answered the queries that filled my head. Caked as they were with the dirt in which they lived, reeking of sweat and their own excrement, I found it difficult to remember that they, too, were children of God. Even more uncomfortable was the knowledge that I had come from stock such as these. Clean clothes, meat each day and a fresh bed at night had engendered the sin of pride which had attached itself to my soul like a lamprey upon some hapless fish.

It was from one of these journeys I was returning one day in October. The earth was still dust, for winter's rains had not yet begun. The orchards were ablaze both with ripening fruit and autumnal foliage and the vines were no more than twisted twigs, having already been harvested and pruned. A cold wind blew from the west, the breath of the new snow I could see on those mountains known as Pyrenees at which the Languedoc ends and the Iberian country of Catalonia begins. I wondered at that time why the knights did not free the lands on the other side of those mountains from the heathen.[3]

On the slope of the mountain called Cardou, I paused for a moment to give thanks to God for a spectacle so rich and to wonder at the majesty that created it in six days' time. I had barely said my "Amen" when a hare, large and fat no doubt from a summer of repasts at the expense of the Brothers' gardens, ran nearly over my feet. It stopped a short distance upwards and away and looked at me with an insolent eye.

The animal robbed me of all thoughts of Him who made us both. Instead, I remembered the summer months which had passed without the spicy flesh I saw before me. I raised my staff and moved forward with caution.

My second step did not stop with what I thought to be firmament beneath wild berry bushes. Instead, I had stepped into a void to the extent that I fell forward. When I stood, reaching for the staff I had dropped, I observed that the bushes obscured an opening in the earth much larger than that into which I had stumbled.

I was facing no mere animal burrow but a cave or shaft in the stone white as the distant snow, a hole so cleverly concealed that, had I not fallen, I would have walked past without notice. Without moving from where I stood, the marks of stonecutters were visible upon the walls. This was, then, no natural crevice or fault in the mountain but one brought about by the hand of man.

Had I but turned and sought explanation of my discovery, I would go to the fate that awaits me in peace. As it is, Satan himself fueled the curiosity that led me forward.

From the light outside, I could see I was in a chamber, a cave, perhaps, crudely enlarged. Darkness prohibited my taking its exact measure, but I could stand upright and my extended arms touched neither side nor ceiling.

In the dimness, I perceived an object in the middle of the rough floor, a block of stone of about the size of a bound manuscript.[4] On this stone were carvings, letters I scarcely could make out which appeared to be of Hebrew characters, perhaps Aramaic, and Latin. I let my fingers explore since there was insufficient light to see clearly.

Could this be the vessel spoken of in the Gnostic heresies? The stone was of a texture like the white of the Languedoc, so it likely had been carved where I found it,[5] a more believable occurrence than transporting such a heavy object from the Holy Land. Without reading the inscriptions, I would not know and I was filled with a lust for that knowledge no less carnal than that which drives a man to seek a harlot.

I needed light by which I could probe the mystery of what I had found. The Temple was but a quarter of an hour away and could be seen from the mouth of the cavern. The light of a single taper would assuage a hunger for knowledge more acute than any my belly had ever felt for victuals.

I ran as though hell itself were behind me, as indeed it turned out to be. I dashed through the portcullis, hardly extending a greeting to those who guarded the entrance. I crossed the cloister at a run that drew the attention of all and did not care of the opprobrium such conduct would bring.[6] Such was my haste that I neglected to cleave to the walls of the arcade surrounding the garth, thereby demonstrating my humility by surrendering the wider path. Instead, I dashed along the middle, caring not which of my brethren were forced to give way. Inside, I suppressed the instinct to snatch the first lighted candle I saw from its sconce. Instead, I found one in my own cell and I stopped in the chapel to light it from those that eternally burn there. In such a haste was I, I nearly neglected to genuflect upon my departure.

My return to the cave was at a more sedate pace than my departure, for, should an errant breeze or a sudden move extinguish the candle, I would have to return to the Temple to light it anew.

Inside the cavern, I knelt beside the stone edifice and shielded my candle. The Latin inscription was of a dialect so archaic I found it difficult to decipher. The stone into which it was carved badly crumbled.

As I contemplated what was written, it was as if the cold hand of Satan squeezed my heart and I swooned into darkness. I know not how long I was oblivious to the physical world but when I awoke, I wished I had not. According to the label carved thereon, this stone contained that which even now I dare not mention. The fire to which I will shortly be consigned will not be hot enough to expurgate my soul of the perdition engraved upon that stone.

I was distraught, knowing not what to do. I must have been possessed by demons, for I first tried to lift the top from the stone. God's mercy made it far too well lodged to come free. Had I succeeded, I would surely have suffered a fate not unlike Lot's wife, for my eyes would have beheld that far more odious to God than the end of Sodom. My next thought was to share my find with those far wiser and more dedicated to God than I, who could surely explain what I had found. I now realize this was the same urge Satan fostered upon Eve to share her sin with Adam, spreading the disease of sinful knowledge like the plague.[7]

I know my mind was not my own, for I left the unused potion of the taper, an extravagance but one of the lesser sins I was to commit because of the curiosity the devil inspired in my soul.

As I gained sight of the Temple, I witnessed an outpouring of men on horseback, among them most of the knights, all clad as though for battle. Among them I recognized Guillaume de Poitiers, Tartus the German and others, being most of the Temple skilled in the arts of war. With them were asses, burdened as if for a long campaign. They were gone before I reached the walls, their memory being little but a cloud of choking dust.

I was surprised to find the portcullis raised and unmanned,

for if the brethren had ridden forth to vanquish the invaders feared by the Holy See, they most surely would have secured their own source of supply.

Inside the walls, all was confusion. Swine and oxen were unfettered, running freely through the cloister gardens as ducks and chickens flapped and scattered underfoot. I could not find Phillipe and presumed he had gone with his master. The cellarer was in the storage area off the refectory, musing over provisions strewn across the floor—wine barrels, their staves crushed—and the litter of haste predominant.

The cellarer was an old man, his love the order in which he kept his charge. His voice quavered as though broken by sorrow.

"They are gone," he said before I could inquire into the tumult and disorder. "A rider from Paris, from Brother de Molay himself.[8] All the brothers otherwise unoccupied were ordered to collect the holy relics, empty the treasury and take such provisions as they would need for seven days. For what purpose, I know not."

This was exceeding strange. Brothers "otherwise unoccupied" would pertain to those knights trained in the art of war, leaving those charged with the actual sustenance of this Temple. Were the departing knights sallying forth to battle, they would certainly not be ordered to subject the Temple's holy relics and treasury to the vagaries of conflict. So full of my virulent discovery was I that I held the whimsy of the Master of the Order to be of little consequence. I only pondered in whom, if at all, I should confide.

It was after Vespers that the wisdom of the Master became apparent. We were gathered in the chapter house, each seated on the stone benches that were carved into its walls, discussing what little business might be left upon the departure of so many of our number. I had in my robes ink, quill and paper, planning to return to my duties when our meeting concluded, though verily my mind had so succumbed to my discovery, I doubt I could have added two figures. I knew not to whom, if anyone, I should confide. The first chapter of the rules of the Order had been read,[9] when the door slammed open. Therein stood the king's bailie for Serres and Rennes. With him were a host of men-at-arms.

"What say you, good brother?" asked the cellarer. As the senior brother present, he was, under the rules of the Order, acting as abbot.

"I am no brother to you," the bailie said.

I knew not his name but seen him at the Temple before, his little swine-eyes peering from a face of corpulence as if he were a merchant about to offer a price for a bolt of cloth.

"What means this intrusion?" the cellarer asked.

The bailie motioned so that the various men-at-arms filled the room and blocked all exit therefrom, though in truth the only exit was into the store closet to which I have referred. "In the name of Philip, by Grace of God King of the French, I order you to stand forth, for you, all of you, are under arrest and all goods herein forfeit."

A murmur of protest ran its course before the cellarer said, "So it cannot be, for we are of the Church, not subject to the laws of God's servant Philip."

The bailie was undismayed. He let out a laugh like the bark of a dog, reading from a document that bore the royal seal, "You are accused by your king of such crimes as idolatry, blasphemy and such physical atrocities as fondling each other, kissing each other upon the fundament and other private places, of burning the bodies of deceased brothers to make powder of the ashes which you then mix in the food of younger brothers, of roasting infants and anointing idols with the fat therefrom, of celebrating hidden rites and mysteries to which young and tender virgins are introduced, and a variety of abominations too absurd and horrible to be named.[10] As such you are forfeit any rights to heard by ecclesiastical courts."

"You will answer to His Holiness," someone said.

"His Holiness does King Philip's bidding," the bailie replied.

With this pronouncement we were roughly shoved and dragged outside, placed in ass-drawn carts and taken away from the Temple and into a night illuminated by a waning moon. The darkness that gripped my spirit was without even this poor light, for the charges made against us were so far from the realm of truth as to be the product of certain perjury. My only consolation was that many of my brothers had been forewarned that very afternoon and I had witnessed their escape.

I could but ponder if the king's men had found the document or if it was still safe in its hiding place. Mere possession of such a writing could have condemned us all.

I knew not whence we were being taken but I had little hope for what would happen once we arrived. I was well aware of the treatment accorded witches, sorcerers and heretics. The heaviest part to bear, though, was that I had just gained the hurtful knowledge in the cave that redemption was not certain. In my own heart, I was a heretic more virulent than had I been guilty as charged.

Translator's Notes

1. Over the two centuries of their existence, the Templars had been given vast estates, most of which contained serfs. Each Temple so invested thereby became a feudal landlord.

2. Though not suitable for motorized vehicles, the course of this old Roman road is quite ascertainable. The first attempt at an accurate survey of France (1733–1789, undertaken by the father and son Jacques and Cesar-François Cassini de Thury) shows it as the main access to the area.

3. Parts of Spain were occupied by the Moors, Berbers, until 1492, although at the time of Pietro's writing Andalus, not Catalonia, was the province under Moslem rule.

4. There was no standard size for the manuscripts monks copied by hand, but a good guess in comparison to the average size would be sixty centimeters by forty and perhaps thirty thick.

5. The writer uses the Latin *in situ*, meaning the original or natural position. Since a carved block of stone is hardly natural or original, the translator has taken a liberty in departing from the original text.

6. Medieval monastic orders frequently had rules of the order prohibiting running, hurrying or other rash conduct that was not conducive to an air of contemplation in the monastery itself. Whether this was true of the Temple is unknown. Perhaps Pietro is thinking about the former monastery.

7. The Black Death, bubonic plague, which wiped out nearly a third of Europe, was still fifty years in the future. More limited outbreaks were not unknown in Pietro's time.

8. Jacques de Molay, Master of the Order 1293–1314. De Molay had, only three years before he succeeded in having Pope Boniface VIII grant the Order exemptions from taxation in England by directive to Edward I, had been given a papal promise that the "moveable goods of the Order will never be seized by secular jurisdiction, nor will their immovables ever be wasted or destroyed."

9. The chapter house was the room where the various chapters of the rules of the Order were read to the brothers and such business matters as concerned the Order were discussed.

10. The original draft of the complete charges, eighty-seven in number, is preserved in the Tresor des Chartres and includes various forms of idolatry such as animal worship and imbuing the Grand Master with the ability to forgive sins.

Part Four

Part Four

CHAPTER ONE

1

London, Piccadilly
0530 hours

Lang's internal clock woke him. For that one instant, yesterday was as ephemeral as the dream he could no longer remember. Pegasus and the Templars were some living nightmare he expected to vanish like smoke. In their home in Atlanta, Janet and Jeff were getting ready for work and school. Lang needed to check his electronic notebook for the day's appointments.

The feminine smell of the room and the sour taste of last night's greasy Chinese were more substantial. Those and his aching hand, bruised from driving it into the man's stomach the night before, were real.

Lang had dropped off without bothering to undress. That, along with a day's beard, didn't show him the image he would have preferred when he checked the mirror over the vanity. He knocked on the door to the adjacent bath.

No response. Not likely any of Nellie's girls were up at—he checked his watch—five-thirty. Once in the small bath, he latched the far door before peeling off clothes that felt as if they had become part of his skin.

He had to fiddle with the knobs and adjust the detachable shower head before he got a decent spray. The floral aroma of the soap—eau de hooker, he imagined—was a little strong, but it did get him clean even if he did smell like . . . well, like he had just come from exactly where he was.

As needles of hot water massaged his back, he planned how to get across London, an international border and through whatever French towns and cities might be necessary. He wasn't going to bet that British rail stations and airports weren't being watched.

He finished his shower, reluctantly using the only towel. It reeked worse than the soap. In the cabinet above the sink he found a cute little pink safety razor. Trying not to think of where it might have been used, he carefully shaved around Herr Schneller's moustache. He had become as accustomed to it as if he had grown it himself.

Dry and dressed, Lang surveyed the results: an ordinary working bloke in rumpled clothes. It would have been nice if he had dared to go shopping for new attire. Nice but too risky.

He left the room to see if anyone else was awake.

In a small kitchenette off the main salon, he found a tall black woman in a shiny emerald dress. The garment's deep neckline and high hem told him she had just come in from a night's work.

"Hullo," she said, her voice husky with a West Indian accent. "What cat dragged you in?"

"Nellie let me spend the night."

She turned to face him, her back to a gurgling Mr. Coffee. A sculpted eyebrow arched. "I hate to think what that cost you, honey."

"And I need to get to Manchester," Lang added as though it were an afterthought.

She twisted her long body to fill a mug with steaming coffee. She had to bend over so that her already short skirt rose another six inches. Lang didn't think the effect was accidental.

"Manchester?" she repeated. "You a long way from home, sweetie. Yo wife sho gonna know you gone 'fore you gits home."

"I'll pay for the ride," Lang said.

"I ain' no taxi service, dahlin'. Jes' got in mysef. You gonna have to take the train like everbody else."

But she seemed to be thinking it over as she sipped from the mug.

"Too bad," he said, making a disappointed face. "I'll have to hire a car. I'm sure Nellie knows a service. . . ."

Eyes the same color as the coffee contemplated him over the mug. Lang felt like a heifer being appraised at a county fair. "You some kinda special friend o' Nellie's?"

He couldn't resist the aroma of freshly brewed coffee. Seeing a cup on the counter, he held it out. "Mind?"

Her head gave a slow shake without her eyes leaving him. "Hep yo'seff."

He filled the cup with the remainder of the pot. "Known Nellie a long time."

She emptied her mug and set it on the counter, smacking her lips as though tasting something particularly good. "How much you gonna pay somebody, drive you to Manchester?"

Lang shrugged. "What's it worth, coupla hundred?"

She treated him to dazzling white teeth. "Lovey, for two hundred quid, I'll make it the most fun ride you evah, evah had."

Lang never doubted she could have, but he just wasn't in the mood. It didn't seem to bother her at all when, several hours later, untouched, she dropped him off at the British Airways terminal in Manchester. It was only after she had driven off that Lang realized he hadn't asked her name, nor she his. In fact, she had exhibited a professional lack of curiosity the whole way, saying nothing when he asked her to stop on a bridge where he could toss the Beretta into the river below.

Using the Heinrich Schneller identity and credit card was too chancy. Lang had to assume the umbrella he had left in Jenson's shop had been traced, but he had insufficient cash for the ticket. Since his destination was an EU country, he didn't need a passport, but he was going to have to have something identifying him as a U.K. resident.

He watched a newsstand and chose his victim carefully, a man about Lang's age and build who purchased a *Guardian* and stuffed his wallet into a jacket pocket. A slight nudge, a polite apology and Lang was Edward Reece, the name on his victim's driver's license. Wearing a pair of newly purchased sunglasses over a face missing Herr Schneller's moustache, Lang picked the busiest counter. Any ticket agent would expect to see his face match that on the license while Lang demonstrated no more than the usual passenger impatience as he shifted his weight and checked his watch.

He tried not look particularly relieved when the pretty woman handed his ticket across the counter. "Enjoy your flight, Mr. Reece. When you arrive in London, ask the agent at the gate for directions to the flight to Toulouse-Blagnac."

Lang slid into the seat with a combination of the apprehension flying always brought and satisfaction that he had pulled it off so far. At Gatwick, he would change from the domestic to international gates without having to pass through security and the scrutiny of the police he was sure were looking for him. He could even use Schneller's Visa card. That was the reason for this specific flight: He wanted to avoid Heathrow, whose configuration would have required he enter the international area through metal detectors, observant cops and cameras.

2

London, Gatwick International Airport
0956 hours

Lang was inconspicuous among the business travelers shuffling along the concourse. Many, like him, carried no baggage.

He might have been a little suspicious had he seen a passenger behind him duck into a restroom rather than continue towards the waiting flights for destinations all over Great Britain. The man entered a stall, shut the door and sat, only to flip open a cell phone.

"He's on the way," the man said.

3

London: Mayfair
1102 hours

Gurt sat in front of the monitor, nodding as though expressing agreement. The Visa card had provided an irresistible source of financing for Lang's quest just as she had known it would. She congratulated herself. Men were nothing if not predictable.

Toulouse-Blagnac? Somewhere in the southwest of France, the Languedoc mentioned in those papers Lang had told Jacob about, the ones at Oxford. Apparently Lang thought he would find Pegasus's secret there, the secret that had almost gotten him killed. Maybe he had right, *was* right, she corrected herself. Had right or was right, he was likely to be in trouble.

She stood and exited the smoke-sensitive computer room, pausing under a "No Smoking" sign in the corridor to light a Marlboro. She needed to call in a few more favors, go see the guys in the Second Directorate, Science and Technology, although what she needed wasn't particularly scientific nor was it exactly high-tech.

But first a phone call on a secure land line. Ignoring the glares of the health-conscious, she kept her burning cigarette as she rode down on the elevator. Outside, a brisk walk brought her to an Underground station and a bank of public phones.

She dialled a number, inserting coins when the other end answered. "You were right," she said without preamble. "He's headed to France. In fact, his plane should be landing about now." She listened for a moment. "Fine, I'll meet you."

4

Toulouse-Blagnac International Airport
1142 hours

As an arrival from a European Union country, there was no customs, no immigration, no reason for the two airport gendarmes near Gate Seven to notice Lang. They were far too intent on the young lady disposing of the morning's breakfast croissants behind the small cafeteria counter. She was living proof of the unfairness of life as evidenced by the diversity manufacturers offer in bra sizes.

Lang had disembarked into a large, modern terminal that, absent the multilingual signs, could just as easily have served Birmingham or Peoria. His companions from the flight dispersed quickly, none exhibiting any interest in him. Departing passengers were herded aboard quickly, the aircraft reloaded with baggage and in minutes Lang was the only traveler left in the gate area. It didn't look like he was being followed.

The bathtub at Nellie's had been more spacious than the Peugeot Junior he had reserved before leaving Gatwick. Good thing he had no luggage; there would have been little room.

It was the only thing Euro Car had, so Lang presented Mr. Reece's license, signed the rental agreement, paid a cash deposit and wedged himself in. He was fairly certain that when Reese discovered his wallet missing, he would notify the appropriate parties of the loss of credit cards long before his driver's permit.

Once Lang found the road, he headed through identical modern high-rises, wondering why modern European multifamily housing was uniformly ugly. Signs led him to the *centre de ville*, or downtown. Medieval stone and plaster replaced contemporary cookie-cutter.

He noted at least one advantage to the car's size as he shoehorned it into a parking place between an aging Deux Cheveux and a Renault. Over the top of the Renault, he could see the pink brick tower of the Basilique St-Sernin, all that remained of an eleventh-century monastery, according to the guidebook he had picked up at the airport.

Although the Peugeot fit into the parking place, there wasn't a lot of room for Lang to open the door and squeeze out. He managed, and walked a block to the town square, which featured the cathedral ubiquitous to European towns. This morning the square itself had been transformed into a small marketplace. Temporary stalls displayed a surprising variety of vegetables for so early in the spring. There were flowers, too, in almost every color, their fragrance mixing with the odor of fish, crustaceans and mussels shining on trays of shaved ice.

Women held small children and haggled with vendors. As in Rome, there were few men in sight.

He left the square and walked down one of the narrow cobbled streets, looking for what he needed. He passed a charcuterie with feathered fowl and unskinned game hanging in the window above fat sausages. Next was a patisserie, its pies and cakes freshly baked along with long loaves of bread. Habit made him check the glass display windows for anyone else on the street. There was no reflection but his.

He found a shop that had camping supplies and a small tent in the window. From its location, he guessed the store had mostly a local clientele.

The Languedoc was, after all, a small, largely rural province pushed against the shoulders of the Pyrenees. From what Lang had seen so far, it attracted few tourists. When people spoke of the south of France, they usually referred to the Languedoc's neighbor to the east, the summer playground of the wealthy, the Riviera. Cannes, Nice and Cap d'Antibes were world-famous. In contrast, few people outside of France could name a town in the Languedoc other than Rochefort, home of the blue-veined cheese.

The nearby foothills and mountains did attract local rock climbers and campers, vacationers very different from those of the Côte d'Azur. The out-of-doors types were typically young, adventurous and unable to afford a trip to the more distant and prestigious Alps.

All of that might have accounted for the proprietor's surliness. That and the fact he was French. Lang didn't look as young as he guessed most customers would be and he hoped he looked a little wealthier. Lang was sure he didn't appear to enjoy the grime, insects and unpredictable weather of the great outdoors, either.

But he did know what he wanted: hiking boots, Mephistos. Best in the shop and certainly the most expensive, judging from the shopkeeper's sudden enthusiasm in showing them. Lang picked out a felt hat with a prestained leather band that Indiana Jones might have favored, a half-liter plastic canteen in a carrying case, two thick cotton shirts, two pairs of jeans, and other equipment any hiker might need such as a compass, a collapsible trenching tool and a flashlight with extra batteries. Finally, he selected two coils of rope, the strong, light-weight fiberglass variety favored by serious mountain climbers. By the time Lang paid for such a large order, probably equal to a week's sale, all trace of French disdain had been replaced by a regular bonhomie.

Two doors down the street, he bought a cheap camera complete with flash capabilities, several rolls of film and a cardboard suitcase for his purchases, acquisitions that he struggled to fit into the Peugeot's limited storage space.

Leaving town, Lang headed south towards Limoux on the D118, two narrow lanes writhing through terrain that was different from any he had ever seen. Green hills alternated with sharp spikes of bare white rock like giant bones reaching from the earth. To his right, the Pyrenees were as ephemeral as a dream in the distant haze.

He had the road mostly to himself, seeing more tractors than cars. He passed vineyards, budding vines defying what looked like rocky soil. Sheep were like cotton on the hillsides. Sunflowers and tobacco were little more than fields of green buds.

The further south he drove, the more ruins he saw, remains of once-mighty fortresses and castles bleaching under the same sun that had warmed Pietro seven centuries before. The thought was spooky, as though he was regressing in time.

Limoux went by. According to the map that came with

the car, it was the last place large enough to be depicted as a town before the coast. Suddenly Lang was winding along the lip of a deep canyon with water sparkling far below. Also below were red tile roofs of villages he hoped were Esperaza and Campagne-sur-Aude. The Spanish-sounding names made him remember something he had read, that this part of the Languedoc had been part of Catalonia before one of those endless wars that had redrawn Europe's boundaries for two millennia.

If there was a sign announcing Rennes-les-Bains, Lang missed it. His first notice he had arrived in the tiny village was a cluster of plastered, tile-roofed buildings that crowded the highway. The place was too small for a cathedral or even a square but he did have to slow to a crawl as he came up behind a tractor. Both driver and machine had seen better days.

Despite clouds of greasy diesel smoke, Lang saw the sign to the Hostellerie de Rennes-les-Bains in time to turn onto a dirt drive lined with flowering fruit trees. In front of him was a pink-washed building on a slight rise. According to the guidebook, it was the only hotel within miles.

He replaced the moustache before leaving the car. The entry was into a limestone-floored foyer. Dark paneling extended to the gallery of the second floor. A rustic, wagon-wheel chandelier hung directly above his head. He was facing a country French desk, its simple pine holding a brass banker's lamp, leather register and polished brass bell. From his left, daylight streamed through an arched doorway, beyond which he could see the hotel's small dining room with a single picture window overlooking the Aude Valley.

He put down his suitcase and wandered over to have a look. A woman was clearing dishes from the continental lunch advertised on the hotel's sign.

Lang startled her when she looked up and saw him. "Oui?"

His French wasn't any better than his Italian. "Chambre?" he asked hopefully.

Lang was pleasantly surprised when he got something resembling whatever he asked for in French. At his only stay at Paris's oh-so-snobby Bristol Hotel, he had used a English-French dictionary, stumbling syntax and a heavy-tongued accent to ask room service to send up a cold drink. Minutes later, he got the cold just fine, only it was a very dead fish. The incident had colored his opinion of both his linguistic ability and the French. He held neither in particular esteem.

"You are American?' the woman asked in perfect English.

"German," Lang replied with appropriate Teutonic stiffness.

She wiped her hands on her apron and smiled as though indicating the difference was insignificant. "We have a room," she continued in English. "One with the view you see here." She indicated the glass behind her.

She led him back to the foyer and opened the register. He reluctantly gave her both Schneller's Visa card and passport. With just a little luck, the passport wouldn't hit the computers in Paris for several days and she wouldn't run the credit card through until he checked out. She seemed disappointed in both. She recorded the number of the passport before making an imprint of the card.

Lang was trying to remember how long it had been since he had seen that done to a credit card instead of an electronic swipe when she handed it back and reached into the key rack behind her and headed for the stairs. Lang had to trot to keep up. Along the gallery, she opened a door and silently motioned him inside. The room was unremarkable other than the promised overlook of the Aude. The travel magazines would have described the view in superlatives, something like shimmering diamonds in the midday sun as the river meandered between chalky cliffs.

As soon as the woman was gone, Lang opened his new luggage and changed into jeans and a heavy shirt. The Mephistos were even more comfortable than they had been in the store. He took out a coil of rope, ran his belt through it and secured the trenching tool to his belt.

Locking the room as he left, he stopped to pull a single hair from his head and use spit to glue it between door and jam. If a visitor came, he wanted to know it.

THE TEMPLARS:
THE END OF AN ORDER

An Account by Pietro of Sicily
Translation from the medieval Latin by Nigel Wolffe, Ph.D.

6

After six days, we reached the destination our gaolers intended. Had I more pigment and paper with which to record it,
this record would be replete with the cruelties and privations
inflicted upon us, but those facts are no longer important.

I know nothing of the place in which we are confined
other than that it is a twin-towered castle of the king in a city
upon a high hill looking down upon a river. Each Brother is
in a sperate cell so that there can be no congress among us.
The cell which is my lot is below the surface of the earth so
that I have no window, its walls so thick I hear nothing but
the scurrying of rodents in the straw which is my bedding and
only furnishing. Water and dampness drip from the walls and
the smell is of rot and decay.

Once a day a trencher of swill I would not have considered
fit for swine is shoved beneath the door without spoon or
knife so that I must defeat the rats in competition and then
eat like a dog. After the third day's confinement, I learned to
thank God for the little sustenance it gives me.

When taken, we were allowed no possessions other than what was on our backs. Had I not kept with me the material with which I intended to labour after the evening meal, I would not be able to record the events that have transpired.

On the first morning after arriving here, I was roughly dragged into a large room and set in front of a high dais, upon which sat a man made known to me as a myrmidon of the Grand Inquisitor of Paris. He read to me allegations similar to those made by the bailie. I denied them, whereupon I was taken forth to another room from which I heard screams and moans.

I supposed this to be the place where I was to be tortured so that I might confess to the falsehoods urged against the Brethren of the Temple of Jerusalem. I know not what was worse: waiting while listening to such suffering in anticipation of my own or the torture which was inflicted upon me.

I wanted to pray God to grant me strength for what I was about to endure but, alas, the knowledge from that accursed cave deprived me of the devotion to do this, for I knew not to whom to pray.

From the room now came quiet and from it was carried the broken form of the old cellarer who had not survived. Indeed, he was one of the fortunate members of the Temple.

I was fastened in an iron frame in a sitting position so that my leges extended toward a screen, on the other side of which was a fire. My feet were greased with butter and the screen removed so that my feet were roasted like venison over a hearth. The screen was moved back and forth to regulate the heat. Each time my tormentors again read the scurrilous charges, which I again denied even though I could smell my own flesh as it sizzled in the flames. I deafened myself with screams before blessed darkness overtook me.

My tormentors would not let me be, but revived me and began anew.

The next day, two of my teeth were drawn out. The day after, I was placed in the strappado.

I know not how long I lay in the straw of my miserable cell, my burned flesh an enticement to rodents and other vermin and my torn muscles making repelling them painful, before a boy appeared before me. At first, I thought he was but a vision, one of many as the pain made me drift in and out of cognizance. Instead, he had been sent to tend to such wretches as I in much the same manner of a stable hand, to replace the straw and to replenish the water, green and stinking in its bucket.

His name is Stephan and he is the fountainhead of any news I receive. Through him, I learned that even the pontiff, Pope Clement V, has abandoned us, banding with King Philip to destroy the Order in spite of the promises of his predecessor. I also learned that His Holiness had proclaimed all the Brothers apostate, the riches of the Order forfeit and the Order abolished. A number of the Brethren, much treasure and the Order's ships have disappeared.

I also learned that brothers refusing to confess to the insinuations and impeachments against them will be burned before the Temple in Paris.

It is an enigma: Whether to perjure myself by admitting the accusations, thereby avoiding further torment but damning my soul, or alternatively to cleave to the truth, suffering further mortification of the flesh and death by fire? Would that I still believed the latter course meant thereby gaining salvation! Then there be no choice indeed. Because of what I learned on Mount Cardou, I know not if salvation exists.

Had I but remained a humble monk in Sicily, had I not lusted after fine victuals and raiment, I would not now be at this pass. Would that I . . .

My transcription of these events was interrupted and I was forced to secret pigment, pen and paper, for they surely would be forfeit were they discovered. I am nearly at the end of the pigment I mix with the foul water to make the ink with which I write. It is as it should be in that I have little left to tell, a short time in which to live and can write only with the greatest of pain, my arms having been wrenched from their joints and my fingers swollen from the forcible removal of the fingernails by my inquisitors.

I anticipated further infliction of pain. Instead, I was taken before the same inquisitor and instructed to divulge my initiation into the Order, a simple ceremony in which I was put before the Chapter during the presence of Jacques de Molay, the Grand Master. I was told that it would be a very hard matter to be the servant of another, meaning Our Lord and the Chapters superiors, having no will of my own. I was required to answer several questions: Whether I had a dispute with any man or owed any debts? Whether I was betrothed to any woman, at which point I and a number of Brothers, remembering I had been but a noviate in Sicily, smiled despite the seriousness of the intent of the question. Had I any infirmity of body? Whereupon the assembled chapter was asked if any had objection to my admission and upon unanimous answer that they did not, I was received into the Order.

My inquisitor frowned as scribes finished their transcripts, inquiring as to the nature of any oaths required of me. I spoke truly, that I swore upon the Book and upon the Cross that I would forever be chaste, obedient and live without property, whereupon the Grand Master kissed me upon the mouth, admonishing me to the following effect: I was henceforth to sleep in my shirt, drawers and stockings, girded with a small cord, to never tarry in a house where there was a woman large with child, to never attend a wedding nor the purification of a woman, to never raise a hand against another Christian except in self-defense, to be truthful.

Upon giving such testimony, I was returned to my cell. Later Stephan told me that my words were the same as the other brothers examined that day, yet the inquisitor found it all to be perjury.

Had not Stephan so confided in me, I would have believed

the multiple inquisitors set upon me who told me my brethren had all confessed. Indeed, these new askers of questions were more fearsome that the original ones who imposed torture, for several showed me kindness, weeping at my fate while cajoling me to purge my soul of corruption and confess, while their alternates slapped my face, threatened and prevented me from voiding either bladder or bowel except upon myself.

Pain is but transitory, while damnation is eternal. I chose not to swear falsely against my brethren or the Order. I pray God may inspire my executioner to strangle me before my body is consumed by the flames. Of more significance, I pray my time in purgatory will be short before my Lord and all his saints receive me into heaven. I pray I may be forgiven the sin of pride which lured me from my original station, which made me seek knowledge I should have not sought, which has caused me to question those things that are a matter of faith and to die in a state of torment of revelation I do not wish to heed.

I ask that you who find this writing pray for me also, for time on this earth and my supply of material with which to write quickly expire.

Conclusion by the Translator

There is no surviving complete list of the Templars who were burned at the stake in Paris between October of 1307 and April of 1310, if there ever was such a document. We know that de Molay made no effort to escape, believing to the last the name of the Order would be restored.

It is likely no such list ever existed, the very anonymity of the victims being part of the terror Philip wished to inspire in those hesitant to confess. To die without name was to die without sacrament or burial in consecrated ground, and, hence, without unction and subsequent hope of resurrection—a fearsome prospect in the early fourteenth century.

Whatever Pietro may have found in the cave that so shook his faith, we will never know, nor is it significant. What matters is his first hand account of life as a Templar, albeit a non-combatant, in the days after the retreat from Palestine.

His narrative will be of interest to historians for years to come.

N. W.

CHAPTER TWO

1

Rennes-le-Château

It was only a few minutes drive to Rennes-le-Château on a road as twisted as a bedspring and almost as narrow. A cluster of stone and plaster buildings clung to the top of a hill. Francis had been right about Saunière being something of a tourist industry. Two or three couples festooned with cameras wandered through narrow, mostly empty streets. A small visitors' center hawked postcards with Saunière's picture and books in multiple tongues on the possibilities of what he had found. Signs in three languages reminded guests it was illegal to dig on public property. Apparently the priest's find had inspired tales of buried treasure.

The small Romanesque church was no larger than the town's other buildings, its only remarkable feature the gilt border around its low door. The Church of Mary Magdalene, the guidebook said, built in 1867.

Saunière's church.

Lang went inside.

Just beside the door, he was surprised by the leering face of a carved stone devil, his twisted body painted red and squatting under the weight of the holy water stoup. The vaulted ceiling was about twenty feet high and richly decorated with painted designs. The church itself was no more than a simple rectangle, with a center aisle dividing eight pews. The single room could not have held a hundred people. And yet every detail was as richly done as the largest cathedral.

The pulpit was carefully carved with the scene of an angel standing beside an empty cave.

The discovery that Christ had left the tomb.

Appropriate.

Everywhere Lang looked, he saw evidence of what had probably been the most skilled artists available. He understood Saunière's intent, to erect a place of quality and dignity that avoided ostentation. The priest had not intended to become an ecclesiastical parvenu.

Lang walked around, making a second inspection, impressed with the craftsmanship, the carving of the oak altar rail and pulpit steps. The altar, white marble, perhaps Carrara, was engraved with a triptych of Christ's birth, crucifixion and, again, an angel in an otherwise empty tomb. Curiously, this latter scene occupied the center rather than the chronologically correct last section.

Stations of the cross marched around the walls. Nothing unusual in a Catholic church, Lang thought. Until he came to fourteen, the last. Christ, half wrapped in a shroud, being carried to the tomb. But there was something . . . Above the figures, the moon. Lang was fairly certain Jewish law required a burial before sundown of the Friday before Sabbath. If so, perhaps the figures were not taking Him to the tomb.

Another message from a dead priest?

If Lang had had doubts as to what the priest had found, Saunière's church dispelled them.

Outside, he left the car parked to walk through the hamlet. A loaf of bread, cheese, sausage and bottled water made lunch, eaten while contemplating the church's facade.

Dusting off the crumbs, Lang cramped back into the little car. Once down the hill and on the other side of Rennes-les-Bains, the road began a steep ascent before it forked. Lang pulled onto a narrow shoulder and consulted the rental company's map. It was too small to have the detail he needed, so he peered in one direction, then the other, as though the answer might be coming down the road.

Actually, it was. Almost, anyway. Lang was turning his head to see when he spotted a stone cross to his left, mounted a few feet up the hillside. Such *calvaire* are common in the countryside of Catholic countries but this one wasn't alone. Beyond it was a statue of Christ, also not unusual. But Lang couldn't recall ever seeing both together. And this stature was a little different: instead of facing the passing motorist, it was perpendicular to the road, staring into the blue haze of the distance.

He got out of the car and climbed up to the cross. It bore no name but the conventional *IN RI* and a date too eroded by years of weather to be easily readable. The statue was life-size and mounted on a plinth as though to give Christ a better view of the hills and valleys. At one time, He had been pointing at something, judging from the extended right arm broken off at the elbow.

Standing on tiptoe to bring his eyes even with the stone shoulders, Lang sighted down the damaged arm. It was aimed at a hill somewhat taller than the others. Even from the poor detail of the map, Lang figured he was looking at

Cardou, the slope on which Pietro had made his discovery.

Was the statue a clue or just one more roadside shrine?

Lang walked back to the cross. Although shorter than the statue, its elevation made the top higher than Christ's head. From a few feet further up the slope, Lang could line up cross and statue like front and rear gunsights. The place on Cardou, the target, was indistinguishable from the surrounding slopes, nothing but white limestone with a scattering of trees tenaciously rooted in the rocky soil.

With his hiker's compass Lang noted he was facing a heading of about seventy-five degrees, a little north of due east. Trying to keep the compass as balanced as possible, he walked around to the front of the cross and squinted closely at the blurred date. It could possibly have been 1838.

Or it could have been the mathematical equivalent of the word puzzle in the picture.

$$1838$$
$$8-1=7$$
$$8-3=5$$

Seventy-five. Seventy-five degrees.

Compass heading or just a date? A few days ago, a week ago, Lang would have seen no encrypted message in a date on a cross. But then, he would never have thought about paintings as maps or Latin anagrams, either.

Magnetic north, of course, was not only different from true north but it also moved a little every few years. Seventy-five degrees in Saunière's time might not be the same exact heading today. Also, every compass had its own unique, built-in, degree of error. Without the correction card that came with the compasses on ships and aircraft, there was no way to know how far off the instrument might be. Or that it might not be off at all.

Returning to the car, Lang picked up the camera and took a number of shots lining the cross and statue up against the backdrop of Cardou.

Then he drove down a steep descent, crossed the Aude just past the point at which the Sals branched off, and turned almost due east. To his left he could see a silhouette dark against the afternoon sun, a tower of Blanchefort on its white pinnacle.

Seeing the old castle was a lot easier than getting there. Twice he took white dirt roads which headed towards the top of the mountain but turned out to be disappointing. One ended in a barnyard, leaving him staring at a pigsty with the occupants staring right back. The second was more devious. It headed straight for the old Templar fort, waiting until it dipped over a rise to make a right-angle turn and intercept the same road that had led him not to the castle but to pork.

Lang remembered something Dawn used to say, that a man would drive to hell before he would stop and ask directions, to which Lang retorted that the last man to ask directions was one of the Wise Men who asked King Herod where the Christ child had been born. The inquiry had a less than salutary effect on a lot of local infants and men haven't asked directions since. Herod notwithstanding, Lang would have inquired if he could have found someone to ask.

The third time was indeed the charm.

No matter how slowly Lang drove, white dust billowed behind the car like a chute behind a dragster. When he stopped to look at the woefully inadequate map, a capricious wind blew the choking, stinging cloud into the Peugeot's open windows. By the time he was pretty well covered with dust, the road became little more than a path and its grade increased enough to provoke mechanical protests from the car's already underpowered engine. The path became a track and the track ended at a level spot a hundred yards or so from the summit.

Lang parked and got out, making sure the Peugeot was in gear and the brakes on. If it took off on an excursion of its own, he was in for a long walk. There were a number of tire tracks in the loose soil but they were rounded, washed out or abraded by the wind, not recent. He began climbing the steep slope to the old fortress, each step sending a cascade of loose dirt and pebbles racing downhill.

Only the single tower he had seen from below crowned the top of the hill, its white stones reaching maybe a hundred feet before ending in steel scaffolding that had a head start on rusting away. Someone's restoration project had been abandoned long ago.

Lang was disappointed.

He had expected more than this, at least some indication where the walls and buildings had stood. Deep down, at that place where all men are part little boy, imagination had pictured a well-maintained cloister behind a huge portcullis. Perhaps a few men in armor, maybe Pietro himself.

Instead, he saw stones scattered where they had been pulled down, probably by the locals as material was needed for their own buildings. Rock already quarried and shaped was far too valuable to ignore. The tower, or what was left of it, had been preserved because it would have been difficult to get to the huge stones at the top and pry them loose. Judging from the accumulation of lime splotches, used condoms and graffiti, the inside of the tower had served birds, lovers and political satirists equally.

Lang smiled at the thought of Pietro and his brethren's reaction to the frenzied fornication that had obviously taken place here.

Steps worn by centuries of feet were carved into the

stone of the tower's inner wall, each smaller than Lang's size tens. At one time, the structure had several stories, as indicated by the square holes cut into the stone that would have held floor joists.

Lang turned his eyes back to watch where he was going. A misstep would have unfortunate consequences.

The deck or floor at the top had also long disappeared. The stairs simply ended four or five feet below the crenellated battlements. Lang leaned against the cool stone for support as he turned and surveyed three hundred sixty degrees.

To his left rear he could see the red tiles of Rennes-le-Château's few buildings. In front and slightly east of north was the town the map described as Serres.

Rennes and Serres.

Pietro had been right: militarily, Blanchefort had not been in a position to defend either. A force sent from here would have had to cross a river, all too easily guarded by a hostile army. Rennes, now Rennes-le-Château, was distant, too far to see what might be happening there. The first notice of an attack to any defender at Blanchefort would have been smoke from a town already sacked and burning.

If not to defend Serres and Rennes, what purpose had this old fortress served?

Cardou was close and in full view. Lang couldn't be certain, but he thought he was looking at the same face of the mountain he had lined up with the cross and statue. From here, he was much closer and could see a spot a couple of hundred yards square where the hillside leveled briefly. It was wide enough to have collected piles of white scree.

Balanced with one hand against the wall of the tower, Lang took the camera out and shot another series of pictures. It was difficult to exchange the compass for the camera while steadying himself, but he managed without doing more than giving himself a good scare when his hand slipped a few inches. Seventy-five degrees again. Accurate or not, the magnetic needle was telling him the cross, statue and tower all lined up to point to the same place on Cardou's slopes.

He had to back down the steps. There was no room to turn around.

The shadow of the tower had grown substantially. There was not going to be enough daylight left to explore Cardou. Lang gave the slope one more glance and got back into the Peugeot.

2

Cardou
1649 hours

It was only when the diminutive Peugeot disappeared downhill that the sniper lowered the weapon. It was the first time the telescopic crosshairs and the blunt, flash-suppressed muzzle had been off Lang since he had emerged from the tower.

The sharpshooter stood, flexing knees that had cramped and gone numb, and put down the Israeli-made Galil. The rifle was not the traditional weapon for long-distance marksmanship. Its light weight made it ideal for carrying but difficult to hold its electronically enhanced Leupold M1 Ultra 10× scope in place for long periods. It required more concentration and control than the heavier, bolt-action .50 caliber Barrett preferred by most snipers despite a nearly five-foot length and thirty-pound weight. But even if the Galil was steadied by a bipod, skill and patience, the sniper's stock in trade, were still required.

The shooter's companion let go of a pair of Zeiss binoculars, letting them hang by the strap around his neck. "You'll never have a better opportunity," he said with a grin.

The marksman folded the rifle's collapsible stock, unscrewed the barrel from the chamber and removed the twenty-round clip before replying, while fitting each component into its own slot in a customized attaché case.

"Too late for remorse," the sniper said, opening the door of an Opel with Paris plates and carefully placing the bag on the backseat. "But tomorrow is a different day."

3

Limoux
1957 hours

It was dark by the time Lang found a shop in Limoux that displayed the red-and-yellow Kodak sign. Using more gestures than words, he elicited a promise the film would be ready in a couple of hours, or at least before the store closed at nine o'clock, or 2100 hours. In southern Europe businesses stayed open late after closing from midday until midafternoon.

In a small bistro, smoky and loud, he took his chances on a less than perfect comprehension of the menu scrawled on a chalkboard. He lucked out with a thick stew washed down with inexpensive and acerbic local wine.

By the time he finished dinner, the post office was empty of workers and devoid of customers other than a young man muttering angrily into a long-distance telephone. Lang fed a few coins into a vending machine and received a prestamped envelope. A few more coins produced additional stamps, enough to send the envelope on a transatlantic voyage. Taking a blank piece of paper from the service counter, he wrote a lengthy note.

He finished just as the young man slammed down the phone with an audible "Merde!" and angrily stomped outside. A woman or money or both, Lang guessed, stepping over to a copier old enough to have served one of the French kings with a fairly low Louis number. The insertion of coins produced a protest of whines and clicks as though the machine resented being disturbed at this hour. Lang copied the written pages, stuffing the duplicates into a pocket. The original sheets went into the stamped envelope and then into the international mail slot.

Lang got the prints at the photo shop, gave them a cursory glance and drove back to the hotel. There, he examined the snapshots in detail. The differences in distance between the two locations from which he had shot the pictures made it difficult to tell if both groups depicted the same spot on Cardou's slope. Difficult but not impossible. A patch of sketchy green in the photos taken from the roadside could be the grove of stunted cedars recognizable from the shots taken from the tower. A white streak in the more distant view matched a stream of crumbled and fallen white rock. He studied the pictures taken from the tower, particularly anything, including shadows, that looked symmetrical or regular in shape.

He was disappointed to see nothing that could not have been created by wind, rain and the exfoliation of rock over the centuries.

Tomorrow he would inspect Cardou in person.

4

Toulouse-Blagnac International Airport
2330 hours

The airport terminal was closed for the night, the next regular passenger flight not scheduled until the 08:24 from

Geneva. Other than a bored watchman who was far too interested in his portable television to pay any particular attention to private aircraft, no one observed the Gulfstream IV when its tires squeaked on the runway and its twin jet engines spooled down as it taxied to the tarmac. Nor was there anyone to notice the slick black Citoën slide out of the shadows like a hawk gliding down on its prey.

There was the pop of an air seal as the aircraft's door swung open and wheezed down. Four men came down the steps, the younger three each carrying a small suitcase. From the care each man exercised with his luggage, an observant witness would have surmised that the bags contained something other than clean shirts.

The oldest of the quartet exited the plane last, carrying nothing other than a raincoat slung over one arm and an air of authority, the manner of a man accustomed to being obeyed. Without a hat, his shoulder-length silver hair reflected what poor light was available. One of the first three deferentially held the Citoën's passenger door open for the older man.

The aircraft's two-man crew stood stiffly on the top step until they were dismissed by a wave of the older man's hand. The plane's door shut and the idling engines began to whine. By the time the Citoën was driving through the airport's open security gate, the Gulfstream was screaming up into the night. It banked sharply to the west and was gone, its strobe lights fading like dying comets.

The older man was seated next to the automobile's female driver, the other three in the luxurious backseat.

"Where is he?" the older man asked in unaccented French.

"Asleep in his room," the proprietress of the Hostellier de Rennes-les-Bains answered.

CHAPTER THREE

1

Rennes-les-Bains

Lang had dreams that left him less than rested. As far as he knew, Dawn had never been to this part of France. Yet she had been waiting for him atop Blanchefort. There was a man with her. Lang couldn't see his face but, with that baseless certainty of dreams, he knew it was Saunière.

Lang knew better than to try to figure out what it all meant, other than the hole Dawn had left in the rest of his life would never be filled. Over ten years and not a day passed he didn't think of her. For that matter, rarely did an hour slide by without his seeing her face. Not the Dawn he had married but the dying bundle of bones and flesh in the hospital. It was becoming increasingly difficult to remember the way she looked before she got sick. Even seeing her that way in his dreams left him with teary eyes.

Memory has a sadistic streak.

The brilliant sunshine pouring through the window was of some comfort. Hard to be gloomy when he looked into the cloudless sky. Below the hotel, fog covered the Aude Valley, shimmering in the sun like a blanket of silver wool. It would burn off by the time he dressed and had coffee and a croissant.

In the hotel's dining room, Lang sipped coffee strong enough to strip chrome off of a bumper. In front of him was the well-wrinkled photocopy of the Polaroid. It didn't matter that the faces were now blurred and the inscription fuzzy. He knew both by heart. It was the background, the shape and location of the distant mountains, he was trying to memorize.

An hour later, the little Peugeot again struggled to reach the flat space below Blanchefort. Yesterday's tire tracks were partially filled with loose dirt, the erasing effect of the wind. Lang searched for any tracks sharper, more defined, that would tell him someone else had been here. There weren't any.

At the base of the tower, he took a compass bearing and set off towards Cardou. Loose pebbles and scrub growth slowed progress along a saddle of rock. Occasionally, he stopped to check the compass and to make sure the rope loop that held the trenching tool to his belt was secure. Twice he sipped from the water bottle, not so much from thirst but because the motion gave him a chance to survey the surrounding slopes from under the hat's brim without appearing to be looking for anything. He couldn't shake a creepy feeling he was being watched, the sort of intuition the people in horror stories have when the spooky villain is about to strike. The only thing missing was background music building to a crescendo. He had seen no reflection from a distant pair of binoculars, no brush moving without a wind, none of the things that might betray a hidden observer.

Overactive imagination, he told himself, too vivid a memory of the grisly last chapter of Pietro's tale.

A flash of reflected sun gave him a start that nearly brought the croissant back up. He jumped behind a boulder, squinting into the glare for a full minute before realizing he had only seen the morning's light on the windshield of a car far below, on the same road he had been on the day before. If he could see the road, he must be . . . Yep, he was. A careful look and he could see the cross, too. The Christ statue was invisible, blending in with the distant trees.

Lang trudged onward until he was standing in the field of scree he had noticed from the tower, loose rock that appeared as a bare spot from the cross. He took the picture of the painting from his wallet and turned it slowly.

The peak to the left, no more than a gray smudge in the distance, had the picture's jagged gap between it and a much closer hill. He leaned over, turning his head to get as close to an upside-down view as possible. The nose wasn't as sharp and the chin had disappeared but the gap could, conceivably, resemble Washington's profile on a quarter. It had been, what, four hundred years or so since Poussin had painted that picture? Plenty of time for geologic change.

This was as good a spot as any.

A very large spot, the size of a football field.

Speaking of which, he had to pick his way around rocks and boulders like a kick returner avoiding tacklers. The goal line was the point where the level space met the edge of Cardou's incline.

Lang stood there for several minutes. One place was slightly steeper than the rest. Steeper, yet the rock was piled just as high. Wouldn't loose stones roll until they reached a flat place? So gravity would seem to indicate.

Lang scrambled over a boulder, leaving a piece of the

skin on his knee on a jagged point. Does anyone hear when you curse alone? Maybe not, but it sure made him feel better.

He was standing in front of a large boulder that seemed to be partially imbedded in the hillside, its top more than head-high. It was the only piece of visible rock that could have been placed over an entrance big enough to admit a man, at least the only rock along the plane where Washington's profile was recognizable. Leaning against its rough surface, his feet scrabbled for traction in the loose soil and pebbles. His entire weight wasn't enough to budge it a centimeter.

There had to be a way. Saunière had done it alone or his secret would not have been kept. But how?

Had to be a matter of simple physics. But nothing about physics was simple. Lang had nearly flunked it in high school.

He stepped back, looking up the slope until he saw a stone fifteen or twenty feet away, one approximately the size of the one in front of him. Climbing up to its downhill side, he took the trenching tool from its rope loop and began to dig at the rock's base. After ten minutes of hard labor, he discarded his shirt. After what seemed like an hour, he had undermined the downslope side of that rock with a trench a foot or so deep. If he wasn't careful, he was likely to be flattened like Wile E. Coyote when he tried something similar to catch the Road Runner. Only Lang wouldn't be around to hear the "beep-beep."

Mopping his face with the wadded shirt, Lang took the coil of rope from his belt, looped it around the rock and tied it off. Then he went back down to the lower stone and did the same thing.

Now he had two boulders, one above the other, connected by the strongest nylon rope he could find. A swig from the water bottle celebrated the accomplishment. He hoped the next step would have made his physics teacher proud.

Picking up the trenching tool, he used it to smooth a path from the upper rock down the slope. Then he went back up and stuck the tool under the boulder, using the shovel's handle as a lever. That didn't work, so he pushed the little spade as far under the rock as it would go and stood on the handle, bending his knees and bouncing up and down like a diver about to leave the high board.

Simple physics, a lever.

He had expected his weight to jiggle the thing loose, but he was doing knee bends for nothing, panting in a fair imitation of Grumps. He promised himself he would start working out as soon as he got home. That's the easiest part of getting in shape, promising yourself you're going to do it.

He was going to have to think of something else to budge that rock. He stopped for another drink.

The sound of scraping metal made him forget his thirst. Something had shifted. Knees flexing, he felt the huge bulk of the stone move so imperceptibly that he thought it might be wishful thinking instead of motion.

As his high school teacher would have said, simple physics: tons of inertia were about to become kinetic.

With renewed vigor, Lang jumped up and down on the tool's handle two more times. There was a groan of rock grinding rock. He just had time to jump free before the boulder slowly moved from its resting place and began to inch downhill. In seconds it had the momentum and speed of a freight train on a ten-mile straight.

Now all Lang had to do was pray the fiberglass rope was as strong as advertised.

It was.

Maybe stronger.

The loose boulder crashed past the lower stone and the

rope sounded like a plucked harp string as it went tight. The power of tons of stone in motion snatched the other rock loose and it followed the first down the mountainside in a fury of scree, vegetation, dirt and noise. Fortunately, there was nothing below but the river.

The place where the lower rock had been imbedded into the hillside was hidden in a swirling storm of white grit. Lang sat on a nearby rock and waited. As the dust settled he wondered if Saunière had used the same method without the benefit of technologically enhanced rope. If so, how in hell had he gotten the rock back into place? Maybe he had simply pulled another boulder downhill instead.

A darkness was emerging behind the dust cloud, a blackness that could only be an opening in the hillside, a cave.

Lang stood, feeling that going-into-action sort of tingle. If he had guessed right, he was about to follow not only Saunière but Pietro.

There was enough water remaining in the bottle to soak the shirt before he tied it over his nose and mouth to absorb as much loose dust as possible. Taking the flashlight from its clip on his belt, he checked to make sure it was working and marched two thousand years to the rear.

2

Cardou

The sniper looked up from the scope. "He's gone into some sort of cave. I can't see him."

The other person took the binoculars from his eyes. "So I see. I'd suggest you keep that thing ready. You may have the opportunity to use it at any moment."

The shooter put a cheek back against the Galil's metal

frame stock and moved the barrel so that the scope's picture was a point a few feet in front of the cave. "I'm not walking anywhere. I'll be ready."

It could have been clouds making shadows on white rock, had there been any clouds in the brilliant blue sky. The angle of the sun to any number of rocks could have also been the origin of the shadows. Or, possibly, the shadows could have been the result of a far-ranging sheep, moving from boulder to boulder so quickly that the eye was unsure if it had really seen movement.

The sniper didn't think so.

The scope moved to a place fifty or so feet from the cave's entrance.

3

Cardou

A haze of white dust threw the flashlight's beam back into Lang's eyes. He couldn't see until he was completely inside the cave. He couldn't see the walls and he certainly couldn't see the low ceiling. He smacked his head against unforgiving rock. At least the impact made him see something, even if only spinning balls of color.

Wary of another collision, he stooped before moving forward. Of course, he thought. He should have known the damned roof would be low. Men centuries ago rarely stood more than five feet. He had never seen a suit of armor that he could have gotten into.

The dust was settling enough that Lang could see chisel marks, the tracks of the stonemasons Pietro had observed. This cave had been enlarged by a process more laborious than Lang wanted to imagine.

He stepped deliberately, placing each foot softly to minimize stirring the powdery white dust carpeting the floor.

Still, there was enough of it in the air that he didn't see it until the flashlight silhouetted it against the far wall. A stone box, squarely carved, about twenty inches by fifteen and maybe a foot high. Only its shape distinguished it from the pieces of rock that had fallen from the ceiling as the centuries passed. An indentation in the coat of covering dust indicated it had a lid. Closer inspection revealed irregularities in its coating of grime that may have been letters. With a tentative hand, Lang rubbed the stone, the slightest touch sending motes whirling into the light's beam. The surface felt warm, almost hot to his touch, in contrast to the cool of the surrounding dark.

He tried to remove the top without success. The lid had been carved to such a perfect fit that aeons of dust and grime had provided a sealant as effective as cement. Once again, Lang experienced warmth that seemed to reside in the box itself.

He squatted, sitting on his heels to bring his face closer to the stone. He closed his eyes and gave a gentle puff as he had in law school to blow dust from a book long unused. When he guessed the ministorm had quieted, he looked.

Much of the carving had cracked, fallen away as the stone had expanded and contracted in response to the cave's temperature fluctuations. One series of characters resembled the Hebrew inscriptions Lang had once seen in a synagogue. Aramaic, the ancient language of the Jews? And Latin, the letters barely legible.

Lang's lungs seemed to expand involuntarily as his surprise made him suck in a mouthful of dust and dirt that sent him into a spasm of coughing. He did not remember going from a squat to sitting splay-legged on the cave's floor, staring at the ancient letters in the halo of the flashlight. Solving the riddle of the painting had been one thing, a cerebral exercise. Finding this was quite another.

His mind was spinning like a fishing reel, unable to even guess at all the implications from this discovery. Saunière, Pietro . . . they must have felt the same as Lang did now.

The cavern filled with light from behind him.

"Very clever, Mr. Reilly. I congratulate you."

For an instant, Lang thought the police had finally caught up to him. Then he was afraid they hadn't.

Forgetful of the low ceiling, he started to his feet.

"Stay right where you are if you want to live, Mr. Reilly. And be sure to keep your hands where I can see them."

Lang lifted his arms, the universal gesture of surrender. There was no point in provoking these people. Not that They needed provocation to kill. Rough hands from behind snatched him to a semistanding position and slammed him against a wall. A quick but thoroughly professional pat-down followed. A hand reached into his pockets, removing all contents before the nearly dry shirt was pulled from his face.

"He's not armed," a second voice said. "But here's a copy of some sort of letter."

The copy made in the post office.

Lang risked looking over his shoulder. All he could see was a blinding light.

"You might want to read that letter," Lang said, "before you do anything . . . rash."

He was grabbed by the shoulders, spun around and shoved towards the entrance, again whacking his head on the low rock as he stumbled into daylight that made him wince after the darkness of the cave.

When Lang's eyes adjusted, he saw a man, perhaps in his fifties, certainly dressed more appropriately for the boardroom than a mountainside in France. He was reading the letter. From his expression, he was less than amused.

It was an old trick, the if-something-happens-to-me letter, not exactly original. But Lang was guessing that, trite or not, the letter was going to save his life, at least for the moment. At this point, he would have been perfectly willing to be saved by lost letters, infants on doorsteps or any other literarily hackneyed device including having the cavalry ride over the hill.

Beside the man in the suit were two more guys, younger and bigger. They looked as though they might have once played some sport where collisions were likely: football, rugby, hockey, something where inflicting pain is encouraged. Their necks overflowed the starched shirt collars and the tailored suits were stuffed as tight as the skin of a sausage. They each wore what Lang guessed to be thousand-dollar-plus Italian toe caps, footwear for the corporate elite. From the sheen of the black leather, those shoes hadn't made many excursions like this one. Their wardrobes were complete with the Heckler and Koch 10-millimeter MP10s they each held, a submachine gun small enough to fit in a briefcase with the stock folded, heavier artillery than the goons in London had. It was the weapon of choice of both the Secret Service Presidential Detail and Navy SEALs. These guys were neither.

Lang didn't turn but was certain the one behind, the one whose push had ejected him from the cave, was from the same mold.

The older man looked up from the letter. Tan under a full head of long silver hair, his face was lean, the sort of face AARP likes to use in its brochures.

"To whom did you send this?" he wanted to know.

"Santa Claus," Lang said. "I'm beating the Christmas rush."

He dipped his chin, the slightest of nods, and Lang's arm was snatched upward from behind, a quick snap that sent a jolt of pain across Lang's shoulders. It hurt enough to make him gasp.

"No one likes a smartass, Mr. Reilly," the man said without a trace of anger, as though he were lecturing a dull child. "I assure you, I will have an answer. The question is, how much will you have to endure first?"

Lang made a show of glancing from left to right. "Don't see the rack, thumbscrews, any of the interrogation tools Philip and the boys used on your people. Sure you can ask questions without equipment?"

Another wrenching of the arm. Lang may have only imagined the sound of tearing ligaments. He was certain he saw stars brighter than when he had banged his head.

"And the answer?" Silver Hair asked.

"And what happens when you get it?" Lang asked. "Don't guess I'm walking out of here with your thanks."

The man in the suit wasn't the first to call Lang a wiseass and Lang devoutly hoped he'd live long enough for this guy not to be the last. But the purpose of the conversation wasn't social banter. Agency training taught that, in a tight spot, stall, play for time in hopes you'll find a way out. With two, probably three men armed with automatic weapons, it looked like Lang was going to need a whole lot of time.

The older guy, obviously the leader, gave Lang a smile that wouldn't have melted ice in July. "Very perceptive of you, Mr. Reilly."

He nodded to the hulk to his left who reached inside his coat with the hand that didn't have a gun in it and produced a long slender box like something from a jeweler. Inside was a hypodermic needle.

"You guys ought to open a clinic," Lang said. "Every time I see you, you want to give me a shot. And you haven't even asked me about allergies."

Silver Hair gave another of those little dips with his chin and the guy with the needle took a step.

"What the hell is it?" Lang asked. "Truth serum?"

"Not quite yet, Mr. Reilly," he said. "Later, perhaps a little sodium pentothal. Right now, we want you sedated, to help you relax and enjoy the ride, as you Americans say."

"Couple of questions," Lang said. "After all, we both know you're not going to turn me loose to write an expose for the *National Enquirer*. You can at least give me the satisfaction of a few answers."

Silver Hair sighed. "And then, no doubt, you will tell me to whom you sent this letter."

"So you can get rid of them just like you did my sister and nephew, kill them like the doorman in my condo building and the antique dealer? I don't think you'd believe me even if I did tell you."

There was a flash from down the hill, not in the direction of the road, the instant of glare of sun reflected off something—glass, metal. Lang wasn't sure he had really seen it. If Silver Hair or his pals had, they gave no indication. Lang looked in the opposite direction, making sure that if something really was out there, he didn't give it away. Whatever it was, it wasn't very likely to be there on his behalf.

Lang might have been more wrong before but he couldn't remember when.

Silver Hair nodded to his flunky to hold up a second. "Then, perhaps you will tell me how you found the cave and its . . . contents. I'd like to make sure no one else does. But be brief with your questions, Mr. Reilly."

The older man sat down on the same flat rock from which Lang had watched the dust settle, the copy of the letter spread open on his lap. Lang felt a slight relaxation of the pressure on his arms. The one that had been twisted felt as though the joint was on fire.

"Templars," Lang asked, "you are Templars?"

Silver Hair spoke as though relating a familiar story. "Quite correct, Mr. Reilly. If you know who we are, you also know our history, that in 1307 the King of France . . ." He scowled as though recalling a personal betrayal. "The perfidious Philip sent orders to his minions to arrest the Knights of the Temple of Solomon and accuse them falsely. Our spies were widespread, were in every court in Europe. They warned of what was coming. As many of us as could leave without raising suspicion fled to Scotland where Philip's lackey, Clement, couldn't reach us. The Scottish king, the one known today as Robert the Bruce, was under papal interdict and no friend of the pope."

His voice had more of an inflection than an accent, although Lang had the impression English wasn't his first language.

"As many of you as could?" Lang was thinking of poor Pietro, left to face the Inquisition on bogus charges. "You deserted a number of your brothers to be tortured, killed, to burn at the stake."

Silver Hair crossed his legs at the ankles. Lang noticed he was wearing those short socks that European men favor. "It was God's judgement as to who went and who stayed, not ours."

Lang was tempted to ask if the choice had been communicated by stone tablet or burning bush. Instead, he asked, "And Clement would have been delighted if he had bagged the entire Order, right? After all, you were blackmailing him just as you are blackmailing the papacy today."

Silver Hair reached into an inside coat pocket and produced a silver cigarette case. He held it out for Lang to see. "Supposedly made from several of the infamous thirty pieces of silver given to Judas." He took out a cigarette and offered one.

Lang shook his head. "Don't smoke. No point in risking one's health."

If the Templar got the irony, he ignored it. " 'Blackmail' is such an ugly word, Mr. Reilly. We prefer to say we guard the pope's greatest secret." He lit up with a gold Ronson.

"And have since you somehow discovered it during the time of the crusades," Lang said.

The older man exhaled a jet of blue smoke instantly dispersed by the light wind. "We have served the True Church for some time, yes."

Lang made no effort to keep the contempt out of his voice. "Some service! Murder, blackmail. Hardly Christian virtues."

If Silver Hair was offended, he didn't show it. "Regrettably, an imperfect world does not allow the consistent practice of Christian virtues. After all, our Order was founded as a military one, trained in the very unchristian art of war. It was necessary then just as an occasional unchristian act is necessary now. Fortunately, we have the sacrament of confession to shrive us of such sins."

"Including killing women and children?"

He stubbed out his cigarette. "We have no time for ideological argument, Mr. Reilly. Suffice it to say that when we held Jerusalem, one of our number came across certain parchments that lead us here, the same that the priest Saunière found hidden in his altar." He let a smile flicker and die. "We know you are aware of Saunière, Mr. Reilly. Why else would you visit such a forlorn little place as Rennes-le-Château? What we found here on Cardou must be protected, no matter who suffers."

"So much for loving thy neighbor."

With one hand he held the letter, using the other to push himself erect from the rock with a spryness Lang would have associated with a younger man. "Mr. Reilly, I answered your question, that yes, we are the Templars. Now you can do me the curtesy of answering mine or . . ." He nodded to the goon with the needle.

4

Cardou

"You best make your shot before he jabs that needle in," the man said to the sniper. "I'd wager it's full of nasty stuff."

The shooter didn't move the scope. "Nothing nastier than the slug Reilly gets in the head should I hurry and miss."

The man bit back a retort. He knew placing a bullet in exactly the desired place from this distance was a skill depending equally on metrology, mathematics, chemistry, physics and biology.

The longer the shot, the more the slightest breeze must be considered. The propellant of the projectile, gunpowder, had to be of the exact quality anticipated to burn at the rate calculated and provide precisely the power needed. Too little and the shot falls short. Too much is likely to overflatten the trajectory, resulting in overshooting the target. Either way, the velocity of the bullet would not be as anticipated, making it more subject to the other variables such as the weight and speed of the slug.

The shooter had to have the physical attributes required to breath in rhythm with the shot, inhale, exhale, hold, slowly exhaling until just enough air was in the lungs to keep the hands steady but not enough to cause the slightest tremor. The tiniest, most minute error, a single centimeter at this range, would send the bullet wide by several feet.

Gravity also affected the trajectory, depending on whether the shot was up or downhill. The variation made precise scope adjustment necessary.

If it were easy, anyone could do it.

He kept his impatience to himself.

5

Cardou
1042 hours

At first, Lang thought the man with the needle was going to pray. His knees bent to the kneeling position so slowly that it wasn't until the crack of a shot seconds later that Lang realized something unexpected was happening. The echo was still circling the mountainsides like a startled pigeon as the Templar slumped face-first to the ground, exposing blood and brain matter where the back and top of his head had been.

With one movement, Lang snatched himself free of a grip loosened by surprise, grabbed the copy of the letter and dove for the ground, landing hard enough on the rocky surface to nearly knock the wind out of his lungs. He rolled downhill, trying to ignore the cuts from sharp stones, until he was behind a boulder big enough to hide him from the sight of the three remaining Templars.

A deafening silence is not an oxymoron. The fitful breeze seemed to have quit rattling sand against stone. There was no noise of cars from the distant road. It was so quiet even the memory of the shot's sound was beginning to fade like a dream. It was as if Lang had gone deaf or sound had ceased to exist.

He could imagine the Templars quietly hiding behind rocks of their own. The flat crack of the shot, almost like a hand clap, announced that the shooter had fired from a distance. He would be peering through a scope, waiting.

For what? Lang was fairly certain he hadn't been the target. If he had, he wouldn't be here behind this rock. For that matter, it would make no sense for the Templars to catch him in the act of violating their secret and then kill him before they found out how he had discovered it and to whom the letter had been sent.

Then who?

Lang gave up. It didn't matter. If only the shooter could keep the Templars' heads down while he slipped from rock to rock downhill to the car . . . And why not? He wasn't any good to the Templars dead; they'd never find out what they wanted. So, if the mysterious rifleman intended Lang no harm and the Templars wanted him alive . . .

Lang wasn't willing to risk his life on the logic.

Good thing, too.

When Lang lunged for another boulder, one of those Heckler and Koch MP10s barked a short burst and rock splinters stung Lang's face like bees. He had no weapon, not even a penknife. He would have felt less naked standing nude in downtown Atlanta. Safer, too.

Lang was trying to figure out exactly where the most recent shots had come from when he heard something other than their fading echo, something crunching in the sandy soil. Someone was moving towards him, moving slowly and deliberately on the soles of those expensive Italian shoes. No doubt whoever was approaching was also trying to keep his head down from the unknown man with the rifle.

Lang put the copy of the letter on the ground, wedging it under the massive stone. If he were captured, its location might become a bargaining chip. Moving around the boulder, Lang kept it between himself and whoever was out there. He picked up a white rock that fit neatly into his palm. It was no match for an automatic weapon, but it was better than no weapon, at all.

Maybe.

6

Cardou
1042.30 hours

"Now what?" the man demanded. "You've made them all go to ground."

The sniper was still intent on whatever was to be seen through the scope. "We wait."

"Wait? For how long?"

"For as long as required."

7

Cardou
1043 hours

Unlike the shoes creeping up on him, the rubber of Lang's Mephistos cushioned any movements he made. Even so, he could play ring-around-the-rock only so long. Assuming these guys had even a modest grasp of tactics, one of them would be circling the rock while another waited for Lang to literally walk into his sights. The unknown was the sharpshooter. They, the Templars, would have to move while screened from the rifle and Lang was going to have to assume it wasn't him the shooter was after.

The toe caps stopped on the other side of the rock before moving slowly to Lang's left. Lang took a couple of steps to his right, still clutching the stone he had picked up. Another couple of steps and Lang would be exposed to the place he had left the Templars. His imagination conjured up the vision of one of the remaining fat-neck twins looking down the stubby barrel of his Heckler and Koch, waiting to center it on his back.

The one thing they wouldn't expect would be for Lang

to go on the offensive. Sticking the stone under his belt, he felt for a handhold on the boulder, anything he could grab. His fingers found a small crevice and he pulled himself up, trusty Mephistos pushing against the rock.

The top of the boulder was maybe twenty feet high, ten feet across, pointed at the far end and ridged too deeply for Lang to lie completely flat but not deeply enough to provide cover. He could only hope that the Templars would look for him on the ground and that he wasn't the sniper's target. Those two hopes were more of a gamble than Lang would have preferred but no one was giving him a choice of odds.

A sound below. Lang squirmed over and looked down. He hadn't noticed one of the Templars had a bald spot. He was edging around the boulder, the collapsible stock of his weapon pressed to his shoulder.

Lang wiggled the stone out of his belt and pulled into the lowest squat he could manage. He was going to have to jump on the guy, not crawl, if he wanted to surprise the Templar with his full weight.

Something made Lang glance over his shoulder just before he leapt. He was looking at one of those Heckler and Koche's about thirty yards away. Lang knew the weapon wasn't particularly accurate at that range but with a thirty-round clip, marksmanship was purely a bonus.

Lang had no time to be certain he was going to land on the Templar below him. He could only spring and hope.

Lang took one last glance as his head and shoulders rose to the ledge that had been sheltering him. Even at thirty yards, Lang was certain he could see the Templar grinning at the sure kill.

The man with the Heckler and Koch aimed at Lang stood clear of the rock to get the perfect angle. It was a fatal mistake.

The guy's head dissolved in a pink mist.

Lang jumped into space just as the rifle's second crack of the day bounced from hillside to hillside like a trick shot on a billiard table.

The sound made the man below look up. He moved but not quickly enough to avoid the force of Lang's weight. The impact knocked the breath out of both men and they went down in a heap. The Templar was struggling to bring his gun to bear. Lang slipped an arm under one of his opponent's and snaked a hand over the man's shoulder to cup the back of the head, giving Lang leverage to force him sideways so the weapon pointed harmlessly at the ground.

With his other hand, Lang had the rock up, ready to pound the Templar's skull.

"That's quite enough, Mr. Reilly."

The words connected with Lang's consciousness simultaneously with cold steel against the back of his neck. He recognized the feel of a gun's muzzle as well as Silver Hair's voice. That had been it, then: one Templar to keep the shooter occupied while the other made himself bait with Silver Hair right behind, both men screened by the boulder between them and the rifleman.

Lang had been had.

"Drop the stone and clasp your hands behind your head. Slowly, now, stand."

Lang did as he was told.

The man Lang had jumped on got to his feet slowly. His sleeves and trousers were shredded and one of his jacket's inseams was torn open. He'd never wear that suit again. That was the only good news, that plus the fact that two of the murderous bunch would never kill again.

Silver Hair kept the weapon, whatever it was, pressed to the back of Lang's skull as he spoke a few words in a language Lang didn't understand. The other man turned his back to Lang.

"Put your hands on his shoulders, Mr. Reilly," Silver Hair ordered.

Lang did as ordered and the trio began a slow walk down the mountainside. With Lang sandwiched between the two Templars, whoever had killed the other two couldn't shoot without a better than even chance the bullet would penetrate two bodies, Lang's included. Clever.

8

Cardou
1047 hours

"Shit!" The man stood, staring through his binoculars. "They're getting away."

For the first time in hours, the sniper looked up from the scope. "Not all of them."

The man grunted disapproval. "Whatever. They're taking Reilly. We should follow and see if you can't bag the other two."

"And risk killing him? Unless they are sick, crazy, they will keep him between them like ham in a sandwich."

"I'm sure he'd be amused at the simile," the man muttered, "but they're getting away."

"Not true. They will not stay around here and when they leave, we will know where."

9

Cardou
1103 hours

They were on the other side of Cardou when Lang and the two Templars came to a Range Rover parked between two outcroppings so large that the vehicle was invisible until they were almost on top of it.

"In the back," Silver Hair said.

Lang was climbing in when he felt a pinprick in the back of his neck. Before he could get into the seat, the interior of the car began to ripple as though he were seeing it through water. His arms and legs were heavy, too heavy to move. Lang knew what had happened, that he should fight the effect of the drug.

But it felt too good to complain.

Then everything went black.

Part Five

CHAPTER ONE

1

Location unknown
Time unknown

When he regained consciousness, Lang had no idea how long he had been out or where he was.

Of course, they wouldn't have wanted him to know, not if they were planning extensive questioning. They were succeeding. All he knew was that he was lying in an unusually uncomfortable bed, staring up at what appeared to be an old-fashioned canopy. And that his shoulder still hurt like hell where his arm had been wrenched upwards on the hillside.

Lang's Agency training taught total disorientation as an effective interrogation tool. Keeping a captive ignorant of day or night, the date or the hour upsets the internal clock just like jet lag. Jet lag, though, goes away once the body accepts the new schedule. To question someone effectively, you make sure nothing is done at the same time twice. Likewise, not letting the subject know where he is may open up all sort of anxieties the questioner can put to use.

Also the lights. You keep the subject in a place without windows and at the same light level twenty-four hours a day. Intensely bright light if sleep deprivation is part of the plan; low light, too dim to see well, if not.

The talk about truth serum had been just that, talk. Outside of some old spy novels, drugs are usually little help. Sodium pentothal, scopolamine, narcotics like that, inhibit the brain's ability to fabricate, to make up lies, but they also are risky. Too little and you still get lies; too much and the subject is either sound asleep or dead. Whatever the drug makes them babble is going to be incomprehensible.

Plain old-fashioned torture was less than reliable, too. It worked for confessions for the same reason it doesn't work to get information: a man will tell any lie just to stop the pain. Lang very much hoped the Templars realized that.

Lang had been taught that modern interrogation consists of simply wearing your subject down, breaking his will. A less polite word for it is a species of brainwashing.

Lang slid out of bed to the floor, some three or four feet down, and walked the perimeter of the small room. The bowed exterior wall made him curious as to the outside appearance of the building. The single window was shuttered and, no doubt, barred on the outside. The only door was fitted with a intricately cast brass lock plate. When he bent over, closed an eye and squinted through the keyhole, he saw nothing. The key had been left in the outside of the lock.

The dim overhead light cast few shadows because, other than Lang and the bed, there was nothing in the room. No pictures on the walls, no window treatment, no rug, nothing. Had it not been for the hand-pegged hardwood floor and the ornate and undoubtedly expensive wall paper, he could have been in a jail cell.

Except . . . He looked for a door he might have missed, an entrance to a toilet. There was none. Bending over, he saw the porcelain jar under the bed. At least he wasn't going to be the guy that had to deal with emptying that. At this point any good news was welcomed.

On his second lap around the room, he counted the pegs in the floor. Keeping the mind occupied was the best defense against disorientation.

Sixty-two pegs later, a key scratched in the lock and Lang raced for the bed, lay down and pretended he was still out cold.

"Come now, Mr. Reilly," an all too familiar voice said. "The sedative we gave you has worn off some time ago. Playing possum, as I believe you Americans call it, will do you no good."

Lang opened his eyes and gawked in surprise. He could have gone back in time. Silver Hair stood in the doorway wearing a suit of chain mail over which was a white surcoat open at the sides with a red Maltese cross emblazoned on the front. Pointed shoes of steel covered his feet.

"Don't tell me," Lang said. "You're on your way to ask the wizard for a heart."

The Templar looked at Lang blankly. "I beg your pardon?" Then he scowled. "I gather you are referring to my attire," he said stiffly. "Templars dress traditionally when in the temple."

Temple? Had Lang been kidnapped by mad Shriners? He wished.

Silver Hair stepped aside. Behind him was another man, this one in what looked like a monk's cassock. Bare ankles were visible above the flip-flops. He was holding a plate from which came the unmistakable aroma of food. Lang suddenly remembered he hadn't eaten since breakfast of whatever day it was that he had been taken prisoner.

Silver Hair said, "You are hungry, no doubt. The cellarer had something brought up from the refectory. It is humble fare, a local dish of salt cod, but you will find it nourishing."

The man in the monk's outfit set a wooden platter on the bed. It smelled even better. White meat swimming in vegetables.

"Go ahead, eat," Silver Hair entreated.

Lang looked from him to the man who had served me. "Got a fork?"

Silver Hair shook his head. "The fork was not used until the sixteenth century. We use only the knife, as did our predecessors. We try to eschew the vanities of the modern world."

That explained the chamber pot.

"Okay," Lang said, eyes on the wooden trencher with the wonderful fragrance, "we won't tell Miss Manners."

The man in the brown habit set the food in front of Lang.

"Afraid you'll have to do the best you can without eating implements, Mr. Reilly," Silver Hair said. "I think you can understand our reluctance to furnish you a knife."

Lang was hungry enough not to care. He scooped up a piece of the fish in his fingers and plopped it into his mouth. He hadn't eaten many things that had tasted so good. He was nearly finished as Sliver Hair and his companion backed out of the room.

"Until later, then," he said as the door closed.

A second later the lock clicked.

Lang was draining the liquid from the platter when the room began to spin. The outlines of the corners got fuzzy and the planks in the floor lost definition. His head was suddenly too heavy to hold up. They had seasoned dinner with something besides herbs.

But why, Lang wondered as his world again grew dim. They could hardly interrogate him if he was asleep.

And he was too sleepy to care.

2

Location unknown
Time unknown

Only his still-full stomach told Lang he had not been unconscious more than a few hours. A bright light was shining in his eyes. Although awake, he was lethargic, and his head weighed a ton.

"Back with us, I see," said a voice from behind the light. "Time for you to answer a question or two."

Lang struggled to get up to a sitting position. "I get to make one phone call before my final answer, right?"

There was no response. Clearly Silver Hair had better things to do than watch American TV.

"I want to know two things, Mr. Reilly: How did you find our secret and to whom did you send that letter?"

"Right," Lang said. "And as soon as I tell you, I walk out of here. Wherever 'herc' is."

"Something can be arranged, I'm sure."

Something like a bullet in the back of the head.

But Lang said, "I've got a few questions of my own. Like, if you wanted to keep the secret of Blanchefort, why have a virtual map of it painted by that guy Poussin?"

"You test my patience, Mr. Reilly, but I will give you an answer as a demonstration of our good faith. We have always faced a choice: risk committing the secret to writing or risk it being lost if enough of our members succumb to any number of unpleasant possibilities. Centuries ago, plague; today mass destruction by heathen terrorists the West does not have the fortitude to destroy first. It was not unreasonable, then, in Poussin's time, the first half of the seventeenth century, to want some sort of record as to where our . . . discovery might be found. Along with the oral parts of our initiation rites, a picture would serve to find the precise location."

Lang's interest made him forget how groggy he was. He sat up a little straighter. "How did you know Poussin wouldn't give away your secret?"

The light shifted enough for Lang to be able to make out Silver Hair's silhouette. He seemed to be sitting but there wasn't anything in the room to sit on besides the bed. Had they brought in a chair?

"Poussin was a Freemason."

"So?"

"Freemasonry is a tool of our order, its members at our bidding. We control it worldwide, always have. Most men of prominence up until nearly the present were Masons, your George Washington, most of your country's founding fathers, for example. Through it we knew nations' most intimate secrets. We don't intend to experience another 1307.

"More directly in answer to your question, Poussin did the painting because he was commanded to do so, a slight variation upon his work that now hangs in the Louvre. He never knew its significance. We had copies made, one for each of our chapters. Last year we moved the London house, sold a number of its goods rather than move them. The movers mistakenly bundled up the picture with the items we had sold.

"Now, I've given you your answer. I want to know where that letter went."

Lang yawned, not entirely an affectation, and moved his aching arm in a slow circle. "Like I said before, so you can kill somebody else? I don't think so."

There was an audible sigh. "Very well, Mr. Reilly. We will leave you for a while to meditate on your situation. When we return . . . well, I fear it will be most unpleasant. We no longer use the rack, the thumbscrew. But we can do amazing things with alligator clips and automobile batteries, simple electrical cooking appliances and human skin. I warn you, though, we have limited time."

So much for Lang's theory on the demise of torture as an interrogation tool.

There was the scrape of the unseen chair as Silver Hair got up. Lang was already relaxing, slumping back onto the bed, when hands reached out from the dark, pinioning Lang's arms behind him. His wrists were quickly handcuffed to the bed as his pants were removed. His shoulder was on fire.

"Now look," Lang said. "Surely we . . ."

Somebody literally had him by the balls. The scrotum's skin was stretched and he felt cold metal. Before he could say anything else, his breath evaporated in a bolt of pain that seared from his testicles throughout his body. His blood was on fire and he could see nothing but a wall of red that was one with his agony.

Lang didn't hear his own scream. Burning, searing pain had replaced the other four senses, cramping, demobilizing, anguish.

It stopped as suddenly as it started. The clamps were removed and Lang's arms released. The fire in his crotch made him forget his shoulder.

"A few volts, a low charge," the voice from the darkness said. "We will leave you to consider the effects of a larger charge, perhaps applied to a metal rod inserted in the anus up to the prostate."

They left Lang with the thought. That and pain worse than any he'd ever gotten from a dirty shot in any sport he'd ever played. Gingerly, he moved onto his side. That was when he noticed the shock had made him wet himself.

3

Location unknown
Time unknown

Lang no longer needed to count floor pegs to occupy his mind. He had to find a way out of here before the guy jump-started his balls again.

Every move set a new fire in his crotch, underlining the urgency of escape. Gritting his teeth against the constant pain, Lang tried the window. The shutters were immobile, probably secured by a bolt outside too heavy to move even if he could reach it. Besides, unless he was on the first floor, jumping out of a window might not be such a hot idea.

Trying the same tactic as with the Templar in his condo in Atlanta was a possibility he quickly discarded. They would be alert to the chance he might try to spring on them when they entered the room, and if there were more than one of them, there would be no chance at all. Lang needed to think of something else. He began another slow circuit of the room.

If there had been a chair for Silver Hair, he had taken it with him. The door was hand-hewn wood, the marks of the chisel on it and the matching frame visible even in the dim light, as were the details of the brass lock plate. Lang knelt to inspect the lock, the posture squeezing testicles already ablaze. He groaned as he peeked into the keyhole again. There was no spring latch like a modern knob would have. Like most old doors, this one would have been kept shut by a simple latch on the inside, a device that empty screw holes indicated had been removed. The keyhole was still blocked but Lang thought he could see the thinnest glimmer of light between the door and jamb. He moved his head up and down. The space extended from top to bottom, blocked only where the lock's bolt fit into the bolt plate.

Careful to jar his crotch as little as possible, he sat on the floor. Removing a shoe, he used the dirt and grime on the sole of the Mephisto to make a nearly invisible mark on the frame just even with the bolt.

The he returned to the bed, this time looking at the bottom of it. Instead of springs, it had old time slats to support the stuffed cotton ticking. For once, Lang was happy to have been uncomfortable. Those slats . . .

It was tempting to stretch out for a few minutes, to give into the pain, but there was no time. Working the end of one slat loose from the bed's frame, he levered the other end up and down until he heard it crack. Slipping the whole board out of place, he picked a splinter from the damaged end and returned the slat to its place.

Lang had done what he could. Now he had to depend on the fickle favors of luck.

Although it felt like he was passing fire, he urinated a slim stream of blood into the chamber pot. Then he beat on the door.

They must have had a guard outside because the click of the lock was immediate.

The doorway was filled with a large man in a white cassock, complete with a hood and a rope belt, something Pietro might have worn seven hundred years before. The light was behind him, preventing Lang from seeing the features of his face although it was adequate to make a halo of his close-cropped blond hair. And to reflect from the automatic rifle slung over a shoulder.

"The pot needs emptying," Lang said, indicating.

Even in the dim light, Lang could see the sneer, nostrils dilating in disgust as he smelled the dry urine on Lang's clothes. "When you fill it, you will empty it, heathen . . . if you live that long."

The accent was Slavic, Russian or something like it. The rifle was one of the AK-47's, Russian or Chinese-made, that the collapse of the Soviets had left all over Eastern Europe. The thirty-seven–round banana clip hung in front of the trigger guard.

The man's distaste was apparent even in his back as he spun and strode from the room.

The door slammed and Lang dropped to his knees. The key was rattling as he picked up the splinter from beside the door and slipped it between door and jamb. He could feel the heavy bolt hit it and prayed the slender bit of wood would hold.

It did.

Lang leaned against the oak, making sure the door had no give should the man outside test it. Careful the un-bolted door did not move, he turned his back against it and slid into a sitting position, hand over his shoulder to hold the splinter in place.

How long to wait? At some point Silver Hair was coming back with the man from Autolite. He glanced at his bare wrist before remembering they had taken his watch. He began slow counts to sixty, trying to keep score of the passing minutes.

Ten.

Twenty.

Thirty.

Carefully, he pushed the door slightly ajar, trying to remember if the hinges squeaked. The first thing visible in the tiny crack between door and frame was a pair of feet propped in a chair. The guard was taking it easy, maybe too easy if the deep, even breathing was any indication. Encouraged, Lang pushed the door a little wider. He wasn't as lucky as he had hoped. His keeper was tilted back in a chair, his legs stretching to a second chair, engrossed in a magazine. The rifle was across his lap.

Beyond him, a dimly lit hall stretched for maybe twenty feet, intersecting what Lang guessed was yet another hall-way like a large hotel. The only thing missing were numbers on the line of doors.

Lang eased the door shut. He needed to move but couldn't chance the door swinging open. Untying a shoe, he jammed the rubber sole between floor and door. Careful to keep the splinter in place, he returned to the bed. The sheets were old linen, bordered with fine lace. Regretting the necessity of destroying something so beautiful, he ripped a couple of long strips loose before returning to the door. He wadded one strip and made a loop of the other.

The guard was still intent on his magazine. Lang opened the door a little wider. If the guard looked up, Lang was finished. With as little motion as possible, Lang lobbed a Mephisto over his keeper's head. It landed with a gratifying thunk.

The magazine fell to the floor as the guard snatched up the AK-47 and sprang to his feet.

There was only a split second before the Templar realized the source of his distraction and turned around. In a single motion, Lang shoved the door wide and lunged. His sudden weight on the other man's back knocked him down, the rifle clattering against the plank flooring. With one hand, Lang dropped the looped strip of linen over the guard's head, past his chin, and twisted it tight, stifling the yell that was beginning in his throat.

Lang's other hand stuffed the wadded cloth into the man's open mouth, giving the embroidered garotte another turn. The keeper was clawing at his throat, trying to loosen the crushing pressure on his air supply, when Lang brought up a knee to put between the man's shoulder blades and pushed down as hard as possible. The human upper esophagus is a muscular tube, hard to close completely, but the keeper's weakening efforts told Lang he was succeeding.

The Templar was limp when there was the sound of approaching footsteps.

4

Sintra, Portugal
2340 hours

From across the winding, tree-shaded street, they had been watching the top two floors of old limestone that could be seen over the wall. The building's windows were tightly shuttered as though the occupants wanted none of the gentle breeze from the ocean ten or so miles distant. The structure could have been described as a castle or palace simply based on its size and the generous acreage upon which it sat. In fact, it was not much grander than its neighbors, all of which were large enough to be regal residences instead of summer homes. Indeed, three dwellings of royal origin had been built on the hillside of this small town.

In the early 1800s, Lord Byron had fallen in love with the area as had a significant segment of Europe's nobility and wealthy. In the last century, increasingly dreary socialist governments and the taxation necessary to implement the illusion of social equality had forced the sale of many of these exquisite vacation homes to the world's new elite: multinational corporations, usually those headquartered in tax havens with corporate anonymity.

Only two people were in sight tonight, ambling with careful indifference along the sidewalk as they gawked at the opulence of what was illuminated behind protective walls. They had stopped in front of one.

"Not a lot of traffic," the sniper observed. "Haven't seen the first tourist today, either."

"You won't," the other person said, studying that part of the facade visible above the razor wire-topped wall. "What few there are come in by bus, eat lunch at one of those restaurants we saw in the town square this afternoon, and leave. After touring the palaces, there's not a lot for 'em to do. The hotels are priced out of the average budget and you have to have recommendations from some pretty obscure people just to get a room."

The marksman frowned. "I'd never even heard of the place until you tracked Pegasus here. How did you do that?"

By unspoken agreement, they both turned as though to resume their stroll as a large Mercedes slowed for one of the road's many turns and effortlessly accelerated up the hill.

"You did. You got someone to hack into the Froggies' air traffic control computer. Only one flight from Toulouse-Blagnac by private aircraft yesterday, the one to Lisbon."

"But this isn't Lisbon."

"No, but it's less than twenty kilometers away. This town, Sintra, has always been a place for those who would just as soon not be officially noticed. I called a Portuguese solicitor I know, had him check the tax records and, presto! Up come the chaps at Pegasus."

The Mercedes disappeared behind yet another wall as it followed the curves of the narrow street. The pair resumed their interest in the building.

"So," the marksman said, "you think he's in there, that round tower sort of thing."

It was not a question.

"Why else bring him here?"

The two hesitated a few moments before continuing the slow pace of sightseers.

"High voltage as well as the concertina wire on top of the wall," the marksman said. "And I will wager you there are motion detectors in the yard. Probably also dogs."

The other verbalized the obvious. "The two of us aren't going to get him out with a frontal assault. We're going to have to watch the place and wait for a chance."

"And if there isn't one?"

He shrugged as he dug in his pockets. "We can only do our best and hope."

The marksman frowned, unhappy with the obvious truth of the answer. "They could kill him before we . . ."

The sniper's companion turned back in the direction from which they had come. "For all we know, they might have already. But I doubt they would bring him all the way here just to kill him. I would imagine they'll be wanting to know how he discovered their secret first. He'll know his life will last only as long as he can keep that information. He's tough; they won't have gotten it yet."

Both moved deeper into the shadows cast by the limb of a huge oak overhanging the wall opposite the gate of the building that held their interest.

"If he does get out," one said, "it's bloody unlikely he's going to just walk through that big iron gate. Maybe we'd better gather our things from the car and make such preparations as we can now."

"Better yet, call for reinforcements," said the other.

5

London
0123 hours the next morning

Inspector Fitzwilliam hated late night calls even more than those that interrupted his evening routine. Although he would never admit it, he was annoyed by the fact that the phone's ring had no effect on Shandon, his wife. After thirty-two years of marriage, the intrusion rarely even provoked her into rolling over.

This particular call made the detective forget his pique.

When the caller gave a name, he sat upright as though on a spring.

"Who?"

The name was repeated. He had heard correctly the first time.

"Where?" he asked, frowning as he heard the answer. "Hold on." He reached into a bedside table for the pen and pad he always kept there. "Repeat those directions, please."

The caller did so and the phone went dead.

6

Sintra
0527 hours

Lang sprang for the rifle and snatched it up from the floor. Slinging it over his shoulder, he dragged the guard's body into the room and shut the door. The close smell of death and the thought that he had killed again made him gag. If there had been time, he would have felt a cold fury for these men who had not only murdered but had made him a killer, too.

The corpse felt heavy beyond its apparent weight as he dragged it to the far side of the bed. Trying to breathe only through his mouth, he stooped and tugged loose the rope at the guard's waist and pulled the robe over the still head.

Even through the thickness of the door, Lang could hear voices tinged with surprise at finding the sentry gone. He tried to move faster.

Dipping into resources of strength he didn't know he had, Lang managed to dump the limp body onto the bed and throw a sheet over it. The door was opening as he lifted the robe over his own head and let it settle over him like a large white bird coming to roost. There was only time to pull up the hood and hide the rifle under his habit before Silver Hair and another man were in the room.

Silver Hair asked something in a language Lang couldn't understand, again Slavic-sounding.

Guessing at his meaning, Lang pointed to the body under the sheet and mumbled.

The Templar asked again, this time with an edge to his tone.

Again Lang nodded, moving around the bed toward the door.

As soon as he was between the two men and the exit, Lang whirled and lunged into the hall, slamming the door behind him. As he had hoped, the key was still in the lock. He felt, rather than heard, two bodies slam into the heavy wood on the other side as the lock's bolt clicked into place. Lang took deliberate care in putting the key in the robe's pocket.

In the hall was a small cart, the sort of thing an auto mechanic might use to carry around a car battery. That was what was on it: the battery with wires and alligator clips. The sight brought Lang's mind back to the pain he still felt and he fought the urge to go back into the room and fry someone else's balls.

Instead, he made sure the hall was empty before taking the rifle out from under the robe and checking the clip. Full with all thirty-six rounds. Too bad the guard hadn't had an extra magazine. Ammunition, Lang mused, was like cash on a vacation: no matter how much you brought, it was never enough.

He risked taking off the cassock long enough to sling the AK-47 muzzle down under his right arm so that, if need be, he could bring it up, firing through the cloth. He wasn't going to get any points for marksmanship that way, but the Russian-designed weapon was intended more for rapid fire at relatively close range than for competition shooting.

Keeping close to the wall, Lang sauntered down the hall as though he knew where he was going. At the intersection, both directions looked the same: dimly lit, with curving walls and regularly spaced doors that, absent the outside latch, were identical to the one he had just locked.

Right or left?

Lang chose left so the rifle was on the outside. If he had to use it, he preferred not to have to fire across his body. Shortly, he came to an arch framing a staircase beneath an arched window, the glass black with night. The steps only went down. Lang was on the top floor.

The stairs were marble. Like the tower of Blanchefort, there was a depression worn in the middle where centuries of feet had passed that way. Also like the old castle, the risers were short, made for short legs. The steps radiated from a center column in a spiral tight enough to make him slow his descent to ease a faint sense of vertigo.

There were landings on each of the two floors he passed, each similar to the others, each with a window. He saw the color of night and an occasional streak of light shimmering through the waves of the hand-blown glass.

A sound floated up the tight circular stairway, so faint Lang was surprised that he had been unconsciously listening for some time. The further down he went, the more distinct it became until he recognized it as a Gregorian chant, Latin sung without tune, but still pleasingly melodic.

Still too distant to make out the words, Lang came to yet another landing. The stairs continued down, but through the window he could see trees, their branches limned against a streetlight. He thought he could make out a wall, too. He stopped. This place—this weird, round building— probably had at least one basement, no doubt complete with dungeons. If Lang was seeing what he thought he saw outside the window, this must be the ground floor.

He stepped into another circular hallway, this one with a ceiling vaulted twenty feet. The cold gray of stone walls was abated by tapestries, their figures life size and mostly gory. In silent agony, martyrs bristled with arrows, sizzled over fires and were devoured by lions. Between the gruesome pictures, suits of chain mail held swords, empty helmet slits squinting into the dim light.

The main floor.

Like the men in the lifeboat in the lawyer joke, he knew where he was but not where that was.

Steps echoed from the stone floor. Lang grasped the rifle under the robe with one hand and tugged the hood down further over his face with the other. There was no need. Like a ghost in his white habit, a figure floated past on the other side of the hallway. His hands clutched rosary beads and he was mumbling what Lang supposed was a prayer.

Once the Templar was out of sight, Lang felt like saying one of his own.

The chanting grew louder until Lang was at its source. To the right, a huge circular room was filled with men in white robes or chain mail armor. In the center of the circle, another man in robes stood before a carved marble altar faced by the standing congregation.

Just as Pietro had described the chapel at Blanchefort.

Past the chapel was what Lang guessed was the door to the outside. To call it massive hardly did it justice. Reaching almost to the ceiling, two single panels were held closed by an iron bar as thick as Lang's thighs. The hinges, shiny brass, were three or four feet in height.

Lang considered making a dash for it but quickly discarded the idea. Two men, one on each side of the door, stood guard, their AK-47's anachronisms against the white surcoats with the red crosses.

They did not appear to be purely decorative.

Both watched with little interest as Lang approached.

Their reply to his motioning for them to open the door was a question in the same Slavic tongue he had heard before. Lang gave an exaggerated shrug to say that he didn't understand. With the international character of Pegasus, surely not everyone spoke the same language, at least not this language.

The man on the left pantomimed reading something and held out his hand, a clear signal that he expected a document or writing of some sort. Apparently the good brothers had to get a hall pass to leave.

The man on the right was staring at Lang's feet. The Mephistos. After throwing the one, Lang had put the pair back on. Everyone here wore the armored solleret or Jesus shoes.

The Templar guard was quick to unsling his rifle but not nearly as quick as Lang in raising the one under the robe. The sound of the shot inside stone walls was deafening. A neat red hole was centered on the cross on the Templar's robe, blood smudging the sterile white.

The remaining guard was as eager as his brothers to die for the cause, scrambling to bring his weapon to bear. Lang again squeezed off a single shot from the hip, aware that he had been forced to kill yet again.

Even before the sound waves reverberating from the domed ceiling stopped echoing in Lang's ears, the chanting stopped. He let the rifle's sling slip from his shoulder to use both hands on the huge latch on the door. He pushed from his mind the possibility this led into another part of the building or a closed courtyard.

Worse than up that well-known creek.

The latch weighed nearly a hundred pounds and Lang had to lift it a good three feet or so to clear the hasp. The exertion sent daggers across the shoulder that had been twisted as well as a lightening bolt to his scrotum that burned away any remorse he might have felt at leaving two more dead Templars. In fact, the pain was so great that he had an instant fantasy of sticking around to kill every one of them.

A sound behind told him he might have that opportunity. He turned to face the entire congregation from the chapel. Gritting teeth against the pain so hard that he could hear molars grinding, he gave the latch a final shove, pushing the door with his foot. The great hinges moved with what seemed glacial speed and there was a three- or four-foot gap between the doors. Through it Lang could see the gray of dawn and feel a slight breeze.

He was almost outside.

A quick glance over his shoulder saw a distinctly unhappy crowd moving toward him. Although unarmed, the intent was clearly hostile. Stooping, Lang retrieved one of the AK-47's from the floor and thumbed it onto automatic. As he slid between the giant doors, he sent a burst into the ceiling. The noise and the shower of plaster had the desired effect of making everyone duck.

Then Lang was running down steps and onto what looked like a driveway.

He had no idea where he was, so he followed the pavement. Semitropical plants, palm trees, Spanish bayonet, succulent cactus and, beyond, a high wall filled his vision. He hadn't thought about the wall, particularly one far too high to jump and topped with razor wire. A closer look revealed electrical wiring, too. Whether these people meant to keep people in or out, they were serious about it.

If there was a driveway, there had to be an exit. Keeping in the dark, Lang paralleled the pavement until he came to the gate. Iron and every bit as tall as the doors he had just come through, it was the only way out of the compound he could see and it was guarded by two men who weren't dressed in costume. But they did carry automatic weapons and one of them held a cell phone to his ear. Lang was willing to bet he wasn't calling out for a pizza.

Squatting behind a bush, Lang surveyed the situation. The warm breeze was heavy with moisture, the smell of salt air and jasmine. Somewhere near the ocean, but what ocean?

The guard with the cell phone snapped it shut and put it in a pocket, speaking to his comrade. They took their rifles in both hands and began to scan the grounds. Lang considered two quick shots. At this distance, a miss was unlikely. No good. The sound would draw everyone and Lang wasn't sure he could get those gates to open. Steel arms on each side indicated there was some sort of mechanism that controlled the movement. If a combination was required or he couldn't find the switch, Lang would be no better off than he was now.

Make that worse off. He could hear the barking of dogs approaching.

Not a lot of time. In the east, the day was brightening. It would be fully light soon.

7

Lisbon, Portela Airport
0624 hours

The twin DeHavilland turned off the runway of Lisbon's Portela Airport to taxi towards a small ramp where a number of vehicles waited. Within minutes, a parade of black Lancias was streaming along the Avenida Marechal through a city not yet quite awake.

From a tinted window, Inspector Fitzwilliam watched the night reluctantly depart Lisbon. The guidebook he had scanned on the plane told him that somewhere out there in the dark was the old city. Briefly, he let himself fantasize:

he and Shandon on holiday, seated at a small restaurant with a view of the Tagus, Lisbon's magnificent harbor, castles brooding on the surrounding hills. Magnificent from the pictures.

Unfortunately, romantic trips were hardly the purpose at hand. He watched as the cavalcade flashed through Campo Grande, white-belted *polícia* holding back the light traffic of delivery trucks from the country and homeward-bound late-night celebrants. Moments later, he was on the divided IC19. A cloverleaf and the suburb of Queluz whizzed by. Even the pink glow of dawn could not improve the monotony of white flats stacked boxlike on barren slopes.

Damnably accommodating of these chaps, the inspector thought. The Froggies would have died rather than invite him along to observe the arrest. The Dons and Krauts would have smothered him with an endless stream of paperwork. Too bad all the sodding EU didn't cooperate as easily as Portugal. And to sweeten the matter, no one needed to suffer the bother of getting a warrant, according to Carlas, his contact here. Just knock on the door and search for Mr. Langford Bloody Reilly all you bloody like.

He settled back in the seat. This was going to be a pleasure. Maybe Carlas could even get the extradition papers in order while he shopped for a gift for Shandon, bring Reilly back the same day.

Now that *was* day dreaming, he told himself.

If only this affair hadn't leaked to the local constabulary in time for them to warn whoever it was that had Reilly. The Sintra police, he understood, viewed their duty as protecting the local gentry. Even against, or particularly against, the national authorities.

8

Sintra
0647 hours

"You sure that you can cut that without getting electro-cuted?"

The sniper held up a piece of uninsulated wire for an answer, quickly clipping it to a small black box that resembled a pocket tape recorder. "And with this, never will they detect the circuit has been interrupted. At least, not for two hours."

The pair had cut a gap in the wire and were sitting astride a section of the wall hidden from the main building by a clump of trees. The missing steel ringlets had been tossed onto the ground on the outside of the wall as soon as they had been clipped. Below the pair was a small gate almost obscured by flowering vines. Beside them was the grappling hook they had used to secure a rope to the top of the wall, a sound the guards had not heard because they had been investigating another noise, one made by pebbles tossed onto the pavement of the driveway.

"What if he doesn't get out of the house in two hours?" the other wanted to know. "We just calmly walk up to the door and ask to see him?"

The sniper was about to answer but instead held up a hand and pointed to the two guards at the gate, their features rapidly becoming visible in the increasing light. The slump of people bored by the inherent tedium of such duty was gone from the way they stood, peering into the shadows shrinking from the morning. It was obvious they had become suddenly alert, one holding a phone to his head. If either person on the wall doubted something was happening, that doubt evaporated with the sound of dogs barking.

9

Sintra
0648 hours

Lang didn't have many choices. With any luck at all, he thought, he should have two or three minutes before the dogs picked up the scent and either led his pursuers right to him or, more likely, attacked. Any reservations he had had about shooting the two guys at the gate were more than outweighed by the thought of becoming Kibbles and Bits. He'd have to get both men with one burst before either could return fire, though. Flipping the switch back to automatic, he took a deep breath and centered the AK's front sight on the chest of the nearest man, exhaled and squeezed.

Nothing.

When his fingers touched the cocking mechanism, a chill of dread went all the way to his feet. The action was open, ready for a full clip. He had picked up the weapon of one of the men inside and hadn't had time to check the magazine. The rifle was empty, useless.

Well, maybe not entirely useless. Maybe he could at least use the butt as a club. Flitting from shadow to dark spot, he made a quick but indirect run for the gate. Behind, it sounded as if the hounds of hell were on his trail. More likely the Dobermans of doom.

Lang was crouching, ready to make a final sprint across fifty feet or so of open space, when he heard something to his rear besides the dogs. As he spun around, he saw a dark object, felt a sharp blow to his head and everything went dark.

10

Sintra
0649 hours

Six cars squealed to a stop outside a ten-foot iron gate.

Before Inspector Fitzwilliam could climb out of the backseat, two men were pounding the butts of what looked like Yank-made M16 rifles against the steel. He saw Carlas speak into a grille beside the gate, and the iron slowly began to swing open.

11

Sintra
0700 hours

Though stunned by the blow, Lang could feel the throbbing pain as though the back of his head might have a meat cleaver in it. He was being dragged to his feet by two men carrying rifles.

Excited voices were shouting. He was being hauled towards the back of what looked like a medieval castle. The sound of engines made him twist in his captors' grasp. Five or six long black cars were gliding up the driveway. Either Lang was witnessing a Mafia state funeral, a pimp's convention was in town, or somebody really important had arrived. His head hurt too much for him to care which.

Then he saw two guys in khaki, either militia or police. Sometimes in Europe it was hard to tell the difference. Even with the pain fogging his thought process, it hit him: Somehow the cops had found him. This time, the cavalry had come to Little Big Horn in time.

His relief didn't last long enough to enjoy. He was being taken away from his rescuers. One of his escorts pressed a rifle against Lang's throbbing head. The unspoken message was clear: if he made any sound that attracted attention, it would be his last. Despair replaced elation. The building in front of them was big enough to hide Lang easily. The cops would never find him.

"Lang! Here!"

Lang recognized the voice calling to him from somewhere along the wall. Was he hallucinating?

If so, the guys on either side of him were, too. They both whirled to their right, rifles pointing away from Lang. He took what seemed to be the only chance he had and made a headlong lunge.

They spun back around, weapons coming to bear. Lang could see the dark hole of the muzzles, was expecting to see a flash, likely the last thing he would see on this earth.

Instead one, then both, of the men pitched forward as though struck with an invisible hammer. At the same time, the whipcrack of the rifle that had killed them bounced from wall to wall.

Stooping, he intended to grab both their weapons, but the same voice urged him on. "Run for it, Lang!"

Ahead, he could see a rope dangling tantalizingly over the wall. He would later come to believe that with proper encouragement a man can equal or break any track record in the books. He knew he did in reaching that rope. Winding hands around it, he used his feet against the wall to climb faster than Tarzan ever had. He didn't even notice the pain in his twisted shoulder.

Painfully aware that he made an inviting target, a dark body against the white wall, he expected the sound of shots any minute. Then he almost sighed his relief. There would be no gunfire. The Templars wouldn't dare shoot unless they wanted a war with the whole Portuguese police force.

There was growling below and something struck at his

feet as he pulled himself up. He could only hope the dogs weren't particularly good jumpers.

Someone was pulling on the rope, reeling it up, by the time Lang reached the top of the wall.

He wasn't surprised to see Gurt, her cheek pressed against the rifle stock in the standard sitting position for competition shooting. He had recognized not only her voice but also her marksmanship. He was, however, astonished to see Jacob beside her.

"You're too old for this," Lang blurted.

"I appreciate your bloody gratitude," the Israeli said, calmly dropping the rope down the other side of the wall, "but you can express it fully when we get down from here." He wrinkled his nose. "And are those your mates down there?"

Below them was a milling, barking, growling mass of fur and teeth.

Gurt held her sniper's rifle in one hand and reached for the rope with the other. "You two may here sit and all day talk. For me, I am getting gone."

She disappeared feet first as she rappelled down the outside of the wall. Lang followed, this time fully aware of the needles of pain jabbing into his shoulder. Supporting even part of his weight tensed his crotch muscles, sending jolts of burning agony from scrotum to stomach.

The three stood in a wooded area beside the wall as Jacob twitched the rope until the hook disengaged. Gurt disassembled her weapon and stowed the parts in an attaché case.

"Shouldn't we hurry?" Lang asked. "I mean, I don't want you guys to do anything that's uncool like running, but shouldn't we be getting the hell out of here?"

They looked at each other and Jacob shrugged. "Possibly, but I doubt it. I expect the lads from the police and Inspector Fitzwilliam will keep your former hosts quite busy for some time. I don't know Portuguese law, but I'll book someone's going to have to explain a lot of illegal arms."

As an American, Lang had forgotten how difficult it is to legally possess anything other than sporting firearms in Europe. "Who's Fitzwilliam?" he asked.

As they crossed a meadowlike area, Gurt and Jacob took turns explaining that and how they had followed Lang to the Languedoc and then to Sintra. Lang had never before been unaware of what country he was in. He found the experience disorienting.

Beyond the open area was another wall, this one without razor wire. They climbed it, coming down in front of the Templars' next-door neighbor's estate, about a quarter of a mile away.

By the time the trio reached the Fiat 1200 parked a street further up the hill, the pulsating of sirens seemed to come from all directions. Two police cars, lights flashing, wailed past.

CHAPTER TWO

1

Rome
Four days later

They took turns driving, stopping only for gas and snacks, until they were back in Rome. There Gurt had access to a safe house, a small apartment on the top floor of a building on the Via Campania. From the window of the tiny living room, they could look across the ancient city wall to the green of the Villa Borghese, Rome's largest public park.

Jacob took the foldout and Gurt and Lang shared the single bedroom. Happily, the shock torture had no permanent effects.

The moment Lang woke up on the third day, he knew it had to be Sunday. Not only were the busy streets quiet, but he could also hear children's excited screams and laughter along the park's walkways and bike paths.

The three managed to keep out of each others' way long enough to prepare a hearty breakfast in the cramped, galley-style kitchen. Either out of consideration for two stomachs not quite at ease with the smell of fish first thing in the morning or merely because he couldn't find smoked herring in Rome, Jacob had foregone the kippers and had fried sausages instead. The spicy *salsiccia* were a welcome substitute for bangers.

Lang was enjoying his second cup of espresso when Jacob fired up his pipe and Gurt lit a Marlboro.

"Jesus, guys," Lang said, futilely waving the smoke away, "there wasn't much point in rescuing me only to give me lung cancer."

Jacob replied, "Demonstrates we can't stay here forever. Exactly what did you have in mind for your future?"

Lang forgot the smoke. "I'm going to expose the bastards, reveal their secret to the world," he said, cold fury in his voice. "Once their secret's out, there'll be no more extortion money. That will be the end of them."

Jacob made a sucking noise through his pipe, noted it had gone out and prodded the bowl with a matchstick. "And spend the rest of your unnaturally shortened life looking over your shoulder? Once the secret's out, that letter doesn't protect you any longer."

"Those sons of bitches killed my sister and my nephew. They follow that act by framing me for two murders I didn't commit," Lang snapped waspishly. "What do you suggest, kiss and make up?"

Gurt had a question but Jacob spoke first, talking between puffs as he applied a new match. "I'd suggest you think of some form of revenge other than exposure. If not for yourself, for a few hundred million Christians. I mean, I'm a Jew, never was too keen on the Church, but Christianity's a stabilizing force in the world. You destroy it and . . ."

Gurt had been following the conversation so closely that she had let her cigarette's ash grow. It fell unnoticed onto the worn rug.

"Destroy Christianity? What . . . ?"

Jacob pointed the stem of his pipe in accusation. "That's what Lang's talking about. Tell her."

"Yeah, tell me."

Lang sighed. "Jacob read the Templar diary, he made the same guesses I did and we were both right.

"The Templar who wrote that diary was familiar with the Gnostic heresy, a . . ."

"The who?" Gurt asked. Her cigarette had burned to the filter and she flinched as she touched the hot ash with her fingers before she stubbed the smoldering butt out in a cracked ashtray.

"The Gnostics were an early sect of Christians. They believed Christ was mortal, by God, not of God. Therefore, His spirit, not His body, ascended into heaven after He was crucified.

"In 325, about the time the Roman emperor Constantine made Christianity the official religion of the empire, various bishops of the church met at Nicea to decide some troubling issues. First, they had to choose among a number of accounts of Christ's life. They selected four: Matthew, Mark, Luke and John. Possibly one of the reasons these were preferred over others is that all four have Christ being resurrected, body and all. Hence, His immortality and triumph over death, the basic Christian message as well as fulfillment of Jewish messianic prophecy. Subsequently, the Gnostics and any others who didn't share the official view were hunted down and liquidated as heretics.

"The Templars discovered the Gnostics were right: Jesus's body had not ascended into heaven or anywhere else. Instead, His brother and wife fled Palestine, taking the body with them."

"That was what was in the 'vessel' Pietro read about in the Gnostic writings," Jacob interjected.

"In one form or another," Lang said. "Jewish funerary custom of the time required the body be allowed to decompose for at least a year. The bones were then put in an ossuary, a small stone box, and permanently entombed. Whether Jesus's body was brought to the Languedoc and his bones then moved or was hidden until only the bones were left, we'll never know."

"Why not leave the body where it was, where it was placed after the crucifixion?" Gurt wanted to know.

Lang shrugged. "I can't say for sure, but I can make a number of guesses. One would be that the Jewish messianic prophesies all called for resurrection of the body. Leaving the corpse would deny messiah status to Christ and stature to his disciples. Second, that would also occur to His followers, who might well take the body themselves if His family didn't. Third, Christ was executed as a common criminal. Tombs were for the wealthy. It would be just a matter of time before the body was dumped or placed in a lesser grave."

"So, the body, or just the bones, is moved to southwest France?" Gurt had another Marlboro in her hand.

Lang nodded. "And the Templars discovered exactly where. You can imagine the havoc the appearance of Christ's remains would have caused the church. The Templars had a good idea. They began to blackmail the Church, the pope."

Gurt lit up, puffed and looked up at Lang. "If you're talking about the Middle Ages, the pope would have been powerful enough to simply go destroy the body, move it where it couldn't be found or eliminate the Templars."

Lang thought a moment. "Again, I'm only guessing, but I don't think the pope was that powerful. He had to hire mercenaries every time he had to go to war. The Templars had what amounted to a standing army and had fortified the area around the tomb with the castle, Blanchefort. Any attempt to take the body would have chanced the Templars making their secret public. Plus, I'd speculate no pope wanted to be involved in desecrating the tomb of Christ, even though they weren't willing to admit it existed."

Both Jacob and Gurt were silent for a moment, no doubt trying to poke holes in Lang's theory.

Jacob asked, "Assuming you're right on, why didn't the Templars just move the ossuary, take it someplace they could keep secure?"

Lang had wondered about this before and thought he had the answer. "To find the tomb, they had to have a clue. They had some sort of documentation that placed Christ's tomb right where it is. If they moved it, the ossuary lost its authenticity."

"You mean, like a picture, a painting no one knew existed, that turns up in somebody's attic without a provenance but with what looks like Rembrandt's signature on it," Jacob said, ruefully regarding a cold pipe again. "You can test the pigment, the canvas, but there'll always be a smidgen of doubt."

"A doubt the Templars couldn't afford," Lang said.

Gurt filled her coffee cup before raising an eyebrow at Jacob.

"No thanks," he said. "That stuff would melt the spoon, you tried to stir it."

"It's espresso," she said. "It's supposed to be strong."

Jacob pushed his cup a few inches away. "It may be authentic Italian espresso, but my nerves can't take any more caffeine." He looked at Lang. "Which still leaves the question of what you plan to do."

He was right, of course. Exposing the Templars' secret would give Lang great personal satisfaction but it would devastate a large part of the world's population. He thought of Francis, how the revelation would destroy his faith, his reason for life, just as it had Pietro's. He remembered the peace religion had given Janet. Who was he to singlehandedly undo two thousand years of good works? Well, mostly good works, anyway, overlooking the Crusades, the Inquisition and a few other unfortunate excesses.

He made a decision. "Gurt, I would be surprised if Pegasus isn't looking for me. I don't think it's to our advantage for them to know where we are, sure not to yours and Jacob's if they connect you with getting me out of Sintra. Are the stores here open on Sunday?"

She regarded him with curiosity. "Most are."

"Could you get me a computer? A laptop, any make as long as it has a modem."

She frowned. "I suppose this will go on my credit card just like your airplane tickets."

She wasn't angry about it, just unwilling to let him forget.

"Okay, okay," he said. "You know I'll pay you back."

"How?"

He didn't get her meaning. "How?"

"I would very much like to see Atlanta, visit Tara and the places in that wonderful book."

Lang was stumped for a second. Then, "You mean Atlanta, *Gone With the Wind*? I didn't know people read it anymore, seeing as it's become politically incorrect. Anyway, those places don't exist."

"I never have been to Atlanta or the American South."

"This time of year, it's hot and the city has the second worst air quality in the country."

"I do not intend to live outside in a tent. I am sure there is air-conditioning available."

"And the third worst traffic."

"I do not intend to drive."

"Sounds lovely," Jacob grinned.

"I still want to see it," Gurt said. "I think you do not want me to visit."

Truth was, he didn't. Visiting would have been fine but the idea of sharing his small condo with a woman for longer than one night was disquieting. He had visions of beauty potions on the bathroom sink, lacy undies in dresser drawers and pantyhose draped over the shower curtain. He had experienced difficulty a couple of times with women who came to visit and were less than eager to leave. On the other hand, he owed his life to Gurt: she had helped him and was about to again. He was not an ungracious person. Particularly when the promise to be performed was in the indefinite future and a stunningly attractive woman was involved.

"Done," Lang said. "Now what about that computer?"

"I can bring one from the Agency," she volunteered.

"No, I want a new one, a machine that's never had any e-mail address other than mine." He turned to Jacob. "And I'll need Pegasus's e-mail address. They are a corporation registered in the Channel Islands, so they would have an address, maybe a Web site for their legitimate businesses."

2

Rome
Two hours later

Pegasusltd@gb.com was the address, found easily enough by Jacob. The sales staff at the electronic store had been very helpful in programming the new computer, including Lang's own e-mail address and password so he could use his existing Internet service.

At the kitchen table, Gurt and Jacob peered over his shoulder as he slowly typed in the message all three had agreed upon:

Wish to meet to discuss matters of mutual interest. Reply before matters made public.
Reilly

Short if not sweet.

An hour passed. Unable to concentrate, Lang reread the same page of Friday's *International Herald Tribune* a dozen or so times. Jacob dozed in front of the window while Gurt listened to a German-language broadcast of what she said was a soccer match. For all Lang knew, it could have been *The Best of Adolph's Speeches*. The reaction by the audience would have been the same.

The *Herald Tribune* is the only place "Calvin and Hobbes" still exists. For once, Lang didn't find the strip amusing. He was too busy trying to think how an e-mail could be traced to a specific phone line.

An hour had just passed when the computer made a sound like a gong and words appeared on the screen. The picture of an unopened envelope made understanding Italian for "you've got mail" unnecessary.

Name time, place, conditions.

That was all it said—brief, succinct. Obviously Pegasus hadn't referred the question to the legal department.

Lang had previously asked Gurt and Jacob for their input in anticipation of just this question.

Church of San Clemente, Via di San Giovanni in Laterano. Rome. Triclinium of Mithras. 1530 hrs. Tues next. One person only.

Gurt had thought of the forty-eight-hour period. In that time, Lang could reach Rome from anywhere, therefore he could be anywhere when the e-mail was sent. The place was Jacob's idea. San Clemente was typical of Rome in that the site contained several periods of history. At street level, or actually slightly below, the simple eighteenth-century facade at the bottom of the Esquiline Hill indicated a church that had been in use since the twelfth century. Beneath the carved altar and mosaics of the drowning of Saint Clement were the ruins of a fourth-century Christian place of worship. Deeper yet were the ruins of a Temple of Mithras, a first-century male fertility cult that drifted into Rome from Persia to become popular among Rome's military.

Lang recalled that the site had been maintained and continually excavated since the seventeenth century by an order of Irish Dominican monks. So far as he knew, they haven't found any whisky yet.

The advantages of the site for a potentially hostile meeting were several. First, few if any tourists knew about the place. Second, the Mithran temple consisted of passages wide enough for only one person at a time. Finally, the church was at or near the bottom of a steep hill where Jacob could keep watch in secret, calling Lang on a cell phone if a trap appeared imminent. Also, Gurt and her rifle could easily cover the only entrance.

3

Rome, Laterano
1530 hours the next Tuesday

Churches in Rome close at half past noon on weekdays, reopening three and a half hours later. Jacob and Gurt had been in a second-story storage area of a shoe store across the Via di San Giovanni since ten o'clock. In the normal Italian manner of doing business, the shopkeeper had accepted a handful of bills without a single question in exchange for use of the premises. After all, it was money the hated tax man would never know about and, therefore, would not take.

With punctuality uncharacteristic of Rome, a brown-robed monk opened the doors at precisely three-thirty. The sharp edges of a hammerless .38 stuck in Lang's belt under a jacket dug into his backside as he followed the brother inside and past the ornately carved choir enclosure to their left.

The monk disappeared and Lang was alone. Approaching the altar, he noted the detailed animals and leaves depicted in the mosaics of the apse. To the right was an open door and a staircase.

The darkness into which Lang descended was interrupted by weak lightbulbs hung every twenty or so feet from the low ceiling. Somewhere below, water was rushing, a reminder that Rome is located on a number of aquifers, so many that almost all of the hundreds of fountains spout potable water. The passageway was square, wide enough for two persons to pass, and hewn through rock that the dim lights gave a reddish color. Lugubrious faces, whole and in part, stared down from pieces of frescoes, most of which had succumbed to time, neglect and moisture.

In what had been the fourth-century sanctuary, there was little other than a slightly higher ceiling that would have announced its purpose to the uninformed. Lang stood still for a moment, listening to rushing water. Anyone who says silence has no sound, he mused, has never been in a dimly lit ancient ruin, listening for the footsteps of a possible assassin.

A winding metal staircase led to the next level, some fifty feet below the streets of the modern world. What was left of the Mithran temple seemed even more poorly lit than the floor above. A narrow space separated ruined walls that barely reached Lang's hips. Around every turn, skeletons of steel scaffolding reached to the low vaulted ceiling. Lang wasn't sure it was there as part of the excavation or to hold up the ancient brick above his head.

This was not a place for the claustrophobic.

Through occasional grates in the outer walls, water black as oil in the dark was visible as it raced by with an roar of anger at its confinement. At every turn, piles of brick and masonry attested to the archaeology in progress, but there was no one at work. The thought of how truly alone he was down here under centuries of ruins added to the chilly dampness that was not entirely his imagination.

At last the narrow path came to a central room. Along each side, a single long bench was carved into the stone walls. In the center was a chest-high block of white marble, the carved figures of Mithras slaying a bull standing in a bold relief caused by the shadows of the few overhead bulbs.

This was it, the triclinium, the room used for ritual banquets. Lang checked the time, squinting to see the luminous numbers on his watch. Three-thirty-seven. Sitting on one of the benches to wait, his only company was the boisterous voice of the water and spirits of feasting Romans dead two thousand years.

There was no breeze to move the string of lights, yet the darkness seemed to creep from the corners, making silhouettes of fanciful monsters on the walls. The jab of the .38 in his belt was no longer uncomfortable but reassuring.

He was about to check his watch again when he heard something other than water. Standing, he turned to get a direction as the sound became more distinct, then recognizable as footsteps on stone.

With the revolver in hand, Lang moved to the far side of the room, putting the altar between him and whoever was approaching. He wished that Gurt had had time to secure a better weapon, a large-bore automatic with a full clip rather than the puny six shots the revolver held. But at least he had the advantage of surprise.

Or so he thought.

Although darkness hid the man's face, Lang recognized the shining silver hair as the Templar stood at the entrance to the room. "Come, Mr. Reilly, there is no need for you to hide. If I'd wanted to harm you, you would not have lived past the first level."

Gripping the gun's butt with both hands, Lang placed the stubby front sight of the .38 squarely on the new-comer's chest. A miss at this range would be unlikely. "Okay, so I'm a little paranoid. You weren't the one who got your balls singed. Now keep your hands where I can see them and away from your body, step forward and place both palms against the altar."

The Templar did as he was told. A quick pat-down revealed no weapons.

"Now that you're satisfied I'm no threat," he said, "perhaps you'll tell me why you wanted to meet."

Lang motioned to one of the benches and sat so that Silver Hair was between him and the entrance. "Someone walks through that doorway and you're history."

The older man sighed deeply. "Again, Mr. Reilly, had we wanted you dead, you would not be here. Can we dispense with the threats and get down to whatever business you have in mind? I gather there is something you want from us or you would not have been the one to initiate contact."

His eyes met Lang's as he made a show of slowly reaching into his coat pocket, producing the silver case and taking out a cigarette. He broke the gaze only long enough to light it.

"You're right," Lang said. "You've been blackmailing the

church for over seven hundred years. Now it's your turn to pay a little hush money."

The Templar showed no surprise. In fact, Lang was certain he had been expecting it. "How much?"

Lang had given this a lot of thought. The sum should be big enough to be punitive but not enough to make it tempting to kill him and take their chances with the letter. Lang was prepared to negotiate, something he had learned well from horse-trading with the prosecution for lower sentences for his clients. But never anything this big. It was going to be like trying to get a charge of sodomy reduced to following too close.

"Half billion a year, payable to the Janet and Jeffrey Holt Foundation."

Silver Hair lifted a gray eyebrow, either surprised or doing a good job of pretending to be. "I don't think I've ever heard of it."

Lang sneezed. The cold of the stone on which they were sitting was beginning to permeate his body. Standing, he kept an eye on the entrance. "It doesn't exist yet. Janet Holt was my sister, the one you people incinerated along with her son when you firebombed that home in Paris."

The Templar nodded slowly. "You'll use a foundation to channel money . . ."

"No! The foundation will be real enough."

Lang had given this subject a lot of thought, too, ever since Jacob had convinced him that exposure of the Templar secret would do a great deal more harm than good. First he had thought of the money he could demand, the vacation homes, yachts and jets that could be his. The truth, plain and ugly, was that the idea of going the same places for every vacation was only slightly more appealing than getting seasick. His terror of flying increased in inverse proportion to the size of the aircraft involved. The Porsche was his choice of car, he lived exactly where he wanted and already made an obscenely large income do-ing what he enjoyed, trying cases. The only thing missing from his life was Dawn and even the Templars couldn't give her back.

Besides, there was no way the sort of money Lang had in mind would stay a secret. It took little imagination to con-jure up the hordes of solicitors lining up to inundate him with timeshares, questionable securities, even more doubt-ful charities and the rest of the telemarketing inventory. He could also see the IRS salivating at the prospect of taking a large part of the money to staunch the eternal government hemorrhage. A charitable foundation both memorialized Janet and Jeff and let Lang spend a huge amount wherever he thought Janet and Jeff might have wanted, perhaps for children like Jeff in poverty-ridden countries.

Sliver Hair smiled coolly. "A true philanthropist, just like your fellow Atlantan Ted Turner."

"Better. I didn't marry Jane Fonda."

It was not lost on Lang that the other man hadn't squawked about the price, a sure indication he should have asked for more. Instead, Lang said, "One more thing . . ."

"There always is," the Templar said, his tone bristling with sarcasm.

"You got me blamed for a murder in Atlanta and an-other in London. I want to read in the *London Times* and the *Atlanta Journal* that those murders have been solved, the culprit arrested."

Silver Hair was looking around for a place to drop his cigarette. He finally ground it out on the stone floor. "That might be difficult."

"I'm not stipulating that it has to be easy. You've got peo-ple who're willing jump out of windows, you can sure as hell find somebody to take those raps."

He gave Lang a nod, an acknowledgement this request,

too, would be met. "And for this, we get to know who has the letter?"

Lang shook his head. "I might have been born at night, pal, but not last night. The letter's location stays with me. I've got too much to live for. Besides, you know I won't go public with your secret; it would end the funding for the foundation."

"We all die, Mr. Reilly. What happens then?"

"If the foundation is to survive me, so will your secret, a risk you'll have to take, that I'll make provisions not to endanger the annual funding of the charity."

The Templar looked at Lang for a moment as if trying to make up his mind about something. "For a half billion dollars a year, Mr. Reilly, I'd think I'd be entitled to hear exactly how you found the tomb. Most of it we know. But the rest . . . I'd hate to have to be paying more money if someone else . . ."

"Fair enough," Lang said. "You know about the Templar diary. That indicated whatever the secret was, it was located in the southwest of France. It was through the painting, or rather the picture of it, that I finally figured it out. The inscription made no sense, *ETINARCADIAEGOSUM* One too many words. I guessed it might be a word puzzle, anagram, so I rearranged the letters." Pulling a city map out of a pocket, Lang wrote on the margin. "I rearranged the letters like this:

Et in Arcadia Ego (Sum)
Arcam Dei Iesu Tango.
Arcam, tomb, objective case.
Dei, God, dative case.
Iesu, Jesus, possessive.
Tango, I touch.

" 'I touch the tomb of God, Jesus,' is what I made of it. As long as the Poussin is around, somebody else is just as likely as I was to figure that out."

"Since you, er, found our secret, all copies of the painting have been destroyed. The original is in the Louvre."

"Okay," Lang said, "since this is question-and-answer time, I've got one for you. How did you, the Templars, find out about the tomb in the first place?"

Silver Hair took out another cigarette. "Very well, then. When we held Jerusalem, one of our number came across documents, ancient Hebrew, Aramaic, it's called today, scratched on parchment, much like the Dead Sea Scrolls. A petition in which Joseph of Arimathea and Mary Magdalene asked Pilate for leave to depart for another part of the Roman Empire, taking the corpse of Jesus with them for reburial. Written across that parchment was approval in Latin.

"Our long-ago brethren recognized the places and rivers in that document and found the tomb, something that would have been an embarrassment to the Church, as Christ's corporeal body supposedly ascended into heaven. The Vatican saw the wisdom of—ah—paying us to guard this secret."

"Why didn't the Vatican simply destroy the tomb and its contents?" Lang thought he had given Gurt the correct reason but he wanted to know for sure.

The man regarded the end of his cigarette. Thinner and longer than any brand Lang had seen, he would have bet it was made to order. The Templar took a long drag before answering. "And commit the ultimate sacrilege, defiling the tomb of Christ? Better the pontiff should have exhumed Saint Peter and thrown him into the Tiber. Bad enough the body of Our Savior had not ascended, that the Gnostics had been right all along. Besides, the pope only saw part of the documents we found. Where Joseph and Mary actually went, we kept to ourselves."

This was the weirdest conversation Lang had ever experienced. He was sitting in the ruins of an ancient temple, conversing like two baseball fans discussing batting averages with the man who had been at least indirectly responsible for the deaths of what family he had—the first person he had truly wanted to kill. And the one person he knew he would not.

"For such a valuable secret, you left a lot of clues lying around. You explained Poussin's painting, but the cross by the side of the road that lines up with the statue?"

"A relatively modern addition, but a clue for those who know what they are searching for—only Templars until you. We may need to remove one or both markers."

The man shifted his seat on the rock, grasped his knees and seemed to be waiting for Lang's next question. The son of a bitch was enjoying this, bragging on the cleverness of the order. Lang not only wanted to kill him, but he would have enjoyed doing it with his hands around the bastard's throat, watching the life leach out of that arrogant face.

Lang's rational self told him that he would be better off to learn what he could. "You must have a pretty large organization to have tracked the painting from London to Paris to Atlanta."

The other man exhaled smoke tinged with red from the lights. The illusion looked as though he were breathing blood. Stephen King would have loved it here. "Not large but very, very efficient. You don't keep an international organization secret for seven centuries without being efficient."

These people, or at least this one, weren't overcome with humility, just as Pietro had observed seven hundred years before.

"Like the Mafia," Lang said.

The corners of the Templar's mouth turned down in disdain and he sniffed at the comparison, totally missing Lang's sarcasm. "Come now, Mr. Reilly. The Mafia is hardly secret, hasn't been for forty years. And most of its members are in prison—or about to be. No, Mr. Reilly, we are much more efficient. We have brothers in every western country, influential members of their societies. Two heads of state, leading politicians. Education, commerce, science. Any field you choose, we have members not only in it but dominant. And sufficient wealth to buy half the world's nations, General Motors, any other large corporations you care to name. Or politician. There has been no single foreign policy in the Western world we have not orchestrated. We cause conflicts including war when it benefits us and peace when it does not."

Now there was a comforting thought.

Or the man was crazy, megalomania on steroids. Worse, he might *not* be crazy. But if half of what he was saying was true, every conspiracy nut in the world was, in fact, an optimist.

Lang had forgotten how cold he was. He stood, stretching joints that were beginning to ache with the damp chill. "As soon as I see the articles in the papers, I'll e-mail instructions about the money, where to send it. Oh yeah, if you've got someone on the papers, thinking about fabricating a story, don't. I get arrested, the Templars'll be the biggest story of the century, maybe the millennium."

Silver Hair also stood, again crushing his cigarette butt under the sole of a very expensive Italian loafer. "May I send you the papers?"

"I'll see 'em. In fact, I'll assume our deal is off, I don't read about it in the next month."

Silver Hair shook his head, tsk-tsking. "You don't give much leeway, do you, cut us a little slack as you Americans say."

"We also say a tit for a tat. Your people didn't cut my sister or nephew a hell of a lot, either."

"Simply business, Mr. Reilly, a matter of survival. Nothing personal." He smiled benignly as though justifying the smallest of transgressions.

The son of a bitch meant it, just like that. Pure animal hatred provided more than enough heat to dispel the damp. Lang fought back the urge to lunge for his throat right there. Only the realization that, if Lang killed him, he would still be a fugitive and there would still be an order of Templars stopped him.

"Well, it's been swell." Lang stepped aside to walk past and out of the room.

"Yes," the Templar said, "I enjoyed our chat, too."

Lang snorted. You can recognize a vampire because they don't cast a reflection in a mirror. You can tell a Templar because, they don't get sarcasm.

Lang was out of the room before he turned, giving in to curiosity. "One last question."

Silver Hair nodded. "By all means."

"You are all men. How do you . . . ?"

The older man's smile was visible even from where Lang stood. "How do we provide a continuing membership without procreation? The same way the Dominicans, Franciscans or any other holy order does: by men joining. The difference is, we recruit, search out the brightest all over the world." He gave a dry chuckle. "Remember: Celibacy in the church of the fourteenth century was more form than function. Even the popes had mistresses and children. We . . . well, I suppose I've more than answered your question."

There were a thousand other questions but Lang wasn't going to give him the satisfaction of knowing he was interested.

Shadows were beginning to stretch across the Via di San Giovanni as Lang left San Clemente. Even the delicate light of late afternoon made him wince after the twilight underground. Glancing at his watch, he was surprised to see he had been gone only half an hour.

Lang felt as though he had arisen from a tomb himself.

CHAPTER THREE

1

Lake Maggiore
A week later

Sara groused when Lang refused to tell her where he was. He wasn't willing to bet his freedom that the line wasn't still tapped. She did agree to send a copy of the *Atlanta Journal* story of his exoneration to Jacob when it appeared. Jacob would e-mail a code word when both articles had run.

When it came, the storyline common to the papers was that both murders had occurred as an attempt to steal a priceless painting by Nicolas Poussin, a French painter who had a small room of the Louvre dedicated to his work. Having possessed it, Lang had been suspected of its theft until the real culprit was identified and apprehended in London. It came as no surprise to Lang that the purported thief likely died in an escape attempt. The hulk of the car in which he had fled was too badly charred from the unusual explosion, resulting from a high-speed crash, to distinguish human remains. Neither piece mentioned that the art dealer in London had been killed after the man in Atlanta nor what a doorman was doing with such a treasure.

Foolish consistences may be the hobgoblin of little minds, Lang thought with a wry grin, but not of newspapers. Otherwise, why would their editorials tout a candidate, then excoriate him a year later?

Lang was almost sorry to learn that the need to hide was over.

He and Gurt had spent the time on the shores of Lake Maggiore at the cluster of summer homes and a gas station called Ranco, hardly a town or even a village. The only inn had but five guest rooms. It had thirty seats for dinner, however, and each was full every night. Lang gained at least a pound a day.

They made love every morning. Afterwards, they lay exhausted, postponing getting up, watching the rising sun paint the snowy tops of the Swiss Alps across the water a blood red. The scene was reflected in the bottomless black waters of the lake until the picture was streaked by the morning ferry.

The days were spent walking like young lovers, which Lang guessed they were, along the shore, admiring the handsome homes built by people who had declined the commercial development of Italy's more popular Como.

After a far too sumptuous dinner, the couple sat on the deck outside the room and watched the stars until the lake's mist reached like fingers to extinguish the celestial show. As soon as one would stand, the other would make a dash for bed where they tore at each others' clothes and made love again until they fell into an exhausted sleep.

Who would want that to end?

It was only on the way to Malpensa that Lang sat up in the seat of the old taxi with a jolt. He had just spent the first day in years when Dawn had not been in his thoughts. The realization made him feel guilty.

But not for long.

2

Atlanta
Two weeks later

Gurt adored Atlanta. She gaped at the huge homes on West Paces Ferry, marveling that any single person could own such acreage solely for a residence. She loved the variety of restaurants in Buckhead. The high-end malls, Lenox Square, Phipps Plaza, were her nirvana, supermarkets her promised land. The multiplicity of choices both delighted and confounded her. On her first grocery shopping trip with Lang, she was unable to make a selection of anything that had more than three alternatives.

They went to a Braves game. The game did not hold as much interest as the beer and hot dogs. She came away viewing America's national pastime as a large, hot, outdoor Oktoberfest.

She adored Grumps, too, an affection equally returned. Once returned from Sara's care, the dog missed Lang's secretary not at all, wriggling with spasms of joy whenever Gurt returned to the condominium from her outings with Lang, leaving him to muse that if the Germans had loved their fellow man anywhere near as much as they loved their dogs, the past century would have gone a lot more smoothly.

In fact, the dog's affection became a source of humor between Gurt and Lang. Any time he put arms around

Gurt, Grumps would grab Lang's shoe, socks or pants, any-thing he could hold in his teeth, growl and try to pull Lang away.

Lang's apprehensions about living with a woman proved unfounded.

The first recognizable blow to his belief in the sanctity of his own space came from Francis.

It started when the priest came by for dinner, hamburg-ers cooked on a grill on the balcony accompanied by the current vintage of Château Budweiser in cold bottles.

After Gurt and Lang gave Francis the somewhat sani-tized version of their recent European experience, Gurt and Francis got into a discussion that wandered from the medieval Church to indulgences to Martin Luther. Lang left them and went to bed about half past 1560—the year, not the hour.

At Francis's insistence, Gurt was included in dinner at Manuel's, the priest sweeping aside Lang's protests that the evenings there had been historically male-only. As the priest pointed out with Jesuitlike logic, that had only been by Lang's choice. Lang was astonished to hear her tell a joke in understandable if halting Latin. He had no idea she knew a word.

Only months later did Lang find the thin book of con-temporary anecdotes with their Latin translations, *Amo, Amas, Amat: Learn Latin and Amaze Your Friends*. She had gone to a lot of trouble just to please him.

There were no potions on the bathroom counter, no feminine silk in the drawers. Although she was always ap-propriately dressed when they went out, the room in Lang's closets had not diminished. He began to wonder exactly where did she keep her stuff. He supposed that years of living in cramped apartments in Europe had made her thrifty with space.

She amused herself while Lang was at work, recounting

a list of the day's activities over dinner: shopping, walking in various parks or simply enjoying Grumps's company.

Lang began to eye the calendar warily, noting the increasing speed with which her date of departure seemed to approach. Too stubborn to admit it, he nonetheless dreaded the thought.

3

Atlanta
A week later

It was one of those early summer evenings in Atlanta when it was easy to forget that the temperature would soon be nudging the high nineties and the slightest stirring of air perceived as a breeze. Lang and Gurt were walking Grumps along Peachtree at a pace slow enough to allow the dog to savor and return each message his predecessors had left in the grassy margin between sidewalk and street.

Gurt was to leave the next day. Lang could think of little else.

"Lang," Gurt asked lazily, "have you named the bene . . . benefic . . ."

"Beneficiaries," he supplied. "Of the foundation? No, not yet. I've narrowed it to Central American relief funds that specialize in schooling and health for children, kids like Jeff. I've had to hire a staff just to screen the applicants. If I interviewed them all, I'd have to give up the law practice."

Gurt stopped to let Grumps explore a particularly interesting few square feet. "I don't understand: if the money comes from the church to the Templars to you, why not simply return it to the church?"

Lang knew from experience she had given this some thought. She rarely asked pointless questions. "Two reasons: First, if it goes right back to the church, the Templars will find out and simply raise their extortion if they haven't already. Second, the church's priorities aren't the same as mine. Not to put too fine a point on it, but in countries with limited resources, kids need to learn about birth control early, safe sex to avoid AIDS, stuff the church doesn't exactly favor."

"And the church, the Catholic Church, will continue to pay this money to these men because they do not want the world to know Jesus's body did not ascend into heaven?"

Grumps lunged forward, almost snatching the leash from Gurt's hand.

Lang reached across her body and grabbed it, reining the dog in. "Not so fast, fella. Yep. I'm no theologian, but it seems Christ could have been divine either way. The church just made a mistake early on that they don't want to admit."

She took the leash back. "To touch the tomb of God's son . . . It must have really been a journey, a trip."

There was something appealing about Gurt's occasional mismanagement of the American idiom, the way she twisted her face into a pout when she wasn't sure she had it right.

"I didn't think of it that way at the time. I . . ." He stopped, putting both arms around her. "Screw the tomb, the Templars, whatever. Gurt, I don't want you to leave."

She rested her head against his shoulder. Another couple smiled as they detoured around them.

"What is the edge, er, point of staying? I had to practically force you to let me come. I know I cannot replace Dawn."

"Nobody can. But you're not a replacement, you're . . . you're you and that's plenty good enough."

"Then I guess I will stay as long as it does you happy."

"That, madam, will be forever."

He kissed her lightly, oblivious to the honking horns and good-natured jeers of passing motorists.

The moment was shattered by the scream of brakes and a gut-wrenching thump.

Gurt shoved herself free. "Grumps! Mein Gott!"

"Shit!"

Each had thought the other had the leash.

A mound of black fur was crumpled on the curb where the dog had landed after impact with a car.

A woman, pale and shaken, got out of a Volvo. "I didn't see him until he ran right in front of me."

Lang and Gurt ignored her, rushing to the still-quivering animal. Oblivious to the blood that ran down her blouse, Gurt scooped him up, clutching him tightly.

"Liebchen, Liebchen," she moaned. "Es tut mir so leid."

Grumps licked her face before his eyes rolled back into his head and he went limp.

Lang had never seen Gurt weep before. The knowledge she had coolly shot and killed made her grief all the more touching. He took the body from her, surprised at how cold it had already become. There was no breath or heartbeat. Kneeling, he gently lowered Grumps to the ground and put his arms back around the distraught Gurt, whispering anything that might be of comfort.

A small knot of joggers, bikers and other walkers gathered, bonded by morbid curiosity, their voices respectfully low.

Later, Lang was unable to remember what happened first, the murmur of surprise or the tug at his pants leg. He looked down, certain he had momentarily lost his sanity. Grumps, growling playfully, had the cuff of Lang's trousers in his mouth. Where the dog had lain seconds before, a puddle of blood was disappearing like the morning's dew.

Neither Gurt nor Lang spoke as they walked away,

Grumps renewing his search of the grass. Lang was thinking of a hillside in France, of the unexplained warmth he had felt from a stone box whose existence most of the Christian world would deny.

Maybe . . . He shook his head, dismissing the thought as impossible. What he felt for Gurt was miracle enough.

THE FIFTH INTERNATIONALE

JACK KING

Stan Penskie is an FBI agent working as the legal attaché of the American Embassy in Warsaw. Robert Sito, an officer of the Polish Secret Service and an old friend of Stan's, needs to talk to him right away. He's found some pretty incredible information regarding various intelligence agencies around the world. But Robert never has a chance to go into detail . . . before he is killed.

Stan knows it's up to him to find the killer and uncover the truth. But as Stan digs deeper, more people are murdered and Stan himself becomes the primary target. Can one man battle a clandestine organization comprised of the most powerful people in the world? Can one man expose the hidden agenda of . . . *The Fifth Internationale*?

THE MOON
POOL
MAX McCOY

Time is running out for Jolene. She's trapped by a madman, held captive, naked, waiting only for her worst nightmares to become reality. Her captor will keep her alive for twenty-eight days, hidden in an underwater city 400 feet below the surface. Then she will die horribly—like the others....

Jolene's only hope is Richard Dahlgren, a private underwater crime scene investigator. He has until the next full moon before Jolene becomes just another hideous trophy in the killer's surreal underwater lair. But Dahlgren has never handled a case where the victim is still alive. And the killer has never allowed a victim to escape.

ABDUCTED

BRIAN PINKERTON

Just a second. That was all it took. In that second Anita Sherwood sees the face of the young boy in the window of the bus as it stops at the curb—and she knows it is her son. The son who had been kidnapped two years before. The son who had never been found and who had been declared legally dead.

But now her son is alive. Anita knows it in her heart. She is certain that the boy is her son, but how can she get anyone to believe her? She'd given the police leads before that ended up going nowhere, so they're not exactly eager to waste much time on another dead end on a dead case. It's going to be up to Anita, and she'll stop at nothing to get her son back.

NOWHERE TO RUN
CHRISTOPHER BELTON

It's too much to be a coincidence. A series of computer-related crimes from different countries, all linked somehow to Japan. Some are minor. Some are deadly. But they are just enough to catch the eye of a young UN investigator. As he digs deeper he can't believe what he finds. Extortion. Torture. Murder. And ties to the most ruthless crime organization in the world.

It's a perfect plan, beautiful in its design, daring in its execution, and extremely profitable. No one in the Japanese underworld has ever conceived of such a plan and the organization isn't about to let anything stand in its way. Anyone who tries to interfere will soon find that there is no escape, no defense, and...nowhere to run.

JOEL ROSS
EYE FOR AN EYE

Suzanne "Scorch" Amerce was an honor student before her sister was murdered by a female street gang. Scorch hit the streets on a rampage that almost annihilated the gang, but it got her arrested and sent away. That was eight years ago. Now Scorch has escaped. The leader of the gang is still alive and Scorch wants to change that.

The one man who might be able to find Scorch and stop her bloodthirsty hunt is Eric, her prison therapist. Will he be able to stand by and let Scorch exact her deadly vengeance? Or will he risk his life to side with the detective who needs so badly to bring Scorch back in? Either way, lives hang in the balance. And Eric knows he has to decide soon. . . .

FOR THE DEFENDANT
E. G. SCHRADER

Janna Scott is a former Assistant State's Attorney with a brand new private practice. She's eager for cases, but perhaps her latest client is one she should have refused. He's a prominent and respected doctor accused of criminal sexual assault against one of his patients. It's a messy, sensational case, only made worse when the doctor vehemently refuses to take a plea and insists on fighting the ugly charges in court.

Meanwhile, a vicious serial killer who calls himself the Soldier of Death is terrorizing Chicago, and it falls to Janna's former colleague, Detective Jack Stone, to stop him. Body after body is found, each bearing the killer's gruesome trademark, yet evidence is scarce—until a potential victim escapes alive. . . .

BODY PARTS
VICKI STIEFEL

They call it the Grief Shop. It's the Office of the Chief Medical Examiner for Massachusetts, and Tally Whyte is the director of its Grief Assistance Program. She lives with death every day, counseling families of homicide victims. But now death is striking close to home. In fact, the next death Tally deals with may be her own.

Boston is in the grip of a serial killer known as the Harvester, due to his fondness for keeping bloody souvenirs of his victims. But many of those victims are people that Tally knew, through her work or as friends. Tally realizes there's a connection, a link that only she can find. But she'd better find it fast. The Harvester is getting closer.
